MW00532092

A
HOLY
Passion

Books by Alicia G. Ruggieri

A TIME OF GRACE
The Fragrance of Geraniums
All Our Empty Places
A Love to Come Home To

The House of Mercy

*A Holy Passion: A Novel of David Brainerd and
Jerusha Edwards*

A HOLY *Passion*

A NOVEL OF DAVID BRAINERD AND JERUSHA EDWARDS

ALICIA G. RUGGIERI

BRIGHTER DESTINY PRODUCTIONS

A Holy Passion: A Novel of David Brainerd and Jerusha Edwards
Copyright © 2018 Alicia G. Ruggieri.
www.aliciagruggieri.com

All rights reserved. No part of this publication may be reproduced, stored in a retrieval system, or transmitted in any form or by any means electronic, mechanical, photocopying, recording, or otherwise without the prior written permission of the copyright owner.

Cover design by Rachel Rossano
http://rossanodesigns.weebly.com

Map illustration by Alicia G. Ruggieri, based upon the 1799 public domain map by Crutwell. Some locations are approximate.

Scripture quotations are taken from the King James Version of the Holy Bible.

Text to "Jesus Shall Reign" by Isaac Watts is in the public domain.

A Holy Passion: A Novel of David Brainerd and Jerusha Edwards is a work of historical fiction. Where historical people, conversations, events, and locations occur, they are used fictitiously.

ISBN-13: 978-1-948171-03-8
ISBN: 1-948171-03-1

With thankfulness to those
who have trodden the pilgrim-path before us.
May we appreciate and follow their example
of obedient, holy faith.

***

And for Alex – May God ever increase
your love for His lost sheep.

"Who is this that cometh out of the wilderness?"

SONG OF SOLOMON 3:6

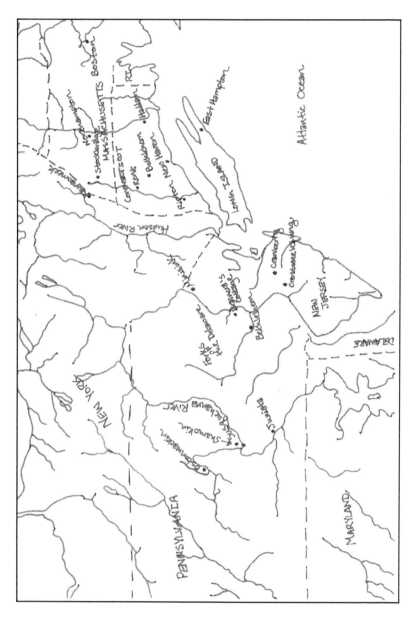

Chapter One

Northampton, Massachusetts
May 28, 1747

"He is here! He is arrived, Mama!"

The exuberant voice of my brother Timothy precedes his entrance by only a moment. Sweat shining across his round face in the warm late-May weather, he bounds into the kitchen, his bare feet slapping the freshly-scrubbed plank floor.

"I thought that you were playing with your hoop in the lane." Esther's voice turns my attention from Timothy for a moment. My sister – younger than me by three years – leans against the doorway behind him, her delicate eyebrows raised beneath her starched mob cap.

Timothy nods with his whole body and takes in Esther and then all of us in the kitchen with excitement-widened eyes. He still gasps for breath, but that does not slow down the delivery of my eight-year-old sibling's message. "I was! But just now I saw a bay horse coming onto Main Street. Oh, and 'tis a beauty of a horse!"

"Main Street? Were you not in the lane?"

Timothy's cheeks color a little. "I joined some of the other children in a race down Main Street. And 'tis a good thing that I did, too, for that is where I saw the horse!"

Esther purses her lips in humor above Timothy's brown-haired head. "There are many bay horses in Northampton. We are not expecting him for another few days."

"Are you certain that 'tis he?" Mama asks, her quick hands stopping their twisting of yarn at the spinning wheel, her foot pausing its *tap-tap-tap* beneath her skirts. Her dark eyes peer up to meet Timothy's. "Many travelers pass down Main Street."

And what is more, my brother has galloped into the house three times already this week, heralding our guest's imminent arrival. Of course Mama and Esther doubt his youthful certainty!

My brother gulps in another breath. His small chest still heaves from the wonderful exertion of running all that way from Main Street. He opens his mouth again, but before he can speak, I hear a pitter-pat of hastened footsteps in the corridor, and our slave woman, Leah, appears, her arm laden with a market-basket. The cloth covering its contents has gone askew from her hurrying.

Relief apparent on her face, Mama turns from my brother to our servant, faithful Leah, to whom Papa gave a more Biblical name after he purchased her in Newport, Rhode Island, some years ago now. Once she was Venus, now she is our Leah. "Timothy says that he has seen our guest approaching. Do you know if this is true?"

"Aye, 'tis he, madam," she assures Mama, her Barbados accent chopping the words, excitement plain on her dark face. "He asked me for directions to the house. I told him, and then I ran all the way here."

At this, my heart begins its slow crescendo. Mr. Brainerd – my Mr. Brainerd – as I have dared to call him only in my head – has truly come. To

Northampton. To my very doorstep. At last.

I set down the silverware I am in the midst of polishing, carefully, afraid that my hands tremble – and fearful that anyone else might notice. How can I yet react this way to the news of Reverend Brainerd's arrival? Why – despite months and even years of commanding my heart to beat normally at the syllables that make up his name – despite lashing my heart with the stark truth that my longing for him will have no fruitful end – despite all of this, why do my hands still shake with agitation?

I look around at my siblings gathered in the kitchen, wondering if any of them have noticed my tension. My elder sister Sarah, Mama's namesake and right-hand, sucks her upper lip into her mouth, her eyes wide with anticipation as she carefully places her carding paddles into the basket near her knees. Beside the hearth, ten-year-old Lucy sets aside her book, its contents forgotten at the news Timothy and Leah have brought, and thirteen-year-old Mary claps her hands and squeals aloud.

Everyone radiates excitement, even Mama, whose quiet control shows her gladness only through the smile curving her lips upward. Why should I appear to be any different from those around me? Why should my excitement give anyone cause to think I have secreted a passion in my bosom for nearly four years – a passion for a man whom I know more from his letters to my father than from the one face-to-face meeting I have had with him?

My breath comes fast. Now, even from within the house, I can hear horse's hooves clomping on the firm dirt road that curves to that of my father's King Street home. Each thud presses into my ears, straight to my brain, and onto my chest, imprinting there as firmly as it ever would on the earth outside. *He is here. He is here!* The words chase each other through every thought, each pulse-beat rat-a-tatting through my veins. Weeks ago, before the last snow powdered our New England world, my father took my carefully-worded suggestion – How bold, perhaps how mad, I was to suggest it! – to invite Mr. Brainerd here to recuperate from the chronic illness that has long troubled him – and that nearly killed him this past winter. He has taken so long to come that I began to believe he would never arrive.

At last I will see him again. He will glance on me – on me, Jerusha Edwards, second-born daughter of Jonathan and Sarah Edwards. And I will feel the sunshine of his smile once more.

Around me, as though in a precious dream that passes too swiftly, my sisters and brother scramble to their feet, the younger ones more than making up for their older siblings' carefully reserved composure. As a bird that catches the flow of a breeze under its wings, I, too, move toward the door, alighting on the excitement surging through the air.

"Jerusha." I am halfway to the door when Mama's voice cuts into my churning thoughts as a dasher through forming butter. "Be sure to take Jonathan." She herself reaches for my youngest sister, Elizabeth, born just weeks ago and nestling now in a cradle near her spinning wheel.

Of all my family, I least wish to meet Mama's eyes in my current state. She will see right past my properly-fastened bodice into the wildly-beating heart beneath. She will discover the reason that I – I, who never ask for anything – urged Papa to invite Mr. Brainerd here. She will know that 'twas not a completely unselfish request. She will know that this independent young man, expelled from Yale for disobedience, this missionary to the frontier Indians, going where only Quakers and Moravians dare go, has snared my heart – though I've never spoken more than a few words to him – though I have surely resisted at nearly every tug. She will find that Mr. Brainerd has woven my affections around his heart, unaware. She will discern that I – Jerusha the dutiful one, Jerusha the dependable and predictable one – have slowly, but surely, deeply fallen in love with David Brainerd through nothing more than his letters to Papa and the paltry moments I have spent in his company.

Surely, she will not approve of such wild recklessness – even if it is kept concealed within my own heart, which it surely must be.

Indeed, I myself do not approve. It is not how methodical, logical Jonathan and Sarah Edwards of Northampton brought up their genteel, conservative daughters to be. Spritely? Aye, we may be that. Outspoken? Even that, if we are in the way of right. But abandoned without reason to their own hearts' emotions?

Never that.

So I keep my deep brown eyes focused on my sleeping brother, Jonathan, named after my father and born a full two years ago. I step over to scoop him up from his place in the cradle for which he is getting much too big, near the banked fireplace. He sleeps on, his yielding body heavy against my own, not about to awaken from his afternoon nap for the sake of greeting a strong-willed man of God he has never met. Esther, Mary, and the others are already going out the door. Timothy has long since left the room and run outside again.

From the passage, the soft knock of knuckles sounds against Papa's closet, the small room in which he studies, prays, and prepares his sermons. Then comes the squeak of a door opening and shutting, and

ALICIA G. RUGGIERI

Papa's quiet, even footsteps join the others echoing down the polished passage toward the front door.

I will be the last to arrive, the last to see him. I nestle the little one against myself, clutching him more tightly than necessary in my eagerness, in my nervousness. Perhaps it is better this way. If I had been the first one out the door, if I had rushed out, Mr. Brainerd's blazing eyes might have landed on me individually, as they once did on that day so long ago in New Haven. And, as on that day, his glance would have penetrated to my heart; I am certain of this. Could I have kept from his powerful, searching gaze the thoughts of him I have long cherished? Thoughts and hopes which I have tried in vain to banish, of which I have not dared to speak even to my own dear sisters and certainly not to Mama, who did not bring up her daughters to become fools.

And a fool is what I am.

Judge you: Am I not a fool to cherish romantic thoughts of this great man – this lofty one who has given up so much, scorning even marriage it would seem, Papa says, for the sake of the gospel?

But a fool I must continue to be, for though I have tried to give up the inclination of my heart, the love I have for Mr. Brainerd have taken root and grown. No matter how much prayer I dedicate to its eradication – even fasting at times – I cannot rid myself of the pressing regard I feel toward a man who, I am certain, does not remember that I even exist, other than as just one more of Reverend Edwards' numerous children. Mr. Brainerd comes now merely at my father's invitation – not through any desire to see me – of the Edwards' girls, certainly not the most amusing or holy or beautiful.

I am a fool.

But even as I tell myself this, I can hear the

trembling words as if someone had spoken them aloud again: *He is here. He is here!*

I float from the kitchen to the passage, with only the weight of the little child to keep me grounded, every limb vibrating with anticipation. The front door stands but a few steps away now. My eager siblings and even my careful parents and Leah left it open when they exited. Fortunate they – they have nothing to hide, as I do. They can show their eagerness outright.

Has he arrived at the end of our lane yet? My pace quickens but then slows as I reach the threshold. *Lord of heaven, help me. Help me to act as I always do with young men – with completely disinterested sisterly love, as I ought, being Mr. Brainerd's sister in Christ. Being the daughter of his minister-friend, my father. And nothing more.*

I step over the threshold just as the proud bay horse turns onto our road, its coat shining in the May sunlight. It is a Rhode Island Walking Horse, a breed coveted for its endurance, a quality Mr. Brainerd has no doubt appreciated these years in the wilderness. I am somewhat nearsighted from too much reading by candlelight, so I cannot see the man who rides the horse as clearly as I would like from this distance. But I remember how he looked three years ago. Three years changes nothing in a man almost a score-and-ten, does it?

My pulse increases as I walk down the hard-packed dirt that leads to our front gate, measuring my steps until I come to the place where the rest of my family gathers. I will see him face-to-face soon enough. My younger brother leaps onto the edge of the gate in his enthusiasm, and Mama steps toward him, pressing a hand of rebuke to the lad's bony shoulder.

A sudden shyness – almost embarrassment -

overtakes me as the man comes nearer and nearer, the small figure growing more real – less a person of my imaginings. Impulsively, I drop a kiss to the cheek of the child sleeping against my shoulder, eager to avoid meeting Mr. Brainerd's gaze as the powerful horse halts before us. I see the dark chocolate-colored hooves of his mount, splattered with mud from the road. Though God blesses us with the sun's light today, it has been a wet spring.

"Mr. Brainerd," Papa greets our visitor formally, as is his wont, though they have been acquaintances for years. Our manservant moves forward to catch the horse's bridle, holding it so that Mr. Brainerd can dismount.

"Mr. Edwards. Mrs. Edwards. I am your servant." His tenor voice has the gravelly, powerful texture of the ocean waves washing over pebbles and broken shells on the sand. There is something else in it, too, that has grown from when I previously heard him speak: a moist breathlessness, as if he has just run the last four miles of his journey on foot rather than sat on horseback. I swallow hard. The illness has indeed grown worse, much worse, over the years. Why does my heart shake in my chest at the thought? Did I not know of this ahead of time? Mr. Brainerd's letters to Papa – and to other men acquainted with him – have said as much. Have said that he was dying, actually, though this seems an exaggeration, if the man were capable of such a thing, given the look of him now. Sickly? Aye. But dying? Perhaps not.

And, even if all appearances indicated such, I do not wish to believe it. Would God waste such a one of His servants? One who has given his life for the salvation of the heathen? Papa invited him here to Northampton in order to cure him – to revive him – not to give him a bed upon which to die. Did he not?

Surely, God will permit Mr. Brainerd's healing in my care.

Our care, that is.

With a swift motion, he dismounts and draws the joined reins over his horse's head. He stands near me, speaking to Mama and Papa, but I find that I cannot look at him. I duck my head, nervous with his nearness, though he pays no mind to me at all. The smell of wool fills my nostrils; his dark, worn coat must be moist from the misty air he has encountered as he traveled from New Jersey through Connecticut, then Rhode Island, and now into Massachusetts. "I thank you for having me come to your home. I hope that 'tis not too great of an imposition, especially considering..." He trails off, coughing thickly. I hear the wetness blanketing his throat.

"God has blessed us in having you come, Mr. Brainerd. 'Tis an honor, truly," Mama answers. Only one familiar with her would hear the pity underlying cordiality in her voice. "I pray you, come into the house. Will you have some tea? Unless you'd rather rest after such a long journey."

"Would you think me very rude if I rested first, Mrs. Edwards? I am not feeling well and would hate to faint away in your parlor." The humor that graces this last bit surprises me. I had not thought of him as waggish at all but only as the passionate, deeply spiritual would-be student I had met so long ago – and then as the relentlessly determined, prayerful missionary.

Mama gives a gracious smile. "Not at all. I will send some tea up to your room."

"I thank you, madam. That is very kind of you."

The group moves as Papa and Mama lead the way with Mr. Brainerd toward our two-story home, built from plank-wood, unlike many of the houses in

Northampton, sitting as it does nearly on the edge of the frontier. Leah has taken her place beside the door, waiting for Mama's next instructions.

I dare to glance up as they move past me, my eyes fixing on the man walking beside Papa. Mary falls into step with me as we shepherd the rest of the children toward the house.

"He is sadly altered, is he not?" Mary's whispered words touch my ear, the warm breath a gentle contrast to the chilly May morning. She has spoken so softly that Mr. Brainerd cannot hear her. Her words cannot hurt him.

But they pierce me. For what Mary says is true, though she has never even seen the man before today. Mr. Brainerd, whose image has flashed like lightning again and again through my head and, I admit, my heart for many months – is indeed much changed. And, as Mary so bluntly stated, not altered for the better. I see this as he turns his head to respond to one of Papa's questions. Anyone with eyes can observe the way his ashy skin stretches taut and dull over his protruding cheekbones. His shoulders stoop slightly, though he seems to try to hold them erect. His dark coat droops across his once-sturdy back in such a way that nothing can be inside the garment but skin-and-bones. He walks as one who has seen twice his years – trying to hide the halt in each of his steps. Is it some secret pain that makes him jolt so, that makes his eyes widen every few paces? My stomach clenches again at the thought, and I worry that my recent meal may come up.

I swallow hard and press Jonathan closer to my bosom, bringing a sleepy whimper from him. "Hush, hush, now." I rub his back to quiet him.

So it is true. All of it is true: Mr. Brainerd's wasting disease has returned with bared fangs this time, the same lung trouble that runs through his family, if hearsay is correct. It killed his brother Nehemiah a few short years ago.

"You know, they say he almost died this past winter when he was in Elizabethtown, staying with Mr. – Mr...."

Mary struggles to remember the name but cannot. As with all things to do with Mr. Brainerd, my brain readily supplies the answer. "Mr. Dickinson. He is the head of the American side of the missionary society in whose service Mr. Brainerd labors. He and his wife are dear friends to him. They nursed him in their home, and thought he might die." I suck in a calming breath. "But Papa says Mr. Brainerd is better. He has recovered before from such episodes." I try to keep my tone confident, hoping that Mary will agree with me, will encourage my optimism.

But Mary's next question hisses into my ear. "How long do you think he has?" Her impertinence stings as lye splashing in my eyes on washday, and I want to snap at her – I want to release some of my fresh pain by inflicting it upon her.

But I am the second-eldest of the Edwards family. I am seventeen: a woman fully-grown by everyone's estimation. And, in my heart of hearts, I love my pretty young sister, overly-gifted with a mobile tongue though she may be. So I swallow the angry hurt that edges up the sand of my soul, threatening to erode it further, and shrug. "God knows," I murmur, keeping my tone neutral as a November sky. "Whatever is His will."

She nods, submissive as I appear to the will of God. But inside, I thrash with the desperation of a caged wild bird flinging itself against its prison bars.

I do not want him to die. Not now. Not while he is within stepping distance. Breathing the same air as I breathe. Living beneath the same roof. Not now. Not while I have the opportunity to get to know him, and for him to know me.

My heart squeezes tight in my chest.

I do not want him to die.

Not ever.

Chapter Two

"He has been in his room all day," Mary states the obvious. We four eldest girls – Sarah, Esther, Mary and I – along with Mama have busied ourselves with work in the kitchen for the past few hours. After Mr. Brainerd's arrival, Papa retreated to his closet. Leah brought a cup of tea to him, but he did not wish for anything to eat. His work was already interrupted by Mr. Brainerd's arrival; I suspect that his candle will burn even longer this evening as he tries to redeem the hours lost.

With a plunk, my sister drops her scrub-brush into the bucket beside her on the floor and sits back on her bare heels. "I thought that we were going to be entertained with tales of missionary bravery. With stories of conversions among the heathen." She cannot – or will not – keep the disappointment from coloring her voice, though she is careful not to show a pout on her exertion-flushed face.

Good for her, too, for Mama glances from the corner in which she and Sarah work at spinning once more. "'Tis for his own rest, not for your entertainment, that Mr. Brainerd has come to us here, Mary." Her tone holds no sharpness, but a warning does nip at the edges, like a dog urging sheep toward the right path. Her fingers continue to twist and feed the wool, her right foot pressing the treadle.

At Mama's gentle rebuke, Mary picks up her scrub-brush once more. Her petite, wiry form stretches out with the vigorous motions of her arms. The *chshuh-chshuh* of the bristles against the floor blends with the whispered bump of the spinning wheel, forming a familiar, comfortable accompaniment to our work. I pick up the next piece of silver, rubbing it with my cloth. Beside me, Esther helps polish as well, her voice adding the low hum of an Isaac Watts hymn to the kitchen.

"Don't let Papa catch you humming that," Mary teases. "He will tell you that people have become too enamored with these new songs and never sing the Psalter anymore."

Esther wrinkles her nose, but once she finishes the verse she was singing, she begins a tune from the Psalter instead.

We work in silence for a few minutes until Mary rises, finished with scrubbing the kitchen floor.

"You are soaked," Lucy observes, her green eyes taking in Mary's wet apron.

Mary only shrugs and picks up the bucket. "I have the passage floor to do yet."

"Sarah Prince says that she does not need to do any housework." This comes from Esther, of course, who is intimate writing friends with Reverend Prince of Boston's daughter.

Mama raises her eyebrows. "Exercise is beneficial for the mind and spirit as well as the body."

She waits until Mary has exited with her light step and half-full bucket. Then she addresses Sarah. "Did you bring the tea up earlier to Mr. Brainerd, as I asked?"

"Aye," Sarah answers, her fingers not stilling in their work. "But there was no answer, and I felt a bit awkward pushing open the door."

I understand this. My eighteen-year-old sister and I have a similar reticence toward those we do not know. We both guard our privacy and feel that everyone else should be entitled to their own as well. But I would think that after seeing the gray look on Mr. Brainerd's face when he arrived, Sarah might have at least opened it a handbreadth to check if he has made it safely to his bed or if he has fainted on the floor!

The thought makes me set aside the silver platter I am in the midst of polishing. My hands tremble as I rise to my feet. Images of Mr. Brainerd lying helpless beside his bed fill my mind. "Shall I go to check on him?" My voice sounds loud in the quiet room.

Sarah raises her eyes to me, surprise clear on her face. My chest tightens with awkwardness. I have spent years trying to squash such a foolish inclination as the one embedded within me, yet with every moment since Mr. Brainerd arrived this afternoon, my lack of success has become more and more evident. Surely, it is merely the admiration of a child for her father's friend, and nothing more. At least, that is what I have been desperately trying to tell myself for the past few hours.

If my inclination shows in any way, Sarah and Mama must think me touched in the head – to be attracted not only toward a man whom I barely know, but also one who may not be long for this world, in all likeliness.

But Mama gives no indication that she suspects anything out-of-the-ordinary. She thinks for a moment, the whir of her spinning slowing. Then she shakes her head, the tendrils of her black hair fluttering in stark contrast to her stiff white cap. "He is probably sleeping, Jerusha. We should not disturb him, poor man. He needs all the rest he can get to heal his constitution."

If he can be healed. Mama doesn't say the words, but I see them in the dark sadness pooling in her eyes just before she returns her full attention to spinning.

I swallow back the argument that springs to my throat. Taking my hard seat again, I polish a silver soup tureen with great fervency until I can see my reflection in it. The extra effort relieves some of the distress that has built up in my heart every time the thought of Mr. Brainerd passes through my mind.

"We'll need that this evening," Mama comments as I set the tureen aside. "Your brother found some turtles in the cow pond."

Turtles... My stomach turns, but I say nothing. Whether I like turtle soup or not makes little difference as to whether it will be served, as it is a favorite dish of my parents. Its strange texture reminds me of a chicken crossbred with a fish. Protesting, however, is not worth the fuss, and it will not alter the menu.

So I will sip my turtle soup submissively, quietly, stealing glances at Mr. Brainerd all the while, praying fervently that it might be the Lord's will to spare him – and me – from the painful Providence that seems to stalk his steps.

***

"I will have Doctor Mather come round tomorrow, Mr. Brainerd," Papa announces. We have had our turtle soup; what a blessed relief when Leah comes to clear away our soup plates and to remove the tureen! She is bringing the meat course now; the beeswax candles flicker on our waiting fine pewter plates.

Mr. Brainerd glances up from wiping his hands on his napkin. I catch a flash of spirit in his hollowed eyes at Papa's commanding air, but he hides or subdues it well and quickly. "I should not wish you to go to any trouble, Mr. Edwards. The doctor in Elizabethtown confirmed what I have long known about my condition. I would not want you to store up any false hopes."

The weariness washes into the caves of his voice and fills them. Pity and something more stirs within my heart. Oh, how I wish that I could make this dear man well again, despite his doctor's grim prognosis!

"One can never be too confident," Papa rejoins, and I know that he is determined to have his way because he knows 'tis the right course of action. And I am glad of it in this case, for I want to hold onto just one thread of hope. "And you seem much better in health than Mr. Dickinson's letter indicated. Perhaps you are improving. You do not know for certain."

Leah returns from the kitchen with a platter heavy with roasted chicken. Papa rises from his seat at the head of the table, ready to carve the plump and well-seasoned bird, selected from our own flock. "Doctor Mather is not a frontiersman hack, such as New Jersey and Pennsylvania boast; he may know of things those in that wild country have no knowledge of."

"Such as Mr. Wesley's new book." This comes from young Mary, sitting to Mr. Brainerd's right, the place I coveted but had not the nerve to attempt to secure. Now, as Mr. Brainerd's hazel eyes turns to join hands with Mary's dancing, dark gaze, I wish that I had more of her vivacious spirit in me – the spirit that causes her to voice her thoughts in a conversation between Papa and our visitor, rather than to sit on the periphery as Sarah and I tend to do. When Mr. Brainerd's mouth rises from its weary setting into a cordial smile, I wish that I had her beauty as well, for Mary is often whispered to be the best-looking of all us Edwards girls, young though she is. No wonder even Mr.

Brainerd grants her a friendly expression, though surely it is one intended merely for a pretty child and nothing more. Besides, does he not regard everyone he meets with a kindly look?

"Mr. Wesley has a new book? Of hymns?" Mr. Brainerd asks, the interest obvious in his voice.

Here Mary is lost, for though she loves collecting and passing along news, she is not careful of details, nor is she a great reader. I am both. Should I open my mouth, kept sealed throughout all of our meal thus far, and reveal what I know of this new book – drawing Mr. Brainerd's attention to myself? My stomach flips over at the thought, and my throat closes up as if I have had a reaction to a hornet-sting.

When Mary sits tongue-tied at Mr. Brainerd's question, Mama interjects the answer in her soft, cultured voice. "'Tis Mr. John Wesley who has penned a new work, rather than his brother Charles." She handed little Jonathan and baby Elizabeth off to one of our servants before the meal was served, so she is free to be hospitable to Mr. Brainerd. "He has published it under a pseudonym, but his acquaintances know, of course, that he is the author."

"*Primitive Physick*, 'tis called," Papa answers, his knife sliding into the tender breast of poultry, slicing off a portion and slipping it onto Mr. Brainerd's plate. "I have not purchased a copy myself but have had the opportunity to peruse it while at a friend's home – specifically with you in mind, Mr. Brainerd. Rational and educated man that he is, Mr. Wesley's advice is sound for a case such as yours – eat light and often, not much before retiring, obtain some exercise outdoors, but nothing strenuous. Such things as you perhaps should have been doing all these months previous – things of which I'm sure your friends advised you and yet you ignored."

Inwardly, I wince. Awkwardness swirls around the room, like a giddy dance gone out-of-control. Mama pretends not to notice it, but I can tell from the strain around her mouth that she is trying to think of something to say that will smooth out Papa's words and give them a more delicate touch.

Across the table, Mary twists her napkin with her fingers. Her fidgeting informs me that she is suppressing a nervous giggle. Beside her, Sarah reaches up a hand to tuck an invisible lock of hair beneath her white cap. Meanwhile, my brother Timothy glances from Papa to Mr. Brainerd and back again, eyes wide in anticipation. My own heart picks up its pace to a rapid trot.

And I had been concerned about protesting against turtle soup.

Mama opens her mouth, and my lungs draw breath again. Good, she must have thought of something that will halt Mr. Brainerd's certain displeasure at Papa's public dressing-down and yet will not raise the slightest disquieting idea in Papa's mind that she is attempting to soften the blow he just tried to deal to Mr. Brainerd's conscience.

But Mr. Brainerd speaks first. His voice is quiet, controlled, and completely void of anger and self-defense. "I am sure that you are correct, Mr. Edwards," he replies. "My health would perhaps have been better maintained had I taken more opportunity for leisure and been more precise and assiduous with regards to my daily consumption of food and drink."

I steal a glance at Papa, who is continuing to carve the bird. His face shows his satisfaction at Mr. Brainerd's acceptance of his admonition, and my heart slows its drumming.

"Yes," agrees Papa, eager to affirm Mr. Brainerd's correct response, "All of your fasting and secret hours of prayer and excessive expenditure of energy... All excellent spiritual discipline for a man of health, but you should have known that such undertakings, while admirable, would entirely defeat your already-weak constitution. Family history informed you of this. Well-intended, certainly, but ultimately, poor judgment."

Everyone has received their portion. Papa resumes his seat, and we each pick up our knives and two-tined forks. Surely we will move from this conversation now that Papa and Mr. Brainerd agree.

I slice off a small piece of the juicy white breast meat and spear it with my knife. I am not hungry, but it is something with which to occupy myself, something to keep my eyes from darting toward the man sitting diagonally across from me. The bite is almost to my mouth when Mr. Brainerd's voice breaks the silence once more. "'Tis perhaps a fault," he begins, friendliness in every tone, "but I have never minded dying. My thought has always been that it would be better to die; shake off this frail, sinful flesh; and fly to God, to be evermore in His presence like one of the angels. Perhaps 'tis why I have been overly careless with my body. I have longed for heaven and for God so greatly that it seemed a little thing to wear out this tent He gave to me."

Papa looks at him, startled, and I see on my father's face – for just the time it takes to draw in a breath – an intense hunger, like that of a man who has not eaten for many days. Strange, for my father has always seemed completely satisfied in his understanding of, and life in, God. I have never seen the thirst on his face that I witness there for just that half of a moment. It so very much mirrors the same craving that I have many times found in myself when I have heard the words of Mr. Brainerd read from a letter or in his published *Journal.* For me, it is this which has driven my affection for Mr. Brainerd from girlish infatuation toward an admiring and at least partly spiritual passion quite against my will. He seems to me to have found that for which my very soul craves – the secret of true joy.

But then, just as quickly as the stark hunger appears on my father's face, it vanishes. He picks up his own fork, and it scrapes the pewter as he methodically stabs his cooked chicken. "We should not hurry to the grave when God has provided means for the continuance of our life," he comments before popping the chunk of fowl into his mouth, chewing thoroughly, and swallowing. "We should endeavor to lengthen our life as much as possible to serve God for as long as we possibly can in this world. It is our Christian duty. Do you not agree, Mr. Brainerd?"

Mr. Brainerd nods, but he has no over-eager expression on his countenance, as some of Papa's other visitors do – longing to please and agree with him, no matter what he says. *He is no respecter of persons.* As I sip my cider, the thought comes to me that this quality in Mr. Brainerd has probably secured my father's scarcely-concealed admiration for him. It is odd for this to be the case, considering my father's position in New England's religious life, Mr. Brainerd's own highly-speckled past, and the difference in their ages and – I suspect – outlooks on many things. Papa thinks of him as an equal, though he seems to not be able to know him intimately as a friend. He wants to be like Mr. Brainerd – and yet he also wants Mr. Brainerd to be more like him.

"I do agree," Mr. Brainerd answers after a pause, "as long as there is no conflict between the more specific duty God has given to us individually and the general duty to care for our health and well-being. The latter must always give way to the former."

And, though Papa says nothing in response, I know that we all hear what Mr. Brainerd left unsaid: that there had been a conflict between those duties for him – and that he had chosen the hard and specific path.

Chapter Three

That evening, as usual, we all gather in the sitting room. Mary sits at Papa's feet, her head against his knees, his hand resting gently on her glossy hair. Across from him, Mama has finally taken a seat, but her nimble hands do not lie idle. Never one to discard beauty along with worldliness, she works on some pretty embroidery for a pillow. Sarah sits beside her, baby Elizabeth cuddled in her lap, while little Jonathan dozes against Esther's chest nearby. My other sisters and I have needlework to occupy our hands and our brother Timothy whittles while we prepare to listen to Papa read from the Scriptures.

As Papa reaches for his Bible, Mary voices the question I wish that I could ask if I did not fear that my voice might tremble. "Why, where is Mr. Brainerd?"

Papa looks at Mama. I catch her shake her head just once. "I do not believe that Mr. Brainerd will be well enough to join us this evening."

Mary's mouth screws itself into a pout, more appropriate for my youngest siblings than for her, though she allows little of her disappointment to seep into her tone. She knows how our parents dislike sulking. "And here I thought that we'd hear stories of the Indian conversions tonight."

"Perhaps another night, Mary," Esther soothes in her sweet-as-molasses-cake way. She finishes mending one stocking and takes up another.

"Am I too tardy to join you?"

I lift my eyes and see Mr. Brainerd standing there in the doorway, a smile raising his lips gently, pain slouching his fine shoulders. Inside me, joy rushes up like an underground spring, bubbling to the surface. I school my features carefully and attend to my knitting. Or at least pretend to. Why must these emotions continue to surface when I should have surely long put to rest my childish fascination with Mr. Brainerd as a man?

Papa rises immediately. "Mr. Brainerd. Come right in and join us. We were just about to begin the Scripture reading."

Without ceremony, Mr. Brainerd takes the chair toward which Papa gestured. 'Tis beside me, and as he sits, he brushes against the blue linen fabric of my skirt. I smell the scent of woodsmoke lingering in his clothing, most likely from his long journey – aye, that and the fragrance of the woods and fields that have surrounded him for years, that have become a part of him. His hands lay flat against his breeches, and I cannot help but eye them surreptitiously. These are the hands of a man who has held bridle reins for many miles and who has taken his own part in manual labor, even building his own homes among the Indians, despite his illnesses, for he has told Papa in letters that he knew that he must live among "his people" – a term of belonging not many other white men would use.

When I have thought of Mr. Brainerd over the years, despite hearing of his exploits as a missionary on the frontier, I have always pictured him as I saw him at Yale those years ago – sturdy, fierce-eyed, but given more to holding a book in his hands than the handle of an axe. Yet, here beside me sits what must be a true example of a frontier missionary. He is courteous, aye, I will not deny that. He sits properly and holds himself well, despite the drooping which he can barely help. At supper, he ate in a mannerly way, though without any pretension. Yet, every inch of him is different from any other gentleman I have ever known, though whether this is a spiritual or physical difference I cannot tell yet. Awe continues to breathe on my soul as I observe him, no matter how I try to suppress it and tell myself that Mr. Brainerd is merely another one of Papa's theological guests and that I must begin to view him thus.

Now, as he waits for Papa to read, Mr. Brainerd's body goes completely still, except for his eyes, which blink more deliberately than most people's do, and his chest, which rises and falls with greater effort. A slight, bubbly wheeze exhales with each breath.

With the firelight glazing his black hair, Papa reads from Psalm 102 and elaborates on its meaning. Then he asks questions from the Westminster Shorter Catechism, directing these mainly to my younger brothers and sisters. Through the nightly exercise, I sit with all quietness as I know I must, trying my best to pay attention to Papa's soft voice.

Yet it is the difficult breathing of the man beside me that continually draws my thoughts away from the Scripture reading. By the time Papa has begun to catechize the younger children, I have started to pray silently, almost through a will other than my own, asking – not demanding, mind you – merely requesting that the Lord God would see fit to heal this man. As my eyes glance at him, I feel as though the pain he must endure moment-by-moment enters my own body, pinning my heart to a board, still alive, as some lads do with butterflies.

His wheezing has softened, probably from resting quietly. In my inattention, I drop a stitch. *Could Thou not merely let him live, even if he is sickly and unable to continue his work with the Indians? We would care for him.*

I swallow. I know what I truly mean... yet what I cannot mean. *I would care for him.* It would be a privilege to comfort him, even if he remains an invalid all his life. My mind wanders, and a scene appears in it: One of Mr. Brainerd and myself, sitting contentedly in our home, of him reading a book of theology, of me sewing some garment for the poor.

Our home? Aye, though my face warms as I realize what I imagined, 'tis truly what I saw. He and I, working for the Lord God in a quiet way, together, with great joy.

I force my mind back to the stocking I am knitting. I must banish such notions from my head and tear up the roots of them from the soil of my heart.

Though God knows that I have tried.

A few moments later, the family prays together, with Papa leading and Mr. Brainerd adding his own prayer at the end. His request drives the spade beneath those roots but cannot upend them.

Raising his hands toward the flame-flickered and shadowed ceiling, he rasps, "Oh, Lord God, may we never outlive our usefulness to Thee!"

My heart warms in my chest at his words, and the hunger that pangs suddenly within startles me – a hunger that I cannot name but the object of which I understand: It is the same hunger that I saw in Papa's face at the supper-table – a hunger for that something more that Mr. Brainerd pants after and has found at last.

I know then, too, that, if there is any future for Mr. Brainerd and me, that God must heal him, for Mr. Brainerd will not be content with the life of an invalid soldier in God's service.

***

"Rushie, Rushie!" Susannah's lisping whisper shakes me from the world of my book. Lifting my gaze from the pages of the *Journal*, my eyes fall on my six-year-old sister, clad in her white shift and barefoot. A rag doll hangs from one hand, while the thumb of the other has already gone back into her mouth. Instantly, I understand why she has come, and a little irritation itches my heart.

"Jonathan will not sleep?" With a silent sigh, I lay aside my book even as I speak and swing my legs over the side of the bed I share with my sister Sarah. It is not yet the time when Mama and we older girls usually turn in, but I often prefer to come apart from the rest of the company, finding a peace in the solitude of our bedchamber. Such was the case this night. Besides, I wished to review what I knew of Mr. Brainerd from his publically-published *Journal.*

Susannah shakes her head, her dark curls bouncing against her slight shoulders. "Leah said to fetch you."

Of course she did. I am the only one of my sisters for whom little Jonathan will go to sleep when he is in a fussy mood.

At least I have not undressed yet. I pick up my candle from the bedside table. "I am coming."

***

Nearly an hour later, I close the children's door behind me. My lips feel weary from humming and softly singing hymns and psalms in Jonathan's small pink ears, yet a thread of joy weaves through my heart with the knowledge that I have helped give him a peaceful night of sleep.

Candle in hand, I tiptoe down the passage, aware that the household has gone to bed – or at least, retired to their chambers now. To my right, the light flickers beneath Mama and Papa's door, and I hear their voices rolling back-and-forth, his low rumble followed by her alto murmur. On my left, the pitch darkness tells me that Esther, Mary, and Lucy have blown out their candle already, probably exhausted from the excitement of the day.

And then, situated diagonally from the room which Sarah and I share, is Mr. Brainerd's guest room. The door remains open a crack, and as I approach, pain-tinged mutterings float out to meet me. My steps become slow as cold maple syrup, and I dare to hesitate outside his door, careful to stay out of the sliver of flickering light cast by his candle.

"Oh, God, dear God, do not make me linger in this state! Do not let me outlast my usefulness. I cannot bear that I should have to remain here on this earth, deprived of heaven's joy for even an hour more, when I can be of no service to Thee!"

The words dissolve into such softness that I cannot understand the meaning. My heart thudding so hard that I can feel its beat against my ribcage, I take a step nearer and peer into the room, keeping my breath still in my lungs.

The man lies prostrate on the floor beside the bed. A Bible, its edges torn and frayed, spreads open before him, and it appears – though I am at such a distance that I could not say for certain – that some of the print has blurred. Could it have been from his tears, now and in times past?

"Do not let the work that Thy Spirit has begun among my people become corrupted. Let it all be silver and gold, none of it dross. Let no leaven be mixed in with the lump. Sanctify Thy people and provide for them good shepherds, who will tend them well."

His people? Does he speak of the natives he left in Cranberry? No other man – well, perhaps other than John Seargent, Papa's distant cousin-in-law and missionary in Stockbridge – has ever spoken of the Indians with such a term of belonging. The affection and sensitivity in his tone toward "his people" – It astounds me, truly. His affection shows that they are worth something, that they are special, despite what everyone around them may believe. And if he loves these once-heathen people in this way, could he not also love me with such warmth and kindliness? I know that if I had the particular love of such a one as Mr. Brainerd, my soul would possess true contentment, knowing that he finds me worthy of his love.

And this is what I have long craved.

A wet, hacking cough wrenches Mr. Brainerd's body with a force and suddenness that alarm me. My sensitivity to pain and others' sorrow – something I have long wished would leave me, for it is often inconvenient – drives the breath from my own lungs in an audible rush, and Mr. Brainerd, his whole frame struggling against the cough that wrestles him, turns a wild-eyed gaze toward the door as he braces himself on hands and knees.

There is nothing for it. I must reveal myself. Embarrassment obliges me to cringe inwardly, but I will not show this on my face as I put a hand to the door, push it open a little farther, and step into the doorway so that Mr. Brainerd may recognize me.

My hand tightens on the candleholder. "I was just passing by – I needed to help with my brother Jonathan, you see – and..." I can go no further with my explanation, for he has begun to hack again, his knuckles white upon the dark wooden floor as he supports himself against the gale buffeting him from within.

My soul bleeds at the sight. I must do something – anything – to help him. Setting my candle down on the table beside his bed, I lower myself to his side. He pays me no mind, utterly overtaken by the coughing and gagging.

"Here." I find the handkerchief tucked away in my sleeve. In his condition, he cannot take it, and I realize how foolish I am. Without giving myself time to think about it, I hold the handkerchief to his mouth. Immediately, red speckles the white fabric.

Inside, I recoil. *He is dying.* The thought makes my bowels turn to water. He cannot die. He cannot.

I will save him. I will...

The cough begins to fade away, not wrenching him so severely each time it wrestles with him. After it has nearly left, he remains on his hands and knees, sucking in air, until he suddenly lifts up a hand and brushes away my handkerchief. "I am all right now." His fist wipes any stray droplets off his mouth. He sits back on his haunches, hands splayed on his thighs, arms stiff beneath the linen shirt that sticks to his sweaty skin.

I crumple the handkerchief into a ball, hiding its spatters not from him, but from myself. Swallowing against the fear that rises like an ocean wave, ready to overwhelm me, I open my mouth to ask if he would like me to fetch him some wine, perhaps, to relax the pain he surely must have.

But he doesn't let me voice the question. Between ragged breaths, he glances over at me for the first time since I entered the room long minutes ago. The coolness in his normally-warm gaze makes me flinch. "I thank you, but I am all right." With great effort, he stumbles to his stocking-clad feet and makes as if to busy himself with some books and papers on his table. "Good-night."

Clearly, I am dismissed. I am not wanted or needed, apparently, even to fetch Mr. Brainerd a cup of water, which he surely must need. My hand tightens around the soiled handkerchief until my fingernails dig into my palm. Grabbing the candlestick with trembling fingers, I retreat to the safety of my own chamber, undress, and crawl into bed beside peacefully-sleeping Sarah, hoping for rest to soothe my confused thoughts.

But my whirling mind will not permit me to enter the world of dreams so swiftly, and I lie awake long, staring up into the blackness, listening to Sarah's even breathing, remembering and then trying to block out the image of Mr. Brainerd hacking and gagging. Why would he not accept my help? Why is he so aloof toward me? He was not that way with Mary at suppertime. He must see some fault in me that disgusts and repels him. At this thought, the pang in my heart causes me to bite the inside of my mouth to distract myself.

As is often the event on such occasions, my inner turmoil turns into a kind of prayer, if pouring out all that is in my heart may be called a proper prayer. 'Tis directed toward God; I take consolation in that, despite its informality. The tears well in my eyes, making me thankful for the darkness, and then leak out the sides, trickling across my temples and dissolving into my hair.

And in the midst of my distress, I sense a Presence with me, comforting me.

Chapter Four

The sunlight streams through the kitchen windows, making the curtains glow as they filter the buttery morning rays. Beside me, Esther overturns a large wooden mixing bowl and the great blob of yeasty dough plops onto the flour-dusted table. Humming a hymn from *The Bay Psalm Book*, I do the same with my mixing bowl, and we both begin to knead, our fingers mushing into the soft mixture.

"Doctor Mather is coming this day, then?"

It is a question to which we both already know the answer. This is just Esther's way to begin a conversation. A conversation in which I must be careful, for I cannot let her know anything of what is in my heart toward one whom we must think of as Papa's friend only – and one who proved his own indifference, nay, aversion toward me last night.

I give the briefest of nods. "Aye," I reply, trying to affect nonchalance and a lack of any more than the casual interest of Esther herself.

"Do you know when? This morning or in the afternoon?"

How can she not know this? Does she suspect…? But when I glance over at my next-in-age sister, her smooth, olive-toned countenance speaks of nothing but innocence. The most talkative of us sisters, and perhaps the most mischievous as well, save Mary,

Esther is only trying to chat with me, whom everyone considers the most reserved. "Doctor Mather has already come," I answer. "He and Mr. Brainerd went above stairs to his chamber a little while ago."

I know this because, when Mama asked our slave-woman to answer the front door earlier, foolish as I am, I made some excuse to hurry through the passage just in time to see the two gentlemen ascending the staircase, Mr. Brainerd's long, bony legs following the stout legs of the doctor.

Esther nods and pushes stray hairs away from her face with a floury hand, leaving a track of white dust on her forehead. She has never been able to enter a kitchen without leaving covered in flour or dotted with grease. "I wonder whether—"

Her words are cut off by the sound of footsteps descending the stairs – not the dainty clatter of my sisters' shoes on the wood, but the firm, heavier step of men. The kitchen door stands open, so the noise of their descent, as well as the low murmur of their voices, wafts into the room. My motions slow and my ears prick up like a startled horse as I try to hear as much of their conversation as possible.

But the only thing I can distinguish is Doctor Mather's low, somber voice saying, "If you wish. Shall we go into Reverend Mr. Edwards' closet, then?"

A knock sounds, followed by the soft creak of the closet door swinging open and then shutting.

My mind cannot focus on the dough any longer, nor on Esther's conversation, which turns to her friend Sarah's latest newsy letter. What does Doctor Mather think of Mr. Brainerd's condition? Will his lungs improve again, as they have in the past – years ago, when he was at Yale, and several times in his wilderness wanderings as well? Or does the doctor think that this time, the dreaded consumption is on a course that cannot be altered? I swallow so hard that my throat hurts. *Oh, dear Lord God, let it not be so!* It is for his sake alone, surely, that I pray it. For Mr. Brainerd's sake and for the Lord's, for is not he one of the Lord's most beloved? But even as I try to convince myself of my disinterested concern, I know 'tis not so.

Footsteps sound near me on the smooth wooden floor of the kitchen. Startled, I glance up from staring down at the dough. Mama stands just beyond the threshold, holding my smallest brother in her arms. Over her finely-stitched everyday gown, she has pinned an apron with a bit more style to it than usual. Little Jonathan grabs at her well-pressed cap, and Mama reaches for his hands, stilling them quickly. "Doctor Mather and Mr. Brainerd have retired to your father's closet. Esther, bring them some refreshment." Unlike some other, more lenient parents, neither Mama nor Papa request an action from us; rather, they command us, for that is how they believe biblical parenthood should conduct itself. Yet Mama's kind smile softens the demand, so that her authoritative manner causes in most of us a desire to obey and please her, rather than to resent.

Thus, at Mama's directive, Esther immediately nods and sets her dough aside. "Aye, Mama." She begins to unpin the now-dirty apron that has protected her dress during our time in the kitchen.

Why did Mama not ask me to bring them the refreshments? If she had, I would have possibly been able to hear first-hand Doctor Mather's judgment of Mr. Brainerd's condition. I tamp down the frustration that rises in my chest. It is foolish; I have no special claim to Mr. Brainerd's private information, and he certainly would not wish to share it with me.

"Esther, you are covered in flour and your hair is coming undone, dear. Be sure to neaten yourself before you go. But hurry," Mama urges, her brow furrowing. She does not like to keep visitors waiting without food or drink, and Esther obviously will require at least a few minutes to clean up.

I speak without giving myself a chance to think. "I will bring the refreshments, Mama."

Mama turns to look at me. I can see the surprise in her eyes. It is not often that I suggest something other than what she or Papa command. I especially am the dutiful one – the obedient one – the daughter who does not question.

"I only have flour on my apron, I think," I add, as though helpful promptness is the only reason I have offered to serve in Esther's stead.

There is no reason for Mama to refuse, and of course, Esther is not given the option of either agreeing or disagreeing with my suggestion. I glance at her, though, to be sure that my sister is not irked with me. Happily, she seems very content to re-pin her apron and continue with the bread-making.

As Mama turns to go, Esther leans over and whispers to me, "Better you than I, sister. Imagine if what he has is catching?"

I wish that all would catch it, then, if it leads to the zeal and fire I witness in him.

***

"I admit, I am surprised to see that you are looking better than I thought you would be, Mr. Brainerd." Doctor Mather's voice rumbles through the wooden door of Papa's closet. Tray balanced on my left arm, I clear my throat and raise a trembling hand to the door.

The knock sounds loud in the quiet passage. The voices within the closet go silent, and I imagine all three gentlemen turning their heads toward the door that conceals me. Then a quick exchange of murmurs ensues.

I hold my breath. "Come in," Papa's steady voice calls out. Swallowing, I compose my features before lifting the latch. The door swings wide, and I am revealed. Papa smiles at me, but I can see the worry underpinning his expression. Doctor Mather stands before Papa's desk, obviously distressed. The object of their concern, however, appears very much at peace as he sits in the only chair other than Papa's, fatigue drawing his features into settled lines. I wonder if Mr. Brainerd has spoken to the doctor about the episode of illness he experienced last night. When his eyes flit over toward me, the expression in them changes to slight irritation.

Ignoring the pang in my heart that comes from his attitude, I glance down at my tray. "Mama sent refreshments for you."

"Just what the doctor ordered." Mr. Brainerd smiles, though not at me, and the sun touches the dry winter earth of my heart, warming me straight to the core of my being. "Well," he adds, glancing at Doctor Mather, "perhaps not *quite* what the doctor ordered."

Doctor Mather chuckles, and some of the tension dissipates. My eyes continue to wander toward Mr. Brainerd's face as I enter the room. Tranquility reigns there – and hope. So the news cannot all be bad. I look up into Papa's face. But Papa does not give any indication of what Doctor Mather has told them. Despite the way the question builds on the tip of my tongue, I do not ask. This is a man's world that I have walked into... Papa's world. I know my place.

Papa quickly confirms this. "Set the tray down, Jerusha. I thank you."

I place the tray on a small table, give a curtsy, and depart.

***

'Tis not until a few days later that I know exactly why Dr. Mather looked so concerned in Papa's closet, and why Mr. Brainerd appears unwise to take the matter lightly.

In the cool late morning, Papa and Mr. Brainerd take a stroll along the path surrounding our house, not realizing that I sit upon the little swing out there, a book of my grandfather Samuel Stoddard's sermons in my lap. Papa often likes to take a short break from his studies during the day; he says that an hour of physical activity is necessary for every man's health and welfare, so it does not surprise me when I hear his voice coupled with that of Mr. Brainerd, a little way off from me, muffled only slightly by the freshly-leafed trees all around me. I ought to immediately make my presence known, but the words catch in my throat as I realize that they speak of a subject most close to me: Mr. Brainerd's health.

"Mr. Brainerd, must I reiterate what the good Doctor Mather told you and me just days ago? You have a confirmed, incurable consumption. You cannot live long. I do not know what it is about this that you do not understand." The controlled exasperation in Papa's voice makes me smile... and wince for Mr. Brainerd's sake.

"I understand it perfectly, Mr. Edwards," Mr. Brainerd answers, his tone mild.

Their feet stop crunching across the dry grass. "Then why should you wish to risk your health further by going to Boston? 'Tis a long and arduous journey. If I may be so plain with you, it opposes common sense. I cannot allow it."

I clap a hand over my own mouth to stifle my gasp

of disbelief. The man can barely walk through the grass! Is it possible for him to ride the long, country road to Boston? Is it necessary?

Several breaths of silence rustle by before I hear Mr. Brainerd's reply, quiet and determined.

"Mr. Edwards," Mr. Brainerd's voice filters through the leafy curtain that conceals me, "the Redeemer's kingdom is all that is valuable on this earth to me. God Himself has a greater regard – infinitely so – and concern for the promotion of His kingdom in this world than I could possibly have. And He will promote His kingdom."

"I agree with you. And you have done much for His kingdom in this world, but now, as Doctor Mather told you, you ought to do whatever would prolong your life. God will take care of His kingdom." Affection rests in my father's words, though they are spoken in command. Some see in Papa only sternness, and that is certainly present, but there is also a deep, private warmth, an enduring personal love for those whom he cares about, and Mr. Brainerd is one of them.

Another long pause ensues. Mr. Brainerd's breaths sound as though they have been torn at the edges as they pass through his lips and down into his roughened lungs. There is a bench on the other side of the path. Perhaps he has taken a seat there to give his weary body rest.

"Even more so then, Mr. Edwards," says Mr. Brainerd, "I should not wish to outlive my usefulness. What is life to me if 'tis not lived for God? And what is it to live for God, but to be used up for Him, to be poured out as a drink offering, even as our Lord Christ was?" He pauses. "I will go to Boston," he says, the conviction solid as stone in his tone. "I would like to meet with some ministers there and see if there is any more work that may be done to further the cause of missions among the Indians. I know of at least two men whom I would recommend that the Society send out. After that… I am not certain yet."

My father's silence sounds loud. Is he angry that Mr. Brainerd has gone against his wishes? Or…? It still surprises me that Mr. Brainerd seems to be able to stand his ground firmly and yet be gracious and gentle with Papa, a deed not many can accomplish. Indeed, I have seen none do it besides him.

Then laughter winks in Mr. Brainerd's voice. "Doctor Mather did tell me that I should continue riding – that it would likely lengthen my days."

"We will deliberate further about this." Papa is troubled. He does not want Mr. Brainerd to go. Knowing Mr. Brainerd's ill health, he may leave for Boston and never come back. He may die on the road. Alone. Cared-for by none. I shut my eyes against the vision, and my heart clenches at the thought. I am not ready to let him go.

I wait until the crackle of grass beneath their feet tells me that they have moved on before I rise, a nearly-unthinkable plan forming in my mind.

Chapter Five

I am sure that Papa will continue to express his strong reservations regarding this trip to Boston.

I am equally sure that Mr. Brainerd has set his face like flint and will try to go to Boston, whether my father believes it is necessary or not. This spirit, not of defiance, but of complete, unreserved determination to do whatever he believes is the will of God, regardless of who naysays him, exhilarates my own spirit.

Yet, like Papa, I cannot allow Mr. Brainerd to go. I cannot allow him to be lost to me permanently.

And the only way to accomplish that prevention is through Mama's persuasion.

My opportunity comes later when I am helping Mama with some folding of linens above stairs. We hear Elizabeth crying in another room, and my sister Sarah calls out, "I am going to her, Mama."

Mama smiles and calls back, "Thank you, Sarah."

We fold quietly for a bit, the only sound the rustling of the sheets as they brush against each other. We fold up, then back, then corner-to-corner, then up, and then finally into one neat, white packet. In the silence, I gather my courage and whisper a plea for help from above, if what I request is God's will. "Mama," I say, my voice surprising me with its stability, "I was sitting outdoors, and I overheard quite by accident Papa and Mr. Brainerd speaking together.

It seems that Mr. Brainerd will not be with us for long but has resolved to go to Boston."

Mama purses her lips, a sure sign that she is worried and is trying to tamp the feeling down. "Aye, he is determined to go to Boston. However, your father does not believe 'tis wise, given Mr. Brainerd's illness. And from what Doctor Mather says, 'tis unlikely that he will ever recover his strength as 'twas once."

A kind way of saying that he is dying – slowly, perhaps, yet dying nonetheless.

I take a deep breath, and the scent of the fresh outdoors in which these sheets dried greets my nose. "Do you not think, Mama," I say and am thankful for the job of folding linen, for it means that the shaking of my hands will not be noticeable amidst the folding, "that you could persuade Papa to prevent Mr. Brainerd from taking this unnecessary risk? Could not someone else go in Mr. Brainerd's stead to accomplish whatever his purpose is in Boston? 'Tis such a far journey, and he is so weakened. 'Tis eighty miles to Boston." Mama already knows this, but there is no harm in reminding her.

"'Tis a long road for an ill man to travel, but Mr. Brainerd appears determined to do it." A sigh escapes Mama's lips. "And he does not seem to be a man easily persuaded from his resolutions. Your father would go with him, but he is too much engaged for such a journey at this time, and Mr. Brainerd wishes to leave on Tuesday. Apart from that, Mr. Brainerd has not yet determined his course after he travels to Boston."

I feel liquid pewter solidify in my stomach. He has not determined his course. Does he intend to travel back to his Indians in New Jersey and resume his work among them, if he grows a little better in Boston? Does he intend to go to stay with his remaining family in Connecticut? It does not seem that he has made up his mind to return to us. My chest tightens. I cannot lose him now that he is physically present among us.

It is time to change my course of argument. "Mama, Mr. Brainerd is a family friend, and I know that my sisters and I look upon him as an eminent servant of the Lord. And we each would be quite willing to go and be what help we can to him." I must phrase it this way at first, though inside I am begging her to let me, and only me, accompany Mr. Brainerd.

Mama does not make the least attempt to hide her surprise at my suggestion. I force my expression to stay steady and innocent, a hard thing, indeed, when I am suggesting that one of us girls, all unmarried females, travel alone with a man who is not our relative on a journey lasting some days.

"One of you girls? Alone, Jerusha?"

I nod as if it is the kind of offer made regularly by modest Christian young women. It is an extraordinary suggestion, aye, but I sense that my purpose is to be found at Mr. Brainerd's side. I cannot bear to think of Mr. Brainerd traveling all that distance alone when I hear his coughing through the night, when I see the frailty of his body, or when I, the one who looks at him most closely, perhaps of all in the family, notice the paleness of his face, the set of his lips against the pain that continually meets him at every turn.

He has spent so long in the wilderness, suffering alone.

No, if he is determined to go to the city, he will not go there to die alone. Not if I may help it.

Yet, I also cannot allow my parents to believe that I harbor a childish affection for this man, an affection which surely I should have long ago forced myself to fold up and put away. If either Mama or Papa suspects such, even the slightest chance that I will be allowed to accompany Mr. Brainerd will disappear.

Mama takes a long while to reply – seventeen shallow breaths, to be exact. "That is a notion with potential," she says at last, slow as cold honey drizzling onto toasted bread. "But I am not sure that your father would approve, given the length of the road."

I want to argue immediately but place a steadying hand on myself. *Wait*...

"Though in the face of necessity, your father can often be brought around to seeing the logic of an idea that he initially has distaste for," Mama goes on, her hands slowing as she thinks. "I would not wish to send Sarah. She is such a help to me with the little ones, especially Elizabeth."

"Sarah does not like to go on long journeys, at any rate," I add, perhaps too hastily. This is true; my elder sister is a stay-at-home if there ever was one. Going to Main Street to purchase chocolate for an after-supper treat is the nearest to adventure she wishes to get, and even for that task, she will not volunteer herself.

Mama nods, agreeing with my assessment of my elder sister, and some of my tension evaporates. *One down*...

"Of course, Esther would wish to go. Reverend Prince's daughter has repeatedly asked her to visit this year, and there has not arisen a suitable occasion."

Inwardly, I wince, but I cannot give the emotion public exhibition on my countenance. Esther is nearly three years younger than I. Why should Mama consider her first, before me? Why are my desires never consulted? It takes supreme effort to stuff the words of protest back down my throat and allow Mama to come to her own conclusion, which I know is necessary. I pick up another pillowcase and fold it with far more concentration than is necessary.

"Yet, given the circumstances, I think it would be better for Esther to wait for a time in which your father may accompany her. If she goes now, I fear that her necessary attendance to Mr. Brainerd would be compromised through her many visits with the Princes."

My breath pulses out audibly, and I hide it with a cough. Ducking my head veils my smile of delight. I am the only daughter left of a reasonable age to be of help to Mr. Brainerd. Surely, Mama will consider thirteen-year-old Mary too young to go. I wait for Mama to continue, anticipation unsteadying my hands.

"That leaves you, Jerusha," she says at last.

Joy trembles up from the tips of my toes.

"'Tis a long journey to Boston," Mama goes on. "Made longer still because of Mr. Brainerd's illness. You would be on the road at the very least for one night, most likely two or three, and must stay at respectable homes along the way."

"There would be no difficulty with that, Mama," I say, as calmly as I can. "I am used to traveling with Papa. Do you remember years ago, when I traveled to New Haven, sitting double with him upon his horse?"

The moment I say this, I regret it. *She will guess...*

Mama's hands become still. She looks at me for a long moment, and then she says, "Aye, I do remember that you went to New Haven. That is where you first met Mr. Brainerd, is it not?"

I lower my eyes to the folds of cloth and force myself to continue the work as if we speak of nothing out of the ordinary. "'Tis. We stayed with my uncle, your brother."

There is another long pause, and I am wondering if Mama has begun to unravel my secret, but she says no more regarding it, and, as we stack the folded sheets high, she affirms, "I will speak with your father. However unconventional, I think that your idea is a good one, Jerusha. There is nothing immoral in it, and you will be of much help to Mr. Brainerd, I am sure. Should Mr. Brainerd wish to take his own path elsewhere after Boston, well, then we will rely on one of our friends in the city to arrange for your return home with a suitable party."

The snag in all of this, however, is that we have not taken into account Mr. Brainerd's opinion of me as his traveling companion.

***

'Tis Pentecost Sunday, and Northampton's First Church brims with congregants. From my seat in the gallery of young women, I spy Mama perching in her usual place of dignity. The pew in which she sits parallels the pulpit and faces the congregation. She wears the beautifully embroidered dress that many of the townspeople – mostly those who are Papa's enemies – say is too gaudy for a minister's wife, and she keeps her gaze fastened on Papa, whose pulpit rises above the congregation. Before him and on either side of the pulpit spreads our local body of Christ: young and old; a few rich, many middling, some poor. In the middle gallery near me, dividing the young women from the young men, servants and slaves join to worship as well; Leah sits there as usual, I know, holding baby Elizabeth.

Nearby, in the children's section of the gallery, I see my small sister Lucy wiggling just a tad on the hard pew, bringing my thoughts away from the sermon for a moment. The long service can be trying for young ones, but the discipline it brings is good for their future lives. As I watch, Lucy slips her hand into her pocket and then brings it to her mouth, as though yawning.

I stifle a smile and hope that the ever-watchful

tithing-man does not spy her and give her a poke with his rod. Lucy must have put some broken pieces of sugar-stick candy in her pocket-bag this morning. The treat will surely make the long minutes pass much more swiftly for her and will bring a literal sweetness to the service.

Papa preaches on the exceeding preciousness of the saving grace of God's Spirit. The sermon deeply touches me with a longing for a closer walk with my Savior – the One who died for sinners, the One who loves sinners… and the One whose personal presence often seems afar off to me, though I wish it were not so.

Below me, a sudden, muffled cough reminds me that Mr. Brainerd sits among us. His place of honor near the pulpit enables me to glimpse his face with ease. There, a look of such rapture sits as I have never before beheld. His attention entirely fixes upon Papa, who stands preaching in a near-monotone as he always does.

Just as my soul is drawn forth by his fire, Mr. Brainerd's soul is drawn forth by Papa's words – I see this in the way that his body sags against the pew, his eyes brighten with tears. This is no quick, unholy passion that leaps up, consuming dry weeds and only flashing for a short time. His is a holy passion for God. A passion whose flame does not go out. I see this, and I know what Papa hungered for the other night as he heard Mr. Brainerd speak: this all-consuming passion for God that drives a man to pour out his life to the uttermost and not allow a drop to be wasted.

And I begin to see that, as much as I long for Mr. Brainerd himself, it is this that I long for as well.

***

Mama made quick work of persuading Papa, as I find at dinner that afternoon.

"My daughter Jerusha will accompany you to Boston." Papa directs his dark-eyed gaze at Mr. Brainerd, who has been caught mid-bite. "She will assist you there."

I stiffen against the back of my chair, for the way that Papa says it makes it appear that Mr. Brainerd is an underaged son at his command rather than a fully-grown man of nine-and-twenty, capable of making his own decisions.

Another man of Mr. Brainerd's strength of will might have answered Papa sharply; indeed, many have done so. But Mr. Brainerd swallows, looks quietly down at his cold meat, and slices off another piece, spearing it. Across the table from him, Papa waits for Mr. Brainerd's protest or acquiescence.

Mr. Brainerd pops the piece into his mouth and chews. He swallows and then takes a sip of cider. "Very well," he says at last. "If you wish, Mr. Edwards."

His eyes do not even touch on me. I feel small. To him, then, any of my sisters would have done just as well as I. Perhaps better than I.

But can I not set aside my childish affection for him? Can I not determine to see him and serve him merely, as I told Mama, as the servant of God, regardless of the foolish fluttering that plagues my heart? Why should it matter to me that he does not give me any particular mind? Why should it matter to me that either Esther or Sarah would have done just as well by his side? It should not bother me. But it does.

Mama speaks now about preparations for the journey, just a day away, and I turn my attention from toying with the food on my plate to her. But when I do so, I find that Mr. Brainerd's hazel eyes have settled on me for the merest fraction of a moment, their

expression dark and inscrutable.
    And I begin to wonder if I have acted in haste.

Chapter Six

When I thrust back the curtains that Tuesday morning, I admit that relief floods my spirit, like a draught of cold water to a thirsty man. If God had permitted it to rain and storm today, I do not know if I could have forced my already-quaking body to mount Mama's mare and follow Mr. Brainerd down the long road to Boston.

But it is a beautiful day. The sun has just begun to rise, the sky spreads out its blue canopy over little Northampton, and the air feels as though it will warm up but not become too hot for riding. "I thank Thee, Lord," I breathe aloud, letting my forehead rest against the pane.

Behind me, Sarah groans. I turn to see her rolling to sit up on our shared bed, her long dark hair slipping out of its braid, her eyes blinking away sleep.

"Sleep well?" I ask.

"Like the dead," she replies as always. "Ugh, I have a headache." But she rises anyway and immediately sets to making up the bed.

I join her, hardly able to keep my fingers under control. Greatest anticipation wars with deepest dread within me, disturbing my concentration. I grab a pillow, plumping its feathery insides. Surely I cannot do much harm to a pillow.

"Today is the day, then." Sarah plucks up her own

pillow.

My eyes flutter over to my riding habit, freshly brushed and spread carefully over a chair. "Aye."

"When are you leaving?"

"Just after breakfast, I think." Mr. Brainerd desired to leave earlier, immediately following our morning family prayer and Scripture-reading time, but Papa – and through him, I – interfered with his wishes.

"'Tis a long journey. I wonder what you will talk about with him."

Immediately, the fearful feelings that I have been trying to keep at bay rise up, clawing at my heart. If Mary or Esther had accompanied Mr. Brainerd, they would have had no trouble finding things about which to converse. They would have spoken with feminine cleverness and gaiety about everything and anything. The road traveled with either of them would not have been stamped with boredom.

I am afraid that he will find me tedious and strange – the bookworm, the one with interests not always considered fitting for a woman – such as the secret, ever-growing desire I have – of which I have told not a single soul – to work among the Indians as he has done, to share with them God's gospel light. Though he will think me strange only if I can get more than a few words to pass through my lips – which very well would be a miracle, when it comes to Mr. Brainerd!

Oh, Lord God, be near to me on this journey, a journey I never could have imagined that I would take! Be close in my heart and mouth and mind. Calm my fears. Be Thou near me.

***

Mr. Brainerd already waits, reins in hand, when I emerge from the front door at last, traveling satchel at my side, my leather mitts pulled up my arms to protect them from the sun. I blink in the bright late-spring light. After the cool darkness of the house, the outside world – especially on this morning of mornings – shines and sings brightly with the promise of new life. In the oak tree near the lane, the chatter and whistles of starlings, sparrows, and red finches pepper the air.

Papa stands by the gate, talking with Mr. Brainerd, no doubt, about whom Mr. Brainerd will see once he arrives in Boston. He holds the reins for my own mount, Mama's sweet mare Cocoa, a round-sided little creature who nods her head at the sight of me and mouths her bit.

In the yard, the younger children are at play, but when I emerge from the house, they abandon their activities immediately and gather around us who are soon to depart. Behind me, Mama and my sisters' steps sound softly on the path.

Mr. Brainerd finally notices that I have come. His eyes catch on my face, like a burr on sheep's wool, but he says nothing and his expression does not change. Then his eyes deliberately push away from me and over to my younger sisters Esther and Mary. On them, he bestows an artless smile. Why not upon me? What have I done? Or not done?

My freshly-bruised heart begins to pound anew with fear beneath the brown fabric of my riding habit. Have I made a terrible mistake in coming along with him? He evidently cares nothing for me – not even as a friend, not even as my father's daughter. Indeed, his face wears thinly-disguised toleration of me and my accompaniment of him. His expression says that I am a nuisance.

But I could not let him go to Boston alone. And I could not allow these last few days to have been the total sum of my acquaintanceship with him. Surely, there must be a way to break through the barrier he has put up between us without reason.

I know this: I must be at Mr. Brainerd's side. So I close my eyes, suck in a deep breath, and tear myself out of my well-accustomed place. "I am ready."

The little ones rustle around me, and I give them a pat on the head here, a little kiss on the cheek there. Then Sarah clasps me against herself, the worry evident in her eyes. "Do not stay in any drafts. And be sure to wear your shoes, even if the weather is warm."

"I shan't. And I shall." Her fears are understandable. Many a girl has left her home never to return, overtaken by disease or sickness. There is no guarantee that I shall ever cross the threshold of our King Street house again, nor that Sarah will be here if I do. Our smiles meet, and for a moment, I wish that I could take Sarah with me, that I could tell her everything that is in my heart for Mr. Brainerd. She, of all my sisters, is the one to whom I am closest and who I think would most understand.

But there is no time to second-guess anything now. Papa has strapped my traveling satchel to the back of my saddle, and he turns to me. "Are you ready, Jerusha?"

I manage to nod, but I cannot force any other words out of my tight throat. And then, with a sudden motion, Papa boosts me up into the sidesaddle and helps me to settle into place. A feeling of elation sweeps over me without warning, and I steal a glance sideways at Mr. Brainerd.

I am really going to Boston with Mr. Brainerd. After years of hoping - wishing - praying that somehow, some way, I might become acquainted personally with this man who has so long fascinated me, ever since I met him just that once at Uncle Pierrepont's home in New Haven - now, with scarcely a day's warning, he and I sit side-by-side on our eager horses, about to embark on a journey together, just the two of us.

I let my eyes travel over my assembled family, a lump rising in my throat. "Farewell, then," I manage. "Pray for us."

Papa stands solemn, as is his way, but at my words, he stretches a hand forward and touches mine. "May God's presence be with you, daughter, no matter what this journey holds for you." The blessing stumbles from his lips, surprising me not with the content, for my father always has entrusted us into God's hands, but with him saying it aloud. Usually, Papa is so much more comfortable with expressing his personal thoughts with his pen rather than his voice.

I swallow down the lump clogging my throat. "I thank you, Papa." *No matter what the journey holds for you...*

Then Mama steps forward, a sack in her hand. Her fingers tie its leather strings to the back of my saddle. "Some more provisions. Mr. Brainerd has a sack as well, but I always think it best to be well-prepared. You do not know what can happen on such a long road." She gives the sack a pull to make certain that it is secure and then reaches up a hand to touch my cheek. "Jerusha," she says quietly, as if she does not want anyone else to hear her. "Take care to listen to God. Do not be afraid to be a help to Mr. Brainerd."

"I will, Mama."

And then we are off. Our horses move through the streets of Northampton with silent riders for some time. 'Tis early morning, and the town is not busy. Mr. Brainerd looks ahead of him and about him, but seldom my way, which is just as well, for I do not think that I could bear his frosty looks continually.

Determined to enjoy this journey, I concentrate on

the fully-leafed trees and the blooming wildflowers growing along either side of the road once we have crossed out of Northampton. Their beauty calms me and reminds me of the Scripture that Papa is fond of quoting. I decide to make an attempt at conversation. Mr. Brainerd is a missionary; surely, he will want to talk about Bible verses.

"These flowers are beautiful, are they not?" I start with a question, one to which he can merely nod if he wishes.

Which he does, giving the shortest nod I have ever received, without turning his head to look at either me or the flowers.

"They remind me of what the Lord Jesus says about the flowers." I dig in my heels, determined to make conversation, as I am sure my sisters Mary and Esther would do. "'And why take ye thought for raiment? Consider the lilies of the field, how they grow; they toil not, neither do they spin: And yet I say unto you, that even Solomon in all his glory was not arrayed like one of these. Wherefore, if God so clothe the grass of the field, which today is, and tomorrow is cast into the oven, shall he not much more clothe you, O ye of little faith?'"

I pause, smiling, waiting for him to share his thoughts on the verses with me, as he has often done with Papa, Mama, Doctor Mather, and even my sisters. To do otherwise would be rude, would it not? And Mr. Brainerd may be strong-willed, determined, not-quite-a-gentleman, even, but he has never been outright rude.

He nods but says nothing, taking a handkerchief out of his coat and coughing into it.

Humph. I decide to forgo my judgment on his behavior. Perhaps his lung ailment prevents him from talking much at the moment. Pity stirs in my breast, but I have already begun down a path on which I feel I must continue – for I must get Mr. Brainerd to notice me. Riding alone at his side does not seem to be accomplishing that.

"I'm sure that in your years as a missionary, you must have found plenty of opportunities to prove those verses true – that God would supply every need you had, that you would want for nothing, that…" I trail off, swallowing down the rest of whatever words I have left. Mr. Brainerd's face has taken on an expression of pained annoyance. The sight of it warms me with humiliation. His disdain for me – nay, dislike seems a better word now – can hardly be concealed. I was a fool to come. I was a fool to think that I could be a better companion to him than my sisters, that he might prefer my company to theirs.

Everything within me desires to turn Cocoa around one-hundred-and-eighty degrees on this lonely road. We are not far from Northampton yet. I have ridden nearly this far by myself many times. I will arrive well before dinner if I hurry. No matter what my feelings, why should I put myself through this torturous journey at the side of a man who holds me in contempt? My sore heart longs to flee, to run from the difficulty, from the pain inflicted by one who does not even know that he causes it.

I open my mouth to speak, to make an excuse so that I may turn around, when I see the edge of the handkerchief he draws away from his mouth after another cough. Scarlet drops dot the crumpled linen. At the sight of this, the realization dawns upon me afresh: I cannot leave him. He may not realize that he needs someone by his side – may even despise the idea of me – but the truth is, he needs me, in case…

In case.

With reality so starkly before me, I set my face for

Boston, determining never again to look back. I will fulfill my duty to Mr. Brainerd – the duty for which I volunteered myself, naively thinking it a way to spend exclusive time in his company. The scarlet dotting that handkerchief tells me that this journey may bring more, much more, than that for which I wished, and I wonder whether this road will see both of our horses or just one when the return journey to Northampton is made at last.

The clomping of hooves adds its steady rhythm to the progression of my thoughts. *Lord, use me as Thou wilt. Do with me here on this journey what Thou wouldst do. But let it be for Thy glory.* My eyes lay steadily on Mr. Brainerd's dark-clad back, two paces ahead. *And let Mr. Brainerd recover.* I feel a bit guilty, as always, making this selfish request, but, if God does what is for His glory, and I have asked for that first, then why should I not also request a good gift from Him? And what a gift Mr. Brainerd's recovery would be. Particularly if...

But I cannot let my mind wander in that direction, especially with Mr. Brainerd's current attitude toward me. "Papa says that we will arrive in three days," I mention, trying to converse once more.

He directs a slight frown in my direction, though without making eye contact. "Two, I think."

"But Boston lies many miles from Northampton. And your illness..."

I let my words trail off because he shakes his head. "I have often – in a much more ill state – traveled fifty miles in a day through the wilderness."

How has he done that? Sheer determination empowered by the Holy Spirit, I suppose, for I cannot imagine the gaunt man riding just ahead of me traveling so hard. "Is it necessary?" I surprise myself by voicing my thought, a contradiction, or at the very least, a questioning of Mr. Brainerd's actions.

I cluck my tongue and urge Cocoa forward beside Mr. Brainerd. I am meant to be his companion, after all, not his servant, bringing up the rear guard. His immediate discomfort at my nearness shows itself in how he straightens himself in the saddle, how his eyes dart from the road before us to me and then down to his hands, loosely holding his reins. When he swallows, his Adam's apple bobs in his throat. "Is what necessary?"

"Pushing yourself so hard. Making such sacrifices as you have. Not many men have done so much in so little time."

"What do you know about my sacrifices?" The question shimmers like too-thin ice in March. I must tread carefully, or I fear that I will fall through into unknown, freezing water.

"I have read your public *Journal.*" I speak tentatively, testing with one foot. "I have read of what you have suffered, laboring to bring the good news of salvation to the Indians – how you first worked outside Stockbridge, then farther west, at last to Crossweeksung. I know that you pressed on, trying to go where few have yet gone, taking with you only native companions. I know–"

"I would have done it all again. I would have pressed harder, gone farther, done more. Those who speak of whether a sacrifice is *necessary* when God places the opportunity before us to do it for His glory, for His Name's sake, know nothing of the love of Calvary."

He sucks in a breath, deep into his lungs. It displaces his cough again. "The last thing on earth that I would desire…" He hacks into the crook of his right elbow, his left hand shaking yet holding the reins. "The last thing I desire is to live useless to God, to be a poor, ineffectual wretch, taking in all of life and giving nothing back to Him who gave all for me. Why should I desire such an indolent life as the one of which you speak?"

Despite the strength of his answer, I cannot allow him to misunderstand what I have said. "Indolent? I said nothing of indolence, Mr. Brainerd. I only wonder if you might have extended your life by taking a less demanding path through it." This is something my father has said of Mr. Brainerd more times than I can count.

"What is my life, or yours? 'Tis but a vapor, a breath that passes away when the sun rises. To extend it for my own sake – that I would never wish. To extend it for God's glory – if such could be done and yet not slacken my efforts but instead increase them – aye, that I would desire. But to increase my lifespan merely to enjoy this life's fleshly pleasures... Nay, that is not my aim and never could be. In the eyes of the world, I have given up much, Miss Edwards, but I have received much more in return from God – I would not go back and change one thing." He swallows hard and gives a cool glance in my direction. "Not one thing. He has known what is best."

With a nudge of his heels, Mr. Brainerd urges his horse forward a few paces so that I again find myself trailing him. I have begun to think that this will set the course for the journey: Mr. Brainerd with his eyes looking ahead, settling on anything except me, and me, riding in his shadow, with my eyes focused on his advancing back.

I can see that Mr. Brainerd has taken out a small notebook and writes in it with a little pencil as he rides. We go on in this silent way for some time until Mr. Brainerd's horse stumbles on a rut in the track. In an instant, the notebook and pencil fly out of Mr.

Brainerd's hands as he grabs for the reins.

I am off my mare before he dismounts. "I think it fell into the grasses to the left." Lifting the hem of my skirt, I step into the hardy, long stems, peering closely.

"No need to trouble yourself. I will find it." He stands at the edge of the road, seeming unwilling to enter the verge while I am in it.

"Nonsense. I am sure that I can find it." And then I spot a little brown square. "Here 'tis – the notebook, at least." I scoop it up, brushing a twig and a smudge of dirt from the cover, and hand it to him.

He receives it from me as if I offer a live snake – and a possibly poisonous one at that. "I thank you. I am certain that I can find the pencil if you will allow me to–"

"Here 'tis!" I announce again, having located the little writing instrument.

He takes this from me as well. "I thank you."

We move toward our horses, who have seized the opportunity to sample the roadside grass while they waited. He mounts.

"I am afraid that I will need your help getting on, sir." Awkwardness fills me to the brim.

He jerks his head around, startled. Slowly, he dismounts, as one moving in a dream from which he wishes to escape but is unable to do so. "Certainly."

"I should have asked to use Mama's other saddle. She and I often ride astride. I do not know why this one was chosen when I would need to have the ability to mount by myself without help." My anxiety has made me babble.

"I will help you." The words come from his mouth, soft as caramel still cooking in the pot. And suddenly I stare at Mr. Brainerd's white linen shirt as he comes to my side. I cannot lift my eyes to his face. It hovers so near to my own that I can feel his warm breath on my forehead.

He hesitates for a brief moment, then seems to realize that there is nothing for it. He cups his hands and squats near Cocoa's side, his long, rough-skinned fingers lacing together.

"Ready?" he asks, his voice strained, obviously anxious to get this ordeal over with as soon as possible. His legs brace for the lift, and the scent of woodsmoke and forest wafts up from his coat – the scent of a man who has gone far and gone fully for Christ.

I nod mutely before realizing that I must speak aloud since he will not meet my eyes. "Aye, I am ready."

How thankful I am that Cocoa is a small mare! With my right hand, I grasp the fixed pommel, making certain that I have a good grip so that we can accomplish this in one attempt. Then, without thinking it over any more, I place my right foot into the embrace of Mr. Brainerd's hands.

Immediately, his muscles tense, and I spring up with my left foot, off the ground and onto Cocoa in less than a moment. His hands drop away immediately, having barely settled me into the saddle. "You can manage from here."

It is not a question. He swivels around and mounts his own horse, leaving me to accomplish my own adjusting. With only a cluck of his tongue and a glance to be sure that I am still on my horse, I suppose, he leads us off down the road once more.

I am tiring of this determined and unnecessary silence. "Do you write often while you ride?"

"Sometimes."

Well, he may be determined to be silent and unfriendly, but I will not be. If he will not converse, then I must merely talk aloud about interesting things. "Papa often writes when he rides as well, but he does not usually use a notebook. He has scraps of paper tucked away upon which he writes his ideas and thoughts, and Mama has given him a little packet of pins to take with him. As he writes each note, he pins them to his coat." I start to laugh at a memory that trickles into my mind. "I remember one time, he even rode into our lane with a few pinned to his breeches. Mama said that he looked like a porcupine that got stuck upside down in a pile of letters."

At this, even Mr. Brainerd must smile, one side of his mouth stretching up of its own volition, the other joining it more willingly. When he smiles, my heart breathes a sigh of delight; heaven has opened and has come down to dwell on the earth.

The quiet settles between us again, but after that touch of humor, it feels more comfortable, more open. I decide to risk another question. Papa seems to be a safe topic, so I will go with that.

"Mr. Brainerd? What did you think of Papa's sermon yesterday?"

He sucks in a breath, and a smile tinged with sadness touches his lips. "'Twas a wonderful sermon and reminds me how little of the grace of God I have, and yet how very precious is even that little bit."

"Little? How can you say that, Mr. Brainerd?" I am surprised at the frankness with which I have spoken, and I tighten my lips against any more words escaping.

Mr. Brainerd glances over at me, surprise showing on his face.

I must clarify. "'Tis only, Mr. Brainerd, that of all men that I have ever known, you are the one who seems to have such a great quantity of God's grace. You are the one who seems most godly of all men I have met. So I fail to see how you can speak of yourself in such a way. You have what I know... all Christian men desire." I wish that I had said *I*. But that would have been too personal, would it not have been?

He is quiet for a long time, perhaps a full mile or more. Then he says, so quietly that I can barely hear him over the soft clip-clop of his horse's shod hooves, "Anything good you see in me is by God's grace alone, Miss Edwards. You have read the published *Journal* in your family, and you hear your father's kind report of me, but you do not know me as I know me. You do not know all the threshing that had to occur to rid me of chaff and make room for God to gain a harvest. You spoke earlier of how much I have given up for God, but you do not know of the still-daily struggles I have against the flesh, even now. I do not wish nor deserve to be on anyone's pedestal. Even the pedestal of grace."

Quiet settles over us again, broken a few minutes later when Mr. Brainerd speaks, this time without glancing at me. "I am feeling uncommonly well this morning. Shall we hasten our pace and see if we might make the journey more quickly than anticipated?"

The alternating trotting and cantering of our horses makes true conversation impossible, and when we finally slow our mounts to a walk, we join a party of traveling ministers, also on their way to the city.

***

In the evening hours, as we gather among the new friends whose homes have been opened to us, whose hearth-fires warm us, I ponder Mr. Brainerd's words that morning when we set out from home: "You do not know me, Miss Edwards."

What does he mean? Perhaps I shall never know, for his behavior ever since we have met has indicated his reluctance to let me – or possibly anyone – deeply into his inner world.

Chapter Seven

The journey takes us three days, much to Mr. Brainerd's thinly-disguised chagrin.

"Where will you be staying?" one of those in the party we joined up with back on the first day of our journey asks as our horses' hooves enter the borders of the ever-sprawling city.

"With Mr. Bromfield." Mr. Brainerd's cheeks are void of color, nearly gray, but determination forces the smile to his face.

"Joseph Bromfield?" one of them asks.

"Aye."

"A most pious gentleman," approves our traveling companion. "And with a house well-suited for guests – very comfortable and spacious. Do you require directions? I know where the gentleman lives."

Mr. Brainerd shakes his head, searching with calloused fingers for something in his coat. At last, he pulls out a square of paper. "I have them here, friend, but thank you."

With that, we part ways with our impromptu companions, and our horses find the road that goes deeper into the city.

I have come to Boston but a couple of times over the years, and the juxtaposition of so many different peoples and cultures has fascinated me each time. When I hear a Dutchman haggling in loud, broken

English with a Scotchman, I let Cocoa lag a bit unwittingly, staring to see who will get his way in the argument.

"Miss Edwards."

Mr. Brainerd's voice startles me, and I urge Cocoa forward to join him several paces ahead, maneuvering around a swath of pedestrians to do so. "I am sorry. I have so rarely been allowed the treat of seeing such a world as this. I will try to not delay you any further."

His stern expression softens for the smallest part of a moment, but then his jaw tenses again and his eyes spark. "If you wished for a sightseeing trip, Miss Edwards, I am sure that your father and mother would have accommodated you at some point. There was no need to attach yourself to my journey here, certainly."

His words sting like lye. Why is he so unkind to me – to me alone?

"I have come only to help you, Mr. Brainerd." The words escape my mouth, strangled by my tight throat. And 'tis the truth, for as much as I have wanted my own affection for him returned, ultimately, first and foremost, I do wish to help him – to care for him – to be of service to him.

"Then it would have been better for you to have stayed at home. Women do not belong on such journeys. They are only a hindrance." With an abrupt turn of his head, Mr. Brainerd kicks his horse into a trot, nimbly guiding it through the traffic, while I follow behind as best I can, smarting from his verbal wounds and proving him correct, I fear, every time he must slow his horse for me to catch up with him.

The sight of Mr. Bromfield's home – solid and stately – brings a scrap of peace to my spirit. My bruised heart pleads without thought: *Lord, let my guest chamber be far from Mr. Brainerd's so that I may hide away there and not see him much for as long as we tarry.*

What have I done in coming here with him?

***

Over the next few days, I see him at some meals, and, of course, we both accompany the Bromfields to the Old South Church on Sunday, but other than that, my prayer is granted.

To my own relief.

To my own sorrow.

He speaks to me as little as is politely possible, only nodding at me if he can substitute that for a verbal acknowledgement of my presence. Can it be that he holds such a grudge against me for merely accompanying him, for suggesting that he could need a *woman's* help? But, nay, his disdain of me came long before our trip to Boston. Why, I do not know.

May God help me to bear it.

***

"Oh! Pardon me. I did not know that you were in here."

I found the library in Mr. Bromfield's home yesterday, and today, Mr. Brainerd found me there, to his surprise, my nose buried in a thin old book, the shelves rising high around me. The air smells of worn leather, unreleased sunlight, and beeswax candles – a most pleasing combination.

At the sound of his voice, I jump to my feet, my skirt bunching against the seat of the armchair.

Mr. Brainerd has already spun around to depart when I speak, politely but without the eagerness that I am afraid used to crowd my voice. "Are you here to fetch a book?"

He turns. "Hm?"

I smile out of courteousness. "You came to the library, Mr. Brainerd. I assume 'twas to fetch a book?"

He eyes me, hesitant as a street cat. "Aye."

I gesture to the shelves. "Then, pray, do fetch it. You are not bothering me." And with that, I sit down again, open my own book across my lap, and begin to read once more.

At least, I fix my eyes upon the text, keenly aware of Mr. Brainerd's presence lingering in the doorway. Apparently, he is undecided as to whether he wishes to be in the same room with me, even to get a needed book.

Then his shoes sound across the smooth wooden planks. Evidently, he has decided to risk being filled with contempt in my company. I do not allow my eyes to drift upward as he slowly makes his way to the bookshelves and peruses the rows of leathery spines for long moments. At last, I hear the sound of a volume being pulled from its snug spot and of his feet pivoting to leave. Soon, I will be able to breathe freely again.

"What are you reading?"

So startled that my mind ceases working, I fear that my eyes have grown to twice their size as my gaze jerks upward to land upon him, standing a few feet away. He clasps his newfound book beneath his arm, against his waist.

"Um…" I desperately try to remember the title of the book I am reading without looking at the spine. After a moment of not being able to recall it, I decide to tell him the content instead, hoping that I will not appear too foolish. "An account of John Elliot's work with the Praying Indians."

A crease emerges between his eyebrows. "You find that interesting?"

"Aye, I do," I reply, honestly. "He was a fascinating

man, much used by God, was he not? His sacrificial, unceasing love for the natives may only be attributed to God's work in him, do you not think so?"

His gaze lingers on the book's pages, yet open. His voice quiets, still waters in green pastures. "Aye, I know so. 'Twas so in me."

Is he speaking to me or to himself? The vulnerability, the openness that I can spy on his face at this moment gives me hope that perhaps, perhaps, there is some way to bridge the extraordinary gap he has determined to place between us, the way he has resolved to hold me at arm's length, as though I am some kind of detestable and dangerous wild creature. When he remains standing before me, silent, for several more breaths, I risk another venture.

"Will you tell me your story, Mr. Brainerd?"

His eyes snap up to meet mine, immediately guarded. He straightens and steps back, and coolness enters the air between us, coming entirely from his frosty demeanor. "What do you mean?"

"How you came, like John Elliot, to have such an intense love for the Indians? So many consider them lower than dogs, but the love you have for the Indians shines out of you whenever you speak of them or pray for them.... How came you by such an all-consuming passion? You seem untouched by anything in this world – its goods, its society, its accolades, and certainly any fleshly appetite."

I have spoken more than I intended, but when shall I have another opportunity like this? I draw in a breath and finish the thought. "I should like to know more, for my own heart beats with a desire to see God's glory spread abroad among the nations as well. Or, at least, a desire for that desire."

He remains silent, expressionless. Awkwardness prickles down my spine.

"Perhaps I presume too much," I add, hesitation creeping like hoar-frost onto the pane of my voice.

The hazel eyes darken with a suddenness I have come to expect of him. "Aye. Aye, you do presume too much, Miss Edwards. If you wish to know of me, you must read my public *Journal.* I have precious little time left on this earth and none at all to spend telling a young girl tales to excite her imagination."

With that, he spins on his heel and strides to the door. I cannot help the tears that rise to my eyes at such a rebuke – such an undeserved rebuke. I duck my head, staring at the blurred text, waiting to hear the closing of the door.

But the door does not close – not yet. His footsteps stop at the threshold. He hesitates a long moment, and I peer up, wondering what level of harshness he will stoop to next.

His breathing rasps, his throat perhaps agitated by the outburst, and his gaunt shoulders rise and fall beneath his coat. At last, he turns, slow as ice melting on a cold April morning. Genuine regret flickers across his face. "I should not have said that. 'Twas unkind, to say the least, and I do not believe that 'tis true of you – that you only wish to hear my story for the sake of gaining a thrill. Pray, forgive me."

Surprise makes it difficult to speak for a moment. Blinking back the remains of my tears, I find my tongue. "Of course I forgive you, Mr. Brainerd." I swallow hard, compelled to go on. "Yet I wish that you believed that I am sincere in desiring to understand more personally what makes a man such as you – one who had every advantage the world could offer him – give up all of his own free will, without any regrets, without struggle... to serve alone in the wilderness, eating bear meat and living in a hut such as the natives do, wearing deerskin... It passes beyond human comprehension and intrigues me, sir. I... I have long had the desire to live within God's will, but you have awakened a yearning within me for the full-fledged soaring in spiritual matters that I discern in you."

Varied emotions pass across his face – swift as storm clouds – emotion that I cannot read, save for brushes of agony and of joy. Quickly, though, he schools his features, manning them with utter self-control. He wets his lower lip with his tongue before speaking. "I...I am glad to hear of your desire, Miss Edwards. But I cannot gratify you or inspire you with my private story. That lies sealed up between me and my God. Anything you wish to know, you must find in my public *Journal.* I am sorry."

Without another word, he slips from the room, shutting the door behind him.

And between us as well.

Chapter Eight

He lasts but a day more in Boston before his illness takes him down with a fury and without warning.

The clatter of footsteps passing by my room awakens me deep in the night, just as one day passes into another. My eyes open to the utter darkness of my chamber, and I lie there, listening for a long moment, wondering what the matter is, whether a rider has come with dreadful news, severe enough to awaken an entire household. Should I rise and see what is the matter, though I am only a guest in a mere acquaintance's household?

The passing of footsteps once more – this time the light ones of a maidservant, perhaps – shakes me from my indecision. I will not sleep until I can be sure that the hub-bub has naught to do with Mr. Brainerd. Pushing back the covers, I swing my legs over the side of the bed and slip down. I reach for my shawl and drape it around my shoulders, despite the warmth of the night, before opening the door and stepping into the passage.

Just then, a servant rushes from the opposite end of the passage, flickering candle in hand. I hear Mr. Bromfield say to her, "And tell Thomas that he must hurry!"

"Aye, sir!" she tries to whisper, but her fright forces the words out of her throat in a near-shout.

I step into the passage as she comes toward me. "What is the matter?"

She stops at the sight of me, her eyes round and white in her brown face. "Oh, miss, 'tis Mr. Brainerd. He has been taken ill."

My heart thuds against my breastbone so hard that it brings pain. "Badly?"

She nods. "Aye, miss. Mr. Bromfield's sending for Doctor Pynchon."

***

Hours later, I stand at the side of Mr. Brainerd's guest bed, the candlelight quivering from the stick held in my left hand, while the doctor and Mr. Bromfield rush back-and-forth, sending for hot water, then for cold, and then moving to a corner to discuss Mr. Brainerd's treatment. I remain here unmoving, shadowed by the bed-curtains, because, as Mr. Brainerd lay convulsing many minutes ago, the blood and gore oozing out of his mouth, he grabbed for the air, grasped and snatched at it like a man drowning. My own heart convulsed in compassion, and, without considering, I reached out my hand and grasped his in mine, as one would offer a floating plank to a man whom the ocean waves were about to swallow. As soon as my hand met his sweating palm, he clasped it, clasped it so tightly that I wondered if he might crush the bones of my fingers. How strange that a man exceedingly weak in body could yet grip so mightily in the midst of his pain. He has not released my hand since.

"He appears insensible." Doctor Pynchon's mutter reaches my ears.

"Aye, that he does," our host agrees.

With his quick, light steps, the doctor comes over

to the bed to count Mr. Brainerd's pulse and breaths. "We'll want that plaster now. Come to my aid, Mr. Bromfield, I pray you."

Mr. Bromfield startles out of his worried, staring state. "Of course."

"Lift him up just a bit... There, now. I will bring it over his head." In moments, they have stripped Mr. Brainerd of his shirt. His thin chest heaves with a naked vulnerability that cannot help but raise my pity. The doctor's practiced hands apply the plaster.

Mr. Brainerd's hand, wrenched from mine when the two men removed his shirt, finds my fingers once more.

My own breath shakes as I suck it in, watching the agony of Mr. Brainerd's breathing. Perhaps it will help. Perhaps a plaster will draw a dying man from the edge of the grave. *Oh, dear God, let it help.*

Having applied the plaster, Doctor Pynchon moves away from the bedside, back to the table where his case rests. He comes back presently with a small pewter cup of what appears to be merely wine.

Mr. Bromfield contradicts my assumption when he asks in his quiet, tight voice, "Opium?"

"Aye." He gestures with his empty hand. "Raise him up, I pray you."

Mr. Bromfield braces Mr. Brainerd's upper body once more. I do not move, for Mr. Brainerd will not release my hand. Yet as the doctor puts the medicine to his mouth, the sick man surprises all of us by knocking it away. "N-n-nay." The word comes out slurred but sure. We all blink.

The doctor tries to put the cup to his patient's lips once more. "It will ease you, sir."

How Mr. Brainerd is able to school his thoughts enough to answer, I do not know, but I marvel. Once more, he pushes away the cup. "My r-r-reason," is all he can manage, half-whispering, half-groaning.

Doctor Pynchon frowns up at Mr. Bromfield. "I think we must compel him."

Though I do not wish to see Mr. Brainerd suffer at all, indignation swells up in my bosom at the notion of these two well-meaning men compelling another man to go against his conscience. "I think you must allow him to be treated as he wishes," I speak up, and my own hand tightens around Mr. Brainerd's fingers.

Oh, Lord God, give me Thy strength to stand up for him! Though not all men – perhaps not this doctor nor our host, Mr. Bromfield – believe females capable of rational, worthwhile thought, my father has always encouraged his daughters to consider their opinions – when schooled by Scripture – on an equal ground with those of men. This stiffens my spine in the face of these two gentlemen's surprised – nay, shocked – expressions.

"'Tis obvious," I continue, thanking God that my voice does not shake, "that he does not wish his reason to be disrupted for the mere sake of comfort. If the opiate were designed to save his life, then I might be persuaded to compel him, but as it is, I humbly suggest that you must desist, sir."

There is silence as Doctor Pynchon and Mr. Bromfield look from one another to me and back again. I can see that they are wobbling, but I cannot be sure upon which side they will come down. With a deep breath, I take courage and speak again, "Indeed, my father, Reverend Edwards, put Mr. Brainerd's physical well-being into my hands on this journey. I will take responsibility should any ill come from failing to administer your treatment."

The doctor raises his eyebrows into tall bushes, then relaxes them into a nearly-straight hedge. "Very well." He puts away the opiate.

Chapter Nine

David

A hand in mine, not tethering me to this life, but comforting me on my journey to the next. Oh, my Lord God, is it Thee who solaces me now? Is it Thy spiritual hand in mine that I sense, that I have sensed the grasp of all these years? Thou alone are my succor, my consolation, my exceedingly great reward!

But strange as 'tis, the hand feels so much like true flesh-and-blood – grasping mine with such a gentle strength, such a focused human love and care as I have not felt since the days of my infancy. It helps me to stand against the agony that sweeps over my body, to not be overcome by its relentless torture. Oh, God, will Thou not send the chariots of Israel for me now?

My hand tightens around the one within it as my lungs and throat drip with burning sulfur. Hell seems to dwell in my very body. Oh, dear God, I care not what I suffer, but that Thou might use me to rescue those who go to perish in that place!

Chapter Ten

Jerusha

The fever remains high all that night and into the dawning day, despite the doctor's attempts, first, to bleed it out and, then, to force Mr. Brainerd to sweat it out by raising the room's temperature with a blazing fire. Now, Mr. Brainerd lies covered only by a linen sheet, his shirt long ago discarded when the doctor applied the plaster. The smelly remains of that treatment bite at my nose from where I sit nestled against the bedcurtains, my hand still wrapped in his unconscious grip. The stain of auburn mucus persists in ringing his gasping mouth, despite my repeated efforts to remove it. A bowl of bloody water sits on the table near me, surrounded by a pile of equally reddened cloths.

"The ulcers in his lungs have burst, I am afraid," Doctor Pynchon loudly whispers to Mr. Bromfield. "That much is certain."

Mr. Bromfield nods, his face settling into grim lines around tired eyes. "Can he survive it, do you think?"

The medical man blows out a breath and licks his plump lips. "'Tis hard to say. I have seen men come out of such before. Indeed, having heard Mr. Brainerd's case history, I am sure that he has had his lungs ulcerate in times past."

There is a pause as the doctor glances toward me and down at our still-clasped hands. Then he looks over to Mr. Bromfield. If I were a blushing woman, I would surely blush now for how this must appear to the doctor – that there is an intimacy between Mr. Brainerd and myself – an intimacy which is not truly there. If my sisters Esther or Sarah were here, it would be one of their hands he would be grasping, not mine. In his distress, a man will grasp at any human contact to comfort him. But the doctor does not know this, and so he hesitates to speak the ugly truth in front of a supposed betrothed.

"'Tis severe," he says at last, pity softening his voice. He begins to pack up the tools of his trade. "In truth, I do not expect him to last another half-an-hour. But then, he could last half-a-year. One never really knows in these cases. I will not bleed him again. I prefer moderation in such measures."

Those who watch surely think that it is Mr. Brainerd who gains comfort from clasping my hand, and yet I also gain a desperate kind of consolation from clasping his, a comfort that finds its refuge in living only in this moment that God has given and not thinking about what tomorrow might bring. I wish that I could beg God to postpone the death of Mr. Brainerd – to make him well enough to come home with me, to live at our house with me by his side, as I am now, all his days. I wish that I could beg this... and in my heart, I do beg it, selfish though I know the prayer is.

In truth, this sickness of Mr. Brainerd's frightens me, shocks me, even. Aye, of course I knew that he was ill, even unto death this past winter. I am no stranger to the sight of consumption victims gasping out their last breaths. 'Tis a common, dreadful sickness, one from which some die every year in every town and village in the colonies. Very few who contract the disease survive its onslaught to live any measure of a full length of days on this earth.

But I suppose that I fooled myself into believing that Mr. Brainerd's case would be different, somehow. Over the years, I built him up in my mind and imagined such wonderful things about the marvelous deeds God would do through him and perhaps through me working with him. Never did I allow the full import of his disease to take root in my mind, to sober my own desires and plans and prayers.

Now I have come face-to-face with the reality of my dreams: a dying man who may not live to walk out of this room; a dying man, who has shown his absolute disregard for my involvement in his life and work and yet who now grips my hand in his, unwilling to let go as he gulps out what may be his last breaths.

I am stunned. And I am appalled at my own selfishness in thought and motive for the weeks and months – nay, years – past.

Doctor Pynchon takes his leave, promising to return when evening falls. After the medical man departs, Mr. Bromfield hesitates a moment, his hand on the open door, his eyes on me. "I have a few pressing matters to which I must attend, Miss Edwards. Is it possible for you to…?"

I do not let him finish his trailing sentence. "I will stay with Mr. Brainerd." A steady knowing has overtaken me: I will not leave his side.

Still, he hesitates. Mr. Brainerd is, after all, a guest in his home. "I dislike leaving you to minister to him alone."

"I will send for you if he worsens," I offer. "I pray that you would believe me: My father sent me along with Mr. Brainerd to aid him in just such a case as this. 'Tis my delight to serve him." And it is.

At last, Mr. Bromfield nods. "All right. May I send

you up some tea and breakfast?"

My throat feels parched and my stomach empty all at once from the long night at Mr. Brainerd's side. "Aye, I thank you."

The ragged rhythm of Mr. Brainerd's breathing provides the only sound in the darkened room. Loneliness creeps over my soul, steady as fog blanketing the ocean. In that moment, my heart cries out for the company and sympathy of my mother and sisters – but they are not here. No one is here who can understand, nor in whom I can confide the fears and sorrows that entangle me as a deer in a thicketed ravine. Tears rise to the rims of my eyes but do not spill over to relieve my pent-up distress.

A few minutes later, a servant brings a tray for me: tea and a plate covered with a linen napkin.

"Set it down there, I pray you." I indicate the little table just behind me, to my right. "And would you change out the water and cloths?"

The girl bobs her head. "Aye, miss." Her hands do not hesitate as she gathers up the blood-stiffened cloths, dropping them into the bowl. "Anything else, miss?"

"Nay, that will be all. I thank you."

With a curtsy, the girl leaves me alone once more – alone with him at whose side I have steadfastly longed to stay, and yet now, here, I experience greater desolation sweeping over my heart than I have ever thought possible. The curtains remain drawn across the long windows, and the air drapes over me with the heaviness of a shroud. Mr. Brainerd's breathing labors on.

Will he die here, now, with his hand clutching mine? In its bleakness, my mind wanders over the past years and months and days of my life, wondering at my unfulfilled desire for this frail, holy man's love – a man whom I have known only through one meeting with him when I was but three-and-ten, a few letters addressed to my father, and the reading of his public *Journal.* I saw in them his love for God, his love for his Indians, his unique ability to be all-consumed by one passion, rejecting temptation to fulfill any fleshly desires.

And, as I sit here, staring nearly unblinking at his gray-skinned face, I realize: I wanted that for myself. Nay, I do not only mean that I wanted a similar love for God and for the lost, though I did indeed desire that – and I believe that God has given it to me in some measure.

Yet, I wanted Mr. Brainerd's love to be directed toward me, too, rather than toward God. I wanted his all-consuming passion to focus upon me. With no thought to Mr. Brainerd's good or wishes, I aspired to be the focus of such a man's affections.

The deep loneliness of this hour presses the truth upon me: I have been selfish and self-centered in my supposed love for him. Utterly so.

And, oh my Lord God, I no longer want it to be so. Out of the depths I cry to Thee. Oh, Lord, hear my voice! Forgive my foolish ways. Cleanse my heart of the self-interest I have nurtured and fed for so long. Give me a new heart of selfless love for Thy servant. Give me a heart that hears Thy voice and obeys, regardless of Mr. Brainerd's feelings toward me. We are both Thy servants. Use me as Thou wilt.

***

Mr. Brainerd sleeps, released at last from the fever that long racked his body and even deprived him of reason. Yesterday, before he became aware, I pulled my hand from his, not desiring that he should wake and wonder why a woman he disdains has taken his hand in hers. Now, his face twitches as his slumber deepens, the firelight catching the lines which hardship and sickness have drawn upon his skin.

Closing Mr. Brainerd's Bible, I creep up from my chair, wincing as the wood squeaks, and stretch out my back, stiff from such long hours sitting by his side. I have not left Mr. Brainerd's chamber since he became ill, except for a few times to use the chamber pot in my own room. The wood in the fireplace crackles as if sap lingers in the fuel, and I dart my eyes over to the sweet slumberer, but he remains asleep, tucked carefully beneath the linen sheets, his fever lower than it has been for days, though not completely gone.

Thanksgiving rises in my heart to God that Mr. Brainerd does not suffer now as he has been in these previous many hours, when his eyes would widen as the shocking pain engulfed him, when he would clutch my hand insensibly, when the verse came over and over again to my own mind: *The last enemy that shall be destroyed is death.* Death has toyed with him, as a cat playing with a mouse, torturing its frail body, and such sorrow washed over me as I saw it. If he lingers long, how can I endure watching Mr. Brainerd's slow demise?

Yet watch it I must, for in the passing hours, I have become yet more convinced that I have been given a task – to serve Mr. Brainerd with utter abandon – and in fulfilling my duty, I will not shirk away from the death that rises to take over his weak body. I will stand beside him; I will minister to him with all that is within me, as if I do it unto the Lord Christ Himself.

Wandering over to the little writing desk that stands on the opposite side of the room, I plan to replace Mr. Brainerd's Bible there where I found it atop a small stack of other books and papers. But just as I go to put it down, my eyes catch on a few small – even tiny – notebooks, clustered together near a quill pen, hastily thrown down, it seems. A few inches away, a handkerchief crumples, the white cloth stained with dried blood and mucus. He must have been in the midst of writing when his attack came in the night.

Writing… These little notebooks are some of his private diaries, I am sure. Not all of them, certainly, for he has told Papa about how he hopes that his brother John may yet bring his diaries to him.

I sneak a glance backward. He still lies asleep, ashen face relaxed against the plump goose-feather pillows. My heart races.

Why have the private diaries drawn me? Is it the way he spoke of them to my father before our journey to Boston, telling Papa how he plans to destroy them, burning them all at once in the fire before the breath leaves his body for the last time? What secrets do they contain? What priceless words will go up in smoke? I do not know, but never before have I been tempted to do something so underhanded as to read a man's diary without permission. I shudder to think of what Papa and Mama would say – and I cannot ignore the knowledge that, even if they know nothing of what I do, Almighty God does. Mr. Brainerd has not given me permission to read his diaries.

I restrain my fingers from touching the books.

I will not read them. I will not betray his trust.

But what a temptation spreads before me!

There the little books lie, their secrets closed within their plain covers. How I long to know this man before his body lies cold! How I long to know – what has made him able – and not only able, but also willing, to give up everything he held dear. What set his soul afire, what even now makes his eyes still blaze out of that solemn, gaunt, heavenward face? And will it set me afire, too, with a passion beyond that which blazes in my heart for him?

Truly, I have never met a man like him, nor do I think I ever shall again. All Christians must be willing to give up their lives at any time that God calls for them. But not all men run toward giving up their lives, holding their most precious thing in opened hands for the Father to take. I know that I do not. Though I am bowed to the will of God in all matters and, indeed, cannot remember a time when I was not submissive to Him, that holy, complete passion for His glory, that filling-up with His joy... that I do not possess.

What has made Mr. Brainerd that way? As my eyes touch the worn cover of the topmost diary, I wonder if these little books could tell me what the man's lips will not.

***

The next day, Mr. Brainerd's fever fully breaks. At last, he lifts eyes towards me, eyes clear of the confusion that has haunted them for the past two days. I am alone beside his bed when he regains consciousness.

When Mr. Brainerd's lids unveil his sight, I am sitting there, reading his *Journal*. No, not his diary – I resisted in the end – but his public *Journal*, the one published to inspire others toward missionary effort and personal devotion, the one carefully void of Mr. Brainerd's own personality – surely meant, on the one hand, to reveal, and on the other, to conceal.

Mr. Brainerd's glance drifts down and sees what I have laid out on my lap, cream paper layered against my apron. His eyes stumble from the book to my face, studying it until I must look away from that penetrating gaze.

"Are you thirsty?" I rise to my feet quickly, so quickly that the book falls, and I must reach down and grab it with a little bustle and titter of embarrassment. He does not answer me, and I realize that he is so weak that he cannot speak, though his lips move a fraction.

But he is alive. He is alive. The relief weakens me as well. *I thank Thee, dear God.* It takes all of my willpower and strength to pour Mr. Brainerd a cup of diluted wine from the pitcher perched on a nearby table.

Clutching the well-made pewter cup with both hands, I bring it over to him. "Thirsty?" I ask again, and he manages to bob his chin in assent. I tuck my hand between his pillow and the back of his head, both sticky with sweat from his fever and the plasters the doctor applied. "Here, let me lift you." I support his head and neck a little bit. He cannot help me at all. He is so weak, weak as a bird fallen from its nest and broken in body.

Sip by careful sip, I get a little liquid into him, and then I release him back against the pillow, his head nestling, exhausted, into the feathery support.

But as I draw my hand away, he grasps it. Not tensely this time as he did before, when he was in a fever, but with the weakness of that same bird clutching its rescuer's finger. My utter shock overcomes any pleasure I might have felt in the encounter. Eyes opening, he breathes in, shallow as a tidepool, and the sound of the blood rattling deep in his lungs and throat drives a stake of fear into my own chest that I must force out again.

"I thank you." The words are so soft, I barely hear them. But when I look down at his face, I see that something has changed between us – for him, at least. A door – or mayhap merely a window – of his soul is open to me that was shut tightly, key safeguarded in his pocket, before now. His gaze does not hand me the key; nay, that he retains, I suspect. But the disdain has left his eyes, and what has come to take its place, I cannot read.

He does not cling to my hand but releases it as quickly as he spoke. 'Twas not a romantic gesture, but 'twas an intimate one – one for which I was not prepared, and it takes me a moment to gather my wits. I turn and replace the nearly-empty cup on the side table, steadying myself against the furniture's edge. With my features schooled, I face the bed once more, but he seems to have fallen asleep in just that moment or two. His mouth hangs slightly slack, his head lolled to the side, his breathing somewhat even.

I press a hand to my chest to steady myself. I focus on what must be done, practically, when he awakens again. And now I – I, who longed for time alone in Mr. Brainerd's presence – feel desperate to have another person in the room when he does. For what happened frightens me.

I cannot allow my imagination to run away with me again. It will mean sure and certain heartbreak – worse than what certainly awaits all of us when he perishes at last. Even now, I have retained my determination to keep Mr. Brainerd at a distance, despite nursing him.

At least, I had done, until he moved to open the door he had shut in my face. Now the feet of my heart long to join him at the threshold of his…. Aye, long to join and also to flee.

These past few days at his side, attending and aiding in nearly every way possible, save with his most personal needs, have announced what I cannot ignore: Mr. Brainerd is a dead man. Or soon will be. And my love for him – if I tend and nurture it and let God rid it of selfishness – will be cut off before it can bloom.

Thus, with every memory of his hand upon mine, my heart beats in heavy thuds of dread, rather than pleasure.

Chapter Eleven

Within days, Mr. Brainerd insists on taking visitors again from his bed, insists on having ink and paper fetched for him, insists on having a copy of old Joseph Shepherd's writings brought to him for editing, in hopes that he can reintroduce them to the world. He is more intent on working for God while ill than most are while well.

I have spent the last few days exhausting myself, perhaps on purpose, in service to him. Mr. Bromfield repeatedly offers a servant to attend Mr. Brainerd through the night, but this I reject – determined to keep my mind and heart from resting enough to think and feel any more than it already does. Mr. Brainerd continues to accept my help. I was uncertain whether he would, but he appears to welcome it, though he never touches my hand again.

I cannot help but take all of this activity in with some degree of worry, as does our host Mr. Bromfield and the doctor who has attended him thus far in Boston. "Mr. Brainerd, you must rest," I urge him more than once when yet another few hours pass in an alternation of him accepting visitors who wish to speak with the author of the *Journal,* to him spending time writing long letters to his brothers John and Israel. Much of the time, he is not able to speak above a whisper, and sometimes not even that. He often must express his thoughts and conversations through written notes.

"Mr. Brainerd, you must rest."

He looks up at me, his skin nearly as pale as the bed upon which he lies. "Rest for what?" he whispers. His eyes glow with a secret joy, though some might rather think his recurring fevers cause the glitter. "For what purpose? Is not the purpose of life to give ourselves fully, body, soul, and spirit, to our Creator?" His lips remain cracked as old parchment, no matter how much balm I apply to them, each time trying to focus merely on nursing him, rather than on the fact that my fingers glide across the mouth of the man with whom I am in love, the man who will never respond – can never respond – in kind.

He swallows back a gurgling cough, and I instinctively reach for the fresh cloth tucked into my pocket-bag for such times. "I do not want to come to the last day of my life, whether 'tis this day or a day ten years hence, and know that I could have done more, that I could have become more fully conformed to Christ's likeness, if I had been more obedient to the working of His Holy Spirit."

A shudder runs through Mr. Brainerd's body, despite the summer heat, and I pull the covers up around his shoulders, trying to bring comfort to the shell of this man, if I cannot heal the core. His eyes squeeze shut and he does not speak for a long moment. At last, he releases a trembling breath, his eyes open, and they rest upon my face, as they have been wont to do since the day his massive fever broke. "If I had one thousand lifetimes to spend, Miss Edwards, I would not do anything differently. I would spend them in the service of my King, my Savior, and my God. I do not regret anything given to Him. Only what I did not give."

I cannot speak in the long pause that follows. I swallow back tears of grief, the depths of which I have not known before now, grief in the face of his joy. Grief for myself, not for him. Taking up my book of sermons again, I prepare to distract myself by reading aloud, but he interposes, "Would you mind handing me another sheet of paper? I think I shall write that to my brother, young Israel. Poor soul, he sees so many of his brothers dying young in the ministry – first our elder brother Nehemiah, now me. I must tell him not to be indecisive any longer. He is no fool who parts with what he cannot keep, when he is sure to be recompensed with that which he cannot lose."

Mr. Brainerd works on his letter, alternately resting and then scribbling a few words. It takes him the better part of an hour to finish. His shaking hands are just passing it over to me to seal when a knock sounds on the door. "Come," I call out. A servant must want to collect dirty linens, of which Mr. Brainerd's illness provides plenty, or perhaps she brings us tea or news of a guest.

But the opening door reveals our host himself. "Ah, 'tis good to see you awake, Mr. Brainerd." Mr. Bromfield holds a letter in his own hands.

A smile touches Mr. Brainerd's lips. "God has preserved my going out and my coming in once more, sir."

The expression on Mr. Bromfield's face, pious man though he is, says that he humbly would beg to differ, given Mr. Brainerd's state. But one does not argue with a dead or dying man, so he merely pauses before turning his attention, unexpectedly, to me. "Miss Edwards, I have news for you. Good news. A friend and his family are traveling home from Boston to Hadley – very respectable folk, I assure you. They depart tomorrow and are quite willing that the daughter of

Reverend Edwards should join them in their carriage. From Hadley, as you know, 'tis an easy distance to Northampton. It will certainly be no trouble for your father to fetch you thence."

His words sink me into silent surprise and dismay. This means, of course, that Mr. Brainerd must not be going back to Northampton with me. He must have made his decision to do otherwise and told it to Mr. Bromfield. But where will he go?

I shake the silly question away. Mr. Brainerd has many friends in Boston and its outlying areas – many friends closer to him than my father – as well as some family that even I know of. Why he ever decided to accept my father's invitation and come to Northampton when he had such connections, I do not understand.

But he is not coming back.

The brittle edges of my heart threaten to break away. *O Lord, be the strength of my heart forever!* I slide my tongue over my lips to wet them and turn away from Mr. Brainerd, lest I must meet his eyes and my heart betrays me. "Very well, Mr. Bromfield. I am most grateful to you for making arrangements and to your friends for their generous offer."

Mr. Bromfield beams. Over the past weeks in his home, I have seen that he is a kind man and likes to see that everyone has been properly looked-after.

"Do you wish to leave Boston now, then, Miss Edwards?"

The invalid's weakly-voiced question startles me. I try to make sense of it. "I came to Boston to help you, Mr. Brainerd," I reply, keeping my answer plain and open and yet feeling as though I am not understanding something.

"I know that, and no one could fault you for declining to assist me further. But I believe that I will be ready to travel again soon, if you would be willing to wait a few more days." His eyes close as he sinks more deeply into the pillows, exhausted.

Incredulity, and again, a further lack of comprehension stills my tongue. What can he mean? Is he asking me to accompany him as he travels? But where to? To his family in Connecticut?

Though I am speechless, Mr. Bromfield is not. He steps further into the room, his well-heeled shoes loud on the polished floor. "You mean to return to Northampton yourself, Mr. Brainerd? For... your recovery?"

Mr. Brainerd's eyes flutter open, and his gaze alights first on me and then drifts away to Mr. Bromfield. "I am dying, Joseph. I did not want to believe it. I thought that, perhaps, like King Hezekiah, the Almighty God might add more useful years to my life." He stops and swallows, his Adam's apple like a stone passing along his thin throat. When he speaks again, his voice holds finality as well as a strength that somehow imparts a whisper of courage to me. "But it does not appear to be His will. I am going back to Northampton to die. I thank God that He spared me the pomposity of a Boston funeral."

He turns his head back to me, and again, something unspoken rests in them that I cannot identify. "Will you wait for me, Miss Edwards, so that we may go back home together?"

***

We stay in Boston for a few more days, delaying to see if Mr. Brainerd's health will improve enough for him to ride. The month of July comes upon us before our horses' hooves touch the road to Northampton again. Mr. Brainerd's youngest brother, Israel, has come up from Connecticut to join us on the journey back.

It takes us five days to retrace the miles across this part of the colony of Massachusetts. And I will admit that I am glad when the journey ends, for Mr. Brainerd has spent the greatest part of it in such pain that it has been difficult for him to speak. Upon reaching our house, he immediately retires to his chamber above stairs, leaning heavily upon his brother's arm on one side and the wall on the other.

I make my excuses as quickly as possible to Mama and Papa and retire to my bedchamber as well, where I cannot help but sink down upon my bed, the door shut behind me, and cry out to my God. I begin to understand the depth of sorrow that David speaks of in Psalms such as the twenty-second.

Why hast Thou forsaken me?

For this is how I feel in the midst of such fear and terror and sorrow and death that plagues this fallen world. I have always known that the world is such a place, for we Edwards children have been taught thus by our parents. But it has now come close to me through Mr. Brainerd. I *know* that God has not truly abandoned me – aye. But my feelings speak otherwise. I open my Bible and read, meditating on His promises, trying so desperately to listen to the quiet voice of the Spirit as He speaks peace over the raging storm in my soul – a storm that has worsened so much since Mr. Brainerd's quiet, "I thank you."

My prayers take me from sitting on the bed that I share with my sister Sarah to kneeling beside it, to begging prostrate at last, nose scuffled on the dusty floor. *Almighty God, be my comfort and my peace.*

The next thing I know, I open sleep-bleared eyes to a twilight-darkened room. A breeze wafts through the partially-open window, blowing back the curtains and ushering in fresh air to replace the stale stillness of the summer afternoon. Over my soul, too, refreshment has come, as well as a new sense of resolve.

Rising to my feet, I move to the wash basin and splash cool water on my eyes. Then, I pin up my hair before going down the passage to Mr. Brainerd's room, knocking quietly to see if he needs something. He accepts my offer of a cup of tea.

Deep within the thoughts of my heart, I know that our journey to Boston was only the beginning of what promises to be a venture deep into the unknown, together.

Chapter Twelve

"Is Mr. Brainerd leaving us, Rushie?"

Timothy's high-pitched voice breaks into the welcome quiet of the sitting room. My hands still over the stocking I am darning. "Why, what do you mean?" Though my little brother's words make no sense at all, the blood begins to thunder through my skull and chest nonetheless. "Why should Mr. Brainerd be leaving? What gives you cause to say such a thing? He plans to remain here until… until he gets better." One way or the other. I do not know how much my parents have spoken of Mr. Brainerd's seemingly inevitable death to my younger siblings. Knowing them, they have spoken of it plainly. Yet, due to Papa's original belief that Mr. Brainerd might find his cure in Northampton and my own long absence during our trip to Boston, I am not sure what they have told the children.

Timothy tosses a pigskin ball up into the air and catches it. Then, as if he remembers our house rule about balls, he glances back at the sitting room door. Relief passes over his face when he sees that Mama has not caught him.

"Timothy, what do you mean?"

He looks back at me, frowning in puzzlement, passing the ball from hand to hand. "About what?"

"About Mr. Brainerd. Why should you think he is

leaving us?"

Understanding clears his face. "Oh, that! Because he is saddling his horse in the stable. And he is wearing his traveling clothes."

He is going back to his Indians. He is leaving us. Sick though he is, this past week has brought mostly good days for him. Apparently, too good. The man believes himself capable of resuming his work! Distress takes hold of me, quick and fierce, and my hands begin to shake. I set aside the stocking and needle. He must be stopped – stopped before he kills himself. Without a word more, I rise and go out the door, Timothy skipping close on my heels.

***

"See, I told you, Rushie."

And, indeed, we find Mr. Brainerd exactly as Timothy described: His horse saddled, Mr. Brainerd feeds the bit into the beautiful gelding's mouth. He glances up as Timothy and I come to a halt, the pair of us a bit breathless from the pace I set hastening from the house.

"Good afternoon," he greets us, bestowing a smile on my brother. When his eyes lift to me, a thoughtful expression fills them. No easy smile graces his lips for me, but not a frown, either, for which I am thankful, for 'tis a change from our first days in each other's company. "And what are you two up to?"

I have caught my breath at last. "We might ask you the same thing, Mr. Brainerd," I say, trying to keep my voice light, without allowing my pressing worry to crowd it. "My brother tells me that you are leaving us."

His back is to us as he checks the girth. "And so I am."

If it is possible, my heart stops its beating. Words

rush to my tongue, but I cannot force my mouth open to argue with his hasty departure.

"I am leaving for at least an hour." A playful smile – the like of which I have not seen on his lips before, yet which seems to fit there so very well – makes his mouth dance, and my heart starts to beat again, quickly as if to compensate for lost time.

My thoughts scramble and then reassemble. "You are going riding? For leisure?"

"Aye." He brings the knotted reins over his horse's head. "*Riding will do him good.* That is what Doctor Mather advised before we went to Boston, if you remember, Miss Edwards."

Relief comes over me – relief and embarrassment. How forward I must have looked, rushing out here with Timothy on my heels! I gather together whatever crumbs remain of my dignity. "Timothy was concerned when he saw you in your traveling clothes and saddling your horse. We came out together to ascertain the true circumstances. And now we have. We wish you a good ride, Mr. Brainerd." I place my hands on Timothy's wiry shoulders to steer him out of the stable, but he escapes from my grasp and runs out into the sunshine independently.

"Would you care to accompany me, Miss Edwards?" Mr. Brainerd's question stops me. Doubting whether I heard him correctly, I turn, my skirt swishing against the fresh, sweet-smelling straw that covers the floor.

"I much appreciated your company in Boston, and you seem to enjoy riding. If you are not otherwise occupied, that is. We will not stay out long – just enough for a little exercise and air – and you can make sure that I do not fall off my horse if I should have a coughing spell." Another smile quirks up the side of his mouth.

Is he in earnest? My heart threatens to burst. The pile of stockings to yet be darned enters my mind, but I push the image aside. I will stay up tonight to finish them, if necessary. I struggle to keep the delight from causing my voice to tremble. "I do enjoy riding. Let me tell Mama where I am going and change my clothes. I will return in a few minutes."

"I will saddle your mare for you." He means Mama's mare, but I do not correct him. My heart dances, giddy as a bird in springtime, as I turn and walk sedately toward the house, breaking into a run after I know that I am out of eyeshot of the stable.

**

And so we ride, Mr. Brainerd and I, he on his sturdy, agile Rhode Island Walking Horse, I on Mama's dainty-limbed mare.

Was it Boston that turned the final tide of this disease, that pushed the pendulum-swing from life to death for the increasingly-gaunt man who rides now at my side? It surely appears that his insistence upon going to the city has brought death's hollow smile of victory nearer to Mr. Brainerd's face. True, the road to Boston is better now than 'twas fifty years ago; my great-grandfather himself saw to that. Wanting to attend the Harvard commencements each year and loathing the ride on a wilderness track to do so, Great-grandfather Stoddard convinced the Massachusetts government to heavily improve the road running nearly from his doorstep to that great city.

Guilt plagues me from time-to-time, heavy and mine to bear by myself, as I can tell no one of the way I schemed to accompany Mr. Brainerd to Boston. I should have relentlessly tried to stop the journey, rather than selfishly have tried to accompany him, desperate to retain his presence. I, perhaps more than any other in our family, knew that he was not well. How could such a journey with its numerous exertions help rather than hinder his getting better?

But, then, who could have argued successfully with Mr. Brainerd? Thus, perhaps the fault lies not completely with me.

And for my part, I was eager to have him to myself – as I thought – for the ride there. 'Twas a selfish, shallow girl who thought to accompany him there, and 'twas a grieved but hopefully wiser young woman who brought him back to her home – who kneels by her bed each night and begs God to have mercy on him… and on her.

For, in my heart, I know that is what I want. I want him well and whole. I want to see the fiery strength burn in his eyes, rather than see pain dimming its glow. Aye, even if naught comes of my affection – which ever-deepens, beyond my control – for this man – even if a mutual love is not the will of the Father for us– I want him to *live*. To live and not die.

What would my world become without such a one as Mr. Brainerd in it, somewhere, even though not by my side? My own chest aches at the thought, and I duck my head, already shadowed by my wide-brimmed straw hat though it is, anxious to cover the tears that smart my eyes.

As I follow Mr. Brainerd's quiet lead down the paths to the river, the Scripture whispers through my mind, echoing down the corridors of my heart, lodging in my very soul: *To live is Christ.*

That is the part of the verse to which my whole being gives assent. The second part that follows is more difficult.

To die is gain.

My heart gives a jerking concurrence instead of a

gentle nod to that.

Gain? Gain for whom?

Not for the Indians at Crossweeksung. Who is there like Mr. Brainerd, utterly selfless and devoted to their good, who will give up all his life and livelihood in order to speak the name of Jesus Christ to them?

Not for the spiritual awakening that still blazes up in pockets here-and-there, all over the country. Does it not need Mr. Brainerd's balancing and yet fervent influence?

Not for the Church as a whole.

And certainly not for me.

This last bit I hardly allow myself to think – for it is too painful to imagine my days without the presence of this hardy-souled man.

Blinking back the moisture from my eyes, I turn my ear away from the bitter contemplations that plague me. Mr. Brainerd may yet recover. He tells us that he has done so several times before now.

He may yet recover. 'Tis my hope.

Yet 'tis also my fear.

For if he recovers, he certainly will go away from us. Perhaps forever. I am not sure that I could bear such a loss, either. But it would surely be better than the alternative. Especially since he grasped my hand that second time in Boston, brushing aside the curtain veiling the secret rooms of his heart, though I had not time to glance within.

Our horses begin wading into the long grass that grows near the river. The brilliant, brown-edged green rises sharply against the cerulean blue of the sky. Mr. Brainerd is more silent than usual – more silent than even I am, the most reserved of the Edwards sisters. He lets his horse walk nearly to the edge of where the grassy earth drops off into a shallow cliff, no taller than a man's height, sloping down to the slow-moving river.

Then he reins in the gelding, giving the horse a light pat on its smoothly-brushed neck, and dismounts easily, despite the disease consuming him moment by moment, hour by hour, like a caterpillar destroys a fruit tree in early spring.

I bring Cocoa to a standstill as well, feeling the leather reins grow taut between my fingers and the horse's muscles bunch near my legs. The strong wind assaults my senses with the scent of water and shade. The sun hangs suspended in the nearly cloudless sky, and I close my eyes for just a moment, enjoying the warmth it brings.

"May I help you down?" He stands beside Cocoa, his hand touching the rein looping nearest him. Even now, his gaze is not upon me, whom he proposes to assist, but upon the far horizon, where the land meets the heavens.

'Tis this that I love most about him.

'Tis this that I resent.

'Tis this that makes my heart run toward him with wide-eyed adoration. And 'tis this that makes my heart recoil from him in fear-filled self-preservation.

'Tis this that makes me remember in the long, dark hours, when I hear him coughing up his lungs, "He who seeks to save his life will lose it."

And whosoever shall lose his life shall preserve it.

'Tis this that he lives for. 'Tis this that makes him unlike any other man I have ever known.

'Tis this single-minded vision of life that causes even Papa to overlook Mr. Brainerd's sometimes uncultured, even countrified speech, his simple – though always gentlemanly – manners… Aye, even his roughened wilderness look – to overlook all that and to wonder at him – as the ancients must have wondered at the prophets, who were spectacles and signs to the whole earth.

I grasp his offered hand, and he turns his attention back toward me. His other hand goes to my waist. I feel only the pressure of his secure grip through the stays I wear beneath my dress. Mr. Brainerd is all gentleness, yet without effeminacy. "Down you come, then," he says with a smile such as he would give to any young woman with whose father he claimed friendship. And half of my heart sighs with relief for his continued reserve. With the sureness of his death sentence coming home to roost while we stayed in Boston, part of me is no longer sure that I wish for him to draw close to me, as I once did.

Though it is I – not Esther or Mary or Sarah – whom he asked to ride with him on these last days of summer. Why, I do not know and dare not hazard any guess.

My feet touch the sun-hardened ground, and Mr. Brainerd immediately releases his hold on me. I would expect no less from a chaste-minded minister, but somehow disappointment still curdles inside my stomach every time he turns away and could have lingered.

No mind. He shall not see that it is so. And why should he not act as he does? He did not come to Northampton to find a wife. He came to get well – so we thought; or to die – as he thought. And I am not here as his riding companion to allure him but to watch over him in case he should have another sudden collapse. Surely that is the only reason he asked me along: He has found that I am dependable and can bear the sight of blood and gore better than many another girl. May God help me to carry out the duty appointed to me faithfully.

Leaving Cocoa's reins with Mr. Brainerd, I move toward the banks of the river, the same river that has flowed through Northampton's territory for as long as memory can tell. Did my own great-grandmother Stoddard come to this riverbank to gather her thoughts? The sunlight swoops through the trees lowing over the water, dappling it with shadow and brightness. Early fallen leaves float here and there on the liquid surface. The river's swirl guides the shed leaves carefully around the boulders dotting their path.

Behind me, I hear Mr. Brainerd murmuring to the horses as he secures their reins to a low tree limb. Then his footsteps crackle through the dry grass until he comes to stand beside me.

I can still remember bumping along behind Papa, as Papa usually brings one of us children with him when he travels to do ministry work. That time, down in New Haven, when Papa was pleading for Mr. Brainerd's reinstatement at Yale, long after his disgrace had transpired, was no different. That time, nearly four years ago now, 'twas my turn to tag along with Papa – and that time, I met a young man with fire for God blazing so in his heart that it shone in his eyes, glazed every word from his lips, graced each movement.

That fire yet burns in the man beside me.

Mr. Brainerd stands, shoulders bowed a bit, eyes narrowed against the pain that I know must dog him. His coffee-colored coat is worn around the edges, where the shoulder pieces meet, and at the ends of his sleeves. When I glance at him, I find that, once again, his eyes are not on me but are set on the far bank. The light glimmers in their hazel depths, reflecting off the golden water below us. I cannot find any words, and he seems in no hurry for conversation either.

Until he coughs, hard and heavy, and my own chest tightens as I hear the way that sound fights a path up from his lungs. *Oh, dear God, not another fit.*

Let him enjoy one day out in the sunshine, breathing the uncloseted air, feeling the earth beneath his boots. "Perhaps we should not be out here," I say.

He cannot answer me, for the coughing continues. It bends him over and then brings him to his knees, and he soon grovels on the moist riverbank, his hands spreading away from either side of his body, whitened fingers grasping the earth. His cough has become a retch, his lungs vomiting bloody matter.

Panic tightens my own throat. *Heavenly Father, help me.* I push away the horror that wraps its arms around me and run into that which I dread. Kneeling beside him, I find my own handkerchief tucked into my sleeve and offer it to him with shaking hands. "Here, use this."

He reaches out for it, choking on his own thick phlegm, and, pressing the cloth to his lips, crumbles to the ground before me. Pity enlarges my heart. I reach over and place my arm around his back, his shoulders. My other hand goes to his other arm, still stretched tautly against the ground. "Mr. Brainerd, hush-a-hush-a. 'Tis all right. It will be all right." My hand rubs his back as though he is my baby brother Jonathan. Indeed, for a moment, that is what it feels like: a maternal, not romantic, love. His coat dampens beneath my hand. "You are sweating," I say aloud.

He nods like a horse with the reins of its bridle pulled too tightly, unable to answer me for the coughing. At last, he sinks back beside me. He cannot speak for a long moment and merely sits there with the handkerchief shaking against his lips.

Gingerly, I pull at his sweat-soaked coat, eager to relieve his suffering in this small way at least. Limply, he lets me guide it off his back. His linen shirt is wet beneath as well, and his neckcloth strains against his throat. Without allowing myself to think of the intimacy of the gesture, I do what must be done: I loosen the knot that embraces the pain-tensed throat.

At the touch of my fingers, he opens his eyes, revealing a peaceful but pain-filled gaze. "I thank you," he rasps. He wipes his mouth, and I make the mistake of glancing down at the cloth. 'Tis covered with blood-tinged mucus. My body tingles with fear.

"We should go back home. You will be more comfortable. I do not know what I was thinking, bringing you to the river," I say, half of me wishing to get away from the dying Mr. Brainerd – to get back to the Mr. Brainerd who is still well enough to read a book and write a letter, to speak quietly with our guests and with Papa and Mama.

But he shakes his head. "The doctor says that the fresh air is good for my condition."

And, as always, when he smiles at me, I forget about the weary pain that lives in the lines of his face.

We stay quiet for many moments, both of us looking down at the sun-dappled water. His breathing gradually eases into its usual soft gasping. "You have given up so much, Mr. Brainerd. Do you ever regret it?" The words come out as a near-whisper, and I stare at my hands, clasped tightly in my lap, as the question sits in the air between us. I know that it is not a right question – that it reeks of rebelling against God's will. But Mr. Brainerd... I sense that – if he chooses to answer – he will be gentle with me, as he must have been with his poor Indians for so many months.

When I look toward him, I see that he turns his head toward me. That slight smile stays on his lips. He strokes the edges of the blood-soiled handkerchief with one rough finger. "You have asked me this question before – back on the road to Boston." He speaks just above a whisper. "Regret? No, Miss Edwards. I do not regret anything I have given up, as you say, to gain the souls of men and women. That has long been my prayer, even back at Yale: that God would give me souls. God merely has redirected me many times into His perfect path."

A relief spreads over me at his response – that, and a shadow of bitter sorrow fluttering its wings against the bars of a cage. "But someone else could have gone to the Indians."

And then you might have stayed in comfort and lived and...

"Someone with better heath, you mean?" he asks, a cough fittingly emphasizing this.

I nod.

"Miss Edwards," he says, "I am all His. My body is His to do what He wills. My choices are not my own, except to choose to follow Him. If He wants to pour me out as a sacrifice... Well, that is His decision, not mine to make. All I have to do is to offer Him all that I am, all that I have. That is all any of us have to do, is it not?"

Again, I nod. Our eyes meet, and a communion passes between us. In this moment, I feel closer to him than I have felt since he took my hand in Boston. His heart appears open to me, not in a romantic way, but in the way for which I asked him, back in Joseph Bromfield's library – to understand personally what has driven him and drives him still to spiritual heights few men or women reach. Will he unveil any of his deepest heart to me now, as he seemed on the verge of doing then?

He looks away, into the green trees, even now tinged with gold on the very edges of their leaves. "I will not say that there have not been difficult things to give up – things for which He asked and which were hard to put into His hand. There were also things – one thing in particular – that He did not *require* me to relinquish, but which I knew that I must if I wanted

His best."

I sit, quiet, waiting to hear more if he will tell me.

He turns his eyes back upon me, and I see a wonder there. "And He has done as He promises in His Word, and more. He says that anyone who gives up houses or lands or family or wives for His sake, and the Kingdom's, will receive them back and more so. God has given me all I desired, and more, Miss Edwards. And when my desires did not fit with His good and perfect plan, He changed them. He changed me. I would not have it other than He has wished." A smile touches his lips, lit by the sun far above our heads. "I am satisfied."

Despite this, my own soul still struggles within me, asking *why* and feeling guilty for asking it.

Chapter Thirteen

When we returned from Boston, I expected my family to swallow up Mr. Brainerd: Papa would wish to spend every waking moment discussing theology in his company; Timothy would ask him – albeit with sideways glances, hopeful that Mama would not see him bothering our guest – to play ball with him; and my pretty younger sisters would, of course, occupy every possible spare moment of his with their witty banter and smiles.

But this does not occur. Papa is much engaged with a book he is writing, as well as his usual many hours of solitary study and prayer. Mama's schedule keeps my youngest siblings, including young Timothy, out of Mr. Brainerd's presence and out of mischief – "The good man needs his rest," I hear her say multiple times each week to them.

As for my sisters... Well, when Mr. Brainerd asks me to accompany him to ride for the third time, I understand why they have kept out from underfoot.

"Are you going for another ride with Mr. Brainerd, Rushie?" Music in one hand, Mama's lute in the other, Mary pauses on her way down the staircase, her bright eyes taking in my riding attire.

I pick up my straw hat with its pink ribbons from the entryway table. "Aye." I do not intend to be short with her, but 'tis difficult for me to speak of Mr.

Brainerd without betraying something of the many emotions and thoughts that swarm within me, calmed only by staying my mind on God Himself. With the hat perched at a slight angle on my crown, as I know is most fetching, I draw the ribbon ties together to make a bow, full and even.

My sister stands there, halfway down the stairs, watching me, so uncharacteristically quiet that I stop tying the bow and look up at her. The solemnity covering her face startles me, and a stone of unease sinks through my innards. "What is it, Mary?"

Bold as ever, she meets my eyes. "There is no hope for this to end well for you, Sister."

My heart thuds in my chest. She cannot mean... She cannot think... "I do not know what you mean." I keep my tone light and begin to tie my bow again.

Mary frowns, shaking her head. "You are falling in love with a dead man."

Her plainspoken words make my eyes dart to all the doorways. Somewhat assured that no one has heard her, I turn away to pull on my leather mitts. "Mr. Brainerd and I are only friends, Mary. You have no cause for alarm. But I thank you for your concern, though 'tis not necessary."

My bristling like this alone would have given me away, but I see when I glance once more at her face that she truly has already guessed my secret. Yet 'tis her love for me, layered behind the frown pulling at her mouth, that drives the tears to my eyes as I step out into the blinding summer sunlight.

***

That afternoon, and many afterward, we ride out together. The dam that somehow silenced him on the road to Boston has broken, and he speaks to me of many things, nearly all of them spiritual, but none of which give words to his personal journey to becoming – unreservedly – broken bread and poured-out wine for our God. 'Tis this that I long to understand. I see the result of his complete relinquishment to God: the amazing and unexpected blessing that God gave in the Indian conversions at Crossweeksung; the holiness in his own life; the contentment with his lot, even in death. But how to get to this place of abandonment… that I do not know, though I want to know with all of my heart. And I want to know *him* as well, deeply, for he knows the secret to this resting in the high place of my God.

We do not always speak as we ride; indeed, often we ride in silence. But when Mr. Brainerd does open his lips, he talks in that beautiful, gentle voice of the glory of God and of how he longs to be perfected and with God and with the holy angels at last. When he speaks thus, the conviction sincere in his every tone, he stirs up in my own heart an answering passion for God, to do His will only, to want His glory only. The question of *Why must he suffer so? Why may my prayer for him and me not be answered?* fades away, replaced by seeming courage.

But the questions in my heart and the longing to keep Mr. Brainerd by me never truly go away, for, afterward, fear sets in.

It sets in when I come upon Mr. Brainerd gasping for breath in the sitting room, weak and pale, straining against the straight back of his chair, his book fallen to the floor.

It sets in when I hear him coughing and choking in the night, when I go to him and raise him up a bit so that he can perhaps catch his breath… and his blood smears upon my sleeve.

And it is this that I fear when I see Mr. Brainerd

slouched over, coughing out the contents of his breast in a bloody mixture of phlegm and tissue: that God has used such a one for His glory among the Indians, but now has decided to discard him – to toss him out like Leah throws the bucket of scraps to the hogs – fattening them up only to be butchered. It makes me weep at night, deeply into my pillow, to think of such a man gone forever. I fear, too, that when he goes into the grave, the glimpse of God as I have never before beheld Him will vanish as well, and such a thought breaks my heart.

Chapter Fourteen

David

Her spirit touches my spirit. I have sensed this from the first day we met. Too, I have sensed the yearning she has – the same yearning that I possess, though in her, 'tis purer, less mixed with lower motives and vices, I am certain. She longs for God Himself. He will be her exceedingly great joy. She will cry out to Him, and He Himself will answer her. He will be her peace, both now and forever.

Weeks ago, she asked me a question: Could she hear my story – the same story told in my private diaries, these tiny volumes so full of my secret thoughts and concerns, these books that mention everything of importance to me?

Everything.

Can I open my heart so much? For so long, I have kept it closed to any save Thee, O my God and Savior – I have reserved myself only for Thee. I have laid each of my Isaacs on Thy altar – and have not spared them the blade.

Yet she has given so much to me. 'Twas her hand that grasped mine in the maw of death itself when we were in Boston – and, unbeknownst to her, I distinguished her voice – gentle and sure as spring rain – refuse to let the doctor there force an opiate down

my throat. 'Tis her presence – and through her, Thine –
that gives me such comfort day-by-day here.

In giving her this, would I perhaps be giving to
Thee as well, but in another way? Giving to Thee
through giving to her?

If it will help her to walk Thy path, I will do it,
though some things must yet be veiled, perhaps until
eternity dawns.

Chapter Fifteen

Jerusha

The hacking sound travels down the stairs and floats into the sitting room, bringing the same horror to my soul as the Egyptians must have felt upon the arrival of the Angel of Death. My fingers stiffen around my embroidery needle, but I try to ignore the coughing. "Here, Lucy," I force my voice to remain steady. "See how I make my stitches even, forming the letter?"

Lucy gives an energetic bounce on the settee beside me. "Aye. After we are finished here, may I go outside to play?"

Another cough comes from above stairs, followed by the sound of a chair scraping across the floor. I swallow. "I think that Mama has need of you after we are finished. Now, concentrate."

Good advice for me, as well – advice I find myself unable to heed.

Lucy sighs, though not loudly enough to warrant a correction from me. She is, after all, only ten years old. I am not so far removed from that age as to forget the difficulty of sitting in a stuffy room, completing tedious embroidery samplers, while my friends ran at liberty in the fresh air.

The coughing continues, this time without any break. I cannot stand it any longer. Tucking my needlework carefully in my workbasket, I rise from the settee. "I must check on Mr. Brainerd. I will return soon."

Lucy moans.

"Keep stitching. You will be finished in no time." The words hardly leave my mouth before my feet are on the stair.

"I do not know why you think yourself alone responsible for him, Rushie," my little sister calls after me.

I ignore her, hoping that her voice has not reached above-stairs, finding its way to Mr. Brainerd's ears. I do not think that I alone am responsible for Mr. Brainerd's well-being; I know that I am. The weight of it presses on me as a yoke presses down the shoulders of oxen. *He must get well. He must. Oh, Lord God, wilt Thou not be merciful?* And even as I plead with the Lord, I am afraid to hear His answer… or, if He is silent, to await what Providence brings. So here I am, once more, running up the stairs, my skirt and petticoat gathered up so that I don't trip, attempting to stave off the black harvest of time that will surely come.

My breath pants harshly from my mouth as I pause in the passage before his door.

Another cough.

"Mr. Brainerd, are you all right?"

"Aye, I am—" Coughing cripples the words as they try to leap from his tongue. "I am well. I thank you."

Silence. I pause, not wanting to be as irritatingly present as a bedbug in a roadside inn. A shiver of unease travels up my spine. "May I get you anything, Mr. Brainerd?"

"Nay, I do not wish to—" Again, the miserable cough interrupts him, yet this time with violence.

A vision of him coughing, his lungs retching bloody mucus on the riverbank some days ago, floods the eyes of my mind and heart. Without waiting for permission, I lift the latch and push open the door.

At the sound, he swivels around from his place at the desk, pen in hand. Papers and books lie scattered here-and-there across the dark-stained surface, along with several blood-spattered handkerchiefs. He stares at me in silence, and I am half-afraid that he will become irritated with me, as he did in those first days that he came to Northampton. I can bear many things, but, when he is irritated with me, my very insides feel ready to crumble like biscuits several-days-old.

"I am sorry that I interrupted," I manage, my eyes skittering away from his. "I was concerned about you. That is, we were concerned about you. When we heard your cough."

Another silent moment tiptoes by. "Pray, excuse me." I back out of the threshold, pulling the door closed behind me.

"Miss Edwards."

His voice pauses my retreat. "Aye?"

"I thank you." His eyes do not meet mine, but stay studied upon the letter he has been writing. "I thank you for caring. Your sincere concern for me these past weeks... has been a reflection of the Divine's care all these years. I do not deserve it."

Surprise, warm and uncomfortable, spreads through my bones. This personal openness from him – from whence has it come? My fingers fidget with the latch. "Any care we give you, sir, is an honor for us."

And for me, 'tis a love-act, besides.

My mouth keeps supplying words to tame the unexpected closeness his speech has brought. "You have given so much for the gospel. You have suffered so greatly for Jesus Christ. 'Tis an honor to serve you."

And not with merely a cold, dead service, but with a warm, blood-filled, beating one, flowing from the deep mines of my heart.

But he shakes his head, obviously troubled at what I have said. "I deserve nothing, Miss Edwards. Certainly nothing good. If you knew the pride, the bitterness, the idolatry that has nestled – that nestles still – from time-to-time in my own heart, you would not say such things. You would turn from me in revulsion, as from a rotting dog, dead in the street."

Confusion falls over me at such strange words. There is a place for humility, for knowing how wretched and sinful we are before a holy God, but these remarks do not match, surely, the man sitting before me. "That cannot be." Visions of all his efforts among the Indians, among the heathen whites, among the spiritually-dead New Englanders combine with what my father has told us children of Mr. Brainerd's fervent prayer-life, fastings, and unremitting steadfastness.

But his eyes latch onto mine and refuse to give way. "'Tis true, I assure you. If you knew – truly understood – how dark my heart can be – how wicked the desires, how selfish, when God has been so merciful to me, so loving, so gentle and good and kind... I do not think that you would hold me in the esteem in which you do." He swallows, his Adam's apple sharp against his emaciated throat.

I think of the private diaries which he has refused to allow anyone save himself to read, of the way in which he has denied seemingly everyone entry deep into his inner world, and a shadow of fear falls over me. So I stand up straight and tall, as the daughters of Jonathan and Sarah Edwards have been so taught to do, and stare back into his eyes. The strength of a lion comes over me. "I think that you should let me be the authority on what I will or will not think of you, Mr. Brainerd. And from the little I know of you, I will continue to think as I do: You are a man of honor, a man like Christ, deserving of my esteem."

With that, I step out into the passage, closing out the brightness of his chamber, my heart pounding yet strangely calm.

***

The sweet melodies of the Psalter hum in my throat as I wait for little Jonathan's long lashes to close over his dark eyes. The house has grown quiet. My sister Sarah is, no doubt, sewing or reading in our chamber, while my younger sisters probably chatter in whispers in their own room. Doubtless, Mama and Papa have retired to talk and pray together over important matters, while the servants have begun to find their own sleeping-places by the banked hearth or in the stable. My head feels heavy with weariness from the day's heat as well as from turning Mr. Brainerd's words over in my mind. My feather pillow will be welcome tonight.

At last, Jonny's eyes shutter. I continue humming and ease away from his trundle bed. With one last look behind me to ensure that my little brother stays asleep, I slip into the darkness of the passage, candlestick in hand.

My feet do not slow as I move past Mr. Brainerd's guest chamber, but my thoughts linger and, with them, a prayer for the man who surely bends his knees beside the bed therein, pouring out his soul for Christ's kingdom to come in every man's heart. Watching the dim candlelight flicker beneath the crack of his door, I cannot believe of him what he would have me to accept: that he is a man unworthy of honor and concern.

My hand has already touched the latch of the

chamber I share with Sarah when the noise of a door opening in the passage behind me bids me to turn quickly, dread filling me at the prospect of one of the younger children having roused and so in need of me to coax them back to sleep.

But 'tis not one of my little siblings' silhouettes that throws a shadow in the passage. Instead, it is Mr. Brainerd who leans out of his chamber, his gaze settling and staying on me, as if he hoped to find that the person passing his door was I.

My heart batters against my chest, but I will not allow him to see that. "Mr. Brainerd, I was just putting my little brother to sleep. I hope that I did not wake you," I whisper, knowing that everything he or I say may very well be heard by anyone still awake behind their thin chamber doors.

He shakes his head. "You did not wake me."

A pause. I open my mouth to say good-night.

"I was waiting for you to pass."

What will come next? This man has been one perplexing layer after another since he has come. I stay silent, my heart on edge, willing myself to breathe steadily.

He steps into the passage, his own candlestick in hand. "Will you come speak with me? I have much to tell you."

I nod, unable to manage words.

"Come, then." He gestures toward the stair.

Every step feels as though I am in another world altogether as I precede Mr. Brainerd down the steps, our feet soft and silent as night animals in the forest. Meanwhile, my mind runs wildly through a tangled thicket of possibilities. What does he mean that he has *much to tell me*? And why in the quiet solitude of night, rather than in the broad daylight with my siblings and parents around to hear as well? I draw in a steadying breath coupled with a wordless prayer as we come to the bottom of the steps. Without consulting him, I step into the sitting room, my candle throwing light before me.

I set the candlestick down on the mantle. There is no fire banked; the night is too warm for that, save in any room but the kitchen, where I know that Leah sleeps across the hearth.

The door shuts, its latch loud in the night quietness. I turn, my body tense with anticipation of what Mr. Brainerd will soon say, and say to me alone.

He stands, silent, his burning eyes staring across the sparsely-furnished room, staring into my own eyes.

Nervousness travels up my spine, and I nearly open my mouth to speak. But before my lips can part, a silent word comes, as if from outside of myself: *Wait.*

Is it the voice of the Lord God, answering the prayer I sent heavenward for wisdom as I preceded Mr. Brainerd down the stair just moments ago? A knowing deep within my soul says that it is. Thus, I stand, waiting for whatever God brings in this strange hour.

Mr. Brainerd swallows hard, though anxiety finds no place to rest on his countenance. "I have much to tell you," he repeats in his quiet, determined voice. "You have inquired of me why and how I came to go among my people, the Indians. You have said that you wish to know the road I traveled to become willing to be poured-out wine and broken bread for them, utterly, with no thought for this world, with no desire left, save to do the will of God, and what is more important, to delight in His will?"

He keeps his gaze steady and waits for my answer.

I nod, slowly. "Aye. I have long admired you, Mr. Brainerd, as you know." I pause, taking stock of what I am about to say. "I desire to be like you, a servant to the uttermost to the Lord Jesus. You make Him appear a good Master, one to whom I would be a fool not to give everything to follow. I want to know the path whereby He led you, but only if you wish to tell it."

Mr. Brainerd remains quiet another long moment, and then he strides forward into the room. "I wish to tell it to you. 'Tis time to tell it." He gestures to the settee. "Pray, be seated. I warn you, though: You may find that I topple off the pedestal upon which you have placed me, Miss Edwards."

Chapter Sixteen

6 Years Ago

David breathed in deeply, and the cool air expanded his lungs, bringing back the familiar ache and then a sudden, knife-edged pain. His stride did not break, but he could not stop the shudder that ran through his skin.

Above, the stars shone out of the black Connecticut sky, peacefully glimmering as he led the group of Yale students down the forest path with a nervous quiet. The eldest of the group at three-and-twenty, David moved with determined – some would say headstrong – steps. His brown breeches blended into the darkness of the natural world around him, but he had already removed his coat because of the July night's warmth, and so his ivory linen shirt gleamed in the moonlight. Above it, his complexion nearly matched his shirt in paleness, and a stranger might have thought fear had brought such a ghostly pallor to his skin, though those who knew him best understood that recurrent illness caused it.

While some of the furtive party might have spines that tingled with fright tonight, David Brainerd was not among them. Excitement, not terror, raced through his limbs.

"Are you giving the sermon?"

The eagerness pulsing through his friend's whispered question infected David as well and distracted his mind from all thoughts of a hurting chest. He turned on the path to glance at Samuel Buell, whose fevered steps nearly tripped on David's heels. "Yes," he answered, "Nehemiah asked me to."

"Your brother doesn't care that you are not ordained?" This came from Henry, a new member of the group, one who had never accompanied them before tonight – and one who showed rather too much nitpicking caution for David's taste. "Will he not get into trouble for allowing you to preach?"

"Nehemiah's one of us," Samuel answered before David could. "A New Light. For a new time. He doesn't worry about all the rules and regulations and licenses, so long as souls are being saved. Is that not so, David?"

David's bosom swelled with pride at the thought of his elder brother, pastor at the Second Congregational Church in Eastbury, Connecticut. "Aye, Nehemiah is one of us, that's for certain." Indeed, his brother, not yet in his thirtieth year, was a most definite member of the new, intensely evangelical faction rising in the American colonies: the New Lights, who emphasized personal conversion and holiness over adherence to tradition. If anyone had doubted Nehemiah's position on the spiritual awakening before now, the invitation he had extended to his not-yet-ordained brother, David, to preach at the series of meetings would wipe away any uncertainties.

"The fire of the Spirit certainly spreads anew," commented another of the party. "First with George Whitefield's tour – Oh, that I could have heard him preach! – and now with Wheelock and the Tennents. James Davenport and Benjamin Pomeroy, as well, of course. And Reverend Jonathan Edwards himself at Enfield a few weeks ago preached a mighty sermon to make any New Light proud."

"Edwards helped to begin the awakening of God's people years ago, in his own town of Northampton. He is not so fiery as Tennent or Whitefield, but he desires true conversion among God's people, just as we do." David paused for a moment, relishing the knowledge that he had taken sides with such men as these: the Tennents, Wheelock, Davenport, and even cautious Edwards, though the final man might not wish to be lumped together with all the rest. "Aye, the fire is spreading," he affirmed, the exhilaration glowing in his voice.

There was huff from behind him. "Aye, and 'tis a fire that such as Rector Clap should like to put out as soon as possible."

David's jaw tightened, hard as a rock. What right had Yale's Rector Clap - a man grasping for the old ways, a Pharisee leading the blind into a ditch! - to stand against the work of God in the hearts of the people of New England?

"He should beware lest God strike him down dead." The words slipped out and a blade of conviction pressed at David's breast, but he pushed it aside. Was it not right? Was it not the truth? The only reason he and the others with him needed to sneak away like this - rather than traveling openly to the meeting - was because of Rector Clap of Yale, who threatened and opposed New Lights whenever he could. Imagine, trying to prevent men and women and children from hearing the Truth!

They came to the edge of the wood, where the ancient footpath met the road running down to Eastbury. Summer meadows spread their dry, grassy blankets over the land straight ahead of them, and then, there 'twas, creeping through the darkness - the sound of an approaching wagon.

"See," grinned Samuel, his wide smile stretching out pale in the darkness. "I told you that our ride would come, Henry."

"Who is it?" This came from yet another of the Yale lads.

David peered into the darkness. His heartbeat matched the rapid clip-clopping of the horse's hooves as excitement raced through his veins. Did those around him feel the same way?

"My cousin, Joseph," announced Samuel. "He favors the New Lights. Went to hear Davenport preach last time he came around here. Aye, even had the man for dinner."

"I know someone who will have *us* for dinner if it comes out that we were attending an irregular meeting," grumbled Henry.

David heard the sand and loose gravel shifting under Henry's reluctant feet. "See here," he turned with a blaze in his hazel eyes that even the darkness of the evening hour could not conceal, "if you are not truly with us, then you are against us. Choose your side, Henry. Let it be known, here and now. There is no room for compromise." So the irregular meetings – meant to fan the flames of the spiritual fires that continued to blaze – had been forbidden. What of it? Obviously, God had given His approval by pouring out His Spirit. Why should anyone require more than that?

The shorter, stouter young man shuffled again, looking down at the ground, not daring to meet his leader's gaze. "Aw, David. I didn't mean anything by it. You know that Rector Clap doesn't look well on this kind of thing at all."

"That's because he's part of the old breed of ministers – the ones dying out, praise God," interrupted Samuel again.

"I cannot afford to be dismissed from Yale." The

whimper on the coward's lips made David's skin crawl. "My parents are expecting me to graduate, and at the top of my class, too. My tuition costs more than my father can afford. I'm…I'm wondering if I should just wait this out for these last months I'm in seminary. There will be time later – perhaps once I am licensed and have my own pulpit – to take such a stand as this."

Henry's proposed compromise tasted bitter as wormwood to David. If a man was not willing to go against the flow of wrong now, when he had much to lose, could he be counted upon to do so when he felt himself secure? And Clap was wrong. All the Old Lights were, the whole lot of them. They had no right to forbid others to partake of the grace of God freely offered, just because they would not come to the Fountain themselves, but would rather trust in their own carefully-cultivated theology and traditions!

"You've not much of a chance of that, Henry," Samuel spoke up, an audible smile in his voice.

"Much chance of what?"

"Graduating at the top of your class. You are competing with David, you know. He's going to outstrip you, that's for certain. I don't mean to dampen your enthusiasm, but…."

David knew that Samuel spoke the truth, and for that, his chest expanded with happiness. He would graduate at the top of Yale's class next year, despite the Rector's dislike of him, and then he would have his pick of any prestigious ministerial position he chose. Someplace where he could read and study by a warm hearth through the long, cold months that made his chest ache and his cough return.

Though, ever since Ebenezer Pemberton had visited Yale last spring, preaching on the vanity of all earthly scholarship and lifting up the example of John Sergeant, missionary to the Indians at Stockbridge,

Massachusetts, the idea of missions work among the Indians always did nip at David's heart and mind. In his private diary, he'd even written about following through on the nagging...

But tonight Samuel's broad, happy voice distracted him. In Sam's company, David was nearly able to forget all about his cough and the niggling pain that refused to let him go. "And, really, will Rector Clap follow through on his promises to punish all the students who follow the teachings of the New Lights? Will he truly, when it comes down to it, oppose an awakening brought by God's Spirit among the Congregationalists?" Samuel shook his head. "Public opinion has slowly been turning toward our way of thinking, and, with it, the views of some of the most eminent ministers. Even Reverend Edwards changed his estimation of Whitefield. I think Clap will bend."

Henry's sigh and subsequent mumble was nearly drowned out by the cart's approach. "I just... I just don't know."

"Well, as the Scriptures say, Henry," David let the words finally march off his tongue, "choose this day whom you will serve."

And he believed it. Truly. Almighty God had touched his own life with saving power in just the last two years. For so long, David had sought for relief from his guilt and sin in his own power – had even tried to devise a way to escape God's righteous judgment by substituting a god of his own making – but had not found the liberation for which he had thirsted. But then God in His love and mercy had given him the true hope of salvation – by grace alone, through faith in His Son alone. Thus, should he now bow to Yale's Rector Clap and refuse to attend – aye, even to preach at, unordained though he was – the evangelical meetings held by his brother Nehemiah and others? Should he disown his new, clearer understanding of salvation because of one man's earthly authority?

No, David would not compromise. Other men might, but not he.

The cartwheels ground to a slow halt just as an owl screeched in the tree above them. From beneath a floppy hat brim, the twinkling dark eyes of their clean-shaven driver peered. "Anybody here heading toward Eastbury?" In the light of the lantern he held up, David could see the man's wide grin – a perfect match for Samuel's.

"We're all going," he announced, taking the mantle of leadership upon his shoulders once again. With his classmates Buell and Youngs graduating this coming September – and with whispers of stricter policies coming at Yale regarding toleration of New Light practices – 'twas up to David to see things through – to make sure that the students stayed afire and alert, ready, as his brother Nehemiah said, to take on the devil's armies. The thought of it thrilled him – sent the rich Brainerd blood pulsing through his veins with the strength of the Connecticut River.

Henry was, of course, the last to scramble up into the cart's bed, slipping and sliding into place. The moon outlined the worry on his round face, perspiring despite the wind. "What will we tell Rector Clap if we get caught? You know that he fined those who followed Mr. Tennent to Milford."

"We won't be caught. Besides, we aren't doing anything wrong," put in Samuel, settling himself beside David. The straw beneath them would make for a softer ride.

"Not doing anything wrong? But the Rector says that this revival of religion is not from the Spirit of God. He disapproves of it. What we are doing will seem to be flouting his authority directly," gulped out

Henry. "Just like those scholars who followed Mr. Tennent to Milford."

Henry apparently did not know that David had been one of those scholars.

"Whether he is in authority or not is beside the point." David held on tightly to the edge of the cart as it took off down the dirt road. His voice softened as it always did when contemplating the deep things of God. "God has given us new light. He is digging up the roots of the trees that have borne no fruit, and He is planting new ones. He has shown us the way to salvation is through faith in Him alone, Henry, and that man must ask God for a new heart before he can commence any meaningful effort at religious practice. You yourself sat down with David Youngs and myself just this past spring. You examined your own heart and found in it nothing to recommend yourself to God, did you not?"

Henry swallowed. "Yes. Yes, that is true."

David put aside his frustration with the younger man and placed a hand on his shoulder. He could feel Henry trembling. Oh, that God would give this generation the fire to proclaim the good news which they had received, no matter what the cost! "So what is the matter, Henry? If you know that of what I speak is true – if God has indeed melted your heart and given you flesh for stone – why do you waver so?"

Henry glanced up but could not keep his eyes on David's. He dropped his gaze back down to the fast-disappearing road beneath the cart. "The cost is so high, David. That is all. I am afraid of what the Trustees will do if they find out that we went to this irregular meeting – and you preached at it, unordained. I – I cannot afford such a fine as the one given to the students who followed Mr. Tennent."

David's heart went out to Henry, who came from a

family with few resources; Henry himself had received financial support from his hometown reverend to attend Yale. "What we are doing is right, my friend," he tried to reassure him. "We are in the right. There is no way that God will allow us to falter."

And with that, they rumbled off into the warm evening mist….

Chapter Seventeen

Jerusha

"So, were you caught?" I cannot keep the question from stumbling off my lips.

Mr. Brainerd turns his face in the flickering candlelight, his eyes meeting mine, and the communion warms the small space between us. The shadows enhance the creases sunbaked into his skin. He pauses a moment. "No." A smile touches his lips. "Not that time at least. We played a dangerous game, you see. The movement of the Spirit had begun in earnest the previous year – really, the first year I was in school at Yale. I had missed part of it due to illness – that same illness that plagued me that night. But I had come back in time to hear Pemberton speak in the spring about the need for evangelizing the heathen – the Indians. Something he said about them – the way he talked about that noble man John Sergeant up in Stockbridge, here in your own colony of Massachusetts." His eyes seem to brighten with an inner fire. "Something in his words set my own heart ablaze, Jerusha."

'Tis the first time he has used my first name without the formal courtesy title of *Miss*. The warmth in his voice caresses my ear. 'Tis a finger stroking my cheek. 'Tis the velvet lining of a cloak touching chilled skin. 'Tis both of these, and yet neither of them, for he cannot have meant it so. He must have misspoken in the emotion of telling such a story.

I hold his eyes for a moment, but then drop my own at the intensity alight in that golden-flecked gaze. Mr. Brainerd is a consuming fire, setting others aflame, even here, in stodgy Northampton. How can I bear it? How can I – little Jerusha, the dutiful, inconsequential second daughter of Jonathan and Sarah Edwards, catch on fire in such a way as he had?

But I ache to. I do not merely long for this man now, but I yearn even more for his God – and mine. For if a man close to the Almighty God becomes such a man as this one, then his God must be yet more worthy of my love and praise than he is.

Mr. Brainerd moves from his place near the mantle, wincing as he steps toward me. I nearly rise to help him, but I know that he will not want the help if he can manage it on his own. He heaves a slight sigh as he finds his seat on a stiff chair just opposite the settee on which I sit.

I keep my hands clasped tightly in my lap, wishing that he would continue the story he has begun. I still feel that I know so little of him, other than what Papa has told us. From that, I know the scholar, I think. And from my own girlish imagination, I have produced a missionary-prince, gilded and suited to fit my fancies. But now... I wish to know the real David Brainerd. And, in my heart, I wish that he longed to know me as well.

"Where was I?" He seems lost for a moment, and I wonder if the incessant pain he bears has caused him to lose track of his thoughts.

"John Sergeant. And Pemberton. The Stockbridge Indians," I murmur with as much gentleness as I am able.

The confusion clears from his eyes, but the tension remains upon his face. "Ah. Aye, Pemberton, that good man. The spring before, just after I had recovered from a bout of illness and returned to the College, Pemberton spoke to the students at Yale, telling us of the great need to reach the Indians. How the English and the Dutch and the Germans had all taken advantage of them. Nearly all, save the Quakers and the Moravians, that is. And, of course, you know of such men as John Eliot, who started the Praying Indian villages long ago."

He leans toward me, and I can see the tears welling in his eyes. "They lived in such bitter darkness, Pemberton told us. Halooing and dancing and pow-wowing with their dumb, useless idols. Such immorality – it oppresses the soul. But I knew of it only secondhand then. I had not come across it face-to-face, as I later was to do."

He falls silent for a moment, hands braced against his legs. I wonder if the pain has launched a fresh attack upon his lungs again.

But another thought comes alongside this concern – a vision of a dying world, and these Indians among them – and so many self-dubbed Christians like myself doing nothing – nothing at all – for them. "Those poor Indians." The words break out of my throat in my astonishment. "With no gospel light, with little kindness shown to them by the white man. No wonder they fear and hate us. No wonder they do not often come to our Savior if we treat them so ill. And yet, hundreds or thousands going to eternal death each year! 'Tis beyond the pale of grief to think of. Why do we so shirk our duty... but for the comforts and pleasures and opinions of this world?"

He nods. "Aye, just as I thought when I heard Pemberton tell of it. I had encountered such dullness in my spirit after a time of such refreshing prior, but then Pemberton's preaching stirred up my soul once more. Suddenly, when I woke in the morning, I was filled with a passion for souls. My last thought before going to sleep was that God would use me to save more souls. My cry, night and day, then, was 'God, give me souls!' I thought of those Indians not as some of my esteemed friends did, as Canaanites to be driven out before us, but as our fellow men and women – lost just as I would be, were it not for the grace and mercy of our Holy God – in need, just as I had been, of repentance and the saving grace of God. And then His Spirit drove my thoughts not only to the Indians, but also to my fellow students at Yale. My friends Samuel Buell and David Youngs encouraged me in this – that same Samuel who came to study with your father, I think, after his graduation."

A smile of soft remembrance touches his lips. I know that he sees the scenes pass before him of days past – cherished memories. "Together, we went to each student and took him to task concerning the state of his soul. God was gracious and blessed the effort. Yale was ablaze, it seemed, with an awakening – true religion toward God in every man's heart."

"But all this seems like a good thing. A work of God Himself, was it not? Why then…?" I trail off, a bit embarrassed, not sure how to ask a man exactly why he had so fallen out with the religious and academic authorities at Yale that they had – from what I know of it – dismissed him.

He looks off into the flaming candle again, seeming to roll my unfinished question around in his heart and mind before answering me. "That part *was* a good thing, Jerusha. There is no evil in wanting men's souls to be saved. There no evil in the Spirit of God working – and I do not believe that we can put artificial man-made limits on how He can work. The only limits there may be are those in the Holy Scriptures." He shook his head. "No, there was no evil in the work. The evil came from the pride bubbling up – that which caused us to begin to judge other men by our own experiences, by outward appearances and not by the behavior that becomes a revived man. We became carried away with the enthusiasm for the thing – for the stirring-up itself – and lost sight of Christ at times. We lacked self-control, became imprudent sometimes, and even overheated. Not all the time, mind. Just at moments. It led me to do and say things in self-centered pride of which I am now ashamed. Things which I thought I did for the glory of God. And then, worse than that, it led me to refuse to accept the blows and unfairness of others with the patience by which God would have wished me to."

He is silent for a long moment.

"Are those the things you wrote of in the diaries which you desire to destroy?"

His throat bobs. "Aye, some of them." It comes out as a whisper. "Thanks be to God that He not only forgave my folly, but He also used it as a rich land in which to begin His deeper plowing in my soul."

He draws in a breath and closes his eyes, as if he is remembering. "'Twas just after prayer that my final blunder – the one that would lead to my dismissal occurred. Nay, I should not use the word 'occurred' – it sounds too innocent – as though I was not the one with the pride-filled words soaking the air before my mouth, as though the foam of self-righteousness had not bubbled up in my heart, as if this was just something that occurred to me and not something that I brought upon myself.

"But thanks be to God who did allow it to happen. Who did allow me to blunder on just far enough away from having my eyes on Jesus to lash me back to the ship. Thanks be to Him for that, for if He had not allowed such a seemingly trivial thing – as I thought it to be at the time but now know that it merely crested the wave of pride that had begun to form in my heart – If not for that, who knows if I would not be here right now – who knows if all that has occurred by His Spirit alone during the past two years at Crossweeksung would have ever happened. No, 'twas a strange Providence that let me veer just enough off-course to be shipwrecked on the island of His mercy...."

Chapter Eighteen

Autumn 1741

Just a few weeks after the fateful decision had been passed by the Board of Trustees – perhaps provoked in part by Reverend Jonathan Edwards' recent commencement address concerning how to identify a true work of the Spirit – Chauncey Whittesley led a group of students in prayer. He did this regularly, gathering with them in the brick Hall.

On this particular evening, the fire in the hearth crackled against the cold night while the beams of the Hall gleamed in the flickering light. Among the many students joining there around the hearth sat David Brainerd, silently despising the man who knelt and prayed aloud.

Tutor Whittesley was a young man, not much older than David, though David was one of the older students at Yale – having entered the school at one-and-twenty. Jealousy mixed with scorn in David's heart as he listened to Whittesley pray. Here was a man who had already entered the academic halls as David knew that he was fitted to do – a man leading all of these students in prayer, leading *him* in prayer!

David's jaw tightened. Swept away into a small corner of his heart, the truth whispered to him: *You should be leading this group of students. You, not he.*

Chauncey was not fit to do so, was he? Too timid to align himself fully with the New Lights, too afraid of Rector Clap and the Trustees. Yet there Chauncey Whittesley dared to kneel, praying with fervency, apparently full of passionate longing after Christ, the same passionate longing that burned within David himself.

Was it not doublemindedness? How could it reckon with true religion of the soul? David's eyes slid open, and he stared for a moment at Chauncey's bent, uncovered head. How dare this man? Did not even Joshua of old tell the Israelites that they must choose whether to serve the Lord or not? Chauncey could not continue forever between the two camps of Old Lights and New. He must either become a New Light vocally... or he would degenerate further into the darkness of the Old Lights.

All at once, the mist cleared: Whittesley was a leavened lump.

David allowed his gaze to drift over the assembled young men, most kneeling as Whittesley did, a few sitting on chairs, all with heads bent and hands clasped together in devotion. So many young men, nearly all destined for the ministry, being misled by this tutor's false piety!

But I will not be misled. I will speak for truth and righteousness. A sense of bravery and nobleness swept over David, intoxicating him. Others might be fooled by Whittesley, but not he. Others might obey the Board's new edict, but David – as the prophet Daniel in the Scriptures – would not.

Whittesley prayed long and ardently that night, his reedy voice interrupted by the sniffle of a runny nose here-and-there, as well as by David's cough, which had continued to trouble him, worsening with the cooling weather, though David perhaps coughed more than was necessary during the tutor's prayer – a prayer of which every word was met with the sword of David's unbridled opinion.

He judged each word, weighed them, and found them wanting. Did Whittesley really mean all he said? If so, would he not have done as David, going to the students one at a time, counseling them toward a life of fresh and renewed commitment? Would he not have stood up for the persecuted New Light students, instead of standing by stupidly, a cold-footed coward, unwilling to risk the wrath of Rector Clap? Would he not have attended the irregular meetings? And where had he been when Davenport came to preach that past summer? Or when Gilbert Tennent had done so? Even when Edwards had spoken a few weeks ago, cautiously encouraging the work of the Spirit, Whittesley's response had been tepid at best, though he gave lip-service to it being, "a very good address, indeed – quite thought-provoking."

He was clearly a fraud. A man unconverted.

Chauncey finished his prayer, tears welling in his eyes. *Surely the tears of Esau.* David pursed his lips and raised his eyebrows just a fraction. He would not be taken in by this man's pretended piety.

The tutor left quickly; he was a quiet man, not given to much social interaction. Besides that, he surely knew of the veiled scorn some of the students held for him. Within moments, the room emptied as the young men went their separate ways, some for studying, others to find some amusement, until only a few – David, Jonah, Henry, and one or two others, all openly New Lights – remained in the shadowed space.

The fire crackled pleasantly in the hearth, its glow warming the outspread walls. Sitting forward on the straight-backed chair, David stared into its glow, restless for... restless for something. There had to be *more*, some step forward in his walk with Christ that he had not yet taken. Sometimes, he felt like a fish floundering on a bank, gasping for breath, with a deep pool of living water just a flop away.

Close to his ear, Henry, who had begun to understand what were the marks of true conversion, eagerly began a low-voiced conversation. "There was feeling in that prayer, was there not, lads?"

A bitterness rose in David's mouth. Even now, could not Henry identify an unconverted man of authority - and thus an enemy to their cause – when he heard one?

But before David could respond, Jonah nodded his agreement from across the table. "Yes, Whittesley's address held an unusually ardent tone. It gives me hope for the college when I hear such prayers from the tutors. Especially in light of the Trustees' recent edict."

Ready to burst, David released his huff aloud and sat forcefully against the chair's back.

All eyes swiveled toward him. Good, he had their attention. David's heart beat quicker in righteous indignation that such a man as Whittesley should be admired. Could they not see through the man's pious veneer as clearly as he did? With intention, he leaned back on his chair, letting the front legs lift off the ground. They would ask him next what he thought. Since Buell and Youngs had graduated in September, David had become the acknowledged leader of Yale's New Light scholars.

Henry licked his lips. The moisture on them shone in the dim light. "Well, David, what do you think of Tutor Whittesley's prayer?"

He felt the small group hold their breath in anticipation and waited a moment, enjoying the feeling of making a judgment that he knew they would accept as final. "Mr. Whittesley?" he asked, as if he cared very little about such a one as the tutor. "He? That man has no more saving grace than this chair upon which I lean."

Slight chuckles broke out among his friends. An uncomfortable glow of guilty self-satisfaction spread through David's heart. Though not without his own sins, at least he was not such a fraud as Mr. Whittesley.

***

"David, he's calling us all in, one-by-one." Jonah's whisper carried fright – genuine terror – in it. The door stood open a crack, Jonah hadn't knocked, and David, of course, had been too absorbed in his work to hear any of his friend's approaching footfalls on the creaky staircase of his landlady's house.

His mind still engaged in translating the Hebrew text before him, David required a moment to transition back to the English-speaking world. Shaking his head, he let his eyes refocus from the books, paper, pen, and ink scattered across his desk to the face of his friend. "What are you talking about? Who? What do you mean?" David had no idea of what Jonah spoke, but even so, a strange tingling fear began to edge up his spine.

Fear opened wide Jonah's eyes. "Rector Clap." He looked behind him, as if sure that someone would eavesdrop on their conversation. But no one stood in the passage, and he turned back to face David, his hands twitching at the buttons on his coat.

Good grief. Such dramatics. And over what would certainly turn out to be nothing more than mere grumblings once more from a surely-unconverted Rector who had no power against the workings of God. Still, David gestured with his pen for the younger man to enter his room fully. "Come inside. And shut the door."

Jonah did so, glancing behind him again, as if fearful that he might discover the elderly landlady listening on the stair. Inside the little solitary retreat, he perched on the bed, the only seat in the room other than the chair upon which David already sat. The ropes beneath the mattress squeaked at even his slight weight, though the straw-stuffed tick muffled it. Jonah's breathing huffed out, as if he had run all the way from the College Hall down to the widow's home where David roomed. His cheeks bloomed scarlet from the exertion. "We shouldn't have done that the other night," he whispered, nodding toward the closed door.

David set down his pen, albeit a little impatiently. He had much work to do this afternoon – and tomorrow as well – if he wanted to attend the next meeting his brother Nehemiah had planned for later this week. He'd promised that several newcomers would be there and had asked his young brother to preach again, unlicensed though David was. Even in the villages and towns outside Yale's bounds, the younger New Lights began to recognize David as a leader among them.

Not that this recognition mattered, of course, but David found it pleasant to think of doing such work for God, of God using him as His instrument in dividing the chaff from the wheat. "By your pleasure, tell me what you are talking about. Or are you going to make me pry it out of you, bit by bit?"

Jonah shook his head. "You will hear about it soon enough, I fear." He bent forward, and David recognized pity new-born in his gaze. "'Tis you he is after, you know. None of the rest of us really matter if he can get you."

The fear wriggled up David's backbone toward his neck. Shuddering against it, he frowned to show Jonah that he had no notion of what he spoke or of whom.

"Rector Clap," Jonah whispered the name again, though they were alone in a closed chamber. "He's taking every one of the lads who were with you and me the other night in the College Hall and examining them. Threatening them."

"For what?" The confusion and fear turned him cold. David hated the feeling, and he despised Clap in that moment for causing it. Though he dashed mentally through the past few evenings, he could think of nothing they had done in the College Hall for which Clap could possibly threaten any of the students. They had been praying. Was that, too, no longer permitted? "In the College Hall? We only prayed and talked–"

"It's about what you said about Tutor Whittesley."

"What did I say?" David tried to recall anything damnable. "The only thing I said about Whittesley was…" He trailed off, unable to remember the exact words he had employed. "Something about his prayer being not very good?"

Jonah leaned toward him until barely a handbreadth divided the two. The scent of the hot chocolate he must have recently imbibed wafted from his mouth, but 'twas the seriousness in his eyes that demanded David's attention. "You said that he," and here he dropped his voice to a mouse's whisper, "that Whittesley had no more saving grace than a chair, David."

Uncomfortable feelings wrapped around David's shoulders, a too-snug coat in warm weather. "Aye, I did." He rose from his seat and strode to the window, anxious to leave his agitation at the desk. "And what of it? 'Twas a private conversation. An opinion, though a well-reasoned one. I did not say it publicly. I do not see how Clap even heard—"

Jonah cut him off, rising from the bed and joining

him at the window. The mixture of moonlight and shadow traced the worry on the younger man's face. "Some freshman must have overheard our conversation – the little spy. Well, it got round to the Rector, and he means to have his pound of flesh now. He will not be flouted as the College's authority anymore."

David sucked in a deep breath. His pound of *David's* flesh; that was what Jonah meant. Clap had been against the New Lights all last year, but he hadn't been able to pin anything on them – nor had he truly tried, not with Samuel Buell and David Youngs standing beside Brainerd, a three-strong cord that could not be broken. Certainly, Clap had fined the scholars who followed Tennent. He had given reprimands. He had even pulled Reverend Jonathan Edwards over from Northampton, Massachusetts, to deliver the commencement address, thinking that cool-headed, logical theologian, the conservative, authoritative minister would stamp down the fires of spiritual awakening.

Clap had been startled – and angered – when Edwards' address had only fanned the flames into a more potent ardor by talking about the distinguishing marks of a true working of the Holy Spirit. Attending students had merely grown in their longing to be part of the work of the Spirit in the conversions taking place all throughout the colonies.

"Flouted? I said nothing against Clap himself." But even to David's own ears, his protest sounded weak. Every student at Yale knew that Clap's concern was not just for himself, but for the Establishment itself – composed of the Old Lights – and its future. He identified himself as one with it. An attack – or even a mere criticism, such as David had given – against any one of those whom Clap thought of as his cohorts, the

Rector would consider as an attack against himself, against Yale, aye, even against true Christianity.

Jonah raised his thick brows. "You know as well as I do the ruling which the Board of Trustees passed in September."

A snort of derision passed David's lips. "You mean, what the Rector wrangled out of them, in his anger that Reverend Edwards did not come down firmly against the New Lights."

Jonah shrugged, discouragement turning his shoulders into soggy haystacks. "Be that as it may, we both know exactly what their ruling says."

Aye, David could remember its phrases word-for-word. They stood like obstacles in his way – waiting for him to jump them, like a horse bolting the bridle. Now, he spoke the reprehensible phrases aloud: "'Voted, that if any student of this College shall directly or indirectly say, that the Rector, either of the Trustees or Tutors are hypocrites, carnal, or unconverted men, he shall for the first offence make a public confession in the Hall, and for the second offence be expelled.'"

Strong words from a strong-willed man in virulent opposition to the direction of New Light thinking – and to any challenge to his own authority.

But David had known this when he had spoken the other evening. And he had not cared. Perhaps he had believed himself invincible. Now doubt began to eat at his self-assurance, but he shoved it away.

"Clap can prove nothing. He was not there," he said, attempting to convince himself of it. "'Twas a private conversation. 'Tis the freshman's word against mine."

Jonah looked away.

David's gut clenched. "Surely, the lads are not divulging information that was part of a private conversation."

Jonah stayed silent for a moment, and then leaned toward his friend, eyes wide with fervency. "They have to, David." Turning away from the window, he retraced his steps and sank onto the bed again. "I had to." The words trudged from his mouth.

"You?" Was it to be believed? How could Jonah – one of the most ardent New Light followers, one who had begun to preach, though not yet ordained – have betrayed him? To Clap?

Jonah rose to his feet in one swift movement, as if the emotion pressed him too much to let his body remain still. "We cannot help it, David. None of us can. Not even I. The Rector already knows everything at any rate. He got it all from that freshman who could not keep his own counsel. Now he just needs witnesses who agree to what the young man said."

"Everything? He knows everything? I cannot understand you." David shook his head. 'Twas too absurd to be possible. "I only said that Whittesley lacks grace. Grace that he might have freely if he came to God for conversion! 'Twas the truth, Jonah. The truth! These Old Lights – they think that by coming after us with chains and dogs and... They think that they can simply quench this awakening that comes from the Spirit of God. How dare they!" His voice grew loud, unusual for him. But anger had overtaken his fear – had obliterated it completely. "They will not do it! They cannot do it, Jonah."

Jonah shook his head, the sadness filling his eyes. "Well, it seems that they mean to try. And they mean to start with you."

"But 'twas a private conversation!" He grasped at this last thread, his hand punctuating the words with a thump on the windowsill. "Even if I was wrong to speak against Whittesley to others in that way, I did it privately. 'Twas a private conversation, and so 'tis a private sin."

Jonah stared, regret on his face. "Not anymore."

David held his friend's gaze for a breath and then strode from the chamber, leaving the door open behind him.

"Where are you going?" called Jonah.

"To Rector Clap – that's where!"

***

The Rector's thin lips spread downward into a near-frown. "Did you or did you not say that Mr. Whittesley was an unconverted man?" The unadorned, dark walls of the Rector's closet loomed high and indistinct around him.

David raised his chin another notch. The fire brimmed up in his bosom. His heart thundered in his chest so loudly he was sure that Clap must hear it. "I don't believe 'tis any of your concern, sir, whether or not I did."

The scowl on the older man's face intensified, causing the pallid skin to shadow into deep creases. "Not my concern, Mr. Brainerd? Are you not a student of Yale? Under my authority? Under the authority of the Board? At least, you have been, up until now."

A threat hovered in his voice. Rector Clap was determined to have his way this time. David knew this. He would try to force David to admit his wrong, with the Trustees' edict bolstering him up. He had been waiting for this moment since Youngs, Buell, and Brainerd, along with the rest of the New Lights, had encountered far more success than he in reaching the minds and hearts of the youths at Yale.

The truth struck David as a blow to the chest: Rector Clap was jealous, quite simply, was he not? Jealous of the work God was doing through the New

Lights. And caught in the past, a past with a dead form of religion.

In that moment, David decided that he would fight against the Rector, though it might cost him everything he had. *I will not give way. No matter what.* 'Twas a matter of principle, of standing up for what was true and right and just. God was on the New Lights' side, was He not?

Squaring his shoulders, David rose to his fullest height – a solid foot above Clap. It felt good to intimidate his oppressor, just a bit. "I am not afraid of you, Rector Clap. 'Tis wrong of you to try to force me to reveal what occurred, and in a private conversation, as I must remind you. You have information already – that is true – but you obtained it by force and threats – all the works of an ungodly man – from my friends."

Not one muscle of Clap's face moved at the charge. "So you do not deny it?"

David said nothing and kept his chin raised. The fire crackled, and a crow gave a long, lonely caw beyond the pane. There was nothing this man could do to him, was there? David was in the right. He was being unjustly treated. *God will not allow Clap to touch me. Oh, Almighty One, be Thou my strength and strong tower!*

Clap sighed, but 'twas not the sigh of one who had given up, but of one who saw that he must take further steps to gain his ends – and would surely take them. "Very well, then, if you will not tell me one way or the other, then I must trust the words of your friends, who told me—"

"Merely because you threatened them!" David could not help but wedge the exclamation into the Rector's self-righteous speech. His breathing quickened, his tightened chest rising and falling with the beat of a racing horse's hooves.

Clap ignored this display of impertinence and continued. "Your friends, who told me that you did indeed say of Tutor Chauncey Whittesley that he is an unconverted man. A tutor of Yale? An unconverted man, Mr. Brainerd? To say such a thing…"

As if much dismayed, the Rector dropped his gaze. A moment later, his eyes, shining bright with unconcealed dislike – met David's again. "You well know what the penalty for such an offense is, Mr. Brainerd. It has not been hidden from you." Clap appeared unable to keep away the smile that crept upon his lips, like the snake into the Garden.

David chose not to answer him, but kept a countenance of stone to match the Rector's earlier one.

The graying man quoted the obviously much-loved words from memory: "If any student of this College shall directly or indirectly say, that the Rector, either of the Trustees, or Tutors are hypocrites, carnal or unconverted men, he shall for the first offense make a public confession in the Hall, and for the second offense be expelled."

The relish lay thick on the man's voice, as if he rolled brandied fruit upon his tongue, anticipating the moment his teeth might gnash it to a pulp. *Clap has long waited for my fall.* He had long waited for the moment when he could put a hand to the unmanageable student's back and push him off the cliff. David's teeth ground together as the tension between him and the Rector seeped into his body.

"Now, Mr. Brainerd, will you publicly confess your sin before the College – before the assembled students and tutors?"

The words bounded to David's tongue without thought, without hesitation. "How could I confess in public a sin, as you call it – I am not sure 'tis so – that was committed in so private a manner?" He sucked in a breath, determined to make his point forcefully. "Is that fair, Rector Clap? Either to me or to Tutor Whittesley, who most likely would never have heard of the offense, as you call it, against his name, if you had not been so zealous to reveal it? Is this Biblical? Or are you merely desirous to get your pound of my flesh?"

The fury burned in the Rector's eyes as the words reached his ears, but he otherwise kept a remarkably calm outward appearance. "Is that your final answer, then, Mr. Brainerd?"

"'Tis." *They will never expel me.* Clap would never force David to do his bidding – Aye, his and that of his contemptible Old Lights – those who led the people ever onward into the increasing darkness of works-righteousness, all in a play for their continued power and esteem.

Blind leaders of the blind...

Yet, despite David's strength of tone and will, Clap easily held the student's eyes without flinching. "Well, then, I know what I have to do. I thank you, Mr. Brainerd. You are dismissed. Expect to hear from me shortly." With that, he turned to his perfectly straightened desk as if David was less than nothing in his eyes, as if the young man no longer existed, which David was sure the Rector wished was the case, indeed.

The powerful feeling he had gained from opposing Clap to the man's stubborn face stayed with David as he spun away from him and strode from the room, his feet loud on the worn wooden boards. He shut the door behind himself with a decisive thud.

As he turned the corner of the passage, Jonah popped out from an alcove in which he had hidden. Worry creased his face. "What happened? What did he say?" His voice was a whisper, despite the emptiness of the passage. David could not blame his friend, poor soul, after the ill way they and the other Yale New

Lights have been treated by the Rector.

Jonah looked to David as a leader – they all did. And David knew that he could not fail Jonah. Nor any of the other fiery New Lights there on campus. "He wants a public confession."

The anger propelled his lanky legs forward down the passage. He needed fresh air. Jonah hurried to tag along. "A public confession?"

"Yes, in the Hall. Before the whole college. Can you imagine how humiliating that would be? Utterly unreasonable. And the Rector knows it, too. It would stifle our whole cause as well. I'm sure that's part of his plan." He stopped, unable to contain his feelings in whispers, not caring who heard what he said now. By his actions, Clap had declared war.

David would take on this new Goliath. He would fell him. Was not God on their side?

The two young men pushed their way out of the door into the compound area. A few students skittered by, eyes focused away from David. Already, he could see that they had heard of the new campaign the Rector had begun – and that he had chosen to wage it against David, whom Clap saw as the general of the Yale New Lights. The more cautious of the students gave them wide berth; some of those whom David knew well and who were on his side greeted him tentatively but hurried on their way, nevertheless.

"Already, they avoid my eyes." The giddiness that had come from defying Clap drained away. David's steps slowed as discouragement seeped into his heart to fill the vacancy. Yet, despite the sudden lowness of his spirits, David's resolve did not soften. "How soon the work of the evil one begins!"

"They are afraid," Jonah replied, his voice soft. "Yale is the only theological school left."

"There is Harvard." Even as he said it, David knew

that most Yale students would not go there because of its increasingly liberal teachings. He shook his head. "Did you know that 'tis rumored that the Tennents' father originally wished to serve as the Rector at Yale, but he was told that his fervency for the gospel might cause a disturbance among the students?"

Jonah frowned. "Would that not be a good thing, if it arose from the working of God's Spirit?"

"Aye, but not according to such as Rector Clap. Things are best if they stay just the way they are." David pulled a dry leaf from one of the trees as they passed it. "Better dead."

"So Reverend Tennent went to Pennsylvania?"

David ripped the leaf in two and dropped it to the ground. "Aye, and he started what some mockingly call the Log College. He said that the west would need preachers and that his sons must be trained to meet that need."

"And that's where Mr. Gilbert Tennent trained? In a log cabin, truly?" Jonah stopped short, gaping and wide-eyed.

A smile played at David's lips, despite the frustration still coiling his muscles. This was the glorious part: How God took the nothings of this world and used them for His glory. "Aye, and Gilbert's brothers as well. 'I say unto you, God is able of these stones to raise up children unto Abraham.'"

They began to walk again, and another student passing by them refused to meet their eyes – a student whom David knew had been warming to the New Light cause only yesterday. His soul cried out in anguish, in frustration. Clap had spread the tidings abroad then, trying to frighten all the students into submission. Now all that was needed to complete the total reversal of all that Tennent, Whitefield, Wheelock, David's own brother Nehemiah, and the rest of the New Lights had worked for was for David to publicly confess that all that they held to as true – that real conversion must occur through Spirit-given, heartfelt repentance – was not true – had never been true. That they were entirely mistaken.

For was that not how the public apology – though directed toward Whittesley – would be taken?

Of course it will.

"Cannot you just give him the confession he wants, though?" Jonah tentatively asked, interrupting David's turbulent thoughts. "He only wants you to say you were wrong about Tutor Whittesley."

"Never." Even as he said it, David remembered the stubbornness on Clap's face – stubbornness that matched David's own – perhaps exceeded it.

A tad of fear crept into his heart. *Surely the Board of Trustees will see reason.* He brushed aside the worry nipping at his heels and marched faster. "How could I go against the freedom of my conscience to say such a thing, especially in a private conversation? If 'twas wrong, 'twas done against God and Whittesley, not against Clap and certainly not against the College!"

"You'll be expelled." Jonah's breath became cloud in the frosty autumn air, white smoke against the brilliant orange of the trees lining the way.

David tried to laugh. "Expelled?" The word sounded foreign. It did not belong beside his name, surely. Not David, who was meant for great things. "For a private conversation?"

But Jonah stared back, his eyes seeming to grow a darker blue with seriousness. "Aye, for that."

Even as David smiled away the idea as foolish, the possibility that Jonah could very well be right haunted him.

But even if he was, David knew that it would not make him retract his position.

Chapter Nineteen

Jerusha

"And do you want to know what the most humorous part of it all was?" Mr. Brainerd rises to his feet and paces, arms crossed behind his back. Then he halts before me, as if waiting for me to respond. A smile twitches at the corners of his lips.

"There is a humorous part to it?" From what I have heard, there does not seem to be. Expulsion from esteemed Yale, the college my own grandfather on Mama's side helped to found, sounds grim through-and-through.

Mr. Brainerd meets my eyes with his own ever-intense ones. "Well, here it is: I was correct about one thing, at least – Whittesley did not even need to hear about any of it! In his fervor to get me punished for bucking the system he so loved, in his fuss over his own authority being upheld, Thomas Clap ended up making poor Whittesley go through much more trauma and heartache than needed to be. After all, no one but myself and a few of the friends to whom I had spoken knew my thoughts on Whittesley's salvation. The freshman who listened at the door had a wagging tongue, unfortunately, as did his landlady, who reported the matter to the Rector. But my friends and I were not going around publicly proclaiming this tutor or that tutor, this Trustee or that one unsaved. Others did such things, proudly and arrogantly in full belief of their own righteousness, but we did not. Again, and I will hold to this, even now, 'twas a private conversation. If any apology had to be made, I believe that it should have been made within the context of that privacy."

"But you did agree to apologize, didn't you? Eventually?"

He smiles, but there is no mirth in it. "Aye, I did. Privately, however, not publicly."

"Even so... May I ask, why? If you so fervently believed that which you've spoken, why did you agree to apologize?"

He opens his mouth to reply, but a bubbling cough rises out of his throat rather than words. He fumbles for his handkerchief like a drowning man grabs for a board to grasp. He struggles to pull it from inside his shirt, and I can see the weakness overtaking him as he fights this inward physical battle. The cough wrestles with him, shaking his already-emaciated torso until he is forced to kneel. Then 'tis all he can do to put one hand on either side of his body, bracing himself against the floor.

My heart pounding, I pull out my own handkerchief and put it to his mouth. My hand comes to rest upon his shoulder. He leans into it, his arms taut as he struggles to expel whatever is clogging his airway. The sweat beads and drops from his forehead as the cough goes on endlessly, a strange interruption to the peaceful quiet of the sleeping house. Every time the cough leaves him, he tries to suck in a breath and the cough returns full-force, shaking his shoulders with the power of a hurricane wind.

The handkerchief grows moist in my hand. I cannot look at it, for fear of the color it will be, for fear that the ulcers in his lungs have burst again. Instead, I look at his face, so darkly shadowed in the dim flickering light of our twin candles. His eyes have closed, curtained with thick brown lashes. I can see the veins in the thin skin of his eyelids, paling now for want of much time spent in the sunshine of late. I put my hand up gently alongside his jaw, right where his neck meets his head, to help support him in his coughing. The skin is wet with sweat and, I am startled to find, slightly grizzled with several days' growth. It must be difficult for him to shave if he is never sure when a cough will overtake him.

The moments tick by. Slowly, the cough drains away, less and less fierce in its attack. It will not take him this time. That is the way with this disease: nibbling away at a man's strength, bit-by-bit, until he has none left with which to fight.

At last, Mr. Brainerd pulls in a breath, his whole torso quaking, and we both freeze in anticipation of the heavy cough that will surely follow. But just a slight hack comes instead. He pauses a moment, his mouth still against the handkerchief I hold to his face. He leans against my other hand, as though it comforts him. Then, sucking air in slowly through his nostrils, he draws away, bracing himself on his arms, shuddering as a man who has been struck with a bullet.

And my own chest aches as well with a nearly physical pain.

I am not sure if I should offer him the handkerchief to wipe away the moisture lingering around his lips. I drop my eyes to look at the linen square and find it wet with bloody mucus. I ball it up in my fist, not wanting him to see it and be ashamed that I had to see the evidence of his physical deterioration... not wanting to see it myself. Fiddling with the side of my skirt, I find the slit there for my pocket and slide the wadded cloth into it.

He has not opened his eyes yet but still sits with his arms stretched out, bracing himself on our carpet. The breaths enter and exit his lungs with shudders, sometimes sharp as if they have caused a pain. His shirt clings wet to his thin frame. I cannot help but remember when I saw him first, years ago; his appearance is so different now. But when he opens his eyes, pain-filled though they are, I see that this is not merely the same man with whom I fell in love – this is a better one than I even thought he was then, in my girlish fantasies. This is one who has been tried in the furnace and has come forth as gold.

"Has it been worth it, Mr. Brainerd?" I cannot help the question from falling from my lips. I am ashamed of it as soon as the words come to life in the air. But though I am ashamed, my heart still thinks it and longs for his affirmation. I must know – again and again from his own mouth – that he still considers the agony of his body worth what he has gained.

I ask it because, in my own heart, I must know for sure. Not only for his sake, for also for mine. For I also have a life that must be lived, must be poured out, and I must know now if this one so dear to my own heart, who has trod the pilgrim path before me, regrets his taking of this very narrowest of narrow ways.

I raise my gaze after a long moment of silence, sure to see censure in his eyes. Yet there is no condemnation there, but merely understanding. And then his hand reaches out. I do not breathe as his fingers brush the edge of my temple and cheek before dropping back to the carpet again.

"Aye, Jerusha. 'twas worth it. He is worth everything I could give and more. How worthless to live for any other end." The words rasp out, a whisper of truth in the night.

Chapter Twenty

1741

A private confession, however – even a private written confession – was not enough for Rector Clap. Suddenly, without Buell and Youngs by his side, having angered the Board of Trustees, David found himself the target of numerous accusations – with the one involving Whittesley crowning them all.

He had attended a separate, unauthorized meeting again in New Haven, after the Board declared such to be unlawful.

He had said that he was surprised that Clap himself did not drop down dead for his actions against the New Lights.

To the Board, Clap represented the New Lights as unrepentant, stubbornly rejecting authority, and divisive – the very last sort of students to whom mercy should be given.

And David, claimed Clap, was their leader at Yale. Cut off the head, and the body would die.

And so Rector Clap got his pound of flesh.

David was expelled.

On the morning he left New Haven, the white mist rose from the Connecticut valleys, hiding his path. His throat tightened against the faint-hearted sobs that threatened to burst from his chest. As the town straggled away into countryside, David could not resist looking back to try to glimpse College Hall one last time. *Will I ever return?*

And if he did not, how would he ever succeed in the ministry to which he was certain God had called him? Where could he serve without a degree and with the scandal of his expulsion darkening his steps?

Where is Thy mercy, O God?

And yet the mercy of God guided David's every step into the mist, away from Yale, away from the fomenting New Light students, away from the misguidance of the Old Light authorities. Though he did not know it then, on that day, God had begun to answer David's prayers for a life of abandoned devotion to Him, putting a knife to His child's self-centered ambitions – ones that acknowledged Him, but gave Him no license to direct him ultimately into whatever path He deemed good. He did not want David for a self-shaped tool – one driven by a sense of his own rightness and that of his cause, one with intellect and reputation backing his claims – no, He wanted him to be shaped in His hands first and then used in the least likely of places that he would ever have imagined or wanted, a place to which David would not have chosen to go if he had remained the same man as the one who left Yale that year.

Shaping on God's anvil is difficult work, painful in ways much deeper than merely the physical. The dross needed to be burned off. David needed to be melted down before God could make him into a vessel fit for His use.

Chapter Twenty-One

Jerusha

Mr. Brainerd pauses. "Even now, I am unfit. I am a worthless servant. I have only done what was required of me."

Sitting there beside him on the floor, our backs against the settee, I watch him close his eyes for a long moment and sense rather than see the shudder of pain that arches through his lungs. His hands clench and then unclench; the sinews in his forearms, grown strong from long hours spent riding, tighten. Then, his eyes open again. His gaze searches my face, filled with a wild passion for me to understand his meaning. I feel almost frightened at such relentless earnestness. "But I pray that my work will not prove to have been in vain."

He goes into a fit of coughing again. He used up my handkerchief last time, wetting it thoroughly with the foul bloody mucus that sometimes slides and sometimes leaps from his throat, so I rise from my place near him as soon as the first cough emerges and rush over to the linen cabinet. I take three rolled napkins, bleached pristine white as Mama would have them, and hurry back to him. This I do not hesitate to place my hand gently on his shaking shoulder and encourage him to lean into the makeshift handkerchief. Shock tingles through me as I realize that his body feels yet frailer each time I touch it, the skin tightening against its bony frame with nothing to cushion in-between. 'Tis an ugly feeling, one that whispers of death.

I am thankful that this fit lasts much shorter than the last one. The disease wrenches Mr. Brainerd's body a final time, as the demon did the boy in the Scriptures, and he sounds as if he is vomiting rather than coughing. His head shakes as the last of the expelled fluid falls into the cloth. The moistness lays on my hand, heavy and thick. 'Tis his life-blood. He gave it up for his God and for his Indians. He gave it up out of love.

My own chest clenches tight again, but not with disease. "You should rest, Mr. Brainerd." I fold the napkin and then, without thought, tenderly wipe the mucus edging the sides of his weary lips. "You must retire to your bed. The night is passing away."

His eyes open, hazy with the confusion that pain brings. Then he shakes his head. "I could not rise to my feet right now. Nay, let us go on talking here, just you and me. It brings me comfort to know that you are here. And there are things I wish for you to know but which are hard for me to put into precise words. Perhaps my story will shed light upon them for you."

At these words, joy sparks inside me, a light in the darkness of grief. I bring him comfort, he says. No, 'tis not a declaration of love – that is for certain; that will never be. But this is a man who has learned not to say anything he does not mean – anything he has not thought through thoroughly. As a result, his words nestle into my heart, attaching themselves as burrs to a woolen petticoat. And so I warn myself that, as burrs, I must not allow them to remain and deepen their attachment, finally catching my flesh and causing me much pain. I have made the mistake once already of falling in love with a man who does not – cannot – will not return my affection. I cannot make the same mistake afresh – and certainly not with the same man. I am here by his side to care for him only.

We should retire.

But, still recuperating from that last bout of coughing, he is yet unable to rise, and I cannot raise him. And he has asked me – Jerusha, calling me by name – to sit with him, to hear his story, to understand him. How can I deny him, a man who has relinquished all, who has lost all for the sake of the gospel… and yet who does not regret any of the giving?

And so I settle my skirt around my feet again, lean back upon my arm, and listen.

Chapter Twenty-Two

1742

He stayed and studied for a time with a minister-friend in Ripton, not far from the shadows of Yale itself. Already, David had given his word to Jonathan Dickinson of the Society in Scotland for Propagating Christian Knowledge – "The Scotch Society" – that he would join their first Indian missionary in spreading the gospel among the natives. Their first missionary, Azariah Horton, had seen good success among the Long Island Indians, and they hoped that David might be well-used of God also.

He knew that he would not. As he walked the wooded groves near Ripton, awaiting the Scotch Society's commission, his stomach weighed heavy with the knowledge of his own utter inadequacy, his own lack of love toward the Indians and toward his fellow man, his own constant failures.

How could he ever do anything for God?

And yet the yearning – soul-deep – remained, that God might indeed use him.

***

Springtime came to Ripton, and with it, the twentieth of April. David's birthday.

The sun swept up from behind the verdant Connecticut hills, promising a day of warmth, of new life, of growth. Yet the grove to which David had retreated to pray remained in shadow, the heavy pines arching over him in condemnation, the cold air threatening his weakened lungs.

His knees fell to the dark soil. Moisture sank into his breeches. His palms hit the ground, then, too, as he prostrated himself. The silent groans of his soul pinned him to the earth.

He was twenty-four.

And how idle and useless all his days had been thus far in his life!

How his sins stood stark, naked, and bleak before him!

How badly had he fulfilled his vow from the previous April, to be wholly God's.

Slowly, the morning sunlight filtered into the grove. Its warmth melted across David's uncovered head. From high in the dark pine tree, a robin released its joy in a gurgling song.

Out of the fog, words came to him, words of life:

He hath not dealt with us after our sins; nor rewarded us according to our iniquities. For as the heaven is high above the earth, so great is his mercy toward them that fear him. As far as the east is from the west, so far hath he removed our transgressions from us.

Something within David clung to the darkness pulling him downward. *Is that not only for those who are His? What if I am not truly His?*

Immediately, the words came again, and his soul filled with delight:

Fear not: for I have redeemed thee, I have called thee by thy name; thou art mine.

He breathed the newly sun-warmed air, mixed

with the scent of the moist earth, and found the strength to push himself up to kneel.

What would the next year bring? A reinstatement at Yale? A path into the wilderness?

Peace settled over David's heart. At least on this day, he was content to do whatever God wished, so long as He allowed him to wear out his life in His service, for His glory – that glory that filled his soul with the same kind of delight that the Shulamite knew in the Song of Songs.

Chapter Twenty-Three

Jerusha

Longing fills my own soul also, hearing him speak in such a way, with such joy at the thought of who God is, and of the delight found in drawing near to Him. I fold my hands in my lap, staring at the smallness of them – thinking of the paltriness of my own love to God, the oft-deadness of my own heart toward Him, all while 'tis always alive and beating for the man who sits before me.

"I wish I had your passion," I say this surely though quietly, intentionally. My words are no mistake, no jumbled thought tumbling out into the listening air. "For years, I have been content with whatever God would do with my life, but I have not had the passion for Him that you have. It has been more a resignation to His will, an acceptance – which is a good start, I suppose – but I long for more. More love for Him who died for me. I wonder if I truly am willing to do what I have spoken of to you – to forsake all for the sake of bringing the gospel to others who have not heard."

His eyes become tender again, looking at me from beneath their weary lids. "Do not think that all must go into the wilderness, as I did. Some are called to that; all are called to forsake all. To forsake all that once filled their hearts and to set their affections fully upon Him who first loved them." He pauses, sucking in a breath. "True, tested love for God comes through trials, not through wishing it into being. Pray for more love for Him, more love for others, and He will send trials from His heart of love your way."

How will trials help me to love Him? But instead of asking this, I say, "Was Yale your trial, then?"

He shakes his head without hesitation. "Nay, not in the way you think. Or, at least, 'twas not my only one. 'Twas merely the door that opened to my trial of the soul, to the threshing floor of my heart. For that is where the real testing takes place – in the heart, in the soul. We are asked by Him, *Do you love Me more than these?* And turmoil bathes our souls as we wrestle with Him to discover the answer. Yale was where Jehovah God took hold of my human strength and began to wrestle with it, as once Jacob did with the Angel. All the while, He only desired to make me go forward in His strength alone, and so with His blessing."

Chapter Twenty-Four

1742

Jonathan Dickinson, commissioner of the Scotch Society, came to Connecticut, hoping to convince Yale's Board of Trustees to allow David to return to the College.

At Jedediah Mills' home, David felt tossed to-and-fro. One morning, longing for rest and quiet before God, he rose before the dawn lightened the sky to gray. Bible snug beneath his arm, he took the often-trodden path into the wooded glen where God had met him in times past – most recently, on David's twenty-fourth birthday.

Four-and-twenty! And nothing to show for it.

In all likelihood, Yale would not permit him to return.

And now word had arrived that even Gilbert Tennent, one of David's New Light heroes, had admitted in a letter that the dramatics of the spiritual awakening had wearied him at last.

How that must have delighted Clap when he heard it! David's own heart crawled into darkness at the thought. The bitterness grew in his soul, a deep-rooted weed. He did not want to draw it out. It would cause too much pain; it would require the relinquishing of too much that he held dear. Pushing thoughts of forgiveness aside for the moment, he found the huge, man-sized rock at which he had become accustomed to praying.

But God was silent that morning. Above David, the sky was tombstone-gray. He could no more sense God's presence than he could the presence of the Indian gods who did not exist. His soul felt empty as a porridge pot scoured clean after breakfast – a breakfast in which he had not partaken, due to fasting. Around him, the birds chirped from their perches high in the trees surrounding the rock. The sunlight appeared, glimmering through the trees as David waited for the inner burst of joy that sometimes followed on the heels of dawn – but nothing in his heart answered it that day.

'Twas Rector Clap's fault, was it not? Aye, and the Board of Trustees. He should not have been so unfairly treated. A public apology required for a private offence! If offence it was! The very idea brought a snort of derision from David yet, startling a scavenging squirrel into running headlong up a nearby oak.

He could not pray. His heart and mind seethed with the injustices dealt to him. *I was at the top of my class, too! If things had continued as they were going, who knew what good I might have done for God and His cause in New England?*

But it had all been ruined by one who wished to destroy God's work in Connecticut!

He should pray. He knew it, but these thoughts plagued him worse than mosquitoes in a humid summer gloaming. At last, as the sun rose higher, David forced his tongue to stagger out a few words, but he could not get past the hazy blur that covered his spiritual vision, nor could he stop the distraction brought by his terrible misfortune at Yale. How would he go on to do great work for God with that disgrace hanging over his head? Without his degree?

They had crippled me, indeed! The anger burned in his heart as the assurance of his own inadequacy soaked through every spiritual fiber of his being. What could God do with such a one as he?

Even when I enter Mr. Mill's church, I can nearly hear the unspoken thoughts of some around me, scorning me – scorning the cause for which I stood. What happened at college – It has opened the mouths of those who oppose the working of the Spirit.

And he was ashamed for his part in that.

David rose to his feet, his heart lifeless as the tomb before Easter morning, unable to pray any longer, unwilling to continue to offer God his dead, cold services.

Chapter Twenty-Five

Jerusha

I look at him wonderingly. "Surely, you did not go to the heathen from a desire for fame? Or from worldly ambition?"

A twinge of embarrassment tightens his pale features. "Oh, Jerusha," he sighs. "I have told you: You think much too well of me. I am a man – a sinful one, redeemed and upheld only by His grace. We do a disservice to the work of God in men's hearts when we paint anyone as either an irredeemable monster or as a sinless angel."

He leans toward me, his eyes intent upon mine. "That is perhaps one of the reasons I feel I must tell you all of this. 'Tis why I also still hold an aversion to your father's idea of editing and publishing my diaries when I am gone."

His gaze goes over to the blazing fire. "I would have them all burned," he says in a low voice. "God works in every man's heart differently and in His own time."

Chapter Twenty-Six

1742

"I have invited Mr. Davenport to Ripton," Jedediah Mills announced as David breakfasted with him one mid-spring morning.

"James Davenport? I had thought that he was in the Middle Colonies – with Mr. Whitefield." David wiped his mouth with the edge of a linen napkin. "I had heard that he was doing much good there. His preaching has been most effective, has it not?"

Jedediah nodded and rose from the table. "Aye, it has been – but we have need of awakening here as much as in the Middle Colonies, do we not? Surely, your recent experience at Yale taught you as much if you were not already aware of it."

David nodded. Aye, New England needed a pouring out of God's Spirit. *And it needs to start with Rector Clap and the Board of Trustees.* Yet in all honesty, he felt weary – weary as Gilbert Tennent said he was of the hullabaloo that surrounded the awakening. "I look forward to Mr. Davenport's visit. We have not met for a long time now. When will he arrive?"

Jedediah deposited his hat on his head, preparing to go for his daily walk. "Not for another week."

A sense of relief flooded David, as the Connecticut River pushing over its banks in the spring, but he hid it from Jedediah. "I will not be here then."

"Oh?"

"I've just received word that a council of ministers wishes to meet with me in Hartford on May thirteenth or fourteenth. They have said that they may intervene on my behalf with Rector Clap and the Board, depending on how goes our meeting. I do not expect to arrive back here before the end of May."

"Ah," Jedediah smiled. "So you plan to do some preaching of your own as well, I would suppose."

David shrugged. 'Twas not safe for Jedediah to know more, though he felt certain that the minister guessed his intent. The return ride from Hartford would not take David two weeks. He would certainly preach in any town or village that asked him.

"Just be careful, my friend." Jedediah had one hand on the door. "The Hartford Legislature is deliberating over some laws regarding unlicensed clergymen. I would hate for you to add another black mark to your name, especially since you are still trying to clear yourself before the Yale authorities."

Agitation rose strong and immediate, but David threw out a good-natured laugh. "I don't think 'tis fitting that you should be the one to warn me. You are hosting James Davenport – and more than likely, his armor-bearer Pomeroy." David looked Jedediah squarely in the eye. "Am I right?"

Jedediah only smiled in return. His fingers fiddled with the door latch for a moment before he spoke again. "We'd best both be careful, aye?"

"Aye," David said, turning back to his porridge, which – in light of his possible reinstatement at Yale due to this council of ministers' interest – suddenly appeared appealing.

Things were looking up, indeed.

***

Yet he felt frightened as he rode out of Ripton. Spring had fully come, spreading its green glory over everything in sight, but the beauty only alienated him.

Was he afraid of the council ahead of him? *Aye.*

Afraid of what Rector Clap's judgment could do to his ministerial career, to his usefulness in God's work? *Aye, that, too.*

And something deeper as well.

He stopped in New Haven and secretly saw old friends. Many of them gave him the news that he had already heard whispered, even in his quiet retreat deep in the Connecticut valleys: The awakening had died down among the students at Yale. David's fear grew. Had it all been in vain, then – his unlicensed preaching, his expulsion, everything?

And, even more frightening was this thought that continually assaulted him: Which one was real? The fire that he felt grow in his soul when he thought of the unreached heathen? Or the numbness that lingered for long days and nights – that made him wish for death itself?

But he pressed on, nonetheless, and rode forty miles to Wethersfield. At dusk, still on the outskirts of the town, he heard angry voices shouting. The sound of breaking glass met his ears and caused his spine to tense.

His empty stomach dropped into his boots as he turned cautiously onto the main village street. A crowd of at least two dozen men milled about. Their faces burned with anger, and several carried clubs. Above the street, many upper-story windows had opened, allowing curious townspeople to observe the hubbub from a safe vantage point.

Though he strained his ears, David could not

decipher the swirl of loud words coming from the throng. He urged his horse to the side of the street and dismounted. Nearby, a potbellied older man leaned against his shop building, observing the riot. The man's leather apron marked him as a smith.

David stopped beside him and nodded toward the milling crowd. "What is going on?" he asked.

The man grunted, keeping his eyes on the group before him. "Foolish young upstarts. They came to Wethersfield a couple days ago. Unlicensed, too. Strollers, the lot of them. Just looking for attention if you ask me, which I do not say you did."

"These men are New Lights?" The disbelief in David's heart pushed away the man's claim. It could not be. He scanned the group, looking for someone he might know – yet hoping not to find anyone. Not in this group. The rebellious looks on their rough faces turned his stomach like rancid milk.

David released a gasp of relief when his informant shook his head. "Nay, not these. I did not say these were the strollers, did I?" He shifted his position so that he could scratch his back against the post upon which he leaned. "These are merely townsmen, angry with those religious fanatics. And they've a good cause to be angry. Those young upstarts have caused a ruckus with their talk of even ministers – God-fearing men – needing to repent!"

Having satisfied his itch, the man bent toward David as if to confide. "We were a quiet town before all these folks came through, stirring up trouble. You have probably got this in your part of Connecticut, too, I would wager. Spreading like the pox, 'tis." He paused. "Where is it you hail from?"

David swallowed down the lump in his throat. "I am studying with the minister in Ripton, currently, but I was at Yale lately."

He should have omitted the part about Yale...

The man sniffed, his large, pitted nose wrinkling up at David's words. "Studying for the church, then? Not going to cause any trouble here, are you? We got enough young hooligans, frantic about religion."

Yet 'twas the townspeople who seemed to be hooligans. What with their yelling, they sounded more like heathen folk than the natives did. David pulled himself up by the bootstraps of his courage. "Surely, the townsfolk could simply reject whatever 'twas that these 'strollers,' as you call them, were preaching. Surely, there was no need for them to riot."

The older man gave a level stare. "Well, say what you like. The young'll always stick up for the young, I suppose. But what I say is this: We've had enough of works of the Spirit." He spat on the ground near David's feet and then turned away without another word.

The mob began to disperse. David knew better than to seek shelter with the Congregational minister in this town; if the man recognized the name *Brainerd,* he would surely not be in a mood to host him, having just been called an unrepentant sinner by some silly young hanger-ons. Had the strollers, as the man called them, been unwanted, rabble-rousing followers of David's fellow New Light James Davenport, who might, by this time, be visiting Jedediah Mills?

'Twas possible. Very possible, indeed.

He found a bed at a local tavern, where he requested and received a hunk of bread, a bowl of thick stew, and a mug of cider. The innkeeper said little; he was busy that night with the remnants of the mob, who after rioting, wished to cool their anger with cider and beer. David was thankful for the absence of human interaction. He felt utterly drained – tired in body, weary in heart and soul and mind. Never more than then had he known such discouragement in the cause to which he had devoted so many long months – a cause that now seemed to have drawn disfavor from the populace as a whole. Tucked away in a corner, he nibbled at the simple meal, the turmoil in his spirit rendering every bite tasteless on his tongue.

Chapter Twenty-Seven

Jerusha

"So you regret your actions and those of the other New Lights?" I ask, my mind struggling to understand the sloughs and plains and mountains of Mr. Brainerd's soul. "Do you believe that all that happened was not a work of the Spirit?"

This is hard for me to comprehend, for even Papa has cast his opinion in favor of the New Lights. After all, one of the first noticeable outbreaks of awakening – complete with cries, fainting, and more – in the colonies occurred after he preached a sermon on the dangerous position of those who have not yet trusted in Jesus Christ.

To my relief, Mr. Brainerd shakes his head immediately. "Nay, that is not what I mean. How shall I explain this?" His eyes close for a moment as if he has fallen into deep thought.

When he opens them and speaks again, it is with a deliberate slowness, every word passing through the sieve of his mind before they alight from his tongue. "As my friend Tennent said, most of us did some foolish things during those years. We listened at times to our own spirits, rather than to the Holy Spirit, and acted in ways in which we ought not have – led by indecent heats in our youthfulness or inexperience or mere excitement. At times, we were led astray by the advice of men of whom we thought most highly – not led astray from their wishes that we be so, but led in that way because 'tis the natural, sinful tendency of a man to confound things – to pervert the right way. Any error resulted from us, not from them.

"Yet I still will say that God brought about that great awakening. A mighty wind blew, and, aye, it caused devastating upheavals. Aye, it divided. But it also stirred the church in such a way as we have not seen for a long time, Jerusha. It angered many in Israel, so to speak. God brought about many real conversions, and men and women went to work for the Lord in ways we may not know until the heavens fold up like a garment."

Chapter Twenty-Eight

1742

The rain poured down the pane, a reminder that the weather had prevented David's usual time of prayer alone in the grove. He tried to tear his eyes away from the soggy world drooping outside the small window of his guest chamber in Ripton, but the gloom called more deeply to him than the consoling words of the book of sermons that lay open on his desk.

I am dead to the things of God.

I am unfit for the work of the ministry.

I am unable to do anything for the glory of God.

The pain – both physical and spiritual – tightened around his chest. His mind churned, a ship lost at sea. *Oh, God, do not forsake Thy servant!*

A tap on the door startled him. Pushing aside the weight, he forced himself to speak aloud. "Come."

The quick, light footsteps on the wood floor told David that Jedediah had entered the room, but misery so dampened his own spirits that he could not turn to face the cheerfulness of the friend who was also his host and mentor.

"I rode out to see old Mrs. Beckham. She is ailing but has placed her hope in God. She remains in good spirits." Jedediah came around to look David in the eyes. "Which is more than I can say for you, my friend."

David's jaw clenched tight against the sorrow sweeping over him, overwhelming him with its strength.

"Do not lose heart, David. You are yet young. There is hope."

He could not repress the laugh of disbelief that leapt to his lips. "Hope? For what? Once more, the Board of Trustees has refused to re-admit me."

Jedediah's brow lowered in sympathy. Even he knew how ridiculous a minister without a degree from Yale or Harvard would appear to anyone who was anything.

David snapped the volume of sermons shut. The musty scent of the old pages rose to meet his nose. "And the awakening has begun to fail. So much good has been done." His voice broke. "And now, due to a few actions of over-zealousness, is it all to be undone?"

Jedediah's hand fell on his shoulder, meant surely to comfort, but David felt nothing but numbing grief. "And worse is the fear that visits me."

"What do you fear, David?"

David rose to his feet and moved toward the window, escaping Jedediah's hand. He did not deserve such comfort. "Due my own indiscretions, will God no longer use me?"

Jedediah remained quiet for a moment. Then, the words came, slow as cold honey. "Do you believe that the message you having been preaching is wrong now?"

David could not agree to that. The truth of what he and the other New Lights – Jedediah among them – had proclaimed still met him every time he opened the Scriptures. "Nay, I believe that we preached truly. Nor do I believe 'twas wrong to preach without a license. Who is the Connecticut Assembly or Yale's Board to tell a man if he should speak the truth publicly or not?

'Tis God who licenses a man, not they." Despite the weight of gloom, David could do nothing but speak honestly.

"Then what is wrong?"

"The party-spirit to which I succumbed – Of that, I am ashamed. I begin to see that my loyalty to the New Lights overrode even my love for Jesus Christ Himself. I see that in how easily I judged Mr. Whittesley because he had not joined us."

David bowed his head until his forehead pressed against the cool pane. His eyes closed. The rain still raced down the glass, even as his own soul wept. *When will God come to me? When will He lift me from the pit into which I have sunken?*

"And yet you will not apologize."

David opened his eyes, and his back stiffened. "I have apologized privately. The matter was a private one. I cannot apologize publicly for a private offense." He turned to face Jedediah. "Would you have me do so?"

Jedediah paused, and then shook his head. "Nay. I would not have you go against your conviction. But it grieves me to see you in such a way. Still, soon the Scotch Society will surely send you off into the wilderness. There will be no time for brooding while you are among the Indians."

Among the Indians. "And there is another source of my wretchedness." The words spilled out before David had thought through them.

Jedediah's face twisted in confusion. "What?"

"I have no compassion for them. Not as I ought to. If I am to go among them speaking of God's love, should not I myself possess at least a drop of it for them?"

"But you have always said that you long to glorify God, and…"

"Aye, I do." David cut him off with unaccustomed roughness. "But is not loving others intrinsic to glorifying God? I know 'tis. And yet I cannot dredge up that love in my heart for the Indians. May God help me, I cannot. He knows I have tried!"

Jedediah approached with the quick steps of a true shepherd aiding a troubled lamb. He reached up to take hold of David's shoulders. "David. Look at me, my friend."

He waited until David finally met Jedediah's tender gaze with a fear-filled, bitter one of his own.

"God will yet use you if you let Him. God delights in using the broken, the inadequate, the used-up, even the mistaken, if they will let Him fill them with Himself. He will give you everything you need – even compassion, even divine love – for the Indians. He has called you, David. He will complete His good work in you. Take heart. Do not fear."

Chapter Twenty-Nine

Jerusha

Silence falls upon us. 'Tis a comfortable quietness.

"Mr. Mills must have been a great encouragement to you," I say at last.

Mr. Brainerd smiles at me. "Aye, he was a Jonathan to my David. He strengthened my hands, truly. I sorely needed it, oppressed from within and from without, preparing to stand for my licensing to preach, anxious that Yale should re-admit me, still battling bitterness toward Clap and the Board, trembling at the thought of me – inadequate, incapable, sin-soaked me – daring to preach to the Indians."

"And you were licensed?"

"Aye."

I hear a twinge of humor in his voice. "What is it?"

He adjusts his position against the settee. "Well, 'twas surely by God's mercy that the council before whom I stood for licensing was composed entirely of New Light ministers. So, aye, I received my license to be an itinerant from the Association of the Eastern District of Fairfield County. Joseph Bellamy was one of the council. I think you know him."

"Aye! He stayed with my family for two years after he graduated from Yale." I had been young then, but I could still recall Mr. Bellamy's round, boyish face and generous nature. "He used to buy sweets for us children and give them to us after supper. He took a pulpit in Bethlehem, Connecticut, did he not?"

"He did, and he welcomed me into his home for all that summer while I waited for the Scotch Society's decision on where they would choose to send me."

Chapter Thirty

1742

"These Indians, you know, are a mixed group: remnants of the Mahicans, Wampanoags, and the Narragansetts. Possibly other tribes as well. Many of them work as servants of the white people who live in the village of Kent." Joseph Bellamy continued the mostly one-sided conversation he had started all the way back in Bethlehem. "Others have preached to them before – including the Moravians, who have had some converts. Still, 'tis a good opportunity for you to try preaching to the natives, to see what the similarities and differences might be between the unregenerate whites and the Indians."

David only half-listened. His backside was sore from the miles-long ride. His mind felt like jam left out in the sun. And his heart... that was his greatest source of trouble.

But riding beside David into the Indian village of Scaticock, Joseph still wore a smile – a smile whose brightness only served to reinforce the darkness that had fallen over David's soul.

How can I do this? 'Tis wrong, so very wrong, to preach to others, is it not, when I myself seem shut off from God? The darkness had begun to threaten a few days before, but only last night, as the prospect of preaching to the Kent Indians loomed near, had it fully arrested him.

Why had he come to preach to these Indians? What a fool he was, to think that God could use such a sinful man as he!

Yet here he was, with Joseph, fifteen miles away from Bethlehem. *And I agreed to preach!* The very notion would have made him laugh, had the seriousness of it eliminated that possibility completely.

Just ahead of him, Joseph brought his horse up to an oak and dismounted. David continued to sit, every muscle frozen beneath the weight that had only worsened as they had traveled.

After tying his horse to a sturdy limb, Joseph seemed to realize that David had not joined him in dismounting. His eyes found David's face, and the smile dropped from his lips. "What troubles you, my friend?"

David swallowed, finding even that action difficult under the darkness that wearied his body. He licked his lips, and his gaze flickered toward the rude huts in which the Indians lived… and from which some of them now drifted toward them, obviously interested in the appearance of two white men on horseback. "I am so vile, Joseph. I have no power to pray. I am shut out from God. I wonder that He does not kill me outright. How can I preach to these people when I know what lies within my own heart?"

"Because these people need to hear the good news of Jesus Christ, and God has called you to preach it to them," Joseph said.

David began to shake his head. Naturally cheerful Joseph did not understand – could not understand – the shadows that suffocated and paralyzed him, often without warning. Shadows that made him question the truth of his calling, of his salvation, and, aye, of his ability to preach. "I do not think that I can preach anymore."

"Nay, you cannot."

Bellamy's affirmative shocked David into staring at his friend. The shadow deepened. What he had thought about himself must be true, then, if Joseph also thought so.

"You cannot preach from your own abilities, David, from your own adequacy. Or because you are holy enough, have learned to pray well, as men think of praying, or are learned enough. You must preach from Christ's sufficiency, from His power. In your weakness, He shall be your strength. Do this in His power, not in David Brainerd's."

The realization that Joseph spoke the truth shook the numb landscape of David's heart and mind. If God wanted him to preach, He would empower him to do it, would He not? *God knows that I have not the power of my own!* His eyes saw the Indians nearing them now – men and women and children who needed to hear of God's Son who had died in their place.

He looked back into Joseph's stark blue eyes and gave a single nod. Weak but willing, joyless yet longing after joy, David slipped his feet from the stirrup irons and dismounted, ready to obey.

God blessed his obedience. Soon, David and Joseph found themselves surrounded by a few dozen Indians, all intently listening to the white men who brought them word of everlasting life, the need for repentance, and the God who had redeemed them in Christ.

'Twas strange. Before he had opened his mouth, David had felt his tongue to be lead, his lips frozen as a pond in January, his spirit lifeless. *Oh, God, help me. I am helpless. Be Thou my help!* His heart cried silently as he stepped forward to obey. His fingers shook as they gripped his Bible, opened to Job 14:14.

Then, as the words came out of his throat, David sensed God's presence lifting the load that rested upon his soul. His Spirit spoke with David's spirit, and David found himself able to pray and to preach with a power that could not have come from himself. He explained the scripture passage, and his listeners, one after another, began to cry out.

Their cries of distress startled him. He continued to preach, feeling as though Someone Else had commandeered his mouth. The tan-skinned faces before him wore expressions of true repentance, of sincere conviction.

This is from Thee, O Lord. This is from Thee alone, and not from myself.

***

The little circle of men gathered near the hearth in Bellamy's parlor. The August sun had long since descended behind the Connecticut hills, and the supper hour had passed, yet these four men bent their knees still on the wooden floor. Two beeswax candles lit the sparsely-furnished room.

David felt the warmth of the bodies beside him – two fervent men of prayer from the Bethlehem community along with his friend Bellamy. His thoughts reached toward eternity as the men, one by one and sometimes all at once, verbally gave themselves up to God with all their hearts. Eternity had never seemed so close to him; the time he would spend in this life had never seemed so short.

His heart bled afresh with the sweet wound of repentance and longing as he pleaded with God to make his heart pure, to make his life a holy one. Soon, he would leave Joseph's home to go on an extended preaching tour, as well as to visit some of his New Light friends. *Oh, dear God, use me, even in a little way. Let me do something for Thee, somehow, by the power of Thy Spirit.*

For he was beginning to see that, as Bellamy said, he could do naught of himself. To look for holiness and power in David Brainerd was to look in vain. *All must come from Thee, but how slow am I to learn this!*

His knees kissed the hard wood as his body bent nearly of its own volition until his face touched the floor. A great desire surged over him, familiar yet with greater strength than it had yet come before now – a great craving after God. The hunger and thirst gnawed at his soul, insatiable. He reached forward, fingers gripping the cracks in the floor, feeling barren and empty, knowing a pleasant inward pain. *I cannot live without more of Thee! Oh, God, make me holy!*

***

The spent leaves of maple and oak trees littered the roads David traveled throughout that golden New England autumn as he iterant-preached throughout that part of Connecticut. All the while, his soul continued to pang after God, after holiness, after the heavenly country in which he knew his desires would gain true satisfaction. The dying world around him drew his thoughts constantly toward the brevity of his life.

And then a letter came, passed along until it caught up with his traveling at last. He recognized the handwriting; 'twas the script of his brother's wife. His hands stilled on the folded paper, unwilling to break the seal, knowing what it contained. *News of Nehemiah's death.*

David swallowed hard against the tears that rose

to his eyes. *I am glad that I made time to stop at his home earlier this fall.* Months ago, his brother had already been suffering from advanced consumption, though they had hoped that he might improve. Apparently, Nehemiah had not done so.

David clenched his jaw and slid a finger under the hardened wax. The seal snapped. *To live is Christ and to die is gain.* He must remember that Nehemiah had lived for Christ; he must remember that Nehemiah's death was a gain for his brother, regardless of the loss David himself felt.

But the letter from his sister-in-law announced not Nehemiah's death but his progressive decline:

Your brother grows very ill. If you wish to see him in this world, make haste to come.

David let his eyes rest on Elizabeth's graceful script for only a moment before deciding: He would go to his brother's home in Eastbury. Perhaps, if God willed it, he would see Nehemiah once more before his brother moved on to that heavenly country.

***

He found Elizabeth sitting beside Nehemiah's bed, her face wearing an expression of grief deepened by great love. David's chest clenched at the sight of it. "How is he?" The question spilled from his lips before he could realize how foolish 'twas.

Still, despite his thoughtlessness, his sister-in-law offered him a weak smile. She did not, however, reply, other than to wipe a hand over her cheeks.

"David, is that you?" The skeletal figure rasped out in a whisper, followed by the tell-tale vomiting cough. How had the disease progressed so quickly? David closed his eyes for a moment, feeling a strange bubbling in his own chest. Death by consumption – It appeared to be the Brainerd family's fate, as 'twas for so many others.

But he could not think of that now. His elder brother's eyes opened just a slit, and he reached a shaking hand toward David.

David stepped toward the bed, his heart quivering. "'Tis I, Nehemiah. I have come. Elizabeth sent for me." He took his brother's gray hand in his, marveling in grief at the smallness of the wasted flesh. "Are you prepared to die, brother?"

Nehemiah's lips trembled at their blood-stained corners and then parted. The air scraped into his lungs. "The Lord has made me a conqueror, and more than a conqueror." He spoke low in resolute gasps. "O death, where is thy sting? O grave, where is thy victory?"

As the night fled and the daybreak came, thirty-year-old Nehemiah's soul returned to God.

Chapter Thirty-One

Jerusha

Mr. Brainerd looks away, into the shadows. "'Tis peculiar. As a child, I always wanted to catch up to my brother Nehemiah in age, but of course, I never could, because, for every birthday I advanced, so did he."

A smile rises to my own lips. "Aye, 'twas the same with me and my sister Sarah. I was so eager for my next birthday, when I would be one year nearer her age, and then…"

He turns to meet my smile with his. "And then she would have a birthday, too," he finishes.

I nod. The communication between us feels so familiar, comfortable, and full of life to me. Surely, he must sense this also – this way in which our souls seem to fit together so well.

Then he rises from his crouched position and does not speak again until he stands before the window. Pushing aside the curtain, he stares out at the night. "Now, I am just a year younger than he was – almost his age – but dying myself. I will never catch up with Nehemiah now. I will meet him rather in the company of angels." He turns, and a smile touches his mouth, but there is a sad joy to it.

Life is indeed a vapor, after all, as the psalmist says.

Chapter Thirty-Two

New Haven, Connecticut
1742

Only a fortnight passed before another letter trembled in David's hand – a letter which promised to change the course of his life.

"Are you well, David?"

He had made the mistake of opening the missive in the sitting room of the friend's home in which he was staying for a few days. David forced a smile to mask the waves of anxiety that began to roil in his belly. "Aye, very well."

Matthew remained quiet for a moment, and then said, "I do not mean to pry, but your shaking hands caused me concern."

David tried to keep his eyes on the bold handwriting, but the pull of his friend's stare compelled him to lift his gaze. "'Tis nothing. Only a letter from Mr. Pemberton of New York."

Matthew stopped cutting chunks from his half-eaten apple and raised his auburn eyebrows. "Nothing? A letter from the Scotch Society, addressed to you, is something."

Indeed 'twas. David's hands began to tremble again; his heart throbbed thick and fast in his chest. An uncharted path stretched before him, a trail leading into the wilderness, hemmed in above and around by towering dark pines – a way into the wilderness, but not a way back out.

"Are they sending you out at last?"

David compelled himself to nod. "They wish to meet with me in New York City." He swallowed. "Regarding the evangelization of the Indians."

"Do they say when they wish you to meet with them?"

"As soon as possible." Even as he said it, fear wrapped its talons around him. These men would see that he was a fraud. They would know that he was not capable of the work they wished to entrust to him. He would fail...

"And what of Yale, then? Are you giving up any hope of returning to the College?"

David's teeth clenched. That chapter of his life seemed yet unfinished. If only he could return to Yale, perhaps he would not be so inadequate. Perhaps he would be better prepared if he possessed his degree... He shook his head. "I do not know."

He looked down at the letter in his hand. He would go to New York.

For now. Who knew what the future might hold for him still in New Haven?

Matthew rose from his seat at the table. "Come. Let me find a few of our friends. We will pray together about this matter of your meeting with the Society."

Gratefulness covered David's heart. "I thank you, brother." His concerns did weigh on him, and he knew from past experience that prayer would provide his only true relief.

***

New York City
November, 1742

His knees shook as he stepped behind the pulpit. His feet, his hands, his mouth, all felt beyond his control. His soul – like Lazarus before Christ raised him from the dead. He took time to lay open his Bible on the pulpit before daring to raise his eyes to look at the assembly, all who had come to hear Mr. David Brainerd preach.

What a dead dog am I! How can they show me any respect? They do not know the vileness of my heart! The thoughts swarmed him, and his heart sank further in dismay. The uplifted faces of the congregants showed anticipation of something worth hearing. *Someone* worth hearing.

I am nothing. I am less than nothing. How miserably disappointed they would be if they knew who I really am inside!

The consciousness of his own sins pressed him down so heavily that he felt that he could not breathe. Fleetingly, his mind returned to his days at Yale, to his lack of love toward those who trusted Christ and yet disagreed with him on a point or two or three. How he had scorned them! *Oh, God, forgive me. How can I not love all my brethren, when I am so much viler than they?*

So many men sat in the assembly, so many much greater than he in spiritual matters, all waiting to hear this sermon that was a final part of David's examination by the Scotch Society before they commissioned him. He gritted his teeth against the cry that threatened to emerge from his tight throat and made it into a silent prayer instead. *Oh, dear God, reward these people with Thy grace. They will get none from me. I am nothing. Thou art all in all. Be Thou my all. Be Thou sufficient for me today. Purify me by Thy grace.*

He opened his mouth and spoke.

Four months later, David received his commission: He was to go to the Indians at Kaunaumeek, New York, a wilderness about twenty miles from John Sergeant's mission base in Stockbridge, Massachusetts.

Chapter Thirty-Three

Jerusha

His legs tremble as he settles down next to me, sucking in a few deep breaths.

My own mind whirls with what he has told me, and my heart already pangs with sharp conviction. How often have I left off prayer because I felt as though God did not hear me? How often have I stopped reading Scripture, never mind having to preach or counsel others, merely because I felt deadness in my spirit? Perhaps the answer to my desire to draw closer to God – to know Him and be known by Him as Mr. Brainerd does and is – lies in this: perseverance such as Jacob demonstrated in wrestling with the Angel in times past, such as Mr. Brainerd has long demonstrated in my own time?

Oh, Lord God, forgive me. Make of me a wrestling Jacob, as this man is, and so leave with me a blessing.

His breathing eases again. He draws his knees up to his chest and locks his arms around them, letting his gaze drift into the darkness of the room. "I labored for nearly a year among the Indians at Kaunaumeek. 'Twas a trying time, a time when in my soul, God asked of me the question, *Do you love me more than these?* And He asked also the question that you have asked me more than once, Jerusha. I had to ask it of myself: Is it worth it? How far will I go for the Cross? What am I willing to give up? What am I truly willing to suffer?"

He swallows hard, the lump in his throat bumping against the tight skin. "'Twas such a time of storm and turmoil in my soul that 'tis hard for me to recount it in words. I have spoken of it in my diary, but even there 'twas hard to describe the thoughts and feelings that swirl when all earthly hope is taken from you, when the consequences of your decision to obey meet you face-to-face."

Silence comes and thickens the air. He appears unsure of how to go on with his story, but every fiber of my being wishes to hear it now – must hear it. So I gently nudge, "You said that John Sergeant lived near you there?"

He startles at the question as though awakening from a dream. "Aye, no more than a half-day's ride, at Stockbridge. Mr. Sergeant made arrangements for me to lodge with a Scotchman who lived near Kaunaumeek."

Chapter Thirty-Four

Kaunaumeek, New York
1743

"An' that's whaur ye can lay doon yer heed."

David stared for a long moment at the sparse, dirty straw scattered across three boards, raised by stones a few handbreadths from the packed dirt floor of the one-room log house. His bed. He looked back up at his host. "Is there... Is there any place for me to put my books?"

The Scotchman squinted. "Books?"

"Aye, my... my books. I have books. I need a p-place for them." David could not help the way his words stumbled and stuttered. Never in his life had he encountered such rough accommodations. And this poor creature of a man and his wife would live and eat and sleep in the same room with him! *How will I ever get any praying done? Or studying?* He eyed the bed again and swallowed hard as he saw small things crawling through the straw. *How will I sleep there?*

His host grunted, exasperation thick in the guttural tone. He strode over to a wooden box crammed into a far corner and rooted around in it for a few moments. Finally, he pulled out an empty sack, the sort that carried dried corn, and shook it, releasing a cloud of dust into the dim cabin light. "Will this dae?"

David stared, his tongue clotting in his mouth. Visions of the glossy bookshelves at Joseph Bellamy's home and at Mr. Mills' – and in his old lodgings at Yale, too, filled his mind.

The Scotchman took David's silence for agreement. He marched across the tiny cabin toward David's bed and shoved the sack at him. "Ye can hang it ower thaur, on a nail. Pit yer books inside."

Without another word, the squat, fleshy man exited the cabin. His wife, who appeared able to speak little English, continued to dart suspicious glances at David as she clattered her stirring spoon in the pot hanging over the low-burning fire.

Numbly, David took the sack and did as his host had directed. A great weariness descended over him, made deeper by the smokiness of the room. Even the smattering of dirty straw appeared inviting to his spent body and mind.

The woman clattered her spoon against the side of the pot again and sneezed more loudly than seemed necessary.

David picked up his Bible. "I will return later."

Like her husband, she only grunted in response, but David thought that he spied relief on her face.

The barrenness of his soul drove him only a little way from the log-house, into a grove of pines that reminded him of the grove he had so loved during his time in Ripton with Jedediah Mills. The April wind blew cold against his face, but David welcomed the harshness. His spirit needed strengthening, needed to stand up against the buffeting.

Oh, God, I am so alone!

The trees towered over him, creaking and groaning. He fell to his knees on the bed of brown pine needles, still moist from the melted winter snows. *I am so ignorant, so weak, so incapable of completing the task before me, of bringing Thy great gospel to these Indians.*

The certainty of his imminent failure weighed him down until he prostrated himself, face against the prickly ground, with no thought of the mountain lions, bears, and wolves that lurked in the forest's shadows. *Let me die. Death is better than life to me.*

He thought of the living situation he must face back at the Scotchman's cabin. The woman's cooking smelled as terrible as the bed her husband offered him.

And all for what? So that he could fail? What a laughing-stock he would be then, what an object of ridicule to all! Why must he suffer in such a way?

Yet, even as he railed against the grievances, he heard a quiet Voice speak within his heart, calling his name. He forced himself to become still so that he could hear, so that he could sense God's presence.

Slowly, in the quiet of the forest, an otherworldly comfort came to him, giving him a measure of rest.

Thou art with me. Thy rod and Thy staff, they comfort me.

***

The sun had barely scrambled over the horizon when David emerged from the log-house, Bible heavy under his arm. The presence of God seemed to have departed again. His heart felt dead to spiritual things. *I am alone in this wilderness, and, what is worse, I do not care if I reach the Indians or not with the news of salvation.*

The trail ahead of him – rough and hardly cleared – led to the Indian village, over a mile away through the lonely forest. He closed his eyes against the bleak prospect before him. *I cannot do this. The Scotch Society does not know what a miserable wretch they sent, how black my sins are, how...*

"Good morning."

David's eyes shot open at the unfamiliar, softly-accented voice, rich and sweet as dark honey, fresh from the comb. An Indian, perhaps ten years older than David, stood before him, a slight smile turning up the corners of his full lips. The man wore a mixture of Indian and English clothing on his sinewy, bronze-skinned body, and he had shaved part of his scalp and smoothed the rest of his obsidian-black hair into a shiny braid.

"You are Mr. Brainerd?"

David managed a nod. "Aye."

The Indian's mouth curved into a true smile, though his eyes remained guarded. "'Tis good that you are here. I am John Wauwaumpequunnaunt. Mr. Sergeant has asked me to be your interpreter with my people." His eyes dropped to David's Bible. "You are on your way to preach this morning?"

"Aye," said David again. He swallowed down the fear clogging his throat. There would be no turning back now.

"Come. My people are waiting." John turned his leather-shod feet and moved down the trail without hesitation.

"They are?" David had not heard whether they knew a new missionary was coming. His heart beat faster. *If I should fail...* He gulped down his fear. *Let me trust in Thee only, O Lord, for I know that I cannot do this in my own strength. I am helpless.*

John slid a glance over his shoulder as he continued leading the way forward. "They have been waiting many generations of men for you, Mr. Brainerd."

***

From then on, John Wauwaumpequunnaunt stood beside David, translating idea by idea from English into the Mahican dialect. When the two came nearly each day, almost all of the villagers emerged from their wigwams and delayed their tasks to hear the missionary talk of this God who called for them to repent and believe in His Name.

Hearteningly, some of them showed signs of concern for their souls. Just a few days after David began to preach, one old woman had come up to David and had told him, through John's translation, that her heart had cried out ever since he began to tell them of this loving Savior. At her words, thankfulness lifted David's heart from the depression into which it had plunged. Perhaps God would use him after all, despite all his sins, despite the darkness that clouded his thoughts more often than not. Perhaps God would come near to him with an abiding presence.

Yet God seemed to hide His face from David, regardless of the seeming progress John and he made in Kaunaumeek throughout that spring and summer.

They started an English school for the Indian children, and the Society appointed John as the schoolmaster.

David moved into the Indian village and began to build his own little hut with his own hands so that he could have some measure of privacy to pray, read, and write.

Yet, throughout the long summer days, grief refused to leave his spirit – a desolation that knew its lack and felt that He who alone could fill it had stepped away.

Chapter Thirty-Five

Jerusha

His eyes have closed in remembrance, but mine remain open, studying him, trying to catch every nuance of each word that passes his lips.

"Continually at this time, I was grieved in my spirit. I often felt no desire for a life of holiness. I was ready almost to renounce my hope of living to God. Everything about me, and more so, within me, looked so dark, so endlessly unholy! I could not endure it."

"But you did endure it." I cannot help but protest the despairing speech. "You stayed in Kaunaumeek until the Scotch Society called you elsewhere."

"Only by God's mercy. In the midst of all my inner darkness, I continued to cry out to God and to meditate on His eternal nature. Jerusha, He never had a beginning! Do you not see what comfort I could draw from these thoughts of His greatness, His power, His perfections, His glory, His holiness in the face of my unholiness? Despite my impotence, my imperfections, my unholiness, this kind of God could and would supply all of my insufficiencies through His own perfections!"

He sucks in a troubled breath, the moist rattling loud in the room's quiet.

I am troubled by his words. So often, I have

allowed discouragement or a slight illness or simply daily concerns to prevent me from praying... and then I have bemoaned the distance between me and God. "I do not always persevere in prayer," I admit softly, unable to meet Mr. Brainerd's eyes. What I say must surely disappoint him. "Sometimes, I am discouraged and the heavens seem shut against my voice, or the business of life crowds out time with God."

He remains quiet for a moment. When I lift my eyes to meet his, to see what he may be thinking of me, I see compassion mingling with the solid truth in his gaze.

"God taught me another thing that summer, too, Jerusha, and mayhap this will help you, as it did me. I learned that 'twas always good, even if I could not persevere in prayer, to persevere in *attempts* to pray. When I do not feel as though I wish to pray, or when the work of life makes prayer seem as merely another thing to add to the list of things to do, that is the time when I should persevere in attempting to pray the most." He pauses, rolling his lips in thought. "And the more that I do in secret prayer, the more I delight to do. The more that I enjoy a spirit of prayer, the more I pray. A great help to me has been understanding that a seasonable, steady performance of secret duties, such as prayer, in their proper hours, coupled with a careful improvement of all time, filling up every hour with some profitable labor, either of heart or head or hands, are excellent means of spiritual peace and boldness before God. Filling our time with and for God is the way to rise up and lie down in peace. He must be the focus of our life in every way, at every time, no matter how we feel."

Chapter Thirty-Six

Kaunaumeek, New York
1743

David fell to the floor of his hut, gasping. His cheek, already dark from several days without shaving, pressed into the hard dirt as he struggled to pull the hot summer air into his burning lungs. Outside, he heard his horse give a whinny of contentment, needlessly reminding him of the source of his distress: He had spent the past several hours laboring to gather hay for the beast in preparation for the cold months ahead.

He opened his eyes, rolling his face down toward the floor, feeling his lashes brush against the cool earth. A groan escaped from his heart. He must spend many more days gathering hay before he would have enough fodder to feed the horse – when he could find the horse, that is. So often, the gelding wandered off into the dense forest, and David could not find him for days. When that happened, David usually couldn't get food for himself, either, at least nothing more than Indian meal cakes.

Why had he thought that life would become easier when he had his own home here? He was utterly alone. God's presence seemed to have vanished, and with it, any feeling of power in his preaching. *When I speak to the Indians, I must be murdering their souls.* The thought filled the mouth of his heart with bitter dismay. He wished that he could crawl beneath the dirt floor of his hut.

To add to all of the darkness from within and without, Yale College still refused to grant him his degree. He had asked more than once and had solicited the help of men connected with the college, but Rector Clap refused to budge. The thought harassed David continually: *What good is a preacher without a degree?*

The pain in his lungs grew sharper. David turned onto his back, willing himself to breath shallowly. Above him, the afternoon light filtered through the greased paper covering his sole window. Soon it would be time for him to go back to the Indian village, just a short walk away, and speak to them again.

What if I attended Yale's Commencement this year? The idea brought fear into his heart. This would have been the commencement at which David himself would have gained his degree. How could he stand by and watch his classmates take their degrees while he himself had no hope of attaining that honor?

Yet, at the same time, the notion would not be suppressed. As he stumbled about the single room, gathering his Bible, washing his face, eating a bite of souring bread, it continued to grow.

What if I went to the Scotch Society first and enlisted their help? And the help of others – others well-connected to Yale, well-respected by Clap and the Board? Excitement fevered his steps as he took the single-file trail toward the village. *Perhaps they could be convinced to grant me my degree based upon my work since I left.*

Though no smile lifted his lips, a little of the heaviness disappeared from his heart as he began to hope once more.

As the summer concluded, David set out for New Haven, Connecticut, determined to settle the matter of his expulsion and degree once and for all.

Chapter Thirty-Seven

Jerusha

My breath catches in my throat, making a little gasping noise before I can silence it. Mr. Brainerd stops speaking, his eyes holding mine in the dim light. His gaze is silent; it says nothing.

I am afraid that mine says far too much.

For 'twas in New Haven that September that we first met, he a wilderness-roughened man, quite too old for me then and so different from, so much more alive than the usual young theology graduates that peppered our lives at home. So handsome, with his wavy brown hair tied back, his tricorn hat beneath his arm, determination in his every step, his every word.

And I? I had been merely an overly serious, reserved girl on the verge of womanhood, very conscious of the pimples with which God had seen fit to mark my chin that day.

Does Mr. Brainerd recall our first meeting? If he does, he has never spoken of it. But now... Will he speak of it now? My heart slowly increases its heavy beat.

He runs his tongue over his bottom lip, moistening it before continuing. "I was not in the sweetest frame of mind as I rode to New Haven. I did not want to appear overwhelmed, as if I had no confidence in God, when I saw my classmates take their degrees, but fear and confusion dogged my steps."

"You did not appear confused or fearful to me," I say. In my heart, I can yet see his upright carriage, his thoughtful expression, his clear eyes as he walked into my Uncle Pierrepont's parlor. As he and my father spoke together, I sat by Papa's side, silently wondering at the passionate sureness combined with humility that radiated from this Mr. Brainerd.

"Only by God's goodness did I appear so. As I watched the Commencement, as all of my hopes and dreams in this world vanished, I found that my mind was calm and that I could resign myself to whatever God willed."

My admiration for him swells as a bud in spring, ready to unfurl its petals to the sun. For was it not this deep-rooted, active peace that drew me toward him at that time? 'Tis a remarkable thing, indeed, to hear of its genesis now. Yet, at the same time, anxious anticipation stretches its tendrils through all my being, waiting to hear what he will say of our first meeting... if he will mention it at all.

Slowly, so slowly that I begin to pray for patience, he continues, "That week, I met with many Christian friends, including your father, who had come to the Commencement. Several of them advised me to write to the Rector and to the Board of Yale and to tell them of my sorrow over the offense that I had given them."

The injustice of this sparks indignation within me, even as I wait for my bit of the story. "But you had already apologized privately. As you said earlier, the offense was a private one. If I may be so bold to say it, it does not seem fair."

A little smile touches his lips and cools the fire I feel on his behalf. "No, 'twas not fair, but they argued that perhaps by that, I could remove the offense that I had occasioned. God granted me the humility to do it.

So I apologized again, not for my ministry while I was at Yale – no, never that, though that might offend them forever, nor for what I believed when I was at Yale. Rather, I apologized for speaking ill of Mr. Whittesley, for making a judgment on one whom I had no right to judge."

"But your apology was not accepted?" The details have grown foggy in my mind.

He smiles. "Oh, they accepted my letter, and my offence was removed."

I frown. "But I thought that you did not...did not graduate." I say the words softly, for even now the shame of not receiving his degree perhaps causes him pain that I know not of.

His face grows serious. "No, you are correct: I did not graduate. The Board required me to return to the college for a full twelve-month if I desired to receive my degree. I could not do that because I had already given my word to the Scotch Society."

"That must have distressed you." A minister with no degree? Such a one could hope of little success or esteem.

"God enabled me to take the news with calmness." Again, his lips curve into a smile, and his hazel eyes glisten, as though lit from within with stars straying from the constellations which brighten the dark sky. "I admit that 'twas at this time, however, that my mind was distracted just a bit in the most pleasant way. Aye, most pleasant to experience, yet also difficult for me to endure."

He falls silent, his brow grows troubled, and I wonder what more powerful event than the denial of his college degree could have occurred in New Haven those three years ago. "What do you mean, Mr. Brainerd?"

His eyes flicker to meet mine, and for a moment he

seems about to refuse to tell me more. But then he sets his eyes on the far, shadowed wall and continues. "I met a young lady, one who attracted my attention in a most compelling, modest, and maidenly way – though she in no way desired to do so, I am certain of that. She walked with a pleasing holiness, with a quiet joy in her countenance. Aye, she was beautiful in every way, though still very young.

"I admit that I had not thought of a woman in such a way since my conversion; my mind had been so engaged in the things of God. Yet, here was this young lady who in her personality, her countenance, and her spirit seemed to meet with me, though we exchanged very few words. And 'twas for the best that our meeting was so brief and that we seemed unlikely to meet ever again, for I had already determined in my heart never to marry."

My heart thumps so loudly in my chest I am sure that Leah in the kitchen must awake from her sleep at the noise. What is this that Mr. Brainerd speaks of? A woman whom he met near the same time as he met me, yet who engaged his attention and interest so much more than I had done? Jealousy and hurt surround my momentarily-unguarded heart, tearing at it with wolf-teeth.

Why did I think that he might have savored a thought of me? Little Jerusha Edwards, barely more than a child at the time, with few words to her tongue and none of them witty and clever. I shift on my crossed legs, covered by the canopy of my skirts. The room suddenly feels too close and hot.

Swallowing back the hurt that pushes me to make a hurried exit, I determine to hear the story to its end – to push through the pain and see what God might teach me through it. "May I ask, Mr. Brainerd, why was that?"

"Why was what?"

"Why did you, ah, determine never to marry?" For if he had married, I would not be sitting here, pining in the depths of my heart over him. I would have set aside all thought of him long ago.

"God called me to the Indians," he replies quickly, as if my question is redundant.

"Yet other missionaries to the Indians have married. John Sergeant and John Eliot are among them, Mr. Sergeant to one of my cousins, in fact." My tongue readily supplies this factual answer. "I say this only because you seem to have, at least at one time, felt a desire for the happy companionship which marriage might have brought you, as it has brought others," I add softly.

He hesitates, and I feel the urge to fill the quiet, thinking space with words, though I know that I should not. Then, very deliberately, he meets my eyes and holds them with his, gently, as one would handle a treasured china cup. "I admit, I did think of going back for that young lady, more than once in the time that followed. Yet I knew that if I should marry, I would be forced to consider my wife's happiness and security alongside the call of God upon my life. Marrying her, I felt, would divide me, would tear me between two passions."

Strangely enough, defensiveness rises in my bosom for the cause of this unknown woman – defensiveness not for her alone, but for all the feminine half of mankind. "Yet you never asked this young woman if she also would sacrifice her happiness and security for the gospel, as you did."

Surprise widens his eyes. "What do you mean?"

"I mean only that, you speak of this young woman as though she would have stopped you from fulfilling God's call upon your life, as though she would have held onto the hem of your garment and hampered your steps forward into danger because she would insist upon a comfortable, protected life."

My mind tiptoes over to the knowledge of that pretty, spoiled cousin of ours, Abigail, who married devoted John Sergeant and did do just that – asking him to build her a small mansion of a house on the main street of Stockbridge, filled with everything to indulge the eyes and heart. *But not all women are of Abigail's mold.*

Mr. Brainerd shakes his head at my words, but my tongue feels compelled to finish. "I believe that you think too little of the fair sex, Mr. Brainerd, and of the mighty workings which God can do in them, despite them being more delicate vessels. How can you know whether this lady would have wished to be spared the troubles of your Christ-led life… or whether she, too, may have wished to lay down her life alongside yours, careless of whatever harm might come to her? You assume that, because she was a woman, she would have hampered you. You assume…"

But his hand on mine, swiftly alighting and then withdrawing, stops the flood of argument streaming from my lips. When I look into his face, only gentle honesty holds a place there. "Nay, that is not so, Jerusha. 'Twas not the fault of the young woman – of any woman – but 'twas – it is – my own weakness, my own strengths that prevented me from doing as you say: of bringing that young lady into the harsh life to which God had called me.

"You see, I know that 'tis in my nature to wish to protect her from all harm and to spare her all hurt. I could never have done that – and yet I would have been tempted to do so and perhaps would have done it in the end, and so have broken my covenant to my God – my covenant to obey Him and to go to the utmost boundaries to win souls for Him. Mine would have been a sorry, broken, failed life, indeed, if I had given in to my heart's desire. At the time, 'twas a choice I had to make: a choice between her who delighted my heart and Him who had created it – and her – for Himself."

He tears his eyes from mine and looks to the candle's flame, now burning low. "I will not say 'twas an easy choice. 'Twas difficult, in the beginning. But then, when the decision was made, how easy to see that, truly, there was no choice. He is no fool who parts with that which he cannot keep, when he is sure to be recompensed with that which he cannot lose."

"Philip Henry." The name of the nonconformist preacher slips from my tongue.

"Aye, he said that, and he was right." Mr. Brainerd pauses. "I must finish my story ere the dawn breaks."

Chapter Thirty-Eight

1743

Thus, from Yale's Commencement David went back to Kaunaumeek, still with no degree to his credit. Yet there was a strange peace that settled over him as the autumn descended into winter – a peace that did not come from his own spirit but from that of Another. He found himself glad to see the Indians, and, to his surprise, he found them glad to see him when he began to preach to them each day once more. John Wauwaumpequunnaunt worked with him on translating prayers into their language, and David began to pray with them directly, rather than through John.

Yet, he continued to feel weak in body and, even more, weak in soul. Temptation besieged him on every side, despite his being secluded from society in general. At times, nearly overcome by the spiritual and emotional pressure within him, he cried out to God for mercy. God answered him, showing him that He was all-powerful and all-sufficient. David knew that his soul could rest on God's grace and power, yet his feelings so often conflicted with this. Renewing his dedication of himself to God, he wanted to keep his covenant with Him but found that he could do it only in God's strength, not his own. Time appeared so very short, eternity seemed so near, and a great name either in this life or after this life, or any earthly pleasure, was an empty bubble to him – a deluding dream.

***

1744

The day came when David planned to preach his last sermon to the little Mahican band. He had received direction from the Scotch Society to move onward to the Indians at the Forks of the Delaware – true frontier country from which he could not be sure that he would ever return.

On his last day at Kaunaumeek, David arrived at the Indian village to find that most of the people had already assembled, sitting or standing in the open area David used for preaching. His heart panged when he saw that several Indians had tears in their eyes.

"What is wrong?" he asked John, who stood by his elbow. "What has upset them?" His inability to converse easily with the Indians, despite his winter language lessons with Sergeant, grated on him at times such as this.

John's often-solemn countenance had become even graver than usual. "They are grieved that you are going away from them, Mr. Brainerd. They say that you are going to tribes who do not wish to become Christians and that you are forsaking those who do."

Guilt chilled David's heart as surely as the late winter air, still smelling of melting snow, brought shivers to his body. "They do not understand."

He drew out a piece of linen from where he had tucked it inside his sleeve and coughed hard into it. Red spackled the cloth when he pulled it from his mouth. The sunset of his own life flashed before his inner gaze, bringing a fresh flood of urgency to his spirit. "My time among these people has come to an end. The men who sent me here have now sent me to different Indians. Tell them that I must obey these men of God. I must go where they send me."

"I will tell them." John turned from David, but not before David saw the interpreter's eyes flit down to the cloth and then fill with concern.

He listened, able to understand some of the phrases, as John spoke to the Mahicans. Their faces did not change but only grew deeper in sorrow.

David stepped up to John's elbow. "Tell them that I have a great affection for them, but that they must be willing to let others hear of this good news that I have brought to them."

John nodded, turned back to the assembly, and spoke again in their language – a language that had once sounded harsh and crude to David's ears but now had become beautiful to him. In these few months, God had put love inside his heart for the people who spoke it. *Some of them now pray to God in that language, and He hears them.*

Would the conversion of a single man, woman, or child's soul ever cease to amaze him? David thought not.

"They say, who will tell them more about Jesus Christ and the way of salvation in Him if you go away from them?" John said, and David could see that this question also lay heavy on the interpreter's mind as well.

"Tell them, I advise them to move toward Stockbridge. Mr. Sergeant will help them greatly. The Lenni-Lenape have no minister to help them at all. I must go to them."

As John relayed the message to the gathering, David let his gaze travel over them, praying for each one silently. There was the woman who had told him that her heart cried out when she heard the gospel preached. On her lap sat her two grandchildren, both of whom had begun to learn English with John and would soon learn the catechism as well. Nearby, a man stood, worn and bent by the difficulties of his sin-saddled life, but in whose face David had seen a light begin to dawn. *O Almighty God, my heart has enlarged with love for them all. Protect and preserve their faith, though 'tis as small as a mustard-seed! Awaken their hearts. Make them alive by Thy Spirit.*

Chapter Thirty-Nine

Jerusha

Pausing for a moment, Mr. Brainerd leans back against the edge of the settee, exhaustion threading through every seam of his body. Pity overtakes me, despite my ravening appetite to hear more of the story that has built the man before me.

Mr. Brainerd's voice has become hoarse. The candle he brought downstairs with him burns low. My own has already extinguished itself.

"Perhaps we should continue another time," I say. "You should not overtax your strength."

He turns his gaze toward me, and I feel drawn toward him as though with a cord. "I wish that I could finish telling my story, Jerusha. Though it depletes my bodily strength, I have found spiritual joy in remembering all these things tonight."

I wish to stay here longer, too. I wish we could prolong this time which surely shall not see repetition – but I see the utter weariness draining Mr. Brainerd's body, though his speaking soul continues to blaze on into the night. Something in my heart stirs – something more akin to a mother with her child, I suppose, than to a woman toward a man whom she holds romantically dear.

I rise, feeling the stiffness from our long talk

stretch out of my limbs. "Come, Mr. Brainerd. 'Tis time to rest. You must be tired from the day. You may tell me more of your story another time."

He gazes into the fire, the glow reflected in his features, in his eyes. 'Tis a radiance I have never seen in any other man, though I have seen the yearning for it in other men's eyes, including the eyes of my father.

But the cost Mr. Brainerd has paid for it is high, too high, for most men, aye, or women, either.

Slowly, he pulls his gaze away from the blaze. "He is a consuming fire, our God." He states it unblinkingly, as a madman might report that the sky rains oranges.

Yet he is not mad. Rather, he is set-apart and other.

I feel inadequate in the face of his holiness, in the face of his rapt attention on God. Aye, for several years now, I have desired nothing other than the will of God myself – but I have desired it without the depth of affection and yearning that I see in this man's eyes. I have desired it because 'tis right to do so – because 'tis pious. Aye, and I have even loved God – in the same way in which I love the king of England. I am wholly loyal to him; I love all he represents. I obey his edicts. But do I love the king in the same way, say, in which I might love a husband? Of course I do not. And thus it has been for me with my God. There has been no personal and passionate love for God Himself. And the sudden thought comes to me – Perhaps this is why I have so sought after Mr. Brainerd's love. He has been the closest I have ever seen to a God with whom I could fall into a true and deep love.

Mr. Brainerd's love for his God – self-giving, intimate, passionate, adoring – makes me feel wholly shallow. Shame trickles through my soul. Yet I do not resent Mr. Brainerd for what his story makes me feel, but yearn to understand how I, too, can have such passion. Such passion for God that it makes me forget all that is in this world.

"Aye," I say, and my response spreads all through my mind and heart. More than ever, I want to touch this man's soul so that I too might catch on fire and burn, but the length of my spiritual arm seems too short. Unexpectedly, tears brim at the edges of my eyes. Fright that he might see them strikes me, and so I turn away from the line of his gaze and rise to my feet.

At my movement, Mr. Brainerd also rises to his feet. Or rather, stumbles, so much so that I rush to his side. I grasp beneath his arms, trying to steady him as, like a newborn foal, he rickets one way and then the other. At last, he stands, the breath pushing his thin chest in and out. The pain has clouded his face again, but then the smile he gives me shines through.

"I thank you," he murmurs.

I nearly release him, but then I sense his trembling unsteadiness despite the brave show. I shift my body so that his right arm slings itself over my shoulder. "Here," I say, "lean upon me."

He hesitates.

"Lean upon me," I insist.

Still he hesitates.

I look up and meet his eyes looking down at me, dulled by pain and darkened by something else, too – some emotion I have not the skill to interpret. "I pray you," I whisper, "allow me help, Mr. Brainerd."

And he does. Together, his candle in my hand, we hobble our way out of the sitting room and move into the passage. Leah peers out of the kitchen. Wearing only her shift, she rubs her eyes in the low glare of the candlelight. She must have heard our shuffling footsteps, though we both try to keep as quiet as we can, lest we disturb the sleeping house.

"Is everything all right, miss?" The whites of her eyes grow wide at what is an unusual sight at an unusual time of night. "Do you need me to fetch Mr. Edwards to help Mr. Brainerd?"

Though Papa's strong arms would make quick work of this task, there is nothing I want less. I smile to assure the servant. "Nay, all is well. I am seeing Mr. Brainerd to his room."

Obviously too tired to offer anything more, Leah nods, muffling a yawn behind her callused hand. "Very good, miss."

She disappears back into the kitchen while Mr. Brainerd and I move across the passage. The staircase confronts us with its sneering, polished brown teeth. Now 'tis I who pause. I had not considered these. "Do you think that you can make it up them?"

The moon sends the soft shimmer of its beams through the leaded glass window nearby. I can just see Mr. Brainerd's soft smile. "Aye, we can make it together, I think, Miss Edwards."

Together. Aye. Fresh strength pulses into my body. "Aye, Mr. Brainerd." Without another word, I press on toward the staircase. The heft of his arm across my shoulders is the weight of joy, I think.

One step.

Then two.

He winces aloud.

Three.

He sucks in his breath. Pausing, I see that his teeth hold his bottom lip in a vice-like grip. "Shall I get Papa?"

Immediately, he shakes his head. "Nay," he says very low. "He needs his rest. He will be awake early tomorrow for prayer and study. I do not wish to disturb him."

"He will not mind…"

Again, he gifts me with a gentle smile. "Let us continue on, just you and I, Miss Edwards. I think we can do it together – if we persevere to the end."

This man is nothing if not determined. And so am I. "Alright," I agree and return his smile. "We are on the third step. That means that there are nine more, Mr. Brainerd."

Four.

Five.

"I would be very glad if you would call me David. But only if you wish to." He gasps this out as we hesitate on the sixth step.

Now 'tis I who lose my breath. "All right." I pause. "Then we must have no more of *Miss Edwards.* You must continue to call me simply Jerusha, as the rest of my family does."

Is it impishness that appears on his dimly-lit face? "I intended to do so, if it met with your approval." He half-smiles and half-grimaces, ending with a wink. "Though I could instead call you *Rushie,* as I hear several of them do, if you wish."

I let my smile meet his. "*Jerusha* will do." The pleasure of his request fills me. To tamp it down, to not reveal it to him who asked, I pretend that I must shift beneath the weight of his arm. "If you are ready, let us keep going up, or the sun will catch us yet on the staircase, Mr. Brai… I mean, David."

***

As I rest in my bed that night, with my sister's body tightly snuggled against mine, I cannot help but be glad that Papa insisted on us all – even us girls – learning at least the rudiments of Hebrew and Greek. For if he had not, I would never have been blessed to know just what I was calling the man who lies asleep in the room down the passage.

David. *Beloved.*

Chapter Forty

The morning sun only nibbles at the horizon of trees when I rise and draw my skirt and bodice over my shift, being sure to tie my pocket beneath. I woke well before dawn with a restless hunger in my spirit. Putting my little New Testament into my pocket, I tiptoe down the stairs and through the passage. Leah has already risen. The sounds of her bustling about, coaxing the fire back to life and starting her duties, float from the kitchen.

I pass into the kitchen. "Good morning to you, Leah."

The servant's head whips up when where she crouches on the hearth. "Oh, Miss Jerusha. You frightened me. I did not think that anyone else was up yet. Except your father, of course. He is always up before the sun." Standing, she wipes her sooty hands on her apron. "Can I get you something?"

"Nay, I'm only using the back door."

She nods, no doubt thinking that I must have a fierce need of the necessary house – so fierce that I do not wish to use the pot in my chamber.

"When Mama asks after me, pray tell her that I have gone for a walk, but I will be back after breakfast, in time for the Scripture reading." Mr. Brainerd does not always come to breakfast now, due to his illness, but in the event that he does this day... Well, something inside me does not wish to see him just yet after last night's talk. There is another One with whom I must speak, whom I must see with my spiritual eyes before I can see the one I love in this mortal flesh again.

Leah bobs her head, accustomed to the early morning walks I sometimes like to take, and with that, I step outside the kitchen door and into the late summer dawn.

The air is fresh but warm still, the leaves just beginning to turn from green to gold and orange and scarlet. My feet quickly make their way through the outskirts of our little town and into the ever-filling graveyard at its edge. 'Tis quiet here, and peaceful. Often, I come here instead of to the river when I desire time alone, apart from the house filled with brothers, sisters, parents, and usually guests as well.

Like a hound dog finding a spot to settle upon for the night, I find my own grassy place and sit. My hand pushes through the slit in the side of my skirt to find the small Bible in my pocket. I draw it out and open it, letting it fall open to my favorite book to read – the Psalms.

And as I read, a prayer comes unbidden to the lips of my heart: *Oh, Lord God, come near to me. Come near as I heard last evening that Thou came near to Mr. Brainerd and were all-sufficient to meet every need, every desire that he has had! Thou hast filled him with Thy living water; he drank and was satisfied. In Thy presence, he found fullness of joy, and at Thy right hand, he found pleasures forevermore.*

I am quiet, still before my God. *Give to me the same spirit that he has. Give to me the same desire to do Thy will – not just as a duty, but as a delight. Use me as poured-out wine, as broken bread, wherever that may take me.*

I rise from sitting to my knees, feeling the soft earth press down. Seemingly of their own accord, my hands open to heaven. *Here I am, Lord. All that I am, all that I have – even my love for Mr. Brainerd – I give it all to Thee, to do what Thou wilt. Make my life a living sacrifice, as his has been, and forgive me for when I have regretted his depth of sacrifice in my own selfishness.*

There is a yielding here in my spirit, an opening of a gate that I perhaps did not wish to give the Savior leave to enter if He so required. Still, a yearning yet clings to the walls of my heart, like ivy to stone, and I hover, asking if the desire itself is wrong.

But I do not think it is. Did not the Lord Jesus Christ ask of the Father to remove the cup from Him, if it were possible?

And so, with the dew dampening through my garments, undemanding, I ask that if it be His will, that He would yet spare my David Brainerd, my beloved.

Chapter Forty-One

September 1747

Just before sundown, I leave the family circle to get our milking cow from the common pasture. She is a small brown-and-white creature, with long, softly-fringed ears that I love to run my fingers along and large moist eyes that peer at me from beneath their dark lashes.

The boy who keeps the gate lets me through, his reddish mop glinting in the early evening sunlight. Though I don't remember his name – there are so many village children – I smile at him, and he gives me a shy grin in return. When the cow comes to my call, anxious to be milked, I lead her to the gate. As I pass through, I notice that the child's unkempt linen shirt wrinkles near his armpits from tightness and that his breeches show signs of wearing through in every place his growing limbs stress them. I will tell Mama or Papa about it; they will see about getting his family something to relieve their apparent poverty.

My bare feet feel the coolness of the green grass slipping between my toes as I urge the cow to move along, using a long, slim branch to guide her. From the road near the meadow through which I bring the cow, the sound of a cantering horse reaches my ears. I strain my eyes to see the rider. Brown-coated and sturdy-looking, even from this distance, I see that, aye, he heads in the same direction in which I am going. Could it be Mr. Brainerd's dear brother, John – who has long been expected but whom I have not yet met?

I quicken my footsteps – and, consequently, the hooves of Madam Cow – through the hazy summer evening, and we arrive home in no time at all. At the side of our house, young Timothy tosses a ball up and catches it. "Timothy!" I call out, still walking down the lane.

He squints through the glare of the setting sun. "Aye?" he asks, tossing the ball again when he sees 'tis only I.

"Would you milk the cow for me? I need to see to Mr. Brainerd."

Timothy hesitates. "Everyone else is inside. They can see to him, can they not?"

"Timothy." I state his name and glower at him. He may be a boy, but I am his senior by eight years.

My dark-haired brother screws up his face but drops the ball. He knows that he must obey me or he will answer to our parents. After he has begun to lead the cow away toward the shed behind the house, I brush off my skirt of any dirt, real or imagined, and head into the house.

Surely enough, the rider whom I saw was Mr. John Brainerd. He and David sit together with Papa in his closet. The door stands half-open. Since 'tis not a private conversation, I pause beside the door, listening.

"You brought the rest of the diaries, John. I am glad. I am so very glad," David says. Do I hear tears in his voice? In the few days since our conversation occurred, we have not spoken alone much. Indeed, I have not dared again to call him by his first name, except occasionally in my mind. Using his name gives pleasure to my heart as the first bite of an autumn apple to the tongue. And what gives my soul even greater pleasure is to lie upon my bed each night, reviewing what he has told me thus far of his story and beginning to wonder with joy whether God might love and use me, might draw as close to me, as He has to David.

"To think that you wanted them destroyed once upon a time." The voice belongs to Papa.

"Aye." David pauses. "And in truth, sometimes I think it would be for the best still. I do not wish for people to read them and pattern themselves after me, you know. I am so deeply flawed, so sinful in every part of my being.... You will see this when you read them, Jonathan. But the one thing I believe that may be taken away from the diaries is this: that God will use a sinful man to bring honor to His Name, by His grace alone. He fills the earthen vessel with His Spirit because He delights in mercy."

"You will allow me to do as I will with them?" Here is Papa's eager, quiet voice.

Again, David hesitates. When he speaks again, determination underscores his every word. "Aye, sir. But I wish to edit them first, in the time God yet allows me. There are many things which the whole world need not know or see, but can be a secret thing betwixt that man and His Savior, aye?"

"Have you the strength to edit them?" This new voice, low and dense and full of life as a spring thicket, must come from his brother. I wait, tense, to hear what David's response will be, for that question also clenches my heart. I do not wish for him to overtax what little strength he still has, to cause himself to fall over the edge of a decline from which he cannot return...

"I think so. I wish to try as long as I might to do something for God. He has done so much for me, and what are these last days of my life worth if I cannot live them for Him to the fullest?"

***

I am little needed by David during much of the week that follows. John's arrival fills him with such joy, he is distracted from all else. Even his continual exhaustion and pain seem to diminish as the two of them – and sometimes Papa as well – remove themselves from the usual hustle and bustle of the Edwards' household, sometimes talking together in the front room or in Papa's closet or in Mr. Brainerd's bedchamber, a new one downstairs, to accommodate his increasing weakness.

Their conversation always circles back to the Lenni-Lenape Indians, whom John Brainerd tends now – "my Indians," as David calls them, or sometimes, "my flock," the affection resonant in his words. He questions John intensely on what spiritual exercises he sets them, whether each convert continues to walk uprightly, and whether John has come across any trouble from the white population surrounding them. 'Tis sweet to hear him talk so and to see the relief his brother's visit has brought him – though it seems I have been forgotten in the process.

"And if ever you need to go away, John, be sure to advise the little flock to go to William Tennent. Be assured, he will do them good," I hear Mr. Brainerd say as I tap lightly on the door of his bedchamber and then ease open the door. He and his brother sit near the window, a Bible spread out on the little table between them, the light spilling across its worn pages

"Ah, Jerusha, there you are." He greets me with a smile, and sunshine pours into the valleys of my heart. "Am I needed for something?"

Distracted by his smile, I try to remember why I am standing here. Oh, aye. "I have come to collect your tray, sir. Also, Mama says that I am to tell you not to overtax yourself. She says that she knows that you have risen early several days this week already, and 'tis not good for your health."

His lips curve upward again, and I fear that the thumping of my heart shows beneath my bodice. "Pray, thank your mother for me, Miss Edwards. Her concern is kind, but surely she knows that I am a dying man already. I wish to do as much for God as I can before my last breath. To burn out for Him!" He turns to John, explaining, "I rose early to edit those diaries you brought me. What a mercy to still have them! How I can see the workings of God's grace in my life through the years. Miss Edwards knows. Do you not, Miss Edwards?"

Startled at his direct address and intimation that he and I have held much personal discourse, I cannot answer for a moment. Awkwardness heats my cheeks as I sense John studying me.

But I am an Edwards girl, one trained to maintain my composure in any situation, however uncomfortable. Schooling my face, I merely nod. "Aye, you have told me of Almighty God's work in your life, Mr. Brainerd."

John's gaze remains on me, but I ignore it and move toward the table beside his brother's bed, gathering the soiled handkerchiefs that always pile up there and heaping them onto the tray with the empty teacups and plates.

After a moment, John rises from his chair, closing the Bible, its tattered pages fluttering. "Still, David, you should not over-weary yourself, as good Mistress Edwards says. We have spoken long enough for today. You should rest."

David does not agree nor disagree but only comments, "You must take care of yourself, too, brother. I have been meaning to tell you that, in the near future, when you return to Cranberry, you must take a companion with you, if at all possible. Someone like-minded. It would be for the best, I think."

As I turn from gathering the cloths, I find that David's eyes fasten upon me, watching me, rather than remaining intent upon his brother, with whom he converses. What can this mean?

Glancing between us, John nods in response to his brother's words and moves toward the door. In much of his aspect and manner, John is very like David when I met him all those years ago, yet there is a quieter, though not-less-hot flame in his eyes, rather than the almost-mad zealotry that yet burns in David's.

Hands clutching the full tray, I step out after John into the passage and pull the bedchamber door shut behind me, hoping that David will sleep while he is alone. When I turn, John stands so close that I bump into him. The odor of woodsmoke and pine-trees still clings to his garments, telling of his time spent taking over for his brother among the Crossweeksung Indians.

"I apologize, Miss Edwards," he exclaims in a low voice, taking a step backward.

"There is no harm done," I reply and move toward the kitchen. Today is laundry day, and there is much work to be done in addition to my on-and-off checking on Mr. Brainerd. Knowing John, he will find something with which to occupy his hours until his brother has finished resting: reading one of the many titles on Papa's bookshelves, perhaps, or walking along the same riverbank where David and I have spent some time this summer. Even thinking of it starts a yearning in my heart – a yearning for those few peaceful days so swiftly past.

"Pray, may I have a word with you?"

Surprised, I stop and turn toward him. "Aye?"

"Would you be willing to walk with me, Miss Edwards?" Matter-of-factness must run in the family. "My brother tells me that the way to the river is very pleasant."

A lump of nervousness rises in my throat, yet I do not allow anything but the most perfect calmness to pervade my countenance. "I have much work to do for my mother this afternoon, Mr. Brainerd, before your brother awakes."

"'Tis important that I speak with you privately before I leave. And leave I soon must." His eyes – brown like the hot chocolate my sister Mary adores, instead of David's intense hazel – have fastened to my face. Like his brother, John has acquired a peculiar tenacity. He is determined to speak with me. A silent sigh fills my chest. I must hear him out. To do otherwise would appear rude.

I nod. "Very well, Mr. Brainerd. But we cannot walk all the way to the river." Something within me resists going that way again with any man save one.

I scurry into the kitchen, depositing the little ball of soiled handkerchiefs in the laundry piling up in a corner and telling my sister Sarah where I am off to. Returning to the foyer, I pluck my straw hat with its strawberry-colored ribbons and my light shawl from their place beside those of my sisters. He takes up his own plain hat, and we are soon out-of-doors.

Autumn has only just begun to tiptoe around the edges of our Massachusetts summer, and the air yet touches our cheeks with a warm breath. The oak leaves hang green above our heads, bearing but the faintest touches of orange, and the last fledglings of the yellow finches land among the seed-bearing flowers bordering our front yard. I let my shawl drape languidly around my shoulders.

"'Tis a lovely day." Mr. Brainerd stops on the stone flags, offering me his arm.

Should I take it? If he decides to stroll through Northampton's busy afternoon streets, many of Papa's congregation will surely spy us. Word will travel that Reverend Edwards' second-eldest was out walking with a young man – with none other than Mr. David Brainerd's brother. In a town this size, gossip takes the wings of a mourning dove, flying high and fast. Yet, on the other hand, Mr. John Brainerd very well may take it as intended rudeness if I refuse his arm, and I do not wish to hurt him, merely to spare myself a little gossip.

I place my hand on his forearm but adroitly turn us toward the back of the property, away from the gate leading to the street. "Let us walk near the house. Then I shall hear if Mama needs me."

"Very well."

We have gained the path that weaves through the herbal beds Esther and I planted together last spring, before David came into our lives, before we knew whether he would emerge from the Indian wilderness alive. The scent of mint touches my senses and combines with that of lavender, thyme, and basil.

Our footsteps – his firm from his booted feet, mine soft from my thin leather slippers – sound loud in the absence of our speaking. I keep my lips sealed. Knowing John Brainerd even for a mere week, I have come to understand that he is not a man given to rash speech. More than once, the two of us have spent an hour in silence, quietly watching by his brother's bed, waiting for David to awake. When the younger Mr. Brainerd wishes to speak, he will do so, and his words will be more worth the hearing because of the rumination.

When we turn around the raspberry bushes, he stops. I glance toward the house and see that the bushes partially conceal us from the view of the kitchen windows. If he were any but an honorable friend of my father and David's brother, I would take several steps forward to avoid that concealment. As it is, I merely drop my hand from where it rests on his woolen sleeve and move inconspicuously a pace back, to put a less-familiar space betwixt us. I fold my hands in front of me, across my apron, wondering what he means to say.

With his gaze fixed on my face again, his eyes narrow in thought, just as I have seen David's do on so many occasions. When he speaks, as with his brother, his voice lacks any hesitation. 'Tis firm as brick dried in the summer sun. "Miss Edwards, I am leaving the day after tomorrow. The Indians need me, and David wishes me to go. I plan to return in but two weeks."

He stops, his gaze probing me. Why is he telling me his travel plans – plans about which I have already learned from David himself? I nod in an effort to prod the conversation forward. Mama will call for me any moment if I do not appear to help with the mounds of laundry waiting to be scrubbed, boiled, and hung. "I know. We will pray for God to grant you a safe journey, both to and from New Jersey. I know that your brother will anxiously wait for your return, but be assured that I will care for him as I would care for –" I almost bite my tongue as I skid to a halt.

I nearly said, *as I would care for a husband.*

John Brainerd stands there, silently, head cocked, eyes still intent on me. I am not one given to blushing, but my nearly-spoken comment hangs unsaid between us. I feel a steady crimson creep up my neck and permeate my face.

"As you would care for a brother," he finishes the

sentence for me, but the look on his countenance shows that he very likely has guessed something of what I nearly misspoke.

I nod, but I can no longer meet his eyes. How must he think of me – a girl who does not wait for the man in question to speak of his own heart before engaging her own? For he must surely know that his brother has not spoken a word of affection to me, no matter the time we have spent together. Does he think that I seek to win his dying brother, and this is why I spend long hours by his bedside, why I accompanied him to Boston?

Without warning, John reaches for my folded hands and wraps them both in his, yet as a friend, not a lover. I shut my eyes, and then, opening them, force myself to meet his gaze.

Understanding rests there, and compassion, too, though what I have done to deserve his compassion and understanding, I know not. "Miss Edwards," he says, "before I leave for New Jersey, I wish to tell you how grateful I am. You have been utterly selfless in your dedication to the care of my brother. You have served him as you would serve the Lord Jesus."

Selfless? No, not I. For 'twas my selfish love – at least in the beginning – that drove my service.

"When you love him, you love the Lord Jesus, you know." He squeezes my hands, gentle and firm as his brother, and releases them.

His intuition startles me, as does his next statement. "I know that my brother thinks of you dearly, Miss Edwards."

"He is dear to us all as well." Oh, how dear to me!

"I mean this, Miss Edwards. You are beloved to him." Then he adds quietly, as if to himself, "And I think I understand why."

Beloved. The word flutters through my mind but

will not roost in my heart. 'Tis not to be believed. Is it? I shake my head. "He has not said thus to me, Mr. Brainerd." Indeed, he has told me of another young woman who once captured his heart, though John must not know of her.

"He may not ever say so, and he has not said thus to me, either. Yet I know my brother, and I would wish for you to understand what is in his heart for you. It changes nothing in this world, of course, but I thought that you would wish to know, in case anything happens to me during my journeys and I could not tell you afterward. After David..." His voice trails off, and we both know what he means. "It may give you satisfaction in latter days," he finishes quietly.

It changes nothing, John Brainerd says. And yet it changes everything. Deep within my heart, a plant that grew in pain and then withered begins to grow once more. Yet 'tis shadowed by the grief of knowing what is to come, unless God answers the prayer I laid before Him several days ago in the cemetery.

We are quiet for a long moment, and then John moves as if he intends to accompany me back to the house. But the words dug deeply into my heart come forth from my mouth. "But your brother is dying."

John turns back to me, and our eyes meet, twin browns. "Aye, he is." He closes the few feet between us. "He is not afraid of death, Miss Edwards, and nor should we be." His gaze searches mine. "May I take the liberty to ask you this? Do you love my brother?"

I answer immediately, honestly, unashamed in the face of his complete sincerity. I feel that in John, as in David, my soul has met a true friend. "Aye, sir. I do love him. I have loved him a long while."

"I thought as much." A smile comes easily, naturally to his lips. "'Tis strange, you know, seeing the two of you pretending that neither means anything more than a brother or a sister to the other. Yet you do mean as much to him as he does to you – if not more. It gladdens my heart to know that God has provided your care and love for him in these last days.

"I would but ask that you love him completely, fully, without reservation, and do not hold him back from the arms of his Savior when He calls for him at last. Will you do this?"

In my mind, my hands, holding so tightly to the dream of Mr. Brainerd and myself together in this life, uncurl. I see that my love for Mr. Brainerd will require loving him enough to fully release him to his God and mine. But if I do this, what will be left inside my own heart, my own soul? Will loving him so unselfishly not strip me utterly? I breathe in deeply and release the air again. I swallow back the pain. "I will do it."

"Thank you." He looks down at the ground and then back up again at my face. "I have one more question for you, Miss Edwards, and 'tis one to which I do not require an immediate answer. Indeed, I do not wish for one."

What can he mean? I wait, listening intently.

"You know that I have taken my brother's place among the Indians at Cranberry."

I give a single nod. What has this to do with me?

"I have watched you all these days I have spent here, as well as heard of your journey with my brother to Boston. I know of your desire to see the Indian nations evangelized. I know that you are a woman of perseverance, courage, and – dare I say? – a significant amount of stubbornness." His usually-serious mouth tilts up into a half-smile like his brother's.

A laugh pops out of my mouth. "Thank you. I think."

"Godly stubbornness, of course," he clarifies, the smile lighting his eyes now. Then suddenly he grows serious – utterly so. "I believe that God has a purpose for each one of us, Miss Edwards, and I wonder if we might each find that ours may be supported by the other."

Can he mean what I begin to think he does? My pulse quickens, though not with love nor fear.

"I do not ask you for an answer now. As I said, I do not wish for one now. You love my brother, and he, you. That is as I would wish. David's comfort is most important at this time. And I do not pretend that my love for you holds the same human affection as his, though I am sure that in time, it will. Neither do I ask that your love for me duplicate that which you have for him. I ask only that you consider marrying me, coming to Cranberry or wherever else God may send me, as my companion and spiritual support."

His words have stricken me dumb. In the space of a few minutes, I have learned not only that David returns my affection, but also that John wishes to marry me, taking me with him into the wilderness not only as his wife but also as his fellow missionary.

The honor of it humbles me.

I do not love him as I love his brother. Could I ever do so?

Yet even as I ask myself this, I am sure that I could do as John asks, that I should, and that, perhaps, I shall.

***

Later, I run to fetch the cow from the common pasture, just as I did the day he arrived. Tears rise and bubble in my eyes, making me thankful for the dusk turning the meadow into a place for the fireflies to play and disguising my countenance.

I asked for the love of David Brainerd, and God has granted me my request, has he not? Yet, now that I possess this gift, how will I bear to lay it down when David releases his final breath?

Chapter Forty-Two

Mr. John Brainerd leaves for New Jersey, promising to return soon if at all possible. The entire Edwards family accompanies him to the gate, where one of the servants has readied his horse for him. In his uniquely quiet, appealing way, he thanks both Papa and Mama again for their hospitality, and then he turns to me.

"Miss Edwards." He gives a small bow of courtesy. "'Twas a pleasure to make your acquaintance. I think that you are a sister to us Brainerds all – a new Jerusha that God has seen fit to send us in His mercy." I know he refers to his cherished older sister's recent passing – his sister who shared my name. Then he adds, much more quietly, "I wish you could be a sister to me in truth. But perhaps there will be another kind of covenant between us one day, if God wills. I thank you for your kindness to my brother."

I stand at the gate, my arm through Mama's, watching as his horse canters away down the road, the dust curling in plumes around its dark hooves.

***

September 13, 1747

'Tis the Lord's Day, and I am attempting to keep my mind and heart much engaged with things above, but David's activity distracts me so that I have only set to memory a few verses in an hour. His new bedchamber – since his growing inability to climb the stairs – lies next to the sitting room in which a few of my sisters and I pass the time as we wait for the start of the afternoon exercises at church. Every few moments, I hear the scrape of the desk chair as he rises, followed by his excited pacing across the floor, then the re-scraping of the floor as he sits again. What is he doing that requires so much activity – activity that drains his strength? And on the Sabbath!

Distraction dissolves into worry, which holds dry kindling to the flame of my anger. Rising to my feet, I smooth down my skirt. "I am going to inquire after Mr. Brainerd," I announce.

Sarah sets down her book, *Pilgrim's Progress*. "Poor man, I should not think he will be able to attend the afternoon exercises, Jerusha. Why not simply allow him to rest?"

"That is precisely what I intend to insist upon," I half-growl, drawing a surprised glance from Sarah. I am not usually so forceful; that is Mary and Esther's work. Before she can say anything more, I stalk from the sitting room and march the few steps down the passage to his closed door.

I hear muttering within the chamber. My heart sinks with the heaviness of an anchor cast from a ship into the depths of the ocean. Has he descended into madness? Once or twice before, especially during the dark days in Boston, I have seen him become delirious, but he has only succumbed to that when at death's-door.

I clear my throat and knock my knuckles sharply against the wood – perhaps too sharply in my anger. "Mr. Brainerd?" I pause, then more quietly, say, "David. 'Tis I, Jerusha."

An obviously distracted, "Come," issues forth.

I lift the latch and push open the door. David sits at the little desk. Because of the pain in his lungs, he bends over like a moon nearly spent. His mouth hangs slightly open in order that he may draw in more breath, his neckcloth cast off so that his strained throat suffers as little constriction as possible. He does not turn when I enter but keeps scribbling away at the paper before him.

When he dips his pen for the third time into the ink-horn, I will wait no longer for him to speak. "We could hear your activity from the sitting room – all this scraping of your chair and pacing." I fold my arms across my chest to show the stubbornness of which his brother John spoke so well.

David scratches out the last bit of something and then dusts the whole thing liberally with sand to absorb the wet ink. Only then does he turn.

His face takes me aback and loosens my fighting stance. Though pale as a dead man's and thin with illness, it glows as if a candle of joy flames high within him. Not a joy resulting from seeing me – Indeed, when he sees the seriousness of my expression, his own sobers but remains blissful. Rather, his countenance shines as Moses' must have after he encountered the Lord God at the burning bush.

"Have I disturbed anyone?" he asks, his first question always one solicitous of others. His voice runs ragged and just above a whisper – a sure sign that he has over-exerted himself. "If so, I apologize."

I shake my head. "Nay, but do you not think that you should rest? 'Tis the Lord's Day, after all." Perhaps I can let guilt goad him into resting – into saving more days, possibly, for him to live – and for me to live in his presence.

"And what better day to do something for God,

Jerusha?" A wince of pain pins down the smile he offers me, as some lads pin down living butterflies. Most likely to distract himself from the knives piercing his lungs, he pushes himself to his feet. The chair scrapes the floor again, as well as my nerves. "I have been writing for some time now today, and, oh, how it delights me to do something for Him again! I have been ill for so long – unable to work – unable to be useful for Him with my body and sometimes even with my thoughts. The pain drives my mind even from prayer at times."

Disappointment with himself darkens his eyes. I hate to see it, but I also despise the physical agony I see him suffer. "Perhaps you should take Doctor Mather's advice," I suggest, yet I am unable to keep the hesitation from shadowing my own voice.

David stares at me for a long moment before comprehension dawns across his face. "You speak of the opiate," he mutters. His hand drops to the back of the chair and his knees shake where his breeches end. His knuckles turn deathly pale as he struggles for the strength to continue to stand.

The sight – and the fear it provokes – *I am losing him!* – gives me the courage to press my point. "It will help with your pain. Doctor Mather –"

"Means well," he interrupts me – a rare occurrence indeed. I must have surely tried his patience thin. He stares down at the floorboards, gaunt shoulders hunched beneath the thin bleached linen of his shirt – a shirt I myself have washed and hung out on the line to dry for him many times now, a shirt which I long to wash and hang out to dry many, many more times.

"I do not wish for you to be in pain," I say, without thinking. For when he is in pain, my own heart aches in sympathy. If possible, I feel it more now, after what his brother has told me of David's affection for me, than I did before.

He glances up, and I see the sudden fire settle to its glowing embers in his hazel eyes. "Pain is not an evil in and of itself. I think that sometimes the Lord God speaks to us most clearly in it, rather than in our times of sensual delight. Make no mistake: I bless the thorn that has driven me to my God, sweet Jerusha."

Did he intend to call me that? *Sweet.*

Without further display of emotion, he turns from me and eases himself into his chair once more. "I cannot take an opiate. It will dull my thoughts, my affections... It will kill all in one, just when I want them most, at the time of my death – when my Lord sends His chariot for me. I would not meet Him with a dull brain, a dull heart, a body dodging the pain He sent."

I cannot speak for the tears and anger that clog my throat. My fingers tighten until the nails grind into my palms. For, though I accept His will, do I not shrink back from the pain He has sent?

Without taking leave of him, I turn and go.

Chapter Forty-Three

When Mama asks who will fetch Mr. Brainerd to come to dinner the next day, I keep quiet.

My poor heart cannot endure any more.

When I stay speechless at Mama's request and continue to baste the mutton where the spit suspends it above the fire, I feel her questioning look directed at me. And no wonder, for I am always the first to rush to help Mr. Brainerd – so much so, that I have overheard Papa say to Mama that there is surely a peculiar bond betwixt our guest and myself. Never the most perceptive man with regard to human relationships, I am sure that Papa does not guess the nature of my feelings toward Mr. Brainerd. But does Mama? Perhaps. If so, she has never spoken a word of it.

"Mary," Mama instructs my younger sister, "go and fetch Mr. Brainerd for dinner."

Mary sits on the floor, playing peek-a-boo with our youngest brother. At Mama's command, she rises to her feet, stumbling over the hem of her skirt. "Come, Jonny-Jonny," she croons in a happy voice. "Come with Sister Mary." Picking him up, she kisses the toddler soundly on each of his round reddish cheeks and settles him snugly against her own aproned waist before trotting from the kitchen.

Mary's feet clatter away toward Mr. Brainerd's room. 'Tis but a moment before they clatter back again, and Mary reappears.

"He said that he may eat something later in his room if that is all right, Mama," she announces.

The touch of concern in my sister's tone worries me, as Mary is normally so carefree. "Does he feel well?" The question tumbles out of my mouth. And what a question.

Mary must think as much, for she gives me a puzzled look. "Of course he doesn't feel well. He has consumption, Jerusha. Mr. Brainerd is dying."

I say nothing more but turn my gaze back to the browned meat. 'Tis ready to pull from the fire, and I am glad for the task to distract my mind.

Again, from her chair where she sits nursing Elizabeth, Mama's gaze seeks me, but I refuse to meet it.

"Mary," Mama says in her steady, quiet way, "your sister meant to ask if our guest is any worse than he has been of late."

"Oh. Well, I do not know. He is writing now. He only said that he would take a little nourishment later in his room, perhaps."

He is writing now. Always, ever working! When he should be resting! Anger fans the fear that burns low in my chest and overcomes my reticence to step into David's room today. "Pray, will you see to the mutton, Esther? I will ask Mr. Brainerd if he has need of anything."

My younger sister takes over for me, but I do not miss the exchange of raised brows between her and Mary, nor the pity that softens their features. Mama lets me go without a word.

***

Sure enough, he sags against the headboard of his

ALICIA G. RUGGIERI

bed, a blood-smeared cloth at his side, a borrowed writing desk on his lap, and the little diary books spread across the coverlet.

I have grown to love and to hate those books – love, because they are David in words; hate, because they represent the price he has paid to become such a servant of God as he is.

Upon my entrance, he glances up with a worn-out smile, but the pen never stops its scratching and tapping. I say nothing but stare at him, feeling unable to keep from displaying my irritation.

"I told your sister that I would take a little something later, perhaps," he says, but this is followed by a retching cough.

In my distressed, angry fear, I refuse to go to his side but allow him to cough out the bloody mucus on his own. Cold emptiness spreads inside of me.

He is dying. And he has brought it upon himself.

I have been cheated, robbed.

If he truly loves me, as John testified, he would not have chosen to forsake me as he does now.

As the coughing ends, he seems to realize that I have not, as I always have before, come to his side to aid and comfort him. His gaze meets mine for a long moment. "Pray, what do you want from me, Jerusha? I see the disappointment in your glance. Surely, I have failed you in some way. But how? I wish I knew, that I might humble and correct myself." I see the tension in his face – the worry at having done some wrong.

But he has done nothing wrong – and everything. Nothing wrong in the eyes of God, surely – and everything wrong for the desire I have to see him well and whole and alive. I am disappointed, aye, but does the cause rest in David?

Or in myself, for being so weak in spirit?

Frustration bubbles up inside me at the words he

speaks. "You should not have gone to Boston in June," I blurt out. I am shocked at my own outspokenness. Usually, Mary is the one to say everything that is on her mind. "Even Papa thought so," I add, less hastily, so that he will not think I speak only from my own heart.

He frowns, and reserve enters his eyes. "Your father is a wise man, and I am indebted to him for all his kindness to me. But he knows that I will not be bound by others' mere wishes, though they are kind ones. I must go where God leads me and do whatever He tells me to do, no matter the cost. I was useful in Boston."

I ignore this and move toward the little table we have placed by his bed for a wash basin. "And the editing of those diaries... all the letters. They sap your strength, the little strength you yet have."

His brow lowers. "The editing of these diaries – the writing of these letters – mayhap God will make them useful, too, after my death."

Useful! Is that all he thinks about? I think of him sweating and delirious in Boston, dying for all we knew. I remember the anguish that clenched my heart like a hawk does a little bird, thinking that death would extinguish him there on that bed. Angry fear causes me to grip the wash basin tightly, feeling its porcelain edges bite into my hands. I stare into the reddish water, seeing the calmness of my reflection, so different from the turmoil I feel inside.

"You nearly died in Boston," I state blandly and turn toward the window. *You are dying now.* And yet he possesses no clinging to life – the clinging that I desperately want him to have. Throwing open the sash, I toss the contents of the basin onto the ground below. Then I stay there, letting the breeze caress my cheeks and dry the perspiration that has broken out on my neck. *Dear God, I do not question Thy will, but why must this man die? Why not choose another?*

There is a long silence. I choose to fill it. "'Twas too great a risk." Why do I do this? Even if he agrees with me, what good will it do now for him to admit that he should not have journeyed to Boston? Yet, somehow, I think the concession will ease my inner agony.

The ropes creak beneath his mattress. He must be rising. I cannot turn now. My eyes have moistened. I close my lids, pushing back the emotion and burying it deep in my bosom. 'Tis time to change the subject. I pull a deep breath into my lungs. "Never mind what I said. If you will not come to dinner, may I read to you so that you will stop working for a little while and rest? Perhaps from the Bible or –"

"Jerusha." The sound of his voice saying my name brushes over me. 'Tis spring sunlight touching the tops of the pine trees, making them a deeper and yet brighter green than they could ever be on their own.

I turn. "Aye," I reply brightly, as if nothing is wrong, wearing my customary smile, the one all the Edwards girls don.

He puts out a hand to use the window trim for support, and I see the bones and veins protruding beneath his flesh before my gaze flickers back to his face. And there, as always, his eyes capture mine.

Looking into them feels as though I look into another world. 'Tis as though I look into heaven. And the thought comes to me: *Surely the Lord Jesus Christ's eyes must have looked like David Brainerd's.*

I do not mean the color or shape or size or any of those outward things at all, of course. No, 'tis something other, something deeper. A light, a fire, a joy – and, aye, a sorrow as well. He is a man who has seen enormous pain and sacrifice and yet has seen something beyond the pain, too. Something that has made all the pain and sacrifice worth it.

"You want me to be content to outlive my usefulness? I cannot be so. I will not be so. The dearest prayer of my heart is that God will not allow me to outlive my usefulness to Him. My whole desire has been to be a flame for God. I would rather burn out than be extinguished." He says each word with precision, not unkindly but with utter firmness. "Why should I want to continue breathing and eating and talking if I can do nothing for God?"

"Would that not be better than death?" The turmoil roiling in my breast makes me nearly shout it at him, and I see the surprise I feel at myself echoed in his face. His hazel eyes clasp mine, searching. Feeling foolish, I look away from him, down into the yard below, and my fingers run across the windowsill. Perhaps that will drain away some of my anger, an anger I know is unwarranted.

He pauses a long moment. Then his answer comes, soft as a pigeon's wing. "Not for me, Jerusha. And not for you, either, though you may think it so now."

He does not understand. He yet thinks of me as that young girl he met years ago, and he thinks that I am afraid of my own death. But I am not. I can honestly say that I have no other wish for my own life but the will of God. And if that means that I should die, then so be it.

But him! I do not want him to die. I cannot believe that 'tis the will of God... I do not want that to be the will of God. The thought of David's death causes me more pain than the thought of my own.

Chapter Forty-Four

"His feet have swollen." Though he addresses Mama, Papa's low-voiced comment reaches my ears at dinner the next day. I sit beside little Eunice, helping to fill her plate with victuals. My heart sinks into a silent dark pool at Papa's words.

"Shall we send for Doctor Mather?" Mama asks as she spoons potatoes onto her own plate.

Papa shakes his head. "Nay, Mr. Brainerd says not."

Methinks that Mr. Brainerd does not know quite what is good for him – good for everyone. Good for me. Who knows if Doctor Mather might have some concoction that would help Mr. Brainerd live longer?

Let me burn out.

The words he so often has prayed in my presence echo in my mind. I press my jaws tightly together and try to smile back at four-year-old Eunice. He does not want to live if he can do nothing for God. He does not want to live for his own pleasure… nor for anyone else's. This last bit carries a bitter tang with it to my mouth. He does not want to live longer, even for me, whom his brother claims he loves, whom he himself called *sweet.* He wants only to enter into eternity.

And, when it comes to it, I cannot open my hands to let him go.

"He mentioned that he wished to see the younger children this evening, if it so suits you," Papa continues to address Mama.

Mama swallows the bite of food in her mouth. "Aye, that would be fine."

***

Later, Mama asks Sarah and me to usher the children into Mr. Brainerd's room, as he requested. I gather Eunice and Susannah from the sitting room, while Sarah, already carrying Elizabeth, goes to fetch Timothy and Lucy. We meet again in the passage and shepherd the little bunch down the narrow way. Eunice clings to my hand as we go. The autumn night has already begun to fall, and both Sarah and I carry a beeswax candle to light our way through the shadows. The honey scent fills the passage.

The chamber door stands open a crack, and I can see that David has taken to his bed. Perhaps the swelling of his feet frightened him enough to force him to rest. Papa stands beside him already, along with Mary and Esther, who holds Jonathan, but Mama is nowhere to be seen. Ah, there she is – tucking the coverlet down deep beneath the mattress so that it will not come undone in the night. Several candles extravagantly cast a warm glow through the small room.

The three older children crowd into the room readily enough, without us needing to urge them forward. Little Eunice retains her surprisingly strong grip of my hand, wordlessly asking me to go in with her. 'Tis understandable. She is accustomed to seeing Mr. Brainerd playful and well enough to at least sit up. To see him as he is now, perhaps as I saw him in Boston... I swallow hard and nod that I will go in with her. We both step forward into the circle gathering around David's bed.

259

I do not immediately look upon his face – His eyes have burned holes in me before, revealed all my secret fears to me with their light. I do not want to be a participant tonight – not in this deathbed utterance. I will only observe, and that reluctantly.

Mama finishes tucking the coverlet and takes a stand behind Lucy, her hands resting on my little sister's round shoulders. "Here are the children, Mr. Brainerd, as you requested."

He struggles to raise himself from reclining to sitting upright against the headboard. Papa immediately comes to his aid, placing hands beneath David's arm sockets and raising up his frail body with little effort. Mr. Brainerd's chest heaves as he settles back, his hands restlessly pulling the coverlet against his waist. "Children," he says, and a rattle shakes his voice. How has he worsened so much in such a short time? Was it not a few weeks past that he and I rode out every day together, him perhaps entertaining secret hopes of recovery and return to the Indians?

But these thoughts distract me from what he says now to my brother and sisters. Despite my initial reluctance to come here, I cannot help but be drawn to his words and to the heart that drives them, as I am always.

Now he holds a hand out toward Timothy, who quickly takes it, the child-heart in him responding to the child-man who sits upon the bed. "I have called you children here to urge you to follow true piety," he begins. "That is the most important thing in life. Timothy, these are the words of a dying man, you see; pay heed to what I say, I pray you."

My young brother draws his lower lip into his mouth. He is more somber than ever I have seen him. Nodding, he edges onto the side of the bed, turning his body so that he can look directly into this beloved man's eyes.

The painful lines in Mr. Brainerd's face soften into a sober smile of affection. He reaches out with his other hand and caresses Timothy's boyish cheek, and my heart throbs in response. What a father this man might have made!

"This is my last sermon. I shall die here, children. Here, in yonder burial ground, I shall be buried. Here, you will see my grave. I wish you to remember what I have said to you. Do not delay the great business of religion, thinking that you may put it off to such-and-such a time or that you may deal with the question of salvation later, when you are grown. The only thing that matters at all in life, at any time of life, is obtaining a true change of heart through believing in Jesus Christ and His atoning death. That alone is the righteousness that God honors – His own righteousness, and 'tis given to you through His Son. Do not rest in anything except obtaining that change of heart – a change of heart that leads to a life of true godliness."

He pauses and then reiterates, "Remember what I have said, when I am gone." He takes each of my younger siblings into his gaze and embraces them with his words.

"But where are you going, Mr. Brainerd? Are you going back to the Indians?" Eunice's bright high voice by my side startles me so that I flinch, bringing the eyes of all in the room to rest on me for a pinpoint of a moment before they turn back to the man on the bed, who answers her.

"Eunice, I am going to heaven to be with God now – to love Him and serve and please Him forever! I wish that I had a thousand lives to give in service to God, ministering in His service. If I had a thousand souls, if they were worth anything at all, I would give them all to God."

I steal a glance around the room, and find that even my sister Mary's usual bounciness has been tamed by his words. She stands beside Mama, utter seriousness cloaking her face, her hands folded against her blue petticoat.

Mr. Brainerd's eyes close, and he continues in a whisper, "But, when all is done, I have nothing to give to Him. 'Tis all of Him who gave His all for me!"

He sucks in a ragged breath. "Oh, my heart goes out to my burying place! It seems to me a place most to be desired. My death is sweet to me, the day of it a glorious day, for I go to be with my Savior and Friend. My soul and my flesh long for the courts of my God."

Now, of course, is the time when people usually tell the dying that they must not give up hope of recovery, that they must fight their illness with all the power that God gives them. But how shall I, or any one of us, say such a thing to this man, whose face blooms with the fierce desire for death, for 'tis only through dying that he will truly live? I hold back the stubborn appeal that rises up in my heart, ashamed to hold him back when he would go forward.

Chapter Forty-Five

When I pass David's room again later, the crack in the door shows me that his candle yet burns. The wood beneath my feet creaks as I hurry past the door on my way to the stair.

"Jerusha? Is that you?" The voice, weak yet still sinewy, comes from behind the door.

My heart leaps up, caught in a bramble of fear and yearning. He must need something. I hesitate. "Are you not asleep, Mr. Brainerd?" Surely, after the long conversation he had with my family, he must be worn to shreds.

I stand there for a moment in the dim passage, holding my candle with both hands, waiting for him to call a goodnight to me. But instead, the door opens by his own hand, revealing his dear face, pale and tired but smiling gently through the pain that clutches his body. His eyes appear to warm when they meet mine, though I don't know why they should, considering our last confrontation over his stubborn insistence on continuing his work.

I lower my head. "Do you need anything? Something..." But the words dissolve on my lips, when David's weak hands suddenly cover mine.

"'Tis you I want." He says it clearly, surely, and quietly. He means it for my ears only, yet he speaks without furtiveness; there would be no shame if anyone else were to hear. "Jerusha." He speaks my name in the same way he speaks of his desire for death, the grave, and heaven. To him, I am sure, our relationship will always be first and foremost spiritually-based – the kind of relationship I wonder if my father had in mind when he wrote that private paragraph about my mother, even before they began courting – the words, written in his plain hand, that I have read more than once in the endpapers in one of Mama's books.

His hands drop from where they cover mine, and I feel the loss of their warmth on my skin. "Come, pray with me now, if it pleases you. And then I will tell you more of my story, if you wish."

I nod, and one of the walls around my heart that I have been steadily reinforcing in recent days shakes. How can I refuse him? I long to pray with him – to hear his steady, sometimes weeping voice beseech God for the spirit of Elijah to come upon the Church and its ministers, as he prayed often when he first came among us. Wordlessly, I follow him into his bedchamber, leaving the door open a handbreadth behind us.

Beside the rumpled bed, he bends to his knees, his engorged, bare feet splayed behind him. I have half-a-mind to tell him that he should not strain his body so, that God will not mind if he sits or lies down while we pray. But, then, I do not think that a man who once prayed out-of-doors all day on his knees while the snow mounded nearly to his neck will hearken to my word of caution. If I have learned anything in these past months at his side, David Brainerd is not a man of worldly prudence but one of reckless abandonment to God.

So I drop to my knees beside him, my skirt billowing and then settling around me. David stays silent, his head bowed low on the bedcover, for a long time – so long that I open my eyes and glance over at him, wondering if he is all right. The look on his face captivates me: Intense wonder and longing surface there. What is he seeing in his inner communion with God that so delights him? What spiritual joys bring this bliss to his soul? Can I know them? And can I make what sacrifice they require?

And then, when he prays aloud, he speaks of awakening in the Church – that God would bring the nations in, that Christ might see the satisfaction of His soul. He ends, as always, with the desire that, "we might not outlive our usefulness."

The tenderness in Mr. Brainerd's prayer softens something in my own heart – melts some of that hardness that has made it difficult for me to pray as I ought in recent days, since hearing from John of David's love for me, since knowing that the return of my own love was assured... and yet denied me. Thus, when I take up where David's prayer left off, I find myself relenting, trusting, and allowing the Holy Spirit room to speak through me instead of trying to find the words to speak myself. I unbutton my heart before God and let Him search it. Mr. Brainerd's manner has awakened some sense in me that perhaps... perhaps, God will do right and good for me, for us, despite not answering my years-long prayers.

That His will is not simply for His glory, but for our good because He delights in us.

I have never prayed thus with any person, and when my heart has emptied itself, I stay quiet for a few moments longer, waiting. The presence of a holy God fills the space that emptied – and not merely a *holy* God, but also a loving God, a merciful God, a God whom all the theologians at Harvard and Yale may attempt to explain but will find themselves unable to do so. A God who longs for us to experience His holiness, His love, and His mercy toward us.

At last, we rise to our feet, still silent, but with a strong sense of peace filling the room. Mr. Brainerd trembles a bit as he unbends his knees and grips the bedpost, his knuckles white. When I look down, I see that his bare feet have swollen even more, puffy as over-risen bread dough and discolored.

The breath catches in my own lungs as I grasp his elbow to give him support. The weight of his body rests on me, a weight heavy as the sorrow that has clung to my heart these past weeks and months. The end is coming. And yet...

Can I trust Him?

Of course – He is trustworthy. I know this as fact. Yet my heart quivers with dread still, despite our peaceful, unexpected time of prayer that ended just moments ago. I remember my sister's words: *You are falling in love with a dead man. There is no hope for this to end well for you.*

From the recesses of my memory, Another's words also come and with them, hope: *Though the fig tree does not blossom, though there is no fruit on the vine, yet I will rejoice in God my Savior.*

In that moment, I continue to make the choice I began to make long ago. *I believe Thee, Lord God my Father. I believe that Thou art good. I not only want Thy will, but I believe Thee now. Though my heart aches, I want to believe; help my unbelief!*

Does David see the trouble flash through my countenance, followed by the calming rain of faith? I do not know. He gives no indication that he knows the depth of the storm that has risen within me since his coming to Northampton. Now, he moves toward the edge of the bed, his neck shining with perspiration, whether from the warmth of the house or the progress of his disease, I do not know.

"May I impart to you more of my story, Jerusha?" he asks, settling back against the headboard. His movements are careful, as if he is afraid of jarring his body. "I will not prolong its telling."

I open my mouth to say, nay, he should sleep. "Aye." The word slips from my tongue, from my heart. "I would like to hear it, if you feel able."

His smile answers me, and I sit down on the chair beside his bed.

Chapter Forty-Six

Spring 1744

"Whoa, there." The rider exerted gentle pressure on the reins. His horse, well-trained to command and eager to stop the continual march forward through dimly-lit forests, halted without argument. Sucking in a deep breath that brought on a wet cough, David stopped to look around him, tremors rivering through his body.

He had arrived at the Indian town of Minisink, not his eventual destination, which was further west, but well along the way. Wigwams spread out before him, made of frames of bent branches covered with either hide or bark. From the holes pocking the center of their roofs, smoke rose lazily into the moist forest air.

Depression fell over David's spirit, quick and heavy as a winter sunset. Who was he to talk to these Indians? Why should they listen to him? *I am nothing. I am no one. I am less than a dog.* The thoughts pursued him as he dismounted and tied his horse's reins to a low-hanging branch. He closed his eyes. *I am Thy servant, Lord. Use me.*

He forced himself not to add, *if Thou can.*

His arrival had excited interest. When he turned back from securing his horse, he found several villagers approaching him. Among them was a middle-aged man to whom the others seemed to show great honor. *He must be their king.*

***

Sometime later, determination strengthened David's feet and put bravery into his heart as he strode toward the wigwam. The Indian king might turn away from him and laugh at the idea of the Christian God, but David would pursue him.

He refused to let himself hesitate at the entrance, no matter how much his knees might quail within his breeches. Bending his tall body, he pushed aside the skin covering the wigwam's entrance and stepped inside.

The murmuring of voices quieted, and once David's eyes adjusted to the dimness, he saw that the king stared at him from across the enclosed space. For a long moment, David could not tell whether the man was truly angered or simply shocked at this white man's persistence. The two had engaged in friendly conversation outside – ending when David had acknowledged that he wished to tell the king about Christ. The king had laughed and turned his back on David before retreating to his wigwam.

Now, standing before the wide-eyed, stone-faced leader, David sought to calm his pounding heart. *His heart is in Thy hands, O Lord. Turn it in whatever way Thou wishes.*

"May I speak with you once more, sir?" David asked.

"About what? Christianity?" Minisink stood at a trail intersection, and the king had evidently found the benefit of learning the languages of those with whom he and the other villagers traded. David could understand the man's English, though 'twas heavily accented.

"Aye."

The king snorted. Not another word emerged from his mouth as he turned his entire body until his back faced David. For a moment, disappointment sank like a heavy stone on the water of David's spirit.

Then, on another hide rug beside the king, a man – surely an advisor – gestured to David to sit.

"Why do you desire that the Indians become Christians?" the advisor asked as soon as David took a seat, cross-legged on the other side of the small fire that burned in the center of the wigwam.

David's heart lifted to hear this question. He opened his mouth to reply.

But the advisor continued. "Why, when Christians are so much worse than the Indians are? Christians lie, steal, and drink. Much worse than the Indians."

David felt the hope drain from him as the man made his argument.

"'Tis these Christians who taught us to become drunk. 'Tis they who steal so much that their rulers must hang them for it. We Indians do not do such things. Perhaps if the Indians become Christians, they will become as bad as the white man."

His dark eyes met David's hazel ones. "Nay, we will not become *Christians*." He said the word as though it tasted moldy. "We will live as our fathers lived, and we will go where our fathers went when they died. Better by far that than to become as those around us who say they are Christians."

The realization turned bitter in David's belly: What the man said was often true of the white people with whom these Indians traded. Tears welled in his eyes. How could he convince this man that not all who called themselves Christ's were His? How could he explain the deception that plagued the white as well as the

Indian understanding of what a Christian truly was?

He tried. As the afternoon sun spent itself, David explained the necessity of rebirth to the man. Yet the advisor remained skeptical. *And no wonder. He has seen so many so-called Christians lie and steal and cheat and drink and encourage the Indians to do so.*

"Will you be my friend?" David asked as he took his leave at last.

The advisor looked at him sharply. "Only if you do not desire your friends to become Christians."

***

He rode onward from Minisink toward the Forks, taking the Old Mine Road. Behind his saddle, a bag contained nearly all he had allowed himself to keep in this world. He had disposed of all his clothes and worldly goods before taking the westward trail.

As he rode farther into the wilderness, the settlements and homesteads – all Dutch – grew ever more remote from one another. His illness increased. His bowels emitted bloody diarrhea, and his lungs coughed scarlet mucus. The rain poured, soaking his coat, shirt, and skin breeches. Beneath his tricorn hat, his hair dripped rivulets of water and feverish sweat down his neck. At such times, hanging over the pommel of his saddle as his horse's hooves jostled his weak body, eternity appeared so near that he could have reached out a hand to touch it.

Oh, dear God, go with me! I cannot go alone into this howling wilderness. My soul sinks within me. Again and again, the words of the king and his advisor at Minisink returned to his mind, and with them, desolation and hopelessness. David reminded himself of the prophets and Christians of times gone by – of how they had lived alone in caves and in scorpion-infested deserts. They had persevered.

The longing for God's presence burned through his soul, as the stars above his head burned through the darkness. *If Thou goest not with me, I cannot go. Enable me to take courage in Thee!*

The Spirit of God empowered him to set his face like flint. He urged his horse onward. There was no time to be wasted with a battle for eternal souls hanging in the balance.

He would reach the Indians at the Forks, or, as the Indians called the place, *Lakhauwotung,* if it killed him.

Chapter Forty-Seven

Jerusha

"You reached them at last," I say.

His eyes meet mine in peaceful joy. "Aye."

"And God poured out His Spirit." The wonder of this – the conversion of souls and Mr. Brainerd – my Mr. Brainerd – being the instrument of it fills my heart with joy.

"Aye, but, if you recall from my *Journal,* He did not bring it right away. He brought it in the time of His good pleasure, not mine. Then I found that the time of His pleasure was also the time of mine, in truth."

Chapter Forty-Eight

1744-1745

David spent a full year among the Indians at Lakhauwotung. He preached to not only the Lenni-Lenape, but also to any whites in the area – Dutch and Irish who lived as though there was no God in heaven who loved and had died for them.

He was utterly alone – one missionary, called by God, sent by the Scotch Society, but completely solitary and without guidance.

He engaged an Indian interpreter, a yet-unconverted man named Moses Tattamy, and began to translate prayers into Unami, the dialect of the Lenni-Lenape.

Yet the work's success appeared dark to him, and his depression pressed him as a heavy, immovable weight, even as he wondered, blindly, if God might do something wonderful among these Indians.

***

On the last day of June, David knelt before God, alone in the room he rented from the Hunter family in the tiny white settlement. Though the log room was small, David felt deep relief to find that he would have a private place to which he could retreat and spend time alone with God. He spread his Bible out on the hide rug, finding that the words printed on the pages before him matched those in his weary soul:

O my God, incline thine ear, and hear; open thine eyes, and behold our desolations, and the city which is called by thy name: for we do not present our supplications before thee for our righteousnesses, but for thy great mercies. O Lord, hear; O Lord, forgive; O Lord, hearken and do; defer not, for thine own sake, O my God: for thy city and thy people are called by thy name.

His heart groaned within him. How the prophet Daniel's agony for the Israelites matched those of David's own heart! *For thine own sake, O my God! Do not defer.*

The tears dripped from his eyes onto the rug. He wiped them away with a roughened hand before continuing to read:

And whiles I was speaking, and praying, and confessing my sin and the sin of my people Israel, and presenting my supplication before the Lord my God for the holy mountain of my God;

Yea, whiles I was speaking in prayer, even the man Gabriel, whom I had seen in the vision at the beginning, being caused to fly swiftly, touched me about the time of the evening oblation.

As the sea when Jesus walked upon it, David's soul calmed. The ears of his heart listened.

And he informed me, and talked with me, and said, O Daniel, I am now come forth to give thee skill and understanding. At the beginning of thy supplications the commandment came forth, and I am come to shew thee; for thou art greatly beloved: therefore understand the matter, and consider the vision.

The veil over his eyes tore. God had called his servants to wrestle in prayer in the past, whenever He wanted to give them any great mercy. *O God, I am ready to wrestle with Thee, if only Thou wilt bless this great work!*

***

And wrestle David did. The task before him – the conversion of the Indians – seemed impossible, but as he stepped forward in prayer and preaching, God enlarged his soul and his faith. He found himself enabled to cry out to God on behalf of the Indians, even when all his feelings told him that to do so was useless. *'Tis impossible for me, but 'tis not so for Thee, O God!* The statement came to his lips over and over again during that year.

Even as his spirit seemed to strengthen, his body grew ever weaker and his illness grew worse. He woke from sleep exhausted still and, more debilitating than that, with a fresh sense of his own inability and sinfulness. Before he could begin to work in prayer for the Indians, he fell down before God to confess his own sins each day.

Slowly, slowly, the distractions of this life melted away as he continued to work, going from place to place, from village to village. He refused to stop, regardless of whether he saw any fruit. His melancholy deepened so greatly that he sometimes wished for death to relieve him of his sufferings. Yet, in prayer, his very bones still cried out that God would get Himself a name among these heathen. He found that he had come to prefer Him above any joy this earth could afford – Everything else paled in comparison to Him, as the candlelight shrivels into nothing before the bold rising sun.

Chapter Forty-Nine

Jerusha

Mr. Brainerd coughs, and the sound rings harsh against the soft night. I rise swiftly to my feet and pour a drink from the pitcher.

He sips at it, and relief spreads through my body as the cough lessens and fades away. After draining the remaining water, he hands the cup back to me, our fingers brushing in the exchange, yet he is so intent on finishing his story that he does not seem to notice.

"Deep in that wilderness, God enabled me to abandon myself entirely to Him and made me find that every true joy could be found in Him. Every joy that this world promises is nothing when seen in the light of His face." He pauses and looks at me a long moment. "And yet, every innocent joy that He gives us, when laid at His feet, grows deeper and more beautiful than it could ever have been by itself."

Chapter Fifty

Forks of the Delaware/Westward
1745

At last, David found that he no longer cared where or how he lived or what hardships he went through, if only he could gain souls for Christ. When his eyes shut in sleep, he dreamed of this. When he awoke each morning, his first thought was of the conversion of the Indians. As he persevered in prayer, he began to experience freedom from sin such as he had never known. God assisted him in his prayers and made them fervent.

As David went among the Indians, he pleaded with them not to fear the conjurers among them, who threatened all who showed interest in Christianity. With his heart pounding in his chest, David put himself entirely in God's hands for safety and deliverance and challenged all the powers of darkness to do their worst upon him. He told his Indian people that he was a Christian and asked them why the pow-wows could not succeed in bewitching him.

Chapter Fifty-One

Jerusha

I suck in my breath at the images swirling in my brain. "That was very courageous of you."

David grows solemn. "I hope that you understand: I did not do it from my own pride or in carelessness. Rather, I saw that the honor of God was concerned. I desired it to be preserved for the testimony of the divine power and goodness and the truth of Christianity – that God might be glorified, loved, and adored by the Indians."

"And did anything happen? Did any harm come to you?"

He shakes his head. "Nay. God did not permit them to harm a hair of my head. And because of that bold stand, God, by His grace, brought about encouraging signs among the Indians at Lakhauwotung – and even farther westward. Yet in the midst of all this, I still longed for the Spirit of God to be poured out on them richly, not only in these drips and drops."

He falls silent. When he speaks again, his voice dips low with emotion. "Sometimes, God brings us the satisfaction of our heart's desire at the time or the place when we least imagine that He will do so. That was the case for me, not only in regard to the Indians, but I begin to see in other ways as well."

Chapter Fifty-Two

June 1745

The end of his eighty-mile ride drew near; he could see the clearing toward which he had directed his horse for the past few days. Yet David's chest felt as though stones had been laid upon it – stones of doubt, disappointment, and fear of failure.

Failure again.

What had he accomplished in the past year among the Indians at the Forks? *Nothing of significance.* There had been no conversions, save that of Tattamy and his wife. No prospect of a great work of God being done seemed to loom ahead. God had not blessed his work, it seemed, with a special display of power, as he had expected. Even David's journeys farther west had met with heartache, illness, and disaster, including the death of his treasured and valuable horse. David's jaw still trembled as he relived the dark day on the trail: feeling his horse stumbling beneath him, hearing the snap of its leg buckling and breaking... and then David himself having to put a bullet through the poor beast's head before continuing toward the mysterious westward villages on foot. He had replaced the horse eventually, but the question of why God would not bless his efforts fully – indeed, seemed to engineer events to impede David's success – haunted him.

Why, O God? Why dost Thou not bless these Indians with an outpouring of Thy Spirit? Only Thou canst do anything to open the eyes of the blind, to heal the ears of the deaf. O God, pour out Thy Spirit! Enlarge Thy kingdom for Thy glory, not that anything should come to me from it.

The horse's body shifted beneath David as he brought his mount to a halt and let his eyes survey the Indian village at Crossweeksung – if it could be called a village. A few hide-walled huts with lazy drifts of smoke emerging from their domes scattered across the clearing before him. A lone woman sat near one of the wigwams, using a pestle to mash something in a wooden bowl. A baby hung at her breast, nursing, as she worked.

A cough bubbled up from David's chest. At the sound of it, the woman became as alert as a deer startled in the forest. Her dark eyes shot upward, and, when she saw David, she scrambled to her feet in one fluid movement, disturbing her nursing baby.

"What do you want?" she asked across the clearing. Her words held a hard edge.

Relief spread through David at hearing the words spoken in English. Though he had learned some of the Delaware Indian dialect while at the Forks over the past year, he still relied heavily upon an interpreter when he preached or translated. For the first time in many days, hope lifted his mouth into a true, though small, smile.

Taking his Bible from his saddlebag, David dismounted and began to walk toward the woman, very slowly. He did not wish to frighten her, as her past experiences with white men may have gone ill. "I have come to tell you about Christ," he said.

Clutching her wailing baby against her deerskin tunic, the woman only stared at David, but he took courage because she did not retreat to her hut.

He stopped when he was a few feet away from her and held his Bible out in both hands. Blood pulsed through his veins. His mind quieted. *Oh, God, only Thou canst give success. Open her heart.* "I wish to talk with you about God's salvation. I wish to teach you what God says in His Book."

The baby's cries quieted to whimpers as its mother rested her hand on the little one's head. The woman's eyes traveled from David's face to the Bible he held toward her. A long silence stretched between them.

She broke the quiet with a shout in her own tongue, so loud that David jumped and his Bible nearly tumbled from his hands. As he regained his composure, he saw the hide covering another wigwam's doorway lift away. Two more women, one just less than middle-aged and another bent and elderly, emerged from the dim interior. Together, they ambled toward David, mild curiosity lighting their eyes. From the shade of the oaks surrounding the village, another very young woman stepped toward him. David realized that she had been invisible to him, standing so silent and motionless beneath the trees. She, too, held a baby in her arms.

The first woman he had met gave another call, and several gangly-limbed children, boys and girls, materialized from the forest around them. Cautiousness ruled over the curiosity in their lean faces. This "village" fringed a large white town, and so David knew that the sight of him by itself was no oddity to these Indians, many of whom lived by trading and selling handicrafts to their white neighbors. However, the sight of a man who wished to speak with them in their own village, seemingly not to profit from them – that was not as usual.

Despite the way that the few Indians gathered

around him, David sought to quell the hope rising in his heart. Others, including Indian converts, had come to speak with the Crossweeksung Indians in the past. They had been utterly rebuffed. *Why do I think this time will be any different?*

He sucked a breath into his panging lungs. He had no reason to suppose it would be so. But he had a God who moved mountains. Perhaps He would move the mountain of unbelief that rested in the hearts of these Indians yet.

Glancing to-and-fro, he spotted a large tree-stump near the middle of the clearing. He stepped onto it and turned to see the few Indians, all women and children, drawing into a semi-circle around him. His heart beat fast. He had no interpreter, only the hope that whatever English these women knew would prove enough for them to understand the gospel he preached.

For 'twas this gospel whereby they could obtain eternal life in Christ.

***

An hour or more later, David felt the strength drain from him as quickly as wine from a skin pierced through with a knife. In the middle of a sentence, his lungs seized. *Not now. Not now!*

But the coughing would not be stopped. As he gagged, he realized that the first woman to whom he'd spoken stood at his elbow. She held out a cup of water. Sinking down on the stump, he took the cup from her with shaking hands. "I thank you," he said between coughs.

Oh, God, strengthen me. All through his talk, he had seen openness on the faces of these Indians such as he had never before beheld – even on those of the children. *Let me finish well.* He drained the cup and began to speak again – of God's just wrath, of His love for sinners, of His Son who died for their redemption, and of the eternal life available through Him.

At last, David knew that he could speak no longer. Rising on trembling legs, he hoped that his knees would not give way before he reached his horse.

"When will you come again?" the first woman asked. Her baby nestled against her, playing with the shell necklace she wore. "We wish to hear more of this Christ."

Joy clogged David's throat for a moment. He swallowed and made no attempt to keep the smile from overtaking his face. "I will come again tomorrow if you wish."

The woman nodded. "That is good. Our people here are scattered in many small places. We will go now and tell others to come to hear you. What you say is good news to us. My heart cries out when I hear you."

He watched for a moment as she went to the other women, urging them to rise. She turned back to David once more as the little group began to hurry from the clearing. "We will go to tell others now and bring them back here."

David nodded, awed at how she, like the woman of Samaria, was so eager to bring others to hear of Christ. Then his knees nearly gave way as exhaustion overtook him again. He stumbled toward his horse, tied to a low-hanging tree branch, and slung himself into the saddle with difficulty.

"For you."

He looked down to find the woman there again, her dark eyes now shining with tears. He had not heard her coming across the pine-needle-blanketed forest floor. She held out an object about the size of her palm, wrapped in leaves. "For strength. Eat it."

David took it from her and unwrapped it, wondering with trepidation what would be inside its green covering. Two pieces of dark reddish dried meat lay there, heavy on his palm. Probably dried bear meat or venison. 'Twas difficult for David to tell the difference by sight alone. He raised it to his mouth and tore off a bite with his teeth. Bear meat, most definitely.

"I thank you." He smiled at her.

She stood silent for a moment, gazing up at him with unblinking eyes. Then, in a flash of movement that would have awakened envy in a rabbit, the woman turned and fled after the rest of the little group of women and children.

***

The women did return with their friends the next day, and David, though still worn in body, spoke to them again. Over the next days and weeks, refreshment poured over his soul as he saw the fruit of his labor budding and ripening as, day after day, and sometimes twice-a-day, he preached to these Indians of the way of salvation in Christ and saw conviction pierce their hearts. Many wept openly and prayed aloud as they sought to repent and take hold of Christ.

As time passed, David felt that he should visit the Indians at the Forks again. After all, the Scotch Society had not sent him to the Indians at Crossweeksung, but to those at the Forks. Yet he found himself torn, fearful that the impressions of the gospel would wear off in his absence.

When he took leave of the Indians at Crossweeksung, assuring them that he would return if at all possible, several of the little congregation that had formed came up to him after he preached to them a final time.

Tears ran down the cheeks of one woman as she faced David. His heart panged as she sought to calm herself enough to speak. Wiping at her eyes with one hand, she pushed her gray-streaked hair away from her face, utterly unconcerned with how broken and vulnerable she appeared.

"What troubles you, my dear woman?" David asked softly, though he knew the answer.

She drew a shuddering breath. "I wish... I wish..." She could not continue for the tears choking her voice.

David enfolded her wrinkled hand in his. "What is it, *ánati*?" he asked again, using the affectionate, familial term for "mother."

She raised her deep brown eyes to meet David's. "I wish God would change my heart." The words came out in a cracked whisper.

How he remembered the pain of knowing that his own heart needed to be remade, all those years past! And how faithful God was to the broken-hearted, to those who knew their true need would be met in His Son, who repented and submitted to Him as their Savior and God!

"Fly to Jesus. He will save you." David pressed her hands gently one last time and turned to the next person waiting to speak to him.

'Twas the old chief. He sagged, head bent over his crouched knees, on a log, thick with green moss. David sat beside him and listened as the man told him in a voice dense with tears how he wished to be saved.

As David spoke with the chief, God put into his heart the hope that He who has begun a good work among these Indians would carry it on to completion, whether David must return to the Forks or not. Though he had passed through so many nearly-fruitless labors, though his hope had been so often frustrated, though his success had been so little in the past, yet here at Crossweeksung, God had shown him that only He could bless David's work. Only He could make it succeed. David learned by experience that only He could open the ears, open the minds, and turn the hearts of these poor, prejudiced pagans to hear the Word of the Lord – these Indians whom he had already come to love with a love that could only come from the Father.

And so he left all in God's hands and returned to the Indians at the Forks.

Chapter Fifty-Three

Jerusha

"But you did not stay among them for long," I say when Mr. Brainerd pauses. I have read this part in his public *Journal*, but how interesting to hear it again from his own lips.

Mr. Brainerd swallows against the cough that threatens to interrupt him. "I stayed at the Forks of the Delaware for about a month. At that time, my interpreter and his wife both gave a public profession of their faith in Jesus Christ. Since his conversion, this middle-aged man had changed in every way. He could not give any distinct views he had of Christ or any clear account that he had accepted Him – which was somewhat unsatisfactory to me – but he knew that he had passed from death into life. And 'twas as though he had become a new man – his conversation, his deportment, were all altered, so much so that even those in the distracted world around him could not help but see such a change in him. I wept at Tattamy's baptism. 'Twas a taste of heaven."

Chapter Fifty-Four

1745

David returned to Crossweeksung about a month after he had left. He found that the Indians had taken his parting advice and gone to see William Tennant, a nearby minister and a friend of David, when they had any questions. Tennant had given the Indians good help, and David's joy overflowed as he saw that the Indians' longings after Christ had continued in his absence.

Over the next few months, the Crossweeksung awakening, which had sprung seemingly out of nowhere and for which David had not looked, grew. One day, forty would come to listen to his preaching. The next day, there would be fifty. Those who came wept bitterly and cried aloud in an agony of soul, longing to gain an interest in Christ. The more he talked to them of the love and compassion of God in sending His Son to suffer for the sins of men, the more David invited them to come and partake of His love, the more their distress was aggravated. They felt themselves unable to come – and yet yearned to do so. David spoke with tenderness, not with terror, yet the sharp arrow of the gospel pierced their hearts.

And slowly, one by one, the Indians obtained assurance that Christ would indeed forgive them and give them a clean heart. Those who obtained comfort and salvation in Christ went to many others, inviting them to give up their hearts to Him.

Meanwhile, David labored without rest – preaching and counseling the members of his little flock individually, eventually building a wigwam among the Indians so that he could dwell among them. Not many months before, David had nearly given up on God using him in any way. He knew that he was worthless, that his heart was foul before Him in and of himself. But God began to show him that this work was not about David Brainerd. The work was not to come from a mortal man. Yet because David was weak, He could show His strength through David. David had found that he was only a very common vessel, yet God could pour out His grace from him, if he was willing.

At last, God had given David what his soul craved: He gave him the souls of the Indians.

Once, David had thought that God would use him to revive the churches of New England.

But then God – in His sovereign and loving plan – did not act according to David's foolish desires, his own plans. Instead, He sent him into the howling wilderness. He sent him among a people that many despised and thought should not even have the gospel given to them.

And, as David stood preaching from his forest pulpit, he knew that he would not trade it for ten thousand lives spent otherwise.

***

The young woman had come among his little flock only to mock them. From his place atop the tree-stump, David could clearly see the derision lying in every twist of her full lips, each squint of her narrowed eyes. A tall youth began to weep noisily as David continued to read the Scripture passage aloud. At this, the newcomer burst into laughter and said something in her own language.

Anger bit sharply into David's heart, but he rebuked himself immediately. *She does not know what she does.* Keeping his focus upon his message, he moved from the Scripture passage into his sermon.

A few minutes into it, he noticed that the bursts of laughter had died away. As his gaze swept over the little congregation, he saw that the newcomer's face had sobered. Her lips now trembled, and, as she met David's eyes, her eyes filled with liquid.

She appeared frozen in place, unable to stop the streams of tears that ran down her round cheeks. After a moment of silent weeping as David continued to preach, the young woman fell to the ground, crying out incessantly. An Indian near her tried to help her to sit, but the young woman seemed to be unable to do so. Her face pressed to the ground, she groaned and cried aloud.

David finished preaching and, as the congregation dispersed into groups for further prayer and encouragement, he approached the young woman. She still lay flat upon the earth, her tears dampening the ground beneath her head.

"I tried to speak with her, but she would not speak," a member murmured as David passed him.

David glanced at the man and then back at the weeping woman. Wonder overtook his soul as he knelt beside her, ready to help her with words if she required it, ready to play the midwife to the heart God must birth in her.

"*Guttummaukalummeh wechaumeh kmeleh Nolah.*"

She was praying, David realized.

"*Guttummaukalummeh wechaumeh kmeleh Nolah,*" she said again, her tears blurring the words.

Have mercy on me, and help me to give Thee my heart.

***

His work continued among the Crossweeksung Indians. At times, the spiritual fires quieted, and David grew concerned lest the work all be for nothing. Yet, always, they would burst aflame again.

And, always, David remained at the task God had set before him, on guard against false impressions that sometimes came with a time of awakening, but striving, too, to stay alert to unusual workings of the Spirit.

***

One night, deep in the month of December, an old woman hobbled into his hut, led by one of those who had come to rebirth early in David's time among the Indians at Crossweeksung. Her feet, clad in leather, shuffled across the hide rugs. Her eyes, clouded, squinted from a face drooping with wrinkles, set atop shoulders bowed by many years.

David rose from where he had been sitting on a skin. Muffling a cough with his arm, he took the woman by her hand. "Good evening, *ánati*," he said. "Do you wish to speak with me?"

"She is a little deaf, Mr. Brainerd," said the man who had led the old woman into David's hut. "You will have to speak loud."

David smiled and cleared his throat, barely hiding the wince it elicited. "Come," he nearly shouted, drawing the woman toward the smoldering fire burning in the center of his hut. Its smoke trailed upward toward the hole in the roof. "Sit with me."

The woman shuffled along, clinging to his hand with her thin-skinned, cool one. Once they sat by the fire, he asked again, "Do you wish to speak with me? About Christ?"

The man who had brought her piped up, "She has had a dream, Mr. Brainerd."

Uneasiness prickled up David's spine. Dreams, visions, trances... These could so easily be from the evil one, appearing as an angel of light. "How did this happen?" He continued to look at the old woman, who appeared very childish in her understanding, but addressed the man.

"She heard some of us talking about the Narrow Way, sir, and she suddenly fell down as though asleep and began to dream. Ask her what she saw. She will tell you."

Oh, Lord God, protect us from Satan's delusions! With a twisted stomach, David asked the woman to tell him what she had seen.

In a very simple way, with the man interpreting, the woman told him: She had dreamed of two paths, one broad and one narrow. As she had followed the narrow path uphill, she had come to a gate. As she had prepared to climb over the gate, she had woken.

"And now, she says, how does she come to Christ? How does she get over the gate?" finished the man.

Gladness filled his voice as David told her about the One who is the Way.

In the days and weeks that followed, David saw that the woman's experience of salvation produced a real, lasting change in her character and actions. There was no doubt about it in David's mind: Would the Spirit of God use such visions and dreams? Would He speak to a broken, old Indian woman in a way she could understand, to lead her to seek salvation in Christ?

David knew now that He would.

***

How strange it was! David Brainerd, who had once thought so much of the opinion of men, was now content to be stared at and mocked by some of the white people. These people came out of curiosity to hear what the babbler would say to the poor, ignorant Indians. Yet God did a work in them also, His words sometimes piercing them as they stood by, gaping and laughing.

Yet as the eternal flourished, the earthly continued to wither. David's body grew weaker until he thought his death drew near. But he had long ago determined that to gain his life, he must lose it. He had already counted the cost.

He had counted it through the many days of fasting.

He had counted it through the long nights of prayer.

He had counted it when he had lost his way so often in the forests and slept out-of-doors, all alone, with wild animals prowling around him.

He had counted it when he had beheld a creature so attractive to him and yet knew that he could not pursue her if he went forward to the Indians.

He had counted it when an esteemed congregation had asked him to become their pastor. On the cusp of venturing toward the Forks, he had decided to go into the wilderness, rather than to stay in useful comfort.

The call of God was on his heart to go, ever to go. It burned there, and he, like a candle, wished to burn out for Him wherever He called and to let Him diffuse His fragrance thereby.

Aye, David had counted the cost. And he knew that the reward of Christ was greater.

He put his faith in Him who promised that He would reward those who diligently sought Him.

He was not a great man. 'Twas only by the grace of God that he had become who he was – a broken vessel, now spilled out for Christ.

Chapter Fifty-Five

1746

A year after he had arrived among the Crossweeksung Indians, a congregation had been established. As his body weakened, David often had to be carried out on a chair to preach. Yet his heart warmed each time he spoke to his people – his flesh and blood in Christ. They started a school, and David obtained permission from the Scotch Society to continue among them.

Continually, he coughed up blood. But he pushed it aside and paid no mind to it. God was in the midst of doing a great work, reaping eternal souls. What did his flesh matter in comparison?

With the congregation established firmly, he decided to set out on a journey to the Susquehanna region again, taking some Indians as native missionaries. He had no assurance that God would see fit to return him home alive. The Susquehanna was a dangerous area; when he had ventured in that western direction before, he had lost his horse and nearly his own life.

The journey was hard on David, harder than he had thought it would be. Many nights, he lay awake on his bearskin, sweating off fevers, his lungs vomiting bloody mucus. Often, he found himself unable to preach in the morning. Secretly, he hoped that he might die quickly and escape from a world that had become so full of pain and grief.

Yet the testimony of his Indians encouraged him, as did the sufficiency he found in God to meet his every need, including the sorrows of his heart. *Oh, dear God, set up Thy kingdom in the hearts of these Indians we meet!*

As the little group traveled on, David grew more and more disordered in body. His mind and heart trembled with the thought that he was not fit for the work; he was not fruitful in it. His spirits sank low.

Despite all of this, he persevered by God's grace alone. From time to time, in between spitting up blood and sweating, he spoke a little bit with various people. If he had been in any doubt before, God used this time to show him that all the work came from Him and none from David's own sufficiency.

At last, the traveling band made their way back from the Susquehanna region to Cranberry, where the Crossweeksung Indian congregation had relocated some time before.

***

David felt ready, in every way, to die. His body ached with fever and rashes from sweating. He could no longer read or write. He prayed in great weakness. Yet still he tried to preach, sometimes for an hour or so, before he collapsed into bed, skin burning and mind confused.

***

"You should desist from your labors, Reverend Brainerd." The town doctor who had come to see David frowned at him. "Your life depends upon it."

David swallowed past the invisible razors that coated his throat. "Whether I should die or not does not depend upon me, my good man."

The doctor's frown sprang into a look of surprise. "Nay? Then upon whom?"

David raised his head from his pallet but then thought the better of it as the interior of his hut spun into a dizzying circle of brown hues. "It depends upon Him who is infinitely wise and infinitely loving. I am willing to rest in His hands."

His heart reached out toward the doctor, a man so taken up with physical health that he appeared to neglect the spiritual. "And I wish that you, too, could know the rest that He gives, Doctor. He says, *Come unto Me—*"

But the doctor cut him off. "Aye, aye, well, do not say that I did not tell you that you should rest, sir!" Pulling his coat back on, the man lumbered out of David's hut with a huff.

He closed his eyes as a cough ripped through his chest again but then opened them as he felt a cool cloth drawn across his hot brow.

'Twas the woman with the baby who had first heard him, many months ago, and the first to obtain assurance of her salvation. Her husband had become a helper and translator, and she herself always sought to bring David comfort in any way she could. He was not surprised to know that 'twas her hand who brought the cooling cloth.

"Are you resting well, sir?" she asked.

He closed his eyes against the pain throbbing through his head and let his heart flee toward God. "Aye, I am perfectly at rest in my own mind, dear woman. I have made my utmost attempt to speak for God. I know that I can do no more than I have done."

At last, when he could no longer aid them in any

way, David left his Indians. His doctors advised him to ride on horseback to save his life, and this he planned to do.

Chapter Fifty-Six

Jerusha

"And so you came to us." The words fall softly between us.

He catches my eyes, holding them gently in his gaze. "Aye, with a few side-trails along the way, I came to you. I came – not as the young strong-bodied Yale student you remembered, but as a worn, broken-bodied soldier of the Cross. I am glad that, after all, God does not need men made of gold to work for Him. He Himself is the gold. He only wants vessels willing to be taken in His hands, allowing His Spirit to fill them, rather than to rely on their own efforts and abilities."

He erupts into a volcano of coughing. The bloody mucus speckles the linen I hold to his mouth until the convulsion calms.

"You should sleep, Mr. Brainerd," I suggest, but, though I search for it, I cannot find that same possessive fear that used to compel me to speak such words. There is peace now amidst the sorrow, a Shepherd's staff guiding me through the Valley. Will it stay? Only time will tell.

David's chest rises and falls with several shallow breaths before he responds. "Aye, perhaps I shall retire now. I thought that I might still edit a few more pages of my diaries, but I may rise early tomorrow instead."

His voice is ragged. He smiles up at me. "Always make good use of precious time, Jerusha." A rumbling choke cuts off his words. This turns into a soggy cough that he muffles by drawing his linen-clad arm up across his face.

The coughing continues, and I pour a cup of water from the pitcher that waits on the table nearby. I sit beside him on the bed as the coughing ravages his body, and my heart cries out to God – Will He not ease the suffering of His servant? Of His son? My heart grows softer with tenderness toward the man beside me; surely, God must feel even greater love toward him than I; surely, God has much greater compassion for him than I. Will He not ease His beloved's suffering? I sit there beside David and ponder this and struggle to trust and to believe, despite what my eyes see. Without hesitation, my arm slips behind the man, and the hand unoccupied by the cup begins to rub his back in what I hope are comforting circles. His spine arches thin and ugly beneath his sweat-dampened shirt.

Death is so very hideous. The tears spring to my eyes as I see the way it lays waste to this man – once so full of life, of vigor – and makes him into a living corpse. The way it thrashes him as a slave-master might beat a rebellious slave to death. And the thought comes to my mind: Is that not what we are as Christians? We have escaped the clutches of our own slave-master – and though sin and death may lash us cruelly, reminding us from what prison we came, we now belong to another kingdom. Death's whip can only drive us onto our King, who has led captivity captive, who has set us free.

Perhaps 'tis this that David means when he speaks of his longing for death.

Slowly, his coughing eases, and the tension in my

own chest lessens as well. Is it wrong to be glad that this will not be the night of his death, I think? Not yet, at least. We will have him with us a little longer. For that, my heart is glad.

He and I sit silently for long moments. Head bowed, he draws long breaths that shudder beneath the hand that I still keep resting upon his back. At long last, he straightens and turns to look me in the eyes. Gratitude pools there. "Thank you, Jerusha," he says humbly.

I meet his gaze. "'Tis a joy to me to serve you in any way, Mr. Brainerd." The quiet words are true – utterly so. I would have served him in other ways – I would have followed him as his wife if he had ever asked me, back to the Indians, to eat bear-meat with him and live in a bark hut. But that is not what has been required of me. What has been required is this: rubbing his back as he edges closer and closer to the place where death and life meet.

"Now," I say at last, breaking the gaze before I say too much, more than I ought, "Let us get you into bed, Mr. Brainerd."

He does not resist as I gently guide him beneath the covers. After the sheet is pulled up to his chest, he reaches beneath the fabric and pulls off his breeches, handing them to me. "All human dignity is lost once we are set on this grim road, Jerusha, aye?" he says with a half-smile. The light still has not gone out of his eyes, but it has dimmed with the pain and exertion of the past while.

He should not be alone tonight. Without another word, I pull the chair from where it stands in front of his paper-flooded desk and set it beside the bed. His eyes stay upon me as he lies back against the pillows, his skin the grayish-blue of a mockingbird's feathers.

"Are you staying here with me?" he murmurs, his

voice gravelly from coughing. Ensconced there on the white linen, he reminds me of one of my small siblings when they are ill.

I reach for the Bible. "Aye, I am staying with you tonight. I think you need a friend beside you." Without meeting his gaze, I open the Bible to Isaiah, and spread it on my lap, thankful for the brightness of the beeswax candles that Mama has provided for this room. She always provides the best of our store for our guests, whether 'tis Mr. Brainerd or Mr. Whitefield or some barely-known student who has come to study with Papa's guidance.

Without waiting for his agreement, I begin to read:

"'Behold my servant, whom I uphold; mine elect, in whom my soul delighteth; I have put my spirit upon him; he shall bring forth judgment to the Gentiles. He shall not cry, nor lift up, nor cause his voice to be heard in the street. A bruised reed shall he not break, and the smoking flax shall he not quench; he shall bring forth judgment unto truth. He shall not fail nor be discouraged, til he have set judgment in the earth; and the isles shall wait for his law.'"

The touch of his fingers on my free hand, the one nearest the bed, startles me. I hesitate in my reading for a moment as I realize that Mr. Brainerd has taken my hand, gently yet firmly enfolding it within his own. When I do not pull my hand from his, he draws our joined hands to rest on the edge of the bed.

My heart stammers, and 'tis only with utmost effort that I am able to continue reading:

"'Thus saith God the Lord, he that created the heavens and stretched them out; he that spread forth the earth, and that which cometh out of it; he that giveth breath unto the people upon it, and spirit to them that walk therein; I the Lord have called thee in righteousness, and will hold thine hand, and will keep thee, and give thee for a covenant of the people, for a light of the Gentiles; to open the blind eyes, to bring out the prisoners from the prison, and them that sit in darkness out of the prison house. I am the Lord; that is my name; and my glory will I not give to another, neither my praise to graven images. Behold the former things are come to pass, and new things do I declare; before they spring forth I tell you of them.'"

His hand tightens on mine, and I turn. The hazel in his eyes glows – I see longing there, longing for another world. "He will come. He will not tarry," David whispers. "I long for His courts. He will come. He will not tarry," he repeats.

Chapter Fifty-Seven

When I wake the next morning, my neck strains with stiffness. Late in the night, I nodded off in the straight-backed chair long after David fell asleep to the rhythm of my voice reading more chapters of Isaiah, then moving onto the Psalms.

During that day and the next, and the next after that, through the rest of the week, David seems somewhat improved, though his feet remain swollen. He is able to walk a little around our fenced yard some days. Much of the time he spends by himself in his room, editing his papers and writing letters to friends and associates. He is always cheerful whenever anyone should pop their head in the door to ask how he is – never unsociable, never showing frustration that he has been interrupted in a task for which he probably has not the time to finish: the editing of his diaries, which he intends to allow Papa to publish after his death if he thinks they will help anyone.

Night seems to be the worst for him, though, when his disease puts on its armor, seeing him at his lowest ebb physically after the strains of the day. Often now, he asks me to pray with him again after everyone else has gone about their evening business – Mama to her sewing, Papa to his closet, the younger children to bed. I do not talk with anyone about these meetings. They are not secretive – something I hide or am ashamed of

– but they are precious and intimate. And what is precious need not be displayed like wash on the clothesline for all of the townspeople to see. As I kneel by David on these nights, my soul seems lifted up to heaven by his words, though they are never many, never eloquent – yet they are always sincerely spoken and directed as though the Savior is there in the room with us – as I have always known that He is, yet have never felt so strongly until these last few weeks with Mr. Brainerd. And 'tis in prayer, too, that my soul and spirit seem most at one with Mr. Brainerd's as well – like we are two halves of the same soul.

After we pray, I usually help him into bed now, where he struggles out of his clothes beneath the sheets, as he did that first evening. I turn my face away into the shadows, waiting until he is ready for my help yet again, preserving what little dignity he has left to him. Then I adjust the pillows and let him settle his weary, often-perspiring head against the downy softness before I take up the tattered Bible from its place always beside him. Many nights, though not all, his hand reaches for mine, twining his fingers with my fingers as I read. Most mornings find me asleep in the chair, my neck stiff, my heart both sore and joyful from the time I have spent in David's presence.

***

"I will take the tray to Mr. Brainerd, Jerusha," Sarah offers as I gather the broth and bread for his light meal.

Possessiveness spreads its wings over and covers me. Careful not to let the ugly emotion show, knowing that sweet-hearted Sarah only wants to relieve me, I smile but shake my head. "Nay, I will do it, but thank you."

Sarah looks concerned. "I do not mind, you know, Jerusha. You care for him nearly day and night now that..."

She trails off, but we both know what she means: *now that he is getting worse.*

"I want to," I answer her, and our eyes catch for just a moment before I let mine drop, self-conscious. "I need to." I let the phrase slip purposely. Sarah and I have been the closest of us older sisters through the years. Sarah has always had a heart of mercy, and of genuine selflessness. These traits have drawn me toward her side, even when my other two close-in-age sisters' fun-loving ways shine brighter.

Will Sarah understand what I mean by that one phrase: *I need to?* Unless I have mistook my sister's character all these growing-up years, she will not push and pull until I tell her more and more, as Mary would have. She will simply understand and let me do as I must.

She stays silent for a moment, and I wonder if my elder sister is going to insist. But then she says, "All right." I hear the compassion in her voice – compassion for me, I think – and I look up again to read clearly in her face that she comprehends something of the relationship between David and me. Loving concern shadows her gaze.

"He does not have much time left, Jerusha," she adds, saying what she and I and everyone else in the Edwards household – in all of Northampton and Boston – already know. But I hear beneath her words the true meaning she intends: *Be careful, little sister. Keep your heart safe.* But she speaks aloud only one more sentence, very quietly, as she picks up a basket full of fresh apples, ready to be peeled: "I do not want you to be hurt."

'Tis too late for that. And, even if it were not, would

I stop caring for Mr. Brainerd? Would I stop if I knew that I could prevent the pain that latched onto my heart long ago now – a wolf-pup of pain with sharp iron teeth? "I am finding that perhaps there is a joy that only comes from suffering, Sarah."

Turning from her direct gaze, I pick up the tray and slip from the kitchen.

Chapter Fifty-Eight

He sits at his desk when I enter his bedchamber. The autumn sunshine floods through the windowpanes and dances across his shoulders and head, crowning him with the gold of a dying world.

When he swivels around to face me, joy blooms in his pale face. It draws his mouth into a smile so wide that an observer would think that he had just received news that he was to inherit a kingdom. And perhaps he has.

He rises to meet me as I step across the room. His hands shake only slightly as he takes the tray from me and sets it down on his desk. If I did not know better, I might think that his health is improving steadily, toward a different end than the doctors say. But I press down the hope that rises in my heart, determined not to allow myself to dream in that merely mortal way again.

"You seem happy this afternoon, Mr. Brainerd," I say lightly. I do not always use his first name, even now, not wanting the sweetness of it to perish with common wear.

With impulsiveness uncommon for him, David reaches for both of my hands. His whole countenance smiles as he gazes down into my eyes. "I am melted with desires, Jerusha," he says, and a quiet joy radiates from his words. "I am melted with desires that God might be glorified, melted with desires to love and live to Him alone. Is that not all that life is worth living for, Jerusha?"

Looking back into that face of joy, the haze of sorrow clears from the meadow of my heart for a long moment. "Aye," I answer, glimpsing that for which he thirsts and hungers continually. "Aye, 'tis." Dropping my eyes from his gaze, I let him keep my hands captive.

But he releases me and moves back to his desk, his motions quick and flickering as a fire blaze. He gestures toward the paper on the desk. "My mind and heart have been taken up with this all morning. I rested a bit around noon, as you, gentle nursemaid, insist," he adds with a smile touched ever so lightly by teasing.

Jitteriness tingles through me at his frame of mind. He is so rarely humorous or teasing; rather he is always driven – going forward – not taking any time for frivolity. Thus, this fresh manner of his startles me – indeed, even unnerves me.

I hesitate a moment, and he turns back to his desk, once more enraptured by the paper spread out there. Losing his attention is akin to having the sun blotted from the sky. Wanting to regain its warmth, I step close to the desk, an arms-length away from David. "Will you not tell me what has so engaged you? Unless 'tis a private matter," I add hastily.

He lifts his eyes, smiling. "'Tis no private matter, Jerusha. Matters of kingdom-work are for all to hear of, at least in due course. What is done in secret – aye, and the secret thoughts of the heart, too – will one day be shouted from the housetops, aye?"

I nod, thinking of the secret thoughts of my own heart and how they will one day be known by the one who stands before me now, just as well as by the One who knows them now.

He spreads his rein-roughened hands across the thick paper. "I have been writing to Reverend Mr. Byram." He pauses. "About how ministers need the Holy Spirit to guide them. How they ought to do nothing of their own accord but only in reliance upon Him, for He guides our lives and breathes and moves inside each one of them who are His own."

As he speaks, his face glows with some inner holy light, and his increasingly ragged breath sounds loud in the silence between us. My soul draws toward him as the water is drawn back to the heavens after the rain.

"Oh, Jerusha," he says so quietly that I can scarcely hear him. "I have tasted it. I have seen His glory. I have known His love in the quiet evenings when I have been all alone save for my God. I have gone into His garden and partaken of His fruits. His love to me has been sweet, sweeter than the choicest of wines. I have wanted for nothing. I am content now to join Him in His heavenly kingdom. Indeed I have been content to join Him there for many years."

Is it possible to be jealous of God? If so, I would be. Is he saying to me that he will miss me not at all? Or are his thoughts not even upon me? Perhaps John misjudged David's affections. Perhaps David thinks of me as nothing but a nursemaid or the young daughter of his fellow theologian, my father.

'Tis strange, for his heavenly-mindedness is what drew me toward Mr. Brainerd in first place. Oh, aye: his flashing hazel eyes, his strong shoulders that seemed meant to carry a burden easily, the kindness that lay ever present on his tongue. Those things attracted me as well. But 'twas the otherworldliness, the sense that he had seen a world beyond this physical one, and that 'twas such a world that he desired, for it contained the most Beloved of his soul – Aye, that was what truly attracted me to Mr. Brainerd, that was what latched my soul to his with a bond that will not let go, though I knew it not at the time. If such is the case, can I begrudge him the lovesickness he displays toward his God and mine? Nay, for it is this that I believe gives him any love worth imparting to me.

At my silence, he continues, "As long as I see anything to be done for God, life is worth having; but how vain and unworthy 'tis to live for any lower end!" He finishes by turning towards me, his eyes glistening with a beautiful joy beyond any that I have ever known, and he grasps my hands in his again. He waits to hear my agreement.

"Aye," I hear the words come out of my mouth, softly but with conviction, from my very heart. They are true, the words my Mr. Brainerd speaks, but oh, why does my heart still ache at the end for which he longs – away from me, down a passage whence I have not yet been bidden to enter? I swallow hard, twice, forcing myself to absorb as much of the light pouring from those eyes as I can. They will too soon darken and close, I know, and I will wish myself back in this moment, here, alone with him, the other half of my own heart beating in his bosom.

"You are right, Mr. Brainerd. There is no other end for which either you or I would wish to live." The tears press against my throat, and I know that I will not be able to hold them back much longer. If I weep before him, he will seek to comfort me. He will tell me that the grave is but a door into eternity, where he will be overjoyed at spending that time with His Savior and mine.

I pull my hands from his, unable to bear the sweet connecting pain any longer. "Excuse me," I barely manage to utter before escaping into the quiet passage and drawing the door shut behind me.

The passage walls stand silent witness as I put my hands up to my face. My shoulders – indeed, my whole body – shakes as several tearless sobs wrench their way from my spirit. The grief tightens, cinching my heart. Behind me, I hear Mr. Brainerd stirring in his room, dragging back his chair so that he may sit again and write and work.

My hands... They still feel as though he holds them. Nearby, in the sitting room, I hear Mama going over the primer with one of my little sisters. From the kitchen, I hear the thump-thump of Leah at the butter churn. And beyond the closed door, I hear the scratch-scratch of David's pen once more. Anxious to make the most of the time he has left... the time I have left with him.

Time presses forward. I cannot escape it.

I rush along the passage, paying no attention to the way my feet clatter on the wood. I must get outside. I need to feel the live wind rush through my hair. I need solid ground beneath my feet; I need to get away from this house – aye, even from him. From the exquisitely painful pressure his fast-ebbing presence exerts on my heart.

For a little while I need to be alone.

When I reach the end of the gate – the gate from which David will no longer exit, the gate from which, as Papa says, he has already exited for the last time – I let the wooden slats slip away from my fingers, let the latch click shut behind me. The gloaming has begun to descend on the street before me, turning the coffee-colored dirt to a strange dark-red hue, the color of blood dried long ago.

As a drowning castaway, I suck in the air, warm with the scent of fires burning in the streets beyond ours and of dry leaves about to fall in showers of red and gold, bronzing the quiet earth. But even this does not calm me, does not distract my anxious mind. I had thought to go for a walk, to clear my mind and heart, to make it ready for the trembling days ahead, but I find that my legs are weak beneath me, limp as unbaked dough, and I take just a few steps beyond the gate before reaching a hand out to the rough wood of the oak tree that keeps watch there, a tree planted by Grandfather Stoddard. Resting against the tree, my shoulders bow with the weight of all that is in my heart. 'Tis so heavy again. So heavy.

I rest my head against the rough bark, feeling the scrape against my skin, but not caring. The shroud of grief has become too great. My affection for David Brainerd, alongside my willingness to let God do whatever was His will, has brought me only pain, or so it seems in this dark moment. "Should I have chosen between Thee and him?" The whisper cracks from my tight throat. Unbidden, the tears press against my eyes, so hard that they hurt as I try to keep them back.

"Yet my affection for this man came without my wanting it, without my willing it. This desire for David's love for me." My voice has quieted. I have never spoken of this aloud, except when I answered John Brainerd's direct question. But I do now, here in the dusk, on our deserted street.

Yet, in the midst of my agony, He enables me to choose to believe.

I will trust Thee. The phrase draws deep-hidden tears to the surface of my soul.

Though He slays me.

I close my eyes against the pressing reality of pain and loss and open them to a greater, truer one – in which lies veritable gain – gain not only in this world, but also in the next.

And even as I pour out my soul to my Creator and

Savior, His Spirit brings a peace to me that I have craved.

Chapter Fifty-Nine

Weary in body but more at rest in my spirit than I have been for some time, I step into the house, intending to go to Mr. Brainerd's room. Perhaps he will wish for me to pray with him again this evening. A new strength has arisen within me, a new desire to pray with him that I did not have before – a desire that goes beyond my love for the man himself and that desires to nestle in the secret place of the Most High – a place David seems to know so well and with which I also wish to accustom myself.

But, when I close the door behind me, Mary's exclamation startles me. "Jerusha!" Mary clatters down the staircase and stops in front of me, breathless. Her eyes widening, she twists her hands into her skirt as she tends to do when nervousness overtakes her. "Where have you been, sister? I've looked for you everywhere."

Beyond her, down the passage, I hear murmuring and groaning. My chest tightens again. "Only out by the gate. I needed some air. What has happened?"

Mary glances over her shoulder at the cracked-open door. "Mr. Brainerd has taken a turn for the worse. Mama went into his room to check on him and found him slumped over his desk, blood trickling across his papers." Her lashes flutter with excitement as she gives me that gory detail.

"Has Doctor Mather been summoned?"

"We sent Leah to run for him, but she has not returned yet."

A moan from the sickroom reaches my ears. I press past Mary, brushing the smooth fabric of her dress, my heart drawn to the one who occupies the chamber beyond. I must go to him, I must comfort him, I must be near if...

I do not want to think of that. Not now. Now I must simply trust the Good Shepherd and hold my beloved's hand as I go through the dark valley with him.

***

Sometime later, the doctor draws away from the bed where Mr. Brainerd lies in a listless half-conscious state, his eyes staring unseeing toward the white ceiling, his linens soaked with sweat and putrid diarrhea. Papa has lingered near the doorway, and now he steps apart with Doctor Mather. Mama and Leah both work to peel away the soiled linens as much as possible and replace them without disturbing or jarring the ill one.

With a strange fearlessness of what others think, I slip my small, trembling hand around Mr. Brainerd's burning one. The perspiration on his skin transfers to mine as soon as I touch it. On the underside of his wrist, where the delicate skin shows his blue veins branching into tiny streams, his pulse jitters against my thumb. 'Tis so quick, like the pulse of the tiny fieldmouse that I once rescued from one of the village cats. I swallow hard against the fear that presses against my ribs. If he dies...

It will be all right. I will trust in Thee.

I see with the eye of my mind a gentle Shepherd leading Mr. Brainerd... leading me, as well. We are together in that picture, one on either side of this Good Man, who walks beside us. His rod and His staff are with Him – He will protect us from every truly evil thing.

And yet a desire remains in me that Mr. Brainerd – David – may yet live. How can I both strive to be at peace with him going and yet yearn for him to stay?

"I do not expect him to last the night." Doctor Mather's voice rumbles, just steps away from me.

"'Tis my sincerest hope that he is prepared for death," Papa replies.

My grasp tightens on Mr. Brainerd's hand. 'Tis not the grasp of lust, but of holy love that will go through the valley with this one who is in his hour of death. One who is beloved of God and of me. I feel the roughness of his skin upon mine like the bark of the oak tree in our front yard. Almost imperceptibly, he tightens his hand on mine slightly.

I hold my David's hand, but no longer will I try to tether him to this world. How my heart fills, full of wishing that he would stay, stay here with me. And yet I have the knowing in my soul that he will go. When, I do not know. Perhaps with the morning sunrise.

And it will be all right.

It will be well.

I will trust in Thee.

***

Papa has disappeared once more into his closet, surely to pray for Mr. Brainerd. Doctor Mather has left to see other patients in this long, dark night.

I stay throughout the whole of the night, barely blinking, hardly breathing, my eyes locked on David's precious face. His countenance, like that first martyr Stephen, seems to glow like the face of an angel, brighter and brighter as death approaches. What does he see? Does he glimpse his Lord and mine?

At times, I wipe his brow and neck and chest, desiring him to have comfort in these last hours. I moisten his sweet lips, lips that have spoken the gospel of peace to so many, and my fingers brush them with ointment. Beneath the thin shirt, his chest rises and falls erratically. Sometimes, his breath does not come for a long time. When this occurs, I myself hold my own breath, not willing to breathe if he cannot. At last, his breath comes again. He gulps it in, as a boy pulls air through a reed in the river, playing a game with his friends, pretending that he has drowned. Yet this is no game. David sucks the air nearly in vain, like a poor fish left to gasp out its life on the river bank. Over and over again, I wipe his brow and neck and chest, my fingers pitying the paper-thin skin on his collarbone. There is no flesh beneath his skin. It has been consumed by the dreadful disease that now takes pleasure in torturing him to death.

***

My hands feel restless.

I must have something to do. My fingers work numbly at my needlework, even as I silently pray.

I cannot sit idly by, watching him become still.

Leah, her lids drooping low over her tired eyes, comes twice to bring me a fresh bowl of water. I dip a cloth into the water, ringing it out, touching Mr. Brainerd's brow, yearning to make him comfortable. I moisten his fevered lips, parched as drought-stricken soil, swollen and discolored, nearly unrecognizable.

I am here alone, except for Israel, so young and visibly unnerved at the idea of death coming for his older brother. My heart pities and understands him.

I am glad that he arrived in time.

Israel rises from the chair that he has set on the other side of the bed. He paces the room, his feet making quiet shuffling noises. Then he leaves and returns a few moments later, a book under his arm. He sits again, the chair creaking beneath his weight, but he cannot concentrate on the book that he has now opened upon his lap. He keeps glancing up at Mr. Brainerd, at me, and then back down at his book.

Mr. Brainerd cannot have long to wait now. The chariots of Israel are coming, as he wished. They are coming swiftly.

Chapter Sixty

He has no control over or knowledge of his personal needs, and so the ever-fidgety Israel and faithful Leah help me to move and dress him many times during the night – to strip the soiled linens from beneath Mr. Brainerd and to replace them as best we can, to remove each newly-fouled shirt from his skeletal frame and to replace it. The stench becomes severe.

"Should we change his shirt this time as well?" As we remove the folded pad from beneath David, Israel speaks more to fill the silence than for an answer. We both know that Mr. Brainerd's shirt is soaked through.

I merely nod and step away once more to go and find a new shirt in the stack of linens. A gradual but steady, sober joy fills my heart as I take the shirt from its place. I am serving him. I am loving him. I will not have the opportunity to do this again in my life. This is the last time. These are the last few hours in which I will be able to serve David. Mine will be the last hands that soothe him.

What a privilege, what an honor God has given to me, of all women.

I bunch the soiled linen pad up and let it drop onto the floor near the foot of the bed. Wordlessly, Israel and I work together, tucking the new folded pad beneath his brother, very gently. I want David's last moments on this earth to be ones of comfort, ones in which he knows that I care for him, even if we have never spoken of this outright.

Israel raises his brother's arms. We pull first one soiled sleeve and then the other over his head. He has become so utterly wasted these past few weeks. His skin draws taut over his body, revealing not only the shape of his ribs but also his veins. I wish that we could take a damp cloth and thoroughly wipe down his entire body, sticky and wet with urine and other body fluids, but we cannot. It will weary him too much, so instead, we bathe him only where we must and then pull the next shirt over his head, guiding David's arms through the fresh sleeves.

I step away from the bed. Israel gently allows his brother to rest back against the pillows that I have plumped. Mr. Brainerd lets out a deep groan, as he rests back. I wonder if it would help if I added another pillow to give him more support. Moving to the chest again at the foot of the bed, I take another pillow out and plump it.

"Here," I say, "let us put this pillow behind him. It might help him breathe a little easier."

At last, we are done. At least for this time, for again, no more than two hours later, we must remove the soiled pad from beneath him. It grieves me for his sake because I know that it costs him every time we must move him. Yet, for my part, 'tis somewhat of a relief, for it breaks up the long, long hours of the night in which we can only wait, hearing his breath rasping in and out, like a farrier's file against a horse's hoof.

***

Near morning, footsteps passing outside the door cause me to awaken. *Leah.* She must be rising to light the fires before dawn, as usual. Blearily, I open my eyes, neck stiff from lying against the straight chair for who knows how many hours.

I meant to watch. I meant not to sleep.

In the stillness, I realize that there is no sound of rasping.

My heart chokes me.

I have missed it. I have missed his final hour. He has gone alone. I have missed saying goodbye to him. Was he awake when he died? Did he see me and Israel sleeping? And wish that one of us would awake, that one of us would accompany him, at least to the shore of the Jordan?

And yet, like the disciples in the garden, we slept in his hour of travail.

My body tense, I rise from the chair. It creaks loudly and slumbering Israel stirs. I look down at the face of the one who lies on the bed between us. 'Tis so peaceful. Gently, I reach down and touch his hand, bracing myself to feel its cold, stiff deadness.

But the warmth of David's hand startles me. I look more closely and find that his chest slowly rises and falls. He has not yet gone. Indeed, he seems to be only sleeping, nearly feverless. He has made it through the night. His worn-out, broken body has rallied once more. How is this possible?

Has love made it possible?

***

Israel has fallen back asleep. Bible open, I sit here, quiet, my hands folded in my lap, waiting as the light touches the windowsill, and spills onto the floor, the fresh milk of the sun sloshing out of its bucket. My hand rests gently on the coverlet. I feel afraid to move. I barely breathe as my spirit blesses God. He has given me the miracle of another day with Mr. Brainerd. He has come back as if from the dead once more.

Should I be glad that his glorious day, as Mr. Brainerd calls it, has delayed its approach? He will continue to suffer until his chariot comes. I am thankful for each moment in his presence – and yet wait to see the advance of his death. How can this be?

An hour or so after the sun rises, he rouses. The light flutters across his eyelids as his short lashes tremble in the sun. Slowly, slowly, his lids open, displaying his still-beautiful hazel eyes taking in this world once more. He seems confused for a moment, almost as if he thought to waken in a different world. Slowly again, his head turns toward the side where I sit unmoving. The confusion clears from his eyes as they focus on me. A slow smile touches his lips.

"Jerusha," he murmurs.

My own face breaks into a smile at the sight of one, weak though 'tis, on his face, and I let out the breath that I did not know I held. The smile on his face strengthens.

"Mr. Brainerd, you need a drink." I rise from my seat, quickly breaking eye contact with him.

Yet, as I move to go, I feel the weak touch again, his skin on mine. He takes my hand, limply. I turn at the touch, my heart dancing in my veins, leaping as King David in the streets.

He is still dying. Never will he put a band around my finger; never will I know the joy of calling him mine truly. But I have begun to know that there is a depth of joy in this kind of sacrificial love, a joy that I could not have found otherwise, perhaps, in the relationship I once longed to experience with him.

And so when I turn to see why he touches my hand and weakly grasps it with his own, I cannot stop that joy from lighting my face.

He sees it. His eyes hold mine for a long moment.

Then he says so simply, as he did that day in Boston, when the first window of his soul opened to me, "I thank you."

The joy pulses from him to me, from me to him. And my heart gives praise to the King of heaven, who has given me this joy where I least thought that I should find it: at the deathbed of my beloved.

'Tis a strange secret: In dying, we live.

***

After I have poured Mr. Brainerd his drink, I hold the cup to his lips, supporting his head with my other hand. I feel his throat move as the water trickles down, cooling the thirst that columns his throat, so scorched by coughing. He cannot take more than a few sips at once before he lays back exhausted on his pillow, eyes closing and drifting off into unconscious slumber.

Now Israel wakens, rubbing the sleep from his eyes. As he stretches, there is a tap on the door, and Mama peeks inside. She carries a tray with porridge on it and some other assorted things, bread and tea among them. Her gaze goes immediately from me to Mr. Brainerd. I smile to reassure her that, aye, he is still alive. "I thought that I would bring you some things for breakfast," she says to Israel and me as she places the tray upon the little bedside table.

"Thank you," I murmur and then glance up at Israel. "You should breakfast with my family, though. You have had a long night."

He smiles at me and shakes his head. "As have you. I believe that you were still awake when I went to sleep."

This is true, but I have no desire to leave Mr. Brainerd's side and converse at the table. "Well, then, we both had a long watch. I pray you, go on."

Israel's will is not as strong as his brothers'. Obviously relieved to leave the sickroom, he agrees. "I thank you."

And for this, I am glad, for it gives me some time alone with his sleeping elder brother, some time to sit here in silence, a quiet understanding between us.

Chapter Sixty-One

A little while after Israel leaves the room for breakfast, Mr. Brainerd shifts his position and opens his eyes once again. I lift my gaze from where it has been resting, reading Psalm 117 aloud so that God's Word might cradle him even as he sleeps. He opens his mouth, but no sound comes out. Frustration shadows his face.

I reach out a hand and rearrange the coverlet. "Hush, do not try to talk. You had a very bad night."

He swallows, eyes closing, then he opens them again, resignation on his face. This time, wanting to comfort him more than anything else, 'tis I who lay my hand over his. Then I continue to read.

As the morning wears on, David sleeps. Setting aside the Bible, I sit, singing a hymn softly and watching him breathe, thanking God for every rise and fall of his gaunt chest. Often, even when sleeping, his mouth moves. I know 'tis in prayer. Though the words are not spoken aloud, I know that he prays for me and for my family, for his brothers and sisters, and always, always for his Indians.

About halfway through the morning, he opens his eyes, dropping my hand seemingly without a thought, and pushes himself up against the pillow. Inching up, he licks his lips. I press the cup of water to them, and he takes a couple of swallows.

"Where is that letter?" he rasps.

"What letter?" I say, placing the cup down with a slight thud on the table. How can he be thinking of letters when, by all appearances, he wasn't supposed to live through the last night? Yet relief floods me to know that he has regained his voice.

He coughs and sucks in a breath. "The letter that I wrote yesterday or the day before… I cannot remember when. The one to Reverend Mr. Byram. 'Twas about the qualifications of ministers. I must fold it. I must address it," he mutters. "I must use what time is left to me. Not idling, but to profit others. To honor God, who has given me so much, who has extended my life."

'Tis on the tip of my tongue to deny him, to refuse to get that letter from the desk where it sits, where I thought his hands would never touch it again. I even open my mouth to say, "No, Mr. Brainerd, you must rest," but the determined look has entered his eyes and hardened them. 'Tis not a hardness that destroys compassion, but the kind of hardness that the Scriptures say the Lord Jesus possessed when He set His face like flint to go toward Jerusalem.

I shut my mouth and nod and get him the letter and the lap desk.

With shaking hands, he folds it and addresses it himself. "You will see that he gets this?"

"Aye."

He closes his eyes and manages a small smile, filled with pain. Just folding and addressing the letter has made the agony surge again, an agony that I can tell arches from his lungs, into his ribs, down his hipbones, through his thighs, and even into his swollen, discolored feet. He stretches restlessly. A moan escapes his lips.

"I will let you rest." I swallow back the tears that

have risen to my throat at the sight of his suffering. How can I have half-hoped that he would linger another day?

***

During the rest of the morning, I help Mama with little chores that I should have tended to long before now: some washing and folding of linens, some cleaning. All through it, I force myself to pray that God would bring Mr. Brainerd's glorious day and relieve him at last.

I am about to go back to Mr. Brainerd when Mama touches my hand. "Why not let one of your other sisters attend him for a while?"

I hear concern for me in her tone. No matter. 'Tis I who must tend him. "I am all right, Mama."

Her eyes study me for a long moment. At last, she nods her agreement, albeit reluctantly.

On the way to Mr. Brainerd's room, I catch a glimpse of my reflection in a windowpane. No wonder Mama sounded anxious. I have not attended to my appearance at all, have hardly eaten, barely slept for days. My hair puffs out on one side and lies flat on the other. My face is pale, and darkness rings my eyes. My lips are cracked from licking them in my nervousness, and my dress is rumpled, to say the least.

Does it matter? Does it matter how I look when Mr. Brainerd's life trickles away in the room just beyond me?

Still, I mount the staircase and go into my own room, where I tip out some water into the basin. Splashing the water onto my face, I am surprised at how good it feels. I have long been numbed by the days of sorrow. I take down my hair. It flows long, nearly down to my knees. I pull the brush through it, enjoying the stroking, and I wonder, so fleetingly, what would David think of my hair if he could see it like this? A pain clenches me as I recognize afresh that he never will know this part of me, that he will never share my mortal, everyday life.

After braiding and pinning up my hair again, I stare into the small mirror, allowing myself to indulge that daydream again that I held onto for the years in which Mr. Brainerd worked as a missionary: the daydream in which he came to Northampton, not as an invalid to gasp out the last few hours of his life, but as a man who sought my hand to join in his.

A stumbling noise and loud banging, as if someone has fallen to the floor, startles me out of my contemplation. What a fool I was to leave him alone so long! My heart chokes me. I throw the brush down with a clatter, and it falls from the table, but I do not stop to pick it up. I rush from my room and find that the others in the house hasten toward Mr. Brainerd's chamber as well.

When I see all the others coming, my step hesitates, and 'tis Mary who thrusts open the door without knocking. Papa and Mama hurry through the doorway, Mama's skirts flying. But I am suddenly frozen, watching as David stumbles about the room, his body lurching to-and-fro. Great hiccups shake his chest. He is straining, straining as if to vomit over and over, but nothing emerges from his mouth except a thin dribble of reddish mucus. His face turns toward me, scarlet with exertion and pain. Sweat pours down his skin, making the sharp angles of his face glisten. Israel and Papa each take one of his arms, ushering him towards the bed. They finally get him to sit on the edge, where his legs dangle, shaking. Mr. Brainerd strains against their hold, not in order to get free of the help, but to heave repeatedly. Still, little comes out except blood and mucus, dripping here and there on the coverlet.

I cannot move. After all of these weeks, I am stunned when I see that the end will not be quiet – the disease may very well not take him in a sudden delirious, mercifully unconscious fever, as last night promised. Rather, the glorious day of which he has often spoken will be vicious and cruel and conscious.

I do not want to see it. I feel strangely sick, as I felt once, when I saw a hawk come down on a squirrel. None of the little animal's struggles availed it. In the end, I pressed my hands against my ears to shut out the poor creature's screams.

And now Mr. Brainerd. My David. My beloved. For all his holiness, for all his piety and closeness to God, he cannot do anything in the face of this vicious disease that tears him apart. Amidst the vomiting, retching, and hiccupping, he struggles for breath, crying out when he can. I confess in my heart, I wish that the end would come to him now. Is this is a selfish desire so that I might not see and experience the pain anymore? Or is it a selfless desire for him, that he may not feel or experience the pain anymore?

Oh, Lord God, let him go!

But he does not go. His soul remains firmly attached to his threadbare body.

As he continues retching and hiccupping, Mama turns to me, for Sarah stands by, holding Jonathan. "Jerusha, come help." Her voice forces me out of my stunned position, and I move forward on numb legs.

Chapter Sixty-Two

From early afternoon until the shadows lengthen and darkness begins to hush a weary world, David continues in a grievous state. After he has somewhat stabilized, though his fever still rages, Mama and Papa leave his care in the hands of Israel and me, instructing us to fetch them if any changes occur.

Finally, Israel himself leaves around suppertime, though only at my urging, for it will not help David for his brother to grow weak. For some minutes, I tend him alone, changing the cool cloths upon his forehead; aye, even taking his hand in mine again.

At last, he rests, asleep.

An urge comes over my person. Rising, I check to be sure that Mr. Brainerd will not need me for a moment or two, and then I scurry from his room, up the stairs on the quietest feet I can muster, and into the chamber I share with my sister Sarah. There, I go to the chest at the foot of our bed. Its latch slips open under my fingers. Rustling through the folded linens and small keepsakes, I find what I seek.

Back down the stairs I fly, into Mr. Brainerd's room. Satisfying myself that he still does not need anything by my hand, I sit in my usual chair, the pace of my errand making my own chest rise quickly beneath my bodice, and I lay the packet I procured on my lap. My fingers undo the burgundy ribbon that holds the linen packet closed, and I gently unfold the fabric.

There they lie, nestled together: two bayberry candles, long and smooth and elegant. I remember when, three years past, I asked Mama if my sisters and I could each have two for our future homes. We had spent days boiling the bayberries, skimming off their natural wax coating, and then pouring that into our candle molds. Mama had been generous in permitting us to take them, for bayberry candles are so time-consuming to make that they are often saved to light just before guests arrive and then blown out within minutes so that the candle can be saved for another time. After it is extinguished, its spicy fragrance lingers in the air all evening.

I inhale deeply and rise again, a candle in each hand, the cloth that swaddled them falling to the floor. Two beeswax candles burn, one on the desk, another on Mr. Brainerd's bedside table. With greatest care but no hesitation, I touch the wick of each bayberry candle to its beeswax counterpart and extinguish the latter, replacing them in their holders with my bayberry candles.

The burning wax fills the room with the inimitable fragrance. In the silence, I take my seat and sit beside David, quiet in the candles' glow.

I will spend them all – use them all up – to honor him.

He still hiccups and coughs a little in his sleep. From time to time, I draw my handkerchief across his mouth to wipe away the reddish spittle that accumulates there. He does not open his eyes, seemingly unaware of my presence, for a very long time. His lips move, though I do not know whether through some wandering of his mind or whether he is trying to speak to me. But at last a whisper emerges from the lips that have moved in the same pattern all evening: "When shall I come to God, even to God, my exceeding joy?"

The question itself, spoken aloud, brings on a gasp and convulsion of his lungs. Then his question turns into a muttered prayer. "Hasten the day," I hear him whisper. "Hasten the day. Then I may come speedily to Thee. Hasten, O Lord."

Seeing his agony, my heart is pierced as with a sword. He coughs again, and fresh blood-tinged mucus bubbles from the corner of his mouth. I hold his hand in mine, unable to do anything else for him. Like a dress ill-stored for decades, his lungs come apart at the seams.

***

At last, he is thoroughly quiet and calm. Even his lips stop moving in their feverish way. His whispered words fade. All is still – very still. Wondering if his fever has died, I place a hand to his brow, pushing aside the wet thatch of hair that has fallen across his forehead. His eyes open then, shining with pain, and turn to me. My heart catches in my throat, swirling with a mixture of sorrow and longing. In his eyes, too, open affection now lies alongside the searing hurt.

I swallow hard and let my hand drop from its place on his face. "May I refresh you with some water?"

Shaking his head, he opens his mouth, coughs, and then murmurs moistly, "What refreshes me most in my soul, sweet Jerusha, is to think of the way God has allowed me to live for Him and to Him in former days. I am useless now, but He did use me once."

"He still is using you now, Mr. Brainerd."

His forehead furrows weakly above closed eyes.

"He is using you here, whether you know it or not."

And then I pull the coverlet up closer to his shoulders, wanting to busy my hands.

But he slows them, stills them, by capturing them in his.

Chapter Sixty-Three

'Tis the Sabbath. I slept in my room last night. Again, Mr. Brainerd felt a little better, and Israel and Sarah offered to sit up with him by turns and let me rest thoroughly through one night, as I have not rested in that way for a long time.

But 'twas no use. I could not sleep. I tossed and I turned for so long my head felt dizzy. Finally, I pushed away the cover and tiptoed over to the window, pushed aside the curtains, and gazed up at the icy moon that stared down at me. When I felt goosebumps travel from my arms down to my legs, I wrapped my shawl closer around me and prayed deep within my soul. Or rather perhaps the Holy Spirit prayed for me. I cannot now remember precisely what I spoke. I know that 'twas a heart-cry. I know that I asked for Mr. Brainerd to be at peace.

The room felt stuffy, like a tomb shut up against the air. I pushed the window open and leaned out, breathing deeply as the wind brushed through sleeping Northampton.

The rooster crowed before I found my way to bed again. The gray dawn already had begun to peer over the horizon and to seep through the trees. Alone in the small bedchamber, I fell into a deep sleep.

Now this Sabbath-day, I wake with a start, hearing the clatter of dishes in the room below mine. I tumble from my bed, pushing aside the covers, and dressing as quickly as I am able before rushing into the passage and stumbling down the stairs.

A tray in her hands, Sarah meets me outside Mr. Brainerd's chamber. Through her tiredness, she gives me her bright, wide smile. "He ate it all," she says. "Every last bit."

I am astonished, for Mr. Brainerd has not eaten well since he came to stay with us. I glance down at the tray as I pass her, but sure enough, she is correct. Even the porridge bowl has been scraped clean. *Perhaps, perhaps God will even now work a miracle. Perhaps this will...*

My heart pounds in my chest, and a smile comes unbidden to my lips as I ease open the door. I can scarcely believe the scene before me: David sits up in bed, the light from the window washing over him, his brother Israel leaning against the bed post. They talk with animation.

David looks up then and holds my gaze with his, quietly, gently, and without demand. "Good morning to you, Jerusha. It gladdens my heart to see you."

A sudden shyness overtakes me, and I barely manage to nod back. "Good morning."

Israel smiles widely at me. He has not the eyes of his brother John, who saw right into my soul and also, perhaps, David's. Considering the circumstances, however, this is for the best, probably.

I tear my eyes away from David's, feeling awkward, yet pleased. I look backwards towards the door. "I see that you ate all your breakfast," I comment, just by way of saying something, anything, to cause the awkwardness to fall away. Two nights ago, I held this man's hand and burned my bayberry candles because I thought that he would not wake to see the light of day again. And now here he sits, as if he might live on for years!

He is still smiling when I look back at him, white and weak against the linen covers, his hands lying limp on top of them. "Aye, aye, I did eat everything, did I not, Israel?"

His brother chuckles and nods. "Every bite."

Could it be that God will yet work a miracle? Could it be that...? I swallow back such a hope.

David pushes against his pillows to raise himself up a bit more. When he cannot manage it, I step to his side and Israel moves to help as well. When he has reached the position he desired, he sinks back, exhausted, with a sigh. "I think my appetite is the result of my approaching death." His eyes sparkle.

A moment ago, I swallowed back my hope. Now I work to push hard against the sorrow that rises in my throat at his words. Aye, sorrow, and perhaps even anger at David – an anger that surprises me, for has not God brought me past such a feeling?

I pause before I reply to what he has said. How can I be angry with a man who only wishes to go and meet his Lord face-to-face? To meet the lovely One, the One whom our hearts should desire above all others?

I am angry because he does not wish to stay here with me.

O Lord God, forgive me, Thy foolish servant once more.

I press my lips together, my hands tightly clasped, my eyes cast down, and say nothing.

But David is not silent. Indeed, he leans forward and takes Israel's hand in his, trembling. His voice quivers with the excitement one about to embark upon a long-anticipated journey. "I was born on a Sabbath day, and I have reason to think that I was new-born on a Sabbath day. Is the Sabbath today?"

I realize that he is looking at me for the answer.

But when I open my mouth, no sound comes out. I make do with a nod.

My wordlessness has no effect on him, but my nod causes him to shut his eyes in bliss. "I hope I shall die on this Sabbath day," he murmurs.

"Patience, my brother," Israel says. But there is no rebuke in his voice, unlike the rebuke that wishes to spring from my fleshly tongue. I clench my teeth, grieved by my own lingering self-interest.

***

After the morning exercises at church have finished, Papa returns home and comes into Mr. Brainerd's room. The door latches shut behind him, and David's eyes creak open. Throughout the morning, while I sat with him, he has slept.

His gaze settles at once upon Papa. His face, usually tightened with pain, even in his sleep, relaxes now with a smile. "Jonathan," he says.

Papa returns the smile and steps towards the bed, where he settles down into Israel's usual chair and picks up Mr. Brainerd's bluish hand. "How are you doing, my friend?"

"I wish I could have gone to the house of God this day." David licks his lips. "But I am almost in eternity. I am almost in His eternal house."

My chest tightens with a painful joy at the anticipation in his voice. I rise from my chair a little suddenly, gathering up the blood-stained cloths. At my movement, Papa turns with a quirk of his eyebrow, but he says nothing.

As I go toward the door, I hear David say, "I am hopeful that a glorious advancement of Christ's kingdom is near at hand, Jonathan."

Again, the blood and mucus break up, and he clears

his throat, fumbling for a cloth to put to his lips. Papa tucks one into his hand.

"'Tis this," David murmurs, "that I think and pray much for. 'Tis this that you will live to see, I hope."

Israel pushes open the door before I can reach for the handle. His quick ears must have caught his brother's words because he enters the conversation as readily as he enters the chamber. "Would you not wish to see the advancement of Christ's kingdom, David? In the flesh, I mean."

The answer is slow but immediate. "I am fully persuaded, Israel," he says, and I do not turn but pause with my back to them, waiting to hear what he has to say, "I am fully persuaded that I will see the prosperity of the Church on earth."

What is this that he means? I do not want to go out the door until I hear. Does he still hold out hope of his recovery? Perhaps the Lord spoke to him by His Spirit? The wild dream rises in my breast, and I cannot keep it down, despite how foolish they appear even to my own heart.

"I will see it advance," David goes on, "from my place at Christ's side. I will rejoice with Christ in the prosperity of His kingdom."

"But, David," Israel protests, "would you not wish to see the prosperity on earth with me and with Mr. Edwards and Miss Edwards?"

"I am willing it should be as it is." The answer, though soft, comes again without delay.

My hope falters, loses its feathers, and drops to the ground.

"But I will say this, that I would not wish to have the choice to make – whether I should go or stay – for ten-thousand worlds."

I turn to catch a glimpse of his dear face before going downstairs. I need to see the faith resting there so that it may bolster my own. Yet when I turn and look at him, to my surprise, he is not gazing at Papa, but past him.

At me.

Chapter Sixty-Four

Papa comes again before retiring to bed. I am glad for it; Mr. Brainerd seems encouraged whenever Papa appears.

I take the opportunity to escape from the room for a few moments. It has grown oppressive to me over the past few hours, hearing Mr. Brainerd's breathing in-and-out, in-and-out, gasping as he sleeps in the half-consciousness of those who are in severe pain, of those who are dying.

Hurrying out of the chamber, my feet are noiseless, and I hear Sarah and Mama talking beyond my view, in the sitting room. They speak in whispers. Normally I would not listen in, but I hear my name.

Sarah, sweet Sarah, says in her concerned, older-sister way, "I am worried for Jerusha, Mama. Truly, I am worried. What will happen when he dies? What will she do?" She says these last few words in the softest of murmurs.

"She will go on," Mama answers.

My back pressed against the smooth wall of the passage, I shut my eyes and nod. I must go on. There will be no choice for me.

"God will give her strength," Mama says. "God always gives what we need. Your sister is a strong woman of God."

Me? I, who am weak and fragile in faith and hope?

I, who was not strong enough to withhold my heart from a man who would not – could not – belong to me?

Sarah does not speak for a moment. Then she says, "Have you seen her of late, Mama? Have you seen the sadness on her face?"

"Not all sadness is from the evil one. There are some griefs that lead to good," Mama answers. "Sometimes God uses a rod to draw us near to His side. Sometimes, what a mercy will not do, He must use an affliction to accomplish."

I had planned to go into the sitting room and speak with the two of them, but now I cannot. My feet turn to the kitchen instead. Silently, I ease open the outside door therein and then shut it behind me. I breathe the freshness of the air, heavy now with the scent of autumn leaves. My back to the solid door, I lean against it, remembering the words of Mr. Brainerd's brother John when he came some days past.

I pray for strength. This strength that Mama and John Brainerd think that I have.

I do not have it. Not in myself.

But in Christ... *Out of Your glorious riches, strengthen me with power through Your Spirit.*

I suck in another breath, turning my thoughts from Mr. Brainerd to the Lord Jesus Christ, who has secured and will secure His strength to me. For I must go back above stairs now. I must face David and the cruel specter of death that stands with its sickle ready behind his bed.

But the thought comes to me, seemingly from outside myself: Is it not God's specter, led about in chains?

Christ Jesus has conquered. I must remember this. The last enemy is death...

And then victory in Him forever.

***

I knock before entering the bedchamber. Papa has taken my seat beside the bed but quickly stands so that I can resume it. "Nay, Papa," I say. "I am going to tidy up first."

He takes the seat again, continuing to talk with David.

I keep my hands busy, for that is one of the ways in which I can keep my mind from straying to worry. My spirit strives to engage in constant prayer. I collect the soiled linens and cloths. I open the window and pick up the bowl of dirty water.

All the while, I listen to what they say with half-an-ear.

"I praise God, Jonathan," David says, "for what a merciful circumstance He permitted in having me to die in Northampton. In your house."

My grip tightens on the bowl's edge, and I let the water splash onto the ground below.

"God has granted me all my desire," he finishes with a gasp. "I can joyfully leave this world."

And I must joyfully let him leave it. Grief coats the inside of my mouth. I set the bowl back down on its table. *Oh, my God, help me.*

Chapter Sixty-Five

He does not die on that Sabbath as he so hoped. Instead, the next day, he feels well enough to make some corrections in his diary, even rising to do it. But he soon grows tired, and his brother Israel helps him back to bed.

By evening, he lies still again, his lips barely moving. His pain agonizes me, and I begin to ask God to give me some of David's own pain, to let me bear his physical burden. For is that not fulfilling the law of Christ?

Into the quietness of the room, his voice repeats brokenly, longingly, as a lover would for his beloved, "Come, Lord Jesus, come quickly! Oh, why is His chariot so long in coming?"

My sisters come with Mama to visit. Together, we sing from the Psalter, which Mr. Brainerd has always enjoyed.

'Tis clear that he will die tonight.

After supper, I am alone with him again. David seems to have gone into that semi-conscious state into which the dying disappear. I sit, my upper body bent over my knees. It weighs heavily on me, this weariness of soul and weariness of spirit.

I turn my head from its cradle in my hands to glance at him. His eyes, glassy with illness, stumble open as a cough seizes him. Lacking the strength to speak, I silently place a cloth near his mouth to absorb the bloody mucus.

At last, the coughing fit ceases, and he sinks back against the pillow, wet with sweat. He sucks in a shallow, gritty breath. "Will you pray for me, Jerusha? It would bring me comfort now, for 'tis hard for me to pray in my mind when the pain overtakes me."

"I am praying for you in my heart, David."

His eyes soften. A little of the pain clears away from them. "I know," he murmurs, "but will you pray aloud?"

And so, pushing aside my weariness, I do, so brokenly that at times I think that David cannot hear me.

But God can hear me, for I surely pray the prayer of the brokenhearted. And so He is near.

When I finish praying, I see that David lies asleep, a more peaceful sleep than he has attained for some days. For this, I thank God from the depths of my heart. Sitting with my hands in my lap, I wait, praying that perhaps God will take him in his sleep, that the chariots of Israel will come not with the clatter of wheels but on the wings of a dove.

'Tis many hours before he awakens. But when he does, some of the pain seems to have abated. By now, I have taken up my book. Israel dozes in the chair on David's other side.

"Would you like some water?" I ask. He nods, and I hold up his head, the back of his skull sweaty on top of my palm. He takes a long gulp, and dread rises inside me as the cough starts again. His gaunt body rattles against my hands as I brace him in an upright position until the fit subsides.

He should not lie in such a moist bed. "We should change your linens, Mr. Brainerd. I will awaken your brother. We were just waiting until you roused."

But before I can move to awaken Israel, Mr. Brainerd puts his shaking hand on mine. "Seeing you here, Jerusha, is like a little piece of heaven."

His words catch on my heart.

"Your prayer for me," he says. "I heard every word."

I force a tiny smile. "Nay, I caught you sleeping. Shame on you, Mr. Brainerd, for sleeping during prayer."

My little jest, poor as it is, makes him smile back. I am glad for it.

"I heard in my sleep. Your every word reached my heart."

Every word of his reaches mine.

***

He fares a little better as the night wears on, and it seems unlikely that this will prove to be the night of his passing, after all. At Mama's urging, I finally disappear into my own room to catch a few hours of sleep. I have spent so many previous nights sleeping upright in a chair that I collapse into a dreamless oblivion.

Chapter Sixty-Six

The sun stretches its golden rays across my bed; the warmth awakens me. Opening my eyes, I lie there for just a moment upon my feather mattress. I feel completely rested and at peace.

And then I remember Mr. Brainerd.

I throw back the bedcovers, rise, pour some water into the basin, and splash my face. After toweling my skin, I pull the pins out of my hair with such haste that they drop from my fingers to the floor. I forgot to take my hair down last night in my weariness. Quickly pinning it into place again, my spirit whispers a prayer: *Oh, Lord God, that Thou would strengthen my heart today.*

I am surprised that Mama did not wake me. All of my sisters must have long risen, including my bedfellow Sarah, and, by the sun's position in the sky when I peer out past the heavy curtains, I know that 'tis well-past time for breakfast and family Scripture-reading. After dressing quickly, I hastily open the door to my chamber and am nearly down the staircase when I realize that loud masculine singing comes from behind Mr. Brainerd's door. The voices are not ones that I recognize. My curiosity rises, but I stay my hand from pushing open the door. Instead, I hasten into the kitchen.

"Where is my mother, Leah?"

Pausing in her work of sweeping out the hearth, the servant twists to look at me from her position on her hands and knees. "Oh, she is out in the garden, miss."

"Thank you."

Indeed, I find Mama squatting down in the herb garden, her gathering basket at her side. She looks up when she hears my footsteps.

"I overslept." I state the obvious and kneel down to help Mama to cut rosemary.

"You looked like you needed the rest yesterday," Mama says. "I did not want to wake you. I fear that you have overtaxed yourself with our guest."

I remember the conversation that I overheard recently between her and Sarah. I shake my head. "I am glad to do it, Mama." Then I bite my lip against the sorrow that presses me all over. I will not have another chance to do such a thing again for Mr. Brainerd.

Mama snips off another sprig, and its piney scent strikes my nostrils. "I fear he is not long for this world. You must prepare yourself, Jerusha."

She knows. I can tell that Mama knows what has transpired in my heart toward Mr. Brainerd. A sweet relief comes with her knowing. Why did I not confide in her long ago?

"I fear nothing can prepare me for this," I say, quietly, very quietly, and wonder if even Mama can hear it.

But she does hear me and pauses in her clipping to rest a rosemary-scented hand against my cheek. Her brown eyes gaze into mine. "I have often wondered," she says after a moment, "how I would go on if your father was taken from me. It would be very hard. Nearly impossible, I think."

Her eyes move away from me toward the house. Is she thinking of Papa, sitting there in his closet? Is she imagining one day when perhaps he will not be there? Will never be there anymore in this world?

Then her hand drops from my cheek and picks up her shears again. "You have been very brave, Jerusha."

I do not feel it. Not at all. 'Tis a forced bravery. I swallow and change the subject. "I heard singing coming from Mr. Brainerd's room."

"Aye, two young ministers came by the house very early this morning, wishing to speak and pray with Mr. Brainerd. He welcomed them, though his strength is so low. I am not surprised to hear that they are singing."

Just at that moment, the sound of a window latch touches our ears. Mama and I both look up at the noise. A window opens, the window of the room in which Mr. Brainerd lies – and the voices carry out onto the cool autumn breeze. They sing Psalm 102 – the psalm regarding the prosperity of Zion.

Chapter Sixty-Seven

Two days later, Mr. Brainerd becomes extremely delirious. Never before has he been like this except when he was in Boston. Israel and I work to keep him comfortable.

I lay a cloth on his fevered brow and stroke his hand from time-to-time. This seems to comfort him. His skin has dried under his feet, and so I take emollients and rub them into his soles and toes, caring for him as I would care for an infant, as I would care for an aged parent.

After a time of great madness and thrashing, during which Israel had to restrain him, Mr. Brainerd sleeps. Israel leaves to have a little supper, and when Brainerd awakens again, I see from the look of his eyes that he has regained his reason. Relief floods my heart.

"How are you doing, Mr. Brainerd?" I ask.

A smile shakily turns up his mouth. He licks his dry lips. I quickly take some salve on my fingers and spread it over them.

"I thank you," he grates out.

I wish that I could comfort him with more than cool cloths and cups of water. "'Tis we who should be thankful," I say, after a moment. "You have given so much to the Church of God. I know that you think that this illness has prevented you from doing good. You have often said that you would not wish to outlive your usefulness, but I wish that you could have heard the two young ministers the other day as they went out the door. They spoke so strongly of their regard, of how meeting with you has challenged them to walk forward with all seriousness in what lives God gives to them. You do not realize how great a blessing you have been to so many."

All these words come out of my mouth before I can reconsider. I do not know how he will take my flood of words, but they have long lain on my heart and mind, especially as I have seen his depression sometimes in the face of what he terms his *uselessness*.

"Your illness has allowed me an opportunity to be useful to you, and through you, to God," I say quietly, taking a seat beside him.

His eyes widen, and I know that a sudden pain grips him. His lips press together for a long moment. Then his face relaxes again, and he turns his head toward me. "I have enjoyed a refreshment of soul which I had not expected to enjoy in this life. And you have been the source of that, Jerusha. For that, for your care of me, I thank you."

The words and the affection I glimpse in his eyes hearten me. I am a woman who may never do great things for God, as the world terms them. But there must be all kinds of usefulness, including this: usefulness in the small things.

"Would you wish for me to read aloud to you?"

He nods.

"From a book of sermons, perhaps, or…"

He shakes his head against the pillow. "From the Bible. I find that the closer I get to heaven, the more other men's words die away and the more I want only that one Book to show me the Way."

And so I pick up his own tattered copy of the Scriptures and read to him until he falls fast asleep again.

***

A knock sounds upon the door. When I turn, Israel pops his tousled head into the room, a smile upon his sun-tanned face.

"Will you come for a walk with me down by the river, Miss Edwards? I asked your mother, and she said that she would send one of your sisters to take your place beside my brother for a while, if you wish."

There is a light in his eyes, an interest there which I have suspected before but which I do not want to see. Is it strange that nothing leaps inside of me at the idea, though he is an intelligent, strong young man, more handsome than his older brothers David or John? The Lord knows that Israel has better prospects in this life at least, from all appearances.

Nay, 'tis not strange, for all of my heart is taken by a dying man who stretches out on the bed, pale as the sheets on which he lies. So when Israel asks me, will I come with him down to stroll along the river, beneath the canopy of brilliant autumn leaves on this fine day, I shake my head. "No, I thank you," I say. "I will wait here with your brother."

A little disappointment gleams in his eye, and I feel slightly sorry for him. Perhaps that is what causes me to say as he turns towards the door, "My sister Mary is above stairs, I believe. She is always eager for a walk."

Mary will be a good companion for him. She is lively and clever and ready for new experiences. But I have already found what my soul loves and will cling to it. Or whom my soul loves, I should say.

Israel shakes his head. "Nay," he says. "I think the solitude will do me good."

"I am sure you are right."

'Tis still early morning, and Mr. Brainerd yet sleeps. After the door clicks shut behind Israel, I look over at Mr. Brainerd. He is sleeping peacefully, calmly. The pain appears to have eased a little. He slept well last night. Would that not be the best way for him to go, if go he must? To go quietly in his sleep, to transfer from this bed of earthly rest into the rest of heaven, into the arms of his Savior?

But, regardless of what happens or how, I must trust my God and Savior. I am beginning to see this now. I am beginning to understand that He must have our best in His heart.

The morning sunlight brushes over the edge of the window and spills down onto his bed. I rise from my chair and go to push back the curtains, letting in more of the rich beams, releasing them to run down as melted butter on the floor.

Opening the window, I breathe in the air. I have not stepped outside for more than a few minutes for several days. And 'tis how I would have it be. There is no sanctuary that I would rather be in than this sanctuary of Mr. Brainerd's room.

I am thankful for these last days with him. I am thankful, and yet I dread each day. How can I be so torn in two?

Behind me, I hear a deep sigh and turn quickly. His eyes are open, the brown lashes sweeping slowly down onto his cheeks. Though I did not give it permission, my heart rises in my chest, so glad to see him alive. We will have one more day together.

Slowly, his head turns toward me and toward the sunlight. "Good morning," I say. "How are you feeling?" I press my hands against my skirt longing for him to say that he feels better, that he feels like he is getting well again. I long for another month's respite as God gave us this summer when we rode horseback through the sunlit hills around Northampton. Nay, if I am honest, I long for whole years of respite.

Years in which we have joy on this earth.

Years in which I wake up to see that smiling face on the pillow next to mine.

Years in which I can see little brown-haired children with hazel eyes running through the grass.

Years in which I can make my home wherever he must go, whether 'tis in a little Indian hut, or here in Northampton, or somewhere else unknown as of yet. If he became well again... who knows what the future might then hold?

He sucks in the air, and I hear the rasp in his throat. The vision of years that we will never experience together fades away as quickly as it came.

He smiles. "My soul is sweetly set on God," he murmurs. "I long to be with Him that I might behold His glory."

And with that I feel a separation from him. His soul, oh, how much more than mine, is so set on the world to come that he does not even think of the world that he yet inhabits!

"Jerusha," he whispers, "Pray with me." He extends his hand toward me. I sit down in the chair by his side and allow him to clasp his hand over mine, tightening in a surprising way for one so ill.

Once more, he begins to pray for his brothers, for his friends, for my family, for his Indians. He speaks of them with so much love! At times I cannot hear his mumbled words. But I am happy that he has included me in his prayer, his prayer for all of his concerns for time and eternity. The words spring fresh from his heart – his great, expansive heart that is so like that of his Savior.

Chapter Sixty-Eight

"Is it the Lord's Day?"

I wipe the last vestiges of sleep away from my eyes as Mr. Brainerd's increasingly-weakened voice meets my ears. Through the dim morning light, I see that his eyes are wide open already. "Aye, 'tis the Sabbath. The first in October."

His eyes close, and a hopeful expression takes its place upon his countenance. "I was born in the flesh on the Lord's Day," he murmurs, "and I have good reason to believe that I was born again in the Spirit on the Lord's Day. I should like to be born in the kingdom of heaven on the Lord's day."

He has said this same thing several times since becoming bedridden, and each Lord's Day, I wonder along with him whether God will perhaps grant him this desire.

Across from me, Israel awakens. Immediately, he rises and bends over his brother before looking at me. "How is he?"

"Much the same." His breathing became more ragged in the night, but it seems to have steadied now, so I say nothing of it. "If you wish, you may go to the morning exercises with my family. I will stay with your brother."

He frowns, surely not wanting to take advantage of my help. "Are you sure? I would be more than happy to stay."

I smile and shake my head firmly. "Nay, go. I will stay." If Mr. Brainerd should pass while the church service is underway, I wish to be here, by his side.

After the family leaves for church, Mr. Brainerd rouses again and asks if I will read to him portions of the Psalms, Isaiah, and John. As I finish the last chapter, a sigh escapes his lips. He smiles up towards the ceiling, his eyes once more seeming to see beyond the limits of his space.

I close the Bible, and, amidst the rustle of its pages, I hear him whisper, "Oh, that His kingdom might come in the world, that they might all love and glorify Him for what He is in Himself, and that the Blessed Redeemer might see the travail of His soul and be satisfied!"

He then turns his head towards me. I set his old Bible carefully on the table.

But he reaches for it, and so I place it beside him on the bed. He hugs it to himself as a child might hug a beloved doll, and tears roll down his cheeks.

I swallow back my own tears. "You must rest, Mr. Brainerd."

Rising, I begin to tidy the room. Israel helped me to wash Mr. Brainerd earlier this morning, before he left. Now, I go about the chamber, glancing towards the bed from time-to-time, straightening this stack of books, those unfinished papers on the desk. At last he dozes, his lips still moving in prayer. After a long while, I take a seat again, happy to see that he rests. Perhaps he will sleep even as long as the morning. Perhaps it will bring him renewed energy. He dearly wishes that he could finish the revision of his papers. But I have heard him speak with Papa already, telling him that he thinks he will not be able to do it, that it must fall to Papa to take on the task. Papa is a man of papers and books and desks.

At last, I take up my embroidery hoop and work on it for some time. All is silent in the streets. Almost the whole town is at church. Through the windowpane, I hear the sweet whistles of the birds and the rustle of the leaves on the trees.

I do not want this to end. My fingers tighten on my needle. I want to sit here always by Mr. Brainerd's side, comforting him, nurturing him, being close to him in his distress. *O Lord, help me. Help me to give him up.* And my throat tightens. I reach for the pitcher to pour myself some refreshment, but I find that there is no water left in it. So I rise from my chair, taking one more glance at him to make sure that he is still asleep, and leave the room.

When I return with a full pitcher, Mr. Brainerd lies awake. He looks at me, quite seriously, where I have paused in the doorway. And I know that he sees me, not past me.

His gaze seems to say that he does not merely see Reverend Edwards' daughter, but that he sees Jerusha Edwards – me – and that he is unafraid of admitting it, at least in this moment, at this time.

The thought of that causes my heart to tense with a throb of held-back joy.

"Jerusha."

Carefully schooling my features, I place the pitcher on the table and walk across the room, not stopping until my skirt brushes against the edge of the bed. "Aye, Mr. Brainerd. What do you need? I did not mean to be gone for –"

His hand coming over mine stops the words from my mouth. "Dear Jerusha, are you willing to part with me?"

I cannot answer him. Is there such a question as being willing or not when the demand will come nonetheless? Is this not what yet, from time-to-time, causes the revolt in my heart? That I must give him up whether I be willing or not? And how could I be willing to give up such a precious one as he?

"I am quite willing to part with you." His voice becomes a whisper. His eyes never leave my face, but his thumb travels over my knuckles, one by one. 'Tis a more intimate caress than that of a friend. Never before today has he touched my hand like this. "I am willing to part with you," he repeats. "I am willing to part with all my friends. I am willing to part with my dear brother John, although I love him the best of any creature living. I have committed him and all my friends to God. I can leave you all with God."

His words break my heart. He is willing to part from me.

Though I know it must be so, though I know the first love of his heart must be his God, my heart still aches at his words. But his love would not be worth having if he did not feel thus. 'Tis a necessary pain.

Yet why does he ask me if I am willing to part with him? Is it so obvious that I am not? Is my affection for him so apparent that he makes bold to question me thus? I have tried so often to keep my affection hidden behind a veneer of true esteem. His caress on my knuckles distracts me. His question disturbs me and ruffles the sense of peace that I had. Must we stir all this up now? Cannot any love that I, and perhaps he, had die with him? Is it not easier that way?

"All is safe for us in God, Jerusha," he says, and there is urgency in his tone. "All is safe with Him who loved us and gave Himself for us. He will not withhold any good thing from us."

I cannot help the bitter sorrow that crawls up my throat, nor the tears that rise and force me to grind my jaw against them. I cannot meet his eyes any longer, those bright spear-points that thrust into my soul. I know he says this to be helpful to me; he does not want me to live in grief. He wants me to have joy in God. 'Tis typical of Mr. Brainerd – always trying to be helpful spiritually to someone.

But the tiniest bit of me wishes that he had some regret. The question comes to my lips, and I give voice to it here alone with him. "You have no wistfulness, then?" I ask, "Nothing you wish you could take with you, or that you wish that you could have done? All is satisfied in God?"

I already know what he will answer me, and so, though I ask the question, 'tis more of a statement. I know that he will say that, aye, he is satisfied with naught but eternity.

Thus, I am surprised by the silence, draping heavy as humidity hangs in the air in the heat of summer. He is probably pondering his academic career and his missionary endeavors, thinking through them to see if perhaps there is something more that he should repent of, something that perhaps he wishes he could do differently, of which he has not yet spoken to me. He will not see the hidden query in my question. The asking of whether there is any person that he might miss.

Whether he might regret leaving me.

And then, as if all the strength has gone out of his own fingers, he drops my hand, though he retains contact with my eyes. Slow and quiet, David answers me. "If I thought that I should not see you and be happy with you in another world, Jerusha, I could not bear to part from you now."

He swallows against a cough. When I reach for the water cup, he shakes his head and renews his hold upon my hand. "It will do me no harm to tell you this now, as I am a dying man. You have probably guessed my feelings anyway. Did I not give them away long weeks ago? When I spoke of the young woman in New Haven for whom I yearned, how could you not guess that I spoke only of you?"

His eyes close for a long moment, and he keeps his grasp on my hand firm. When he opens his eyes again, they glimmer with unshed tears. They shine like the stars in the dark firmament. "But we shall spend a happy eternity together," he rasps and releases my hand. Without another word, he turns his head to the side and closes his eyes, the moisture seeping from their corners.

I cannot speak. I must move out of this room before the emotions that rise in my soul flood out. "Excuse me," I murmur and hurry from the room, the clacking of my shoes loud in the silent house.

***

My feet find their way outside into the golden world of early October. 'Tis strange how time keeps plodding onward. The sun continues to shine. The birds sing. The path that leads from the house to the garden is still there. The old oak tree still pitches its deep roots into the earth. Everything is the same as 'twas yesterday, last year, early this morning.

And yet everything has changed. The unseen and unfelt sun has broken out from behind the cloud inside me and, slowly, the heart-sickness that I have long felt begins to mend. I can feel the wellness flooding through me. Thanksgiving rises in my heart.

God did not have to give me this gift of knowing that David truly returns my affection. He has laid his love for me clearly in the open at last, after many weeks of hinting at it but never committing it to words. After all these weeks when I thought that the young woman of his history was not I, but some other lady.

But now…

We shall spend a happy eternity together!

And heaven looks brighter to me. David and I will meet there as simple, honest hearts once more. I do not mean this in a romantic way, for heaven is the place where our true romance with the great God of the universe will commence in full reality. But of this I am sure: We shall be able to establish the deep friendship there, the deep knowing of one another that we would have had on this earth, no, yet deeper than we would have had on this earth, had we more years together.

The gratitude overflows, and I fall to my knees, the damp soil soaking through my petticoat. I care not. *I thank Thee, Lord God. I thank Thee.* The tears well up and spread down my cheeks, dropping onto the earth and watering it.

John Brainerd spoke truly. My love has meant something to David. It has meant more than the love of a sister and a brother. I have meant more to him than merely my position as Reverend Edwards' daughter. David has desired me, Jerusha. He has wanted to take me to himself, but he was not willing to sacrifice any portion of his time on this earth to meet his own desires.

But we shall spend a happy eternity together.

Joy spreads through my heart where sadness once ruled. Strange though it sounds, now I am able to grieve with joy. His love applies a balm to my heart, a lifelong balm, an eternal one, for love is of God. Even when Mr. Brainerd goes from this earth, the love will remain mine. And I realize that, in this, God has indeed granted me my request.

The church bell rings, and so I stumble to my feet.

Wiping away the remnants of the tears from my eyes, I look down the street. No one comes yet, and so I turn and hurry inside. Leah and the other servants have gone to church, and so 'tis just Mr. Brainerd and I in the house.

Quietly, I enter his room, hoping that he is asleep. Sure enough, when my gaze falls on the bed there, he lies content. His eyelids, delicate and thin and blue-veined, rest closed. Even his breathing, always ragged, emerges from his lungs relatively untroubled.

In that quietness, with the sun shining through the windows and splashing upon the floor, I sense the Holy Spirit speaking to me in the quietness, telling me to trust Him yet again, to believe Him. Like Gideon with his fleece, God has given me a sign. He has asked me to trust Him before. But now He has given me this, this precious gift of spoken love from Mr. Brainerd.

And perfect love casts out fear.

I step across the room to Mr. Brainerd's side and gently pick up his hand. Raising it to my mouth, I kiss the fever-warmed skin. *Aye, Lord, I will trust Thee.*

Chapter Sixty-Nine

Across from me, Israel slowly awakens from his sleep. He looks down at his brother and then up at me. Our eyes meet, and Israel blushes. "Sometimes," he says, "I feel like one of the disciples sleeping in the garden. You, Miss Edwards, are always awake, always caring for him."

I shake my head. Love knows not the word sacrifice. "I just awoke myself. Don't feel badly."

"He is worse today." He states the obvious.

The end is drawing near. I feel it. I sense it in my spirit, which now lies at peace in the midst of this storm – because the Lord Jesus is in it and bids the waves be still.

Israel leans over David, concern written across his face. "If only he could hold on a little longer, at least until our brother John gets here. He wishes so to see him. John is the one that he is close to, the one that he looks to as a fellow worker. I am just the younger brother."

I look at up at him, unable to conceal my surprise at his words. "Do not say that, Israel. Mr. Brainerd has often spoken so well of you. He thinks much of you and has high hopes for you in the ministry. He believes that God's hand is on you."

Israel stares at me. "David said that?"

I nod. Turning to dip one of the cloths in the water

bowl, I wring it out. "Aye, he did."

The disbelief on Israel's face turns slowly into a humble kind of pleasure.

As I wipe Mr. Brainerd's brow, neck, and chest with the moist, cool cloth, he begins to roll about on the bed, or I should say, twitch, for he would roll if he could in the agony that this disease puts his body through. But his weakness no longer permits such movements, so instead, his limbs move to-and-fro nervously across the sheets.

I settle in for a long morning and begin to pray to the God of my life, the God who knows each of our moments and has written them in His book, who knows the day and hour of Mr. Brainerd's death, and of Israel's, and of mine.

Late in the afternoon, we hear hooves cantering down the road. Israel raises his head from the book he has been reading and meets my eyes.

Joy spreads across his countenance. "'Tis John," he says. "I can hardly believe it. He has come. He has made it."

He rises and goes towards the door, but before he can even reach it, we hear the footsteps come heavy on the passage floor, and John bursts into the room. His wilderness clothes – buckskin breeches and knee-high boots – are full of dust. His face shines with sweat, and his hair hangs moist beneath his worn hat. His eyes travel from me to David. "I am not too late." He releases a deep breath. "Is he still conscious? Can he still understand me?"

I nod. "Aye, overall, he has remained coherent."

Relief fills John's face. "Thank God." He pulls off his hat.

I stand from my place beside the bed so that he may sit there. He takes the chair without a word, its legs scraping the floor as he sits. His hearty, travel-stained hands wrap around his older brother's now-thin-and-delicate ones. "David," he says, "David. I am here."

David, who has not opened his eyes for most of the day, edges his head in the direction of his brother's voice. His lids unfurl, and joy shines in his countenance again, spreading slowly and then all at once, when he realizes that this is not a confused dream or fevered hallucination. John truly is here, this one whom he says there is no one as like-minded to himself.

"John, my brother," he murmurs. Their hands tighten together. I am relieved. I know that I can leave him with John and Israel, and so I turn to fetch a cup of tea for the weary traveler. As I leave the room, John says, "I am so sorry that I am late. The Indians had a sickness, and so I was delayed."

As I close the door behind me, Mr. Brainerd murmurs in response, "Do not fret on that. The souls of the people required your delay. Oh, but how seeing you refreshes me!"

***

Delirium grips him for most of the next day. My heart feels pressed as in a vice that the cobbler uses to hold his shoe together while he works on it. John has taken Israel's place by David's side. Israel appeared relieved to give place to his older brother. He still, of course, comes in and out of the room, but it has been a long wait for death for the younger brother. I cannot blame him for his eagerness to get away from time-to-time, for even I have felt the need to escape.

But I know that I will not sit here for much longer on Mr. Brainerd's other side with my sewing in my lap, while John holds David's hand. My father comes in and out of the door, and Doctor Mather visits. Both shake their heads and whisper to John that it will not be long.

As the strong autumn sun wears its way across the sky, Mr. Brainerd gains more control of his reason. At first, 'tis a relief to see his eyes clear. But soon, I almost long for him to be delirious again, for when his wits leave him, his pain appears to lessen. The agony makes it difficult for him to speak, but he finds enjoyment in hearing John talk about his continuing work among the Indians.

Now, in the early afternoon, Papa enters Mr. Brainerd's bedroom again. John rises to his feet at my father's approach. "Mr. Edwards."

Papa nods his head at him and gives a smile, although a solemn one.

Mr. Brainerd struggles to open his eyes when Papa's footsteps approach the bed.

"How are you doing, my friend?" Papa says as a way to begin the conversation, I suppose, for 'tis obvious to all how Mr. Brainerd does.

Mr. Brainerd cannot even manage his customary smile. I wonder if he will be able to respond to Papa's question, for he has not spoken for a few hours. At last, he pants, "'Tis impossible for you to conceive of the pain in my breast. 'Tis... 'Tis a different thing to die than men think!"

With those words, he gives a great gasping cough. Bloody mucus flies out of his mouth and lands on the coverlet. I rise quickly, take up a cloth, and wipe his mouth and chin. How I wish I could stop this dreadful disease!

But I cannot. No one can. 'Tis as Mr. John Bunyan has said: Consumption is that great captain of all the men of death, always conquering, unable to be vanquished.

After the cough settles down, Mr. Brainerd speaks

again, keeping his eyes closed. "I expect to die this night," he says in a sputtering whisper, "but I fear a long delay. Yet I will not fear. What can death do to me?"

He raises a shaking hand from the coverlet, grasping towards Papa. Papa, glancing first at me and then at John, clasps Mr. Brainerd's hand in his.

"Pray for me, that I might not dishonor God by impatience in my... in my extreme... agony."

***

Even in his torment, David thinks not primarily of himself, for Reverend Mr. Billings chooses this night of all nights to pay a visit. Mr. Brainerd speaks to him not of his pain, but murmurs about the great importance of the work of the ministry. After this, he spends some time speaking in a rasping whisper with John about the Indians.

How can he do it? I do not know, other than that his whole soul and body and mind are given over to Christ Jesus so that Christ lives through him and in him, so that Christ only pulses through his body and soul each moment, overpowering everything in its path. Seeing this, the affection and esteem I hold in my heart for him – freed by his own admission – now increases tenfold.

His pain obviously grows during the evening. Mama and Sarah draw the younger children away, trying to keep them as quiet as possible so that Mr. Brainerd might die in peace. The end is surely coming now. We have had false alarms before, but this is not a false alarm. Mr. Brainerd knows this. John and Israel and I know this.

A few hours after darkness comes over the world, Mr. Brainerd's hand stretches out toward me. John holds his other hand, while Israel sits nearby. I embrace Mr. Brainerd's hand with mine, clasping his still-living one for what I know may be the last time.

The Bible sits next to me on the little table, beside the bowl full of his bloodied linens and the wash basin. In this dreadful hour, in this holy moment, when the veil between death and life is about to be torn back, when Christ is about to welcome Mr. Brainerd into His holy heaven, I pull his Bible onto my lap with my free hand. It opens to the Book of Revelation.

"'And I saw a new heaven and a new earth: for the first heaven and the first earth were passed away; and there was no more sea. And I, John, saw the holy city, new Jerusalem, coming down from God out of heaven, prepared as a bride adorned for her husband. And I heard a great voice out of heaven saying, Behold, the tabernacle of God is with men, and he will dwell with them, and they shall be his people, and God himself shall be with them, and be their God. And God shall wipe away all tears from their eyes; and there shall be no more death, neither sorrow, nor crying, neither shall there be any more pain: for the former things are passed away. And he that sat upon the throne said, Behold, I make all things new. And he said unto me, Write: for these words are true and faithful. And he said unto me, It is done. I am Alpha and Omega, the beginning and the end. I will give unto him that is athirst of the fountain of the water of life freely. He that overcometh shall inherit all things; and I will be his God, and he shall be my son....'"

When I fall silent, John begins to sing a song of Zion, one of Mr. Brainerd's favorites. Taking the wings of sorrow, I fly toward joy and let my voice fall in with his and with that of Israel.

***

And so we stay here, as the evening hours chime by, as the last sands of time sink through the timepiece of Mr. Brainerd's life. I will remember these moments always, of all the days leading up to this. I will remember this night; it will be inscribed in the book of my memory.

Tomorrow has not yet come. David is still with us – with me. And He who is the King of all of my yesterdays, all of my todays, and all of my tomorrows, still sits on the throne.

What is more, He still sits here, present with us three, travailing through the birth-pangs of death-into-life.

A little after 8 o'clock, Papa brings a chair into the chamber and sits down. He and John pray aloud for the Church on earth and especially for the Indians, which they know are close and dear subjects to David's heart, above all else.

And then, a little after midnight, David's eyes stare toward the ceiling and do not move any more. He continues like this for the rest of the night, insensible and silent. Each one of his painful gasps echoes in my own heart.

At six in the morning, on the ninth day of October, in the Year of Our Lord 1747, David Brainerd takes his last breath in this world. He passes through the veil. The chariot comes for the Elijah of our day.

Chapter Seventy

I go to his funeral, aye, and I say my public, albeit silent, goodbye there with my hand inside that of my little sister Eunice. Sarah and Esther stand on either side of me, their dark dresses blowing across mine in the brittle October air. My sisters' faces are wet with tears, but I find my own well sealed this day.

We inter Mr. Brainerd in Northampton's burial ground, far from his own family's graves and far from his beloved flock of Indians. John and Israel throw sprigs of rosemary – for remembrance – into the grave first, and then some of the large assembly of mourners do as well. A few shovelfuls of dirt thud on the top of the wooden coffin before we turn and head back home.

***

Early the next morning, I wake even before the rooster breaks open the shell of the dawn with his crow. Pushing aside the covers carefully, lest I wake Sarah sleeping beside me, I rise from my bed. My cold feet find my leather slippers. I will not bother with stockings right now. I move towards the wash basin and splash my face with haste. Something stirs inside of me. It makes me want to go down to the burial ground.

I draw on my skirt and then slip into my bodice,

pinning its front closure with quick fingers. 'Tis strange, sleeping in my own room again, and 'tis equally strange, having so much time to myself – so much time to think.

Silently, I open the door of my bedchamber and then glide down the stairs. I do not want to look down the passageway and glimpse the room where he breathed his last breath here. The sounds of Leah stirring the fire to life come from the kitchen, and I know that Mama will soon come down the stairs. I plan to be back before I am needed.

Catching up my thick shawl first, I open the front door and shut it behind me. Once outside in the foggy early morning, I pull my shawl over my head. Without pause, I go down the walk and out through the front gate, turning to the right and hurrying down the street until I come to another turn. Few townspeople are out this early except for hired hands. I do not take the trouble to greet anyone, though I do spare any women or children a smile as I walk by them.

At last, I am at the place where the graves pock the ground. I take my time walking toward the spot upon which my heart rests its eyes. His headstone has not been put in yet. Only the mound of fresh-packed dirt indicates his burying place. Beyond it, where the ground rises a little bit, Papa's grandfather and grandmother lie beneath their table monuments. They were much beloved, more beloved than my father is by these Northampton people.

This day, however, my eyes do not stray much beyond the packed dirt, the only sign left of the man whose hand I held in death, whose fingers touched mine. Here lies a man whose heart beat only for heaven, and that is where he now resides. I sit down next to the grave, feeling the coolness of the brown earth and dying grass beneath me. As I run my fingers oh-so-gently through the soil covering his resting place, quietness steals over me, and I let out the breath that I did not know I was holding, the breath that perhaps I have held since I was thirteen years old.

It is finished. He has lived his life for God. He has counted the cost and found it worth the prize. And here, sitting at the bottom of the little rise with the husk of what was my Mr. Brainerd, I begin to see more clearly than I have seen before, that it was – it is – worth it.

Christ is worth everything that Mr. Brainerd could give or that I could give. And there is nothing that we could be asked to sacrifice in this life that will not be given back to us one hundredfold in the life to come – the eternal life that I already have within me, this eternal life that made Mr. Brainerd's eyes shine with joy, even in the midst of suffering. It made him willing to give up the thought of me for the joy set before him. It now makes me willing to surrender him.

Tears rise and blur my vision. There is a sorrow in them, but 'tis not a sorrow unto death. 'Tis a sorrow onto joy and onto life. Gently, I ease my body back until I am lying down on the ground beside Mr. Brainerd's grave. I let my hand rest there above him, on the cold earth, and close my eyes in the light of the dawning day. Very quietly, I sing the words to Mr. Watts' hymn:

Jesus shall reign where'er the sun
Does its successive journeys run,
His kingdom stretch from shore to shore,
Till moons shall wax and wane no more.
To him shall endless prayer be made,
And praises throng to crown his head.
His name like sweet perfume shall rise
With every morning sacrifice.

People and realms of every tongue
Dwell on his love with sweetest song,
And infant voices shall proclaim
Their early blessings on his name.
Blessings abound where'er he reigns:
The prisoners leap to lose their chains,
The weary find eternal rest,
And all who suffer want are blest.
Let every creature rise and bring
The highest honors to our King,
Angels descend with songs again,
And earth repeat the loud amen.

A rare joy steals through my bones. We have said goodbye, but 'tis not forever. 'Tis only for the blinking of an eye. In the quiet dawn, I can almost hear his voice say to me, *We shall spend a happy eternity together, Jerusha!*

The tears seep from the edges of my sealed eyelids and track their way down the sides of my face until they soak into my hair. I lay there in such a state while the sun rises, casting its golden rays upon my skin.

At long last, my tears stop. I have been given a glimpse into eternity for these few short months with David Brainerd, with my beloved. And I would not trade it for any happiness that this world could offer me. I rise and brush off my dress, letting the dead leaves and dry grass fall from my skirt onto the dust.

"I love you still." At long last, the words that have lain buried in my heart for so long emerge from their chrysalis, taking to the air so softly that they dissolve into the autumn breeze. "And we shall spend a happy eternity together with the Lord, beloved."

As I turn to go, it seems as though the leaves above me whisper back a single sentence, one that I know so well:

He is not among the dead but among the living.
I take the path out of the burial ground and make my way home.

Jerusha Edwards died four months later, on February 14, 1748, while she was still only seventeen years old. Her death was caused by a sudden fever, possibly connected to tuberculosis.

***

Her grave lies beside that of David Brainerd in the family plot of the Northampton, Massachusetts' Bridge Street Cemetery and may still be visited today.

***

The inscription on her stone carries a verse that was one of David's favorites: "I shall be satisfied when I awake with Thy likeness." Psalm 17:15

A Note to Readers

Dear friends,

Looking back on the journey of writing *A Holy Passion*, I can't help but wonder at how God brings the pieces of a story together...

A few years ago, when we still lived in New England, my husband and I went adventuring in the region in which we both were born and grew up – a place of ancient, crumbling graveyards and of houses with three centuries of history within their walls. One weekend, we stayed at a lovely inn. The guest rooms had been named after 18th-century inhabitants of that town, and our room had received the name of a young woman who had been taken captive by American Indians during a raid. At the time, I remarked to my husband that I would like to write a story about her.

Well, I didn't write a story about that young woman, but the idea of telling a colonial American tale still appealed to me. Soon, I remembered the little book one of my sisters kept on her bookshelf – a book I had never read, but what I knew of the author – a missionary named David Brainerd – intrigued me... in particular, his passion for God that drove him to sacrifice his entire life for the gospel of Jesus Christ. I remembered having heard that he and Jerusha Edwards, daughter of theologian and pastor Jonathan Edwards, may have been romantically attached to one another in his final days.

That little book – which I then read – was *The Life and Diary of David Brainerd,* an account that inspired the work of John Wesley, Jonathan Edwards, Henry Martyn, William Carey, J. Hudson Taylor, and Jim Elliot, to name only a few.

And so the inkling of this novel took root and began to grow, albeit slowly. As I wrote, God continually awed me with how David – and Jerusha – counted the cost of following Him. On the heels of this awe came – and comes – conviction.

Friends, do we count the cost of following Christ and find Him worth giving up – literally – everything? Are we – am I – utterly surrendered to the Holy Spirit's working in every corner of our – of my – life?

He is worth it. Those who have gone before us testify that this is true. Will we believe? Will we obey the truth that we say we believe?

My prayer for you, friend, and for myself, is that we would see with the eyes of our souls how greatly God can use each one of us when we put ourselves entirely in His hands; that we would hunger and thirst for Him as David Brainerd did; and that He would be the beautiful and complete satisfaction of all our true desires.

***

David Brainerd lived during the First Great Awakening, a spiritual revival that swept across the American colonies from the early 1730s through the early 1740s. This movement of the Holy Spirit is a fascinating time about which to learn; it set the stage for many things that followed, including the Second Great Awakening that occurred a little less than 100 years later, and in which another Brainerd took part:

James Brainerd Taylor, who also died of tuberculosis at the even younger age of 27.

The subject of David and Jerusha's relationship continues to be an area of debate, with scholars taking various positions. Some believe that Jerusha cared for David solely out of duty. Others believe that a romantic affection could have existed between them, even to the point of a secret engagement. I've chosen to present the relationship between David and Jerusha as I have because it makes the most sense to me based on the diaries as well as the circumstantial evidence. Ultimately, I don't believe that the state of their relationship can be proven beyond doubt in either direction.

Historically, I have striven to represent characters as they appeared to me through primary and secondary documents. This means that Jonathan Edwards, Jerusha, David, and the others in this cast are flawed people. My desire is that you, friend, would see in these sinful yet redeemed men and women the victory and worth that Christ alone gives. He Himself is the precious ointment, held in weak and earthen vessels.

Those who are familiar with David's diary and life may notice that I have reordered a few events toward the end of his life, as well as have omitted several incidents, such as the debate in which he participated on the road from Boston to Northampton and the presence of fellow New Light Eleazar Wheelock in the Edwards' home when Brainerd first arrived. These deviations were made to streamline the story.

You may wish to know that John Brainerd continued to serve as a missionary and pastor for many years, dying in late middle age. He was known to be as devoted to Christ as his older brother had been, though perhaps less fiery. He married a few years after his brother's death and named one of his children after David. His consideration of Jerusha as a wife is one of the parts of this story that does not have any direct historical support but which I felt was not impossible. Young Israel Brainerd died of a sudden illness about two months after David's death.

***

A writer's hands are upheld by many Aarons and Hurs. Thank you to those of you who have encouraged me by telling me that you are praying for me, by recommending and reviewing my books, and by giving good advice. You are each a blessing to me!

Thanks are due as well to my mom for giving me a push forward when I lagged in diligence and for building in me a love for beautiful graveyards; and to my dear sisters, who have read drafts, given excellent suggestions, and enthused about David and Jerusha with me. Thanks, Bekki, for the original copy of David's diary that I found on your bookshelf, and thanks, Londie, for the wonderful guidebook to New England's spiritual heritage that you gave me. Thanks to my husband, Alex, who helped me brainstorm, read drafts, and was always willing to visit one more ancient New England graveyard with me!

What a blessing my fellow writer-friends are to me! In particular, thanks to Anita for making truly helpful suggestions, as well as for continually encouraging me to keep going with the many rounds of revisions. I've also been blessed with a wonderful gathering of readers in my street-team and on social media. Thanks to everyone who has helped to get the word out about David and Jerusha's story!

If you are interested in learning more about David Brainerd and the time of the Great Awakening, you will find a resource list following this note.

***

Thanks for reading! If you have questions, comments, or would just like to chat, please feel free to contact me via my website or on social media. I would love to hear from you.

Grace and peace in Christ alone,

Alicia G. Ruggieri
http://www.aliciagruggieri.com

Selected Resources for Further Reading

Brainerd, David. *The Life and Diary of David Brainerd*, edited by Jonathan Edwards, 1749 (public domain).

Brainerd, Thomas. *The Life of John Brainerd*. Presbyterian Publications Committee, 1865 (public domain).

Cosby, Brian H. *David Brainerd: A Love for the Lost*. Christian Focus Publications, 2011.

Dodds, Elisabeth D. *Marriage to a Difficult Man*. Auduborn Press, 2005.

Edwards, Jonathan. *The Life of Reverend David Brainerd*. Baker Book House, 1978.

Marsden, George M. *Jonathan Edwards: A Life*. Yale University Press, 2003.

Panik, Marie. *A Guide to Jonathan Edwards' Northampton*. Historic Northampton, 2013.

Piper, John. *The Hidden Smile of God: The Fruit of Affliction in the Lives of John Bunyan, William Cowper, and David Brainerd*. Crossway, 2001.

Jonathan Edwards Center, The. The Jonathan Edwards Center at Yale University. http://edwards.yale.edu/.

Rosell, Garth M. *Exploring New England's Spiritual Heritage: Seven Daytrips for Contemporary Pilgrims.* The Harold John Ockenga Institute, Gordon-Conwell Theological Seminary, 2013.

Wilkinson, Gary, producer, and Christian History Institute. *David Brainerd: Missionary to the American Indians.* Gary Wilkinson Productions, 2013.

Wynbeek, David. *David Brainerd: Beloved Yankee.* Eerdman's Publishing Company, 1961.

Did you enjoy this book?

If so, please consider letting others know about
it by word-of-mouth or by reviewing it online.
Thank you!

87299434R00213

Made in the USA
Lexington, KY
22 April 2018